THE WALLS OF JERICHO

Leadbetter

✗ ✗ ✗ ✗ N.

Prospect

THE WALLS
OF JERICHO

by

Paul I. Wellman

J. B. LIPPINCOTT COMPANY
PHILADELPHIA AND NEW YORK

To *Katema*

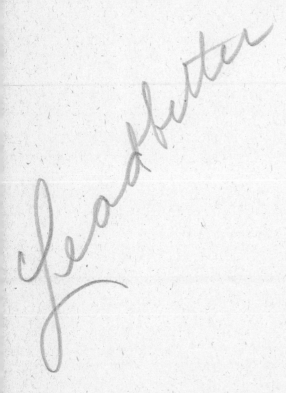

There is no such city as Jericho, Kansas. None of the characters of this book ever existed, except in imagination. But the country of which this novel tells, does exist. To some, the flat plains of America may appear monotonous and uninteresting; but to those who know them, they are sometimes exciting and often very beautiful, and they are peopled by a race as distinct as the Yankees of New England—whom they much resemble—or the mountaineers of Kentucky, or the cattlemen of the West. Except for the general character of the High Plains and the people who live upon them, however, this novel is entirely fictional, and any resemblance to real persons or events, of the past or present, is purely coincidental.

PAUL I. WELLMAN.

THE WALLS OF JERICHO

CHAPTER I

1.

HE paused momentarily at the front door before stepping out into the night, and took his pipe from his mouth while he felt in his coat pocket to make sure his keys were with him.

A delicate pale thread of smoke rose from the bowl of the brier in his hand, pleasantly prickling in his nostrils. As his fingers encountered them, the keys clinked dully on their ring. At the same time Belle's voice came, lagging, from the sitting-room.

"You're going . . . to the station?"

"Yes," he said. "Tucker would be disappointed if I didn't show up on the reception committee."

He said it with a lame attempt at humor; but Belle did not answer. Her mother moved out into the hall in her pink wrapper. Mrs. Dunham was an immensely fleshy woman, and she wore garments festooned with ribbons and lace that accentuated her corpulence. She stood, wordlessly listening, as if awaiting something further from Belle, her great breasts moving, under their flimsy fabric, with her breathing. Something accusing was in her silence; in her daughter's silence. Tucker Wedge was bringing home to Jericho a new wife; an outlander whom nobody in the town knew. The man standing on the porch could feel the heavy disapproval of his wife and his mother-in-law.

David Constable closed the door carefully behind him, shutting off the light from the hall. Half-feeling with each foot before he set it down, as a man will whose eyes are still unaccustomed to the night, he went thoughtfully down the front steps until he felt the roughness of the brick sidewalk. The elms spread over him an opaque canopy of foliage, ink black, shutting off the early stars; and against the dying brightness of the west where the twilight still dwelt, an exquisite dry point of branches and feathery leaf sprays was sketched briefly.

Beauty was in the night. The earth brooded in quietness; yet the warm stillness was relative only.

On closer attention he heard, a block away, the tinny rattle of the Horsts' mechanical piano. From the narrow circle of light beneath a street lamp on the next corner pealed a shrill whinny of laughter, where a knot of high school girls, like a herd of young mares, endeavored to attract the attention of a ranging group of youths of their own age which they had glimpsed momentarily at a distance. High in the dark branches above, a summer locust let go its whirring wings in a mounting series of lazy, rasping sounds, until it passed exhausted back into silence. And from far down over the horizon, made deeply musical by miles of Kansas prairie, came the mournful wail of a distant, speeding train.

Dave turned his long steps toward a bright nimbus of light which showed above the nearer houses, indicating where "downtown" Jericho was. The genial warmth of human activity drew at him powerfully.

As he turned a corner, a sudden pattern of colored lights, coming into view against the darkness, gave him a thrill of pleasure.

Church windows.

A wail of voices. High-pitched women's voices:

> And he walks with me
> And he talks with me,
> And he tells me I am his own;
> And the joys we share
> As we tarry there
> No mortal has ever known . . .

Church hymn at prayer meeting. Why, thought Dave with a curious surprise, it's a *love* song. A woman is telling of her lover. . . .

The shrill voices ached. . . . Odd for such a song to be disguised as a hymn. Or was it odd? Human hunger, seeking to translate the ineffable into terms of experience . . . the ache in the women's voices seemed suddenly a confession.

. . . *Joys we share . . . no mortal has ever known . . .*

But they *are* mortal, he said to himself, and they feel cheated. Because they do not know the joys they sing, in the sere drabness of their mortal existence. He half-smiled in sympathy for the women. For all the brave women who hide their disappointments over the manifold imperfections of life, and show them so rarely and in such unconsciously pathetic ways.

He suddenly lengthened his stride. Prayer meeting at the Community Church started around seven-thirty. It must be nearing eight o'clock now; and that train which had just sent to him its long, far sound would be Number Nine—with Tucker Wedge on it, bringing home a bride to Jericho.

Dave swung out on Main Street toward the railroad station. In Jericho, a native rarely hurried after nightfall. Yet, at this late hour, a good many stores still were open—because the wheat harvest was imminent and the farmers were in, loading up the last of their supplies for that climactic effort of the year. Wagons, buggies, and a few automobiles moved in the street, making way for each other or blocking the road in a leisured, easeful manner. On the cement sidewalks men idled, comfortable in the knowledge that they could always find a friend to fill their time while the womenfolk inside attended to the last shopping.

This was an hour Dave always enjoyed—the pleasant ease, the dawdling gossip, the salty and good-natured humor. But tonight he had no time to linger. Through the throng he made his way rapidly, a tall, loose-jointed figure with a long, humorous face. Acquaintances and friends jerked heads at him. It was easy to see that David Constable was an important man in the community, and well liked—he was a second-term county attorney, of whom great things were expected politically—Congress, perhaps, or the governorship even.

Politics was the lifeblood of conversation in Kansas. Constable knew that his name eddied through every discussion as he passed down the street. It gave him comfortable pleasure. To be known and liked by many people is an agreeable thing.

2.

Overalled men purposefully drew hand trucks piled high with dingy mail sacks beside the railroad tracks. In the hot waiting-room of the squat red-brick depot building a few women nursed babies or fanned themselves; but most of the crowd lingered on the brick platform without, the majority present for the idle purpose of "watching the cars," a favored and well-recognized pastime in Jericho.

Against the wall of the station leaned a small, rawboned man who sported a drooping, tobacco-stained mustache. Dave knew him: Andy McAdam, the town drayman. He was awaiting whatever business the express train from the East might bring him.

At various times Andy McAdam had seen the back doors of nearly all the houses in Jericho. It is not at the front doors, but at the back doors that you come to know a town. The flower beds are at the front doors—and the new paint. And the "Welcome" mats.

But the back doors look out on the garbage pails and the ash cans. At weeds running along slipshod back fences, and the family wash hung out to dry. And at the back doors a town drayman delivers, at one time or another, all manner of things.

Because of his vocation, Andy knew as much about the internal life of Jericho as did, say, Dr. Nathan J. Patterson, the old, town physician, who had felt pulses and scolded and prescribed for most of the population these thirty-odd years. Andy knew, for example, that John Farthing, the undertaker and an elder of the First Church, received every month a box marked BOOKS, from Kansas City. And that the "books" were liquid, although John Farthing claimed to be a strict teetotaler, and was an active member of the Anti-Saloon League.

Andy knew also when Banker Porter Grimes's pretty, shallow-minded young wife had had enough of the old man's overbearing ways, and was going home to Wichita where her mother would pet her and sympathize with her, and finally send her back to the husband who was almost old enough to be her grandfather.

The little drayman could tell just when Doc Patterson's no-good son, Chick, was coming home again—bounced out of another college—by the returning baggage. And a great many other matters that he took care never to reveal: because a drayman must be as secret about his customers as, say, a doctor about his patients.

At the sight of David Constable, Andy grinned cavernously and affectionately. They were old friends.

"How ye, jedge?" he asked.

Dave grinned back. "Giving me a title I don't deserve as usual. I've no hankerings to be a judge; I'd rather be a drayman."

"Shucks!"

"Suitcases are a lot easier to handle than law cases."

Andy chortled. "Dressed up this evenin', I see." His eye had taken in Dave's coat. In Jericho, to don a coat in midsummer, was to be "dressed up."

Dave grunted a noncommittal assent.

Andy ruminated. His mind jumped two or three obvious intermediate comments. Finally he asked:

"What kind of a heifer has Tucker got hisself, anyway?"

It was the fortieth time that question, phrased in different ways, had been asked Dave. He shook his head.

"Wish I knew," he said. Then he added: "She must be something extra special magnificent to get Tucker."

"Reckon so," agreed Andy. But his long years of observation as a drayman had tinged him with pessimism. "Mostly," he qualified presently, "I notice that in marriage things appears to get scrambled up. Fine women gets worthless husbands, an' swell gents gets Jezebels——"

Dave nodded. "That's why, when a man's best friend takes a wife, it's a good idea to put up a sort of a prayer . . . that she's the right one."

3.

Tucker Wedge, the editor and owner of the Jericho *Daily Clarion,* had until very recently been accounted a "confirmed" bachelor: which is to say that over a period of ten years he had shown a sprightly agility in escaping the wiles of the marriageable girls of Jericho. This was the more aggravating to the city's match-making matrons, because Tucker, by general agreement, was Jericho's most "eligible" bachelor from all the standpoints—of money, position, and celebrity—by which eligibility is decided by calculating mothers.

To have this glittering matrimonial prospect suddenly snatched away, by an unknown woman a thousand miles distant, had been enough to create fevered conversation in Jericho for days.

Because he and Tucker Wedge were friends who, proverbially, were believed to confide fully in each other, David Constable had found himself not a little discomfited in being confronted by questions he could not answer.

What kind of a woman was the new Mrs. Wedge? How old was she? Was she pretty? Did she have money, as was rumored? Was it true that she was a grass widow? Above all, why had Tucker found it necessary to marry a woman in Peoria, Illinois, when there were so many fine, charming, well-trained girls right at home—each ready, willing and able to make him an agreeable wife?

None of these questions could Dave answer; and he felt amusement slightly tinged with annoyance at the way most people seemed to resent his confessed ignorance. He did know her name:

Algeria Westcott Wedge.

It sounded rather formidable. In the last two weeks it had been repeated over and over in Jericho: at dinner parties, in business offices, at teas, in little gossiping conversations following Sabbath worship, over back fences. And endlessly over the telephone—which is such a boon to femininity.

Not in all Jericho's history had a woman, an utter stranger, appeared on the horizon, clothed with such immediate consequence. The *Daily Clarion,* as a newspaper, was the pride and boast of Jericho. It was a journal with a reputation over the state. Its editor was a man to be reckoned with, a business leader, but more importantly a political force, a moulder of public thought.

Whatever the wife of Tucker Wedge might be like, she was certain to make a stir. Everything she said or did would be discussed and assayed. It would be no easy existence for her—at first, anyhow.

David Constable had been more completely surprised by the marriage than anyone. Tucker had uttered not one word about any such plan when he left for Peoria to attend an Editorial Association meeting. He was to give a talk there—on the art of "paragraphing," in which he had achieved some celebrity, being frequently quoted in *The Literary Digest*.

The telegram came a few days after Tucker's departure. Dave had read it twice before he could believe it:

> WANT YOU TO BE FIRST TO KNOW AM GETTING MARRIED AL-
> GERIA WESTCOTT. GREATEST GIRL IN WORLD. ANNOUNCEMENT
> IN THE CLARION TOMORROW. HOME IN TWO WEEKS. TUCKER.

After he had recovered sufficiently, Dave sent a lamely whimsical reply:

> ALWAYS TOLD YOU THAT BEING BORN NOT MARRIED IS BREAK
> A MAN OUGHT TO IMPROVE THROUGHOUT LIFE. SERIOUSLY,
> DEEPEST CONGRATULATIONS. HOPE ALL HAPPINESS TO YOU
> BOTH AND LOOK FORWARD TO MEETING BRIDE. DAVE.

And now Tucker Wedge, that blithe and carefree spirit, was coming home. A family man: a man with a wife.

4.

The locomotive headlight hunted toward them through the dark. With hiss and clank and the splintering *ding-dong* of a brazen bell, the train pulled in at the platform.

Dave hurried down the train toward a black porter in a starched white jacket and blue trainman's cap, who was placing a stepstool beside a rear car.

Ahead of him he saw the figure of Porter Grimes, Jericho's most important man of affairs, a determining figure in politics. Porter Grimes was a young-old man—sixty, or thereabouts, with a potbelly and shrunken legs, but with a kind of youthful vitality that belied his years. All Jericho knew him; a man with a hard eye and thin lips, wearing his stained little gray hat perched over one eye. He was the very image of adventure plus shrewd calculation.

Even at his age, the banker-politician had a secret pride in his sexual durability. He never had been a debauchee—he was too careful for that. But his endurance had worn out two wives. The woman walking down the platform with him was his third—Clarissa. She was young, in her twenties, and weakly pretty, with an oversupply of fluffy blondish hair and an inclination to chiffons and crepe de chines.

Just now she was fluttering ahead, down the long row of cars, and

Porter Grimes strode beside her, uttering no word in reply to her chatter, or even seeming to notice that she was with him.

5.

All at once Dave saw Tucker—beyond the Grimeses—short, quick moving, alert as usual, gazing about eagerly.

Good old Tucker. He was shaking hands with Porter Grimes. His face lit up at the sight of Dave's tall, approaching figure. He pushed his way through the crowd, shepherding a woman.

She certainly knows how to dress, thought Dave.

He kept his grin as Tucker advanced toward him with the fatuous smile of the newly married, holding the woman's arm, reaching his free hand out to Dave.

"Dave! God, am I glad to see that old Merino sheep profile of yours! I told Algeria you'd be here—didn't I, darling?" He had a high, nervous edge to his voice. Not exactly like Tucker. "This is David Constable, darling." He pulled forward his wife. "No good—I warn you against him. Drinks nothing but bourbon, plays nothing but stud, and he's the greatest creative liar in Kansas——"

Dave laughed. "Forgive my blushes, Mrs. Wedge. And I want to say, in return for all that, that the first redeeming evidence of intelligence I've ever observed in Tucker is in the kind of a lady he picked out for a bride."

He had a quick, sweeping impression of Algeria Wedge. She was fragile, feminine; not exactly pretty, but he caught in her an elusive charm. She wore her green traveling suit and tiny, straw sailor-hat with a kind of elegant witchery. About her was a sense of triumphant grace. Daring—that was what she had. It gave her a rare sparkling loveliness.

She looked up at him with an odd sidewise smile, and he admired her capable wide mouth, and the grayish eyes which seemed almost to crackle with some hidden determination.

"So this is David Constable," she said. She let him hold her hand a moment. It was cool and soft. Her voice was smooth and rich. "You're the one who thinks that 'to be born unmarried is a break a man ought to improve throughout life.' Aren't you?"

She gave him another smile and released his hand. He noticed how very exactly she had quoted his telegram. If she had memorized the words so carefully, they must have meant something to her. He wondered if she disliked him. . . .

"Where are you staying?" He turned to Tucker. "Why not come to my place?"

Tucker shook his head. "Thanks. Got rooms already at the hotel.

Going to take the Hudspeth house as soon as we get squared around."

Dave did not press the invitation. Tucker's refusal had given him a slight sensation of relief—not that he had been insincere in his offer, but there was Belle. . . . Entertaining seemed a monumental task for her at best, and this newcomer might be a little daunting to an even more skillful hostess.

Clarissa Grimes launched a sudden spate of chatter at Algeria while her husband looked silently on. Tucker seized the chance to take Dave with him to the baggage-room.

"What do you think of her, honestly, Dave?" the bridegroom asked eagerly, in the tone of a man who knows that nothing but extravagant praise can possibly be forthcoming. Without giving Dave an opportunity to answer, he hurried on. "Algeria's going to be a revelation to Jericho. She's none of your hayseed queens. Knows just what, and how to do it. What I've been needing all my life—background. Agree?"

Dave nodded, faintly troubled by his friend's excited, overgay manner. "Your message certainly flabbergasted me," he said.

"Almost as much surprised myself," confessed Tucker. "Hadn't a thought of marriage when I left here. Knew Algeria before, of course, but only casually. Married then. Husband died last fall. Niceish sort of chap—wholesale grocer—but a lot too old for her." He darted a glance at Dave. "You two'll like each other."

"Depend on it."

Tucker nodded, as if at a certainty. "Algeria had charge of social arrangements at the Editorial meeting—wonderful organizer, thinks of everything. We were thrown together a lot; discovered mutual interests; got to liking each other—more than liking. Don't know how the subject came up—mutual decision, I suppose. One evening, sort of found ourselves in each others' arms." He grinned with embarrassment. "Lot of guff, eh?"

"No. It happens that way—lots of times."

"Well—she was the one with all the realistic viewpoints. We're neither of us goslings. She's got property in Peoria, but I have the *Clarion*. She had big decisions to make—giving up her life there, friends, things she was used to. Never wavered a second. Characteristic of her courage. You've got to love her, Dave. You two are the most important things in my life. . . ."

When they returned to Algeria, she was still chatting brightly with Grimes and his wife.

"Mr. Grimes has his car here," she told Tucker. "He's offered us a lift——"

"The Apex House, I suppose?" said Grimes.

"Yep."

Dave saw them into the car. They waved as they drove away, and he smiled back.

But as he turned toward his own home, the smile faded. He wished suddenly he had never sent that telegram.

Apex House. The Apex House, he remembered, was where he had first met Tucker Wedge. . . .

CHAPTER II

1.

IT was on a bitter January afternoon, eight years before, that another train had slid to a stop at the Jericho station. David Constable climbed down to the lowest step of his car, then hesitated before stepping out into the full bite of the blizzard wind.

On the level cinders below, the brakeman shivered in his threadbare blue overcoat, his eyes watering until tears trickled down into his frayed brown mustache and turned into ice there.

"Jiminy, how cold!" said Constable, still hesitating.

"Gawd yes, mister," responded the brakeman miserably.

"Is it like this much of the time here?"

"If it ain't like this, it's jest the opp'site—hotter'n the hinges of hell. An' *dry*—lime kilns is simply dribblin' with moisture compared to it. Stoppin' here long, mister?"

"I aim to live here."

The brakeman stared. "Gawd!" He spoke with a sort of broken-spirited incredulity. "Gawd, what a country to have to live in!"

Not very reassuring; but Dave managed a grin and stepped down. Other passengers crowded. A gross woman, whose hat, with a frightful artificial bird, canted down over her forehead, halted at the bottom step, clutching an infant to her vast bosom while two slightly older children peered around from behind her.

"Papa!" the woman suddenly shrieked. "Boys, there's your papa!"

A florid, big-framed man in an old-fashioned buffalo coat hurried toward them. He embraced the woman and the three children one by one; then took them off to a waiting carriage, the side curtains of which were tightly buttoned against the cold.

Dave watched, half-envious. Nobody was there to greet him—nobody was even remotely interested whether he was in Jericho or not.

Yet he was a man to whom friendship had always been easy, and to whom it had essential values.

He stood on the cinders beside the track—tall and not ill-made, although he gave the impression of excessive thinness. His shoulders were wide and bony, and he had a baseball player's limber swing of the arms; but he was so lean in the loins that his greatcoat blew

voluminously about him. He was twenty-five, and his habitual gait
was indolent. Yet he was capable of great activity when he wished;
and he had an unabashed carriage of the head, and a cheerful expression, chiefly compounded of a humorous mouth and a companionable
gray eye.

In what he beheld about him, there was little to inspire cheer. The
day was sharply cold but bright; and a level, thirty-mile gale blew
unceasingly. To one side of the tracks, a frozen, yellow-gray land-
scape stretched illimitably away to the horizon, with here and there a
splash of dazzling white where some depression had caught a skift of
snow. The sun still stood high in the pale afternoon sky: at its very
weakest in power to give warmth, but bright.

Dave turned from the open prairie to the town which bunched its
buildings east of the tracks.

So this was Jericho. Jericho, Kansas.

It appeared bleak and inhospitable, but the young man gazed upon
it with anticipation, his eyes growing keen. This was to be his town.
His town.

From the depot issued a frozen-faced agent with a plaid woolen
muffler tied over his railroad cap and wrapped under his chin. He
waved impatiently to the conductor.

" 'Bo-o-o-oard!"

A series of protesting snorts, and the locomotive lurched into motion. Past Constable's nostrils twisted a whiff of greasy steam. The
shivering brakeman swung gratefully aboard the last of the moving
cars, and creaking and squealing, the miserable little prairie accommo-
dation puffed southward toward Oklahoma Territory.

For a moment the station agent watched the train go; then he went
in, slamming the door behind him. Alone beside his luggage, Dave
vainly looked around for some equipage to take him to the hotel.
None was visible, so he lifted his two suitcases and entered the depot.

The waiting-room was empty. Already the agent had retreated into
his small cubicle, where he was fenced off from the world by the impersonality of a brass-barred wicket. From behind the wicket issued
the chatter of a telegraph key.

Dave set down his bags and thawed his hands at the stove. His idle
glance passed around the four walls. Brown paint, blistered in places.
A large calendar bore the date: January 9, 1901. Railroad posters: the
Royal Gorge; a snow-capped range of Colorado peaks; a high trestle
bridge with a train of cars and a bell-stacked engine standing diminu-
tively on it. A blackboard with chalked train arrivals and departures.

Dave's gaze came to the wicket, passed on, hesitated, returned. He
almost started. Eyes regarded him unblinkingly from behind the
wicket.

The agent. Staring, he stood there so silently that Dave had been unaware of his presence.

For a moment the young man returned the stare. Then he nodded cordially.

"Raw outside," he ventured.

Not a muscle thawed in the agent's face.

"I said," Dave repeated, "it's cold outside."

The agent's mouth opened. "You kin stay till you get warm. But I'm goin' to supper, an' I gotta lock up."

"I see."

"Drummers generally goes to the Apex House."

"I'm not a drummer. I'm a lawyer."

"Huh!" The agent considered this. "I reckon," he said at last, "the Apex would take you anyhow."

"Thanks."

With a faint feeling of surprise Dave buttoned his overcoat, picked up the bags, and stepped out. A key grated in the door behind him.

2.

Icy wind frayed his skin. He set down one bag so that he could shelter his eyes with a hand in order to read the signs down the street. Nearest the station was a large red barn with a crudely lettered legend straggling above its double doors:

O. K. LIVERY
R. J. McCurdy, Prop.
Rigs for Hire   Feed and Grain   Sales

In a corral at the back two or three miserable horses huddled, their hair roughed out by cold. No human beings were visible.

Beyond the livery stable other buildings receded down the street in the arctic air. Brick, cement block, frame—most of them were unpretentious one-story structures of a commercial nature. But a distant two-story yellow edifice with an ugly mansard roof caught his eye. On the railed gallery running around it at the second story was a decipherable sign: APEX HOUSE.

Dave lowered his head to the wind, pulled the collar of his greatcoat up about his ears, and seizing his bags, set off. He walked fast, but before he reached the distant inn, his ears were numb with cold.

An odor of warm, stale, tobacco-laden air greeted him as he opened the door of the hotel. In the middle of the lobby he saw a huge stove throwing out heat, and surrounded by a ring of chairs occupied by town loafers. These talked drowsily; and solemnly took turns at spitting against the side of the stove. One would spit, and all would watch complacently as his spittle fried and sizzled until it disappeared leaving a small stain behind. Then another would spit. There were many stains on the hot stove-belly.

Dave closed the door on the winter outside, and crossed the warm lobby to the reception desk. There he set down his bags and slapped his chilled hands together. A sad-faced individual with a bottle nose and bleached mustache stood, leaning, behind the desk, picking his teeth with a quill.

"I'd like a room, please," said Dave, after a moment.

The man with the bleached mustache surveyed him sombrely.

"Full up," he said, and turned away his gaze, while the quill toothpick resumed its plying.

Dave waited, then politely said: "I'd count it a great favor, if you'd tell a stranger where he might get accommodations elsewhere."

With a hint of annoyance, the clerk turned to him again.

"Mister, this here's just a little primitive town. We ain't got but the one hotel. Jericho's that crowded, account of the land boom, she ain't got a spare room in the hull place."

"I've got to find some place to sleep."

"That's your hard luck, mister."

Dave thought that over for a moment.

"No," he said, solemnly, "it's *your* hard luck."

The clerk goggled in surprise.

"Only think, my somewhat less than urbane friend," continued Dave with odd, owlish dignity, "of the generations of innkeepers who have waxed fat off the earnings of their taverns—simply because some remote forebear recognized the magic moment when a George Washington, a Harriet Beecher Stowe, a John L. Sullivan, or a Jesse James stood before their doors. They gave lodgings; and future generations came reverently, paying lordly sums for the privilege of sleeping in the apartments these personages had hallowed. How do you know that such an opportunity does not at this very instant stand before *you?*"

The quill toothpick had ceased its activity. "Mister," said the clerk, querulously and uneasily, "I ain't got the least notion what you're drivin' at, but there still ain't no rooms——"

"I ask your pardon," said a voice directly behind Dave.

He turned, and was looking into the eyes of a young man very near his own age—a short, amiable, breezy and cocksure young man.

"My name is Tucker Wedge," said the stranger. "Couldn't help overhearing. Immensely diverted, if I may say so, by your rodomontade delivered at the, I fear, not very appreciative head of our honest but duffle-witted Murdock."

"Now you look here, Tucker—" began the clerk plaintively.

They ignored him.

"Thank you," said Dave, heartily pleased. "I'm David Constable, lawyer."

They shook hands, measuring each other. In the background, the clerk made indeterminate sounds of injury or bafflement in his throat.

"I'm inspired to make a suggestion," said Wedge. "I've a room— not here, a couple blocks away. If you don't mind sharing a bed for a night or so until you find better quarters——"

"Why—thanks—" Dave glanced at the pleasant, aggressive grin. "I hate to put you out—but I accept in the spirit of your offer." He turned to the clerk. "Boniface, farewell!"

"The name's Murdock," said the clerk sulkily.

3.

The freezing wind clawed and bit at them like a hungry thing, so they hurried, each carrying one of Dave's suitcases.

"Three boardinghouses in Jericho—all run by widows," volunteered Tucker Wedge, gasping with the cold.

"Curious," commented Dave. "You'd think after a woman's spent half her life feeding one man, she'd shy off from devoting the other half to feeding a gang of 'em."

"Not our landlady. Feeding men gives Mrs. Dunham a chance to boss 'em!"

They arrived at a two-story frame house badly needing paint. A couple of straggling locust trees swayed bare winter branches before it.

"In here," said Tucker.

As they entered, a fleshy, gray-haired woman rose from a large rocking chair before the base-burner, to greet them.

"Mrs. Dunham, this is Mr. Constable," said Tucker.

She was afflicted by a goitre which swelled her neck out almost to the point of her chin, she wore her hair in a high topknot, and her face was doughy, like a fresh baking of bread just put out to rise. A small, unhealthily fat, yellow pug dog, with a tail curled tight as a watch spring, barked wheezily through a supercilious nose.

"Girlie! Be quiet!" said the woman. Then she informed Dave that he might share Tucker's room for fifty cents the night; and thirty-five cents for supper.

"It's highway robbery!" snorted Tucker as he led the way upstairs. "But she's got you, and she knows it. Notice her eye when she talked money? Greed."

He was interrupted by the appearance of a girl at the head of the stairs. She squeezed aside to let them pass in the narrow hall: Dave had a quick impression—plump, insinuating body, face that in the semigloom seemed withdrawn but not unattractive.

"Hi, Belle." Tucker's voice was carefully indifferent.

"Hello." She ducked her head and hurried down, so quickly that Tucker had no chance to introduce his companion.

"Old lady's daughter," said he to Dave's stare. "Queer one."

"Bashful?"

"Or a man-hater. Helps around the place—fixes beds and what not. Waits table. Never has much to say. Not bad-looking—with a bosom like that you'd think she'd have a little fire. But all the boys say no."

"Speaking from experience, are they?"

"Well, you can bet Belle Dunham's going to let nobody tumble in the hay with her—without taking the legal obligations on."

"Can you blame her?"

"I suppose not. Certainly there's never a man in this house with an honorable intention to his name—barring Judge Marty Hutto, maybe. And that's only because he's too old and has arthritis, to say nothing of two hundred pounds of wife already."

"The rest are all bachelors?"

"None of us can afford a wife. Now that you get me thinking about it—Belle does have her side, doesn't she?"

Tucker ushered Dave into a room. It was scantily furnished. But its bareness struck neither of them. Instead, with mutual interest, they turned toward one another.

They contrasted oddly. Dave's six-foot, loose-jointed frame was almost a head taller than Tucker's quick, stubby figure. Where Dave was leisurely and humorous, Tucker was alert and decisive. The lawyer's face was long and whimsical, with gray eyes and a sandy cowlick which hung down on his forehead. His new friend's nose and jaw were short like a bull terrier's, his eyes were sharply black, and his dark hair already was receding from his forehead, to his growing despair. He was a careful, almost dandified dresser; and in their later acquaintance he was often to rail indulgently at Dave's slovenliness.

"Lawyer, eh? Well, I'm a newspaper man," said Tucker.

"Editor? Jericho paper?"

"Yep. Own and operate it. The *Weekly Clarion*—every Thursday —with a nice line of printing on the side."

"Sounds mighty good."

"Sounds maybe better than it is," said Tucker with sudden, disarming candor. "Bought it on a shoestring. Running it on a shoestring."

"But you sound confident."

"Well, I *am* confident. I'm banking on this country. Constable, you're plain lucky—getting out here when you are. Unlimited possibilities. You've seen how crowded Jericho is—she's been that way for months, full to the gizzard with newcomers after the last cheap land in America. It's a big country, and growing like wildfire. We're on the ground floor, you and I!"

Constable nodded, struck and pleased by his new friend's boundless enthusiasm and assurance.

4.

They washed their hands and faces at a blue-flowered china bowl with a large water pitcher to match, and went down to supper.

"Meals here won't bewilder you with their variety," said Tucker. "Some advantage in knowing what you're going to eat."

All the boarders were men, and all but one were young. A slightly irreverent, good-humored crowd, inclined to hunting and athletics; so youthful that they still quoted Robert G. Ingersoll, with an air of recklessness (though never in the hearing of the formidable Mrs. Dunham) as the acme of freethinking defiance, and looked upon Omar Khayyam as the apotheosis of philosophy.

There were several temporary boarders, but the "regulars," with whom Dave was to grow well acquainted were: Chaucer Gatchell, in the jewelry business; Clark Kelly, an excavating contractor; Charley Van Atta, a surveyor; and Jud McManus, manager of one of Jericho's five lumberyards.

As they were sitting down to supper, an old man entered and took a chair. He had a hawk nose, a harsh, pale face, a wintry blue eye, and his white hair and eyebrows bristled aggressively. Because his back was cruelly bowed from arthritis, he walked slowly with a cane; and he never seated himself, or rose from a chair, without an effort and a grimace.

The seat he had taken was next to Dave's, and Tucker introduced them.

"Dave Constable—Judge Marty Hutto, by the grace of God and the Democrats, judge of the district court."

"I'm interested," smiled Dave. "A Democrat holding political office in Kansas? I thought the game laws were out on all Democrats."

"A few of us, sir, still manage to survive—even in Holy Kansas," said the judge. "Do I understand you are a lawyer?"

"Yes, sir."

"Jericho's well crowded with members of the profession, sir. I expect we come near to having the highest per capita of lawyers in the country. But you'll find the competition easier because a good many members of the Jericho bar have a wrong notion of the meaning of that word 'bar.' Our legal lights are most open and free about enjoying their forty-rod."

Dave was pleased to be sitting next the judge; but after that brief opening pleasantness the old man lapsed into silence and offered no more observations.

As a matter of fact, all the boarders ate more or less wordlessly. Dave also plied a knife and fork with honest relish. But presently he became aware of the presence of Belle, the landlady's daughter.

The girl waited on the table, silently and without expression. He covertly watched her. She seemed to be a year or two younger than he, and she was almost pretty in a full-blown blonde way, plump and voluptuous, lazy and careless in manner. When a jocular remark was addressed to her from the table she appeared not to hear it.

Back and forth from the kitchen she went and came, her wide hips swaying, her shirtwaist tightly pulled over her full bust, her face, with its fair skin, short upper lip, and rather prominent eyes, emotionless. Her physical quality carried a definite appeal, but Dave made no effort to speak to her. He was sure she would snub him.

After the meal he went with Tucker back to the room upstairs.

5.

How does the friendship of young men begin?

Perhaps David Constable and Tucker Wedge should have grown to know each other slowly, in a manner decorous and orderly, with a mutual regard slowly erected on a solid foundation of esteem based on tested virtues and qualities.

Unfortunately—or perhaps fortunately—such seemly processes seem rarely to occur to young men. Youth is too impatient to await the gradual flowering of a friendship. Youth offers its hand boldly and impulsively, where cautious age deems it wise to hesitate, to examine for flaws, to weigh advantage against disadvantage. But who is to say that the rash friendships of youth are inferior to the careful friendships of maturity?

David Constable and Tucker Wedge got drunk together that night. Their friendship dated from that somewhat reprehensible occasion.

The room had a Franklin stove, and it was going when they returned from supper; but the place was drafty.

"Makes a fellow almost wish he had something to warm his insides, doesn't it?" said Tucker innocently.

Dave's eyes twinkled. "If it's whiskey, I'm your uncomplaining dupe."

Tucker grinned, relieved. "Didn't know your principles. Kansas is prohibition, you know."

He brought a box from a bureau drawer, unlocked it, and took from it a bottle and two glasses. These he set on a small table by the stove. They drew up chairs, and with the bottle between them, looked into each other's eyes.

As simply as that, it began. An hour later they still sat at the table. The bottle, much lowered in contents, still stood between them. But the room seemed to have acquired a pleasing warmth for all the howling wintry wind outside. Their tongues were loosed, and under the mood of the hour all things spoken seemed superbly wise or witty.

At the height of this, after the fourth drink, Tucker suddenly began to tell of his life. He spoke of Lawrence, the seat of Kansas University, and the beauty of its elm-shaded streets, and how William Clarke Quantrill, the guerrilla, burned it down in '63.

He mentioned the brick university buildings crowning Mount Oread.

"Ugly as sin, you know," he confided. "It's a wonder Quantrill —or somebody—hasn't burned *them*. Architect's nightmares, every one of 'em. But somehow you get to love the place."

He dwelt upon his exploits on the football field, and how he had played quarterback one entire game with three broken ribs taped up. And of his prowess with the girls of the campus and the town.

Tucker went on to tell of how, having almost been expelled for extracurricular fraternity activities, he left the ivied halls and labored for a time on the Kansas City *Star*, "for a bandy-legged, pot-bellied, half-pirate and half-statesman named William Rockhill Nelson. And from him I learned more of the rudiments and essentials of the newspaper business in two months than in four years of college."

Finally, having received a little money from his family, he "took a flier" by making a down payment on a decrepit newspaper—the *Clarion*. And so he was in Jericho.

After that David Constable spoke of the green Cumberlands in Tennessee where he was born, mourning a youth of few pleasures in which he labored long days with a hoe, "chopping cotton" to eke out the family living. And he told of a day when he picked cotton on a wager and weighed in three hundred and ninety-six pounds of the fluffy stuff—a notable exploit which won him the plaudits of his fellow workers. But his father, a stern, lean man, who worked beside him, gave him no praise, because he said he should have picked four pounds more and thus made it an even four hundred.

And Dave told of the mists in the morning valleys, and the glory of the sunset, and how the whip-poor-wills chanted the whole night through. After his father died under a falling tree and his mother went to her grave because of lung fever, he sold the hillside farm for a pittance and went to college to study law. But his money ran out, and he worked as a lawyer's clerk in St. Louis, playing a little semi-professional baseball on Sundays for the few dollars he could earn, and continuing to read law until he finally passed the bar examinations.

And having discovered that the way is hard and slow for a young attorney seeking to breast competition in a large city, he sought another place. And so came to Jericho.

Whereupon they drank to Jericho which had brought them together. And they continued matching drink for drink, in exceeding amity, until the room seemed to grow dim and the furniture and walls moved in majestic circles about them. And when they could no longer talk they smiled at one another. And when they could no longer smile, they slept at last together on the bed without bothering to undress, like children, forgetful of the world, the flesh, and the devil.

CHAPTER III

1.

THE second-story room at Mrs. Dunham's became a permanent double establishment. Dave Constable's stay with Tucker Wedge, originally an overnight arrangement, extended into weeks, then months; at last they simply forgot about living apart.

Dave rented a cheap office just off the courthouse square and hung out his shingle:

DAVID CONSTABLE
Attorney-at-Law

But though he viewed that new-painted symbol of his professional career with hope, he only sat and killed time for what seemed eternities, for his legal practice seemed to have died a-borning.

He grew to know the town and the country about it. The high plains at first gave him an overpowering impression of emptiness. Never before had he beheld such a sky—the cosmic vault of blue appeared to occupy a good three fourths of the world, making small and unimportant the scattered farmhouses with their meager clumps of ragged trees and inevitable windmills.

But though the vastness at first oppressed him, eventually it distilled in him a sensation of fetterless freedom which he grew to love almost jubilantly.

Jericho itself was remarkable chiefly for the extreme width of its windswept streets and the poverty of its architecture. Most of its dwellings were small frame houses, gone gimcrack to an incredible degree, with fretted, pierced, and scrolled gables and eaves. The most consequential structures were the courthouse and the water tower.

The latter was an institution; almost a personality. It stood on a low elevation back of the town, from which it could be seen for miles in every direction—a landmark which guided wayfarers on the plains as a headland guides a ship at sea. Once it had been barn red, but now it was weather beaten to a neutral brown. And it was bent out of plumb, like an old man with a crick in his back—from the pressure of the prevailing southwest winds. Of wood, huge and round,

its immense staves were bound by wide hoops of iron, and it was upraised on six great posts.

The water tower had been built during an early boom, at a time
when Jericho was filled with community pride and hope. A system
of water pipes was even put in, including fire hydrants for a pre-
sumptive fire department. But that boom was short lived. Pumping
equipment never was installed; the wooden tower on the hill dried
out slowly. Its staves shrank and warped so that bats flew in and out
of the wide cracks at dusk, nested in the tank by hundreds during
the day, and deposited on the bottom a rich layer of guano. Some
of the fire hydrants now rusted in cow pastures. But in this they
were only typical of the general state of the town.

Jericho had been laid out on a grandiose scale by its early townsite
boosters. Far out on the prairie could still be found old bleached
stakes, like ancient bones, marking the location of lost dreams—the
site of a library, a college, a packing plant, or railroad shops, none of
which had progressed beyond the stage of imagination.

One other municipal eccentricity Jericho had—it possessed two
distinct business centers, about eight blocks apart, called, locally, Jerrytown and Jugtown. Between them smouldered a cantankerous business and political rivalry.

They were relics of the county-seat war which had been fought on
these plains a generation before—a battle for survival, since the county
was too poor to support two towns and the county seat would be the
one which would live. Men bushwhacked and gunned for each other,
a few were killed, the militia came down and restored order, and
Bedestown, the defeated rival, gave up the ghost, dragged its dried-out
shacks over the prairie and moved in with its quondam rival.

But the communities could not quite bring themselves actually to
become one. Jerrytown—the old Jericho center—remained aloof,
Republican, and a little superior. Jugtown—so called because the old
Bedestown crowd had many Texas Democrats among them and liked
red liquor—was sardonic, Democratic, and independent.

Dave found the citizens of Jericho much to his liking. The men
were inclined to casual attire, dry humor, and chewing tobacco. The
women sometimes were awkward and ungainly, and given to squawk-
ing laughter. Few social artificialities as yet existed. The banker's
wife did not look down her nose at the grocer's wife; indeed, both
probably did their own cooking, belonged to the same sewing club,
and exchanged recipes and household articles. A man was sized up:
if he proved able and industrious, he was accordingly respected; but
if he were found spendthrift or lazy, he was put down as "trifling."
Dave liked it. He was willing to abide by the eventual judgment on
himself.

2.

The political leader of the Jugtown Democrats was Judge Hutto, whom Dave had met at Mrs. Dunham's boardinghouse. Shortly after Dave's arrival, the judge's wife returned from the visit she had been making in the East, and the old man left the boardinghouse.

Temporarily, therefore, Dave lost touch with the old gentleman, but he shortly met Judge Hutto's opposite number in the Jericho political arena—Porter Grimes, the leader of the Jericho Republican organization.

Porter Grimes was president of the Jericho National Bank, and it was on Dave's instance that Tucker introduced them.

"I have a left-handed sort of interest in politics," Dave told his friend. "It's the lawyer in me, I guess. Lawyers take to politics like preachers to fried chicken. And running for office is a lawyer's best way of advertising himself. You run for office—even when you're licked, you've got your name before the people. *Quod erat demonstrandum.*"

Tucker nodded. "And Porter Grimes is the man to see—he's money, and he's wheat, and he's cattle, and most important of all, he's politics in this end of the state."

"Republican politics?"

"Strictly."

"That's me. My family was Republican—Tennessee Mountain Republicans."

"*That's* all right. You can't get anywhere in Kansas with the Democrats. This is a G.A.R. state."

"So I've heard."

"You'll find Porter Grimes pretty impressive. But don't talk any funny liberalism to him."

"Why?"

"He's a Mark Hanna Republican."

"Oh?"

"But use your head, agree with him, and he'll give you a start. With Porter Grimes behind you, it would be a mighty big boost for your legal career."

Dave was anxious to make a fair start. The description of Grimes was formidable, but when the young men called at the bank next day, they found him urbane, even affable.

The banker smiled, and Dave had a slightly disconcerting sensation—the man's whole face never smiled at the same time. His mouth smiled, but his eyes did not warm.

"So you're interested in politics?" asked Grimes.

"In an amateur sort of way," replied Dave.

"That's good," purred Grimes. "Just the right view. We're all amateurs out here—don't have the professional politician you see in eastern centers. It's a game with us—but on the other hand, when you're in a game you like to win. I look on our little organization as a kind of team—and I don't want to brag, but I think we know how to manufacture victory."

"Your record speaks for itself, sir."

Grimes was pleased to accept this as a compliment.

"It takes work," he said, "but a young fellow like you has a pretty good prospect—if he plays ball with the team. All you have to do, Constable, is take orders. Carry out assignments. Above all, stay away from the wild-eyed enthusiasts and hysterical theorists."

"Yes?"

"Of course I needn't ask how you stand on the tariff."

"Why—" Dave paused uncomfortably. "I'm—undecided."

"*Undecided?*" barked Grimes. "Young man, the high protective tariff is the foundation stone of this country's industrial expansion!" He paused, stared at Dave suspiciously, then asked as if it were a test question: "How do you happen to feel on the railroad-rate laws?"

Something in Dave bristled. Grimes's overbearing attitude antagonized him. He glanced over to Tucker. As plainly as if his friend were speaking, his face said: Be careful, keep your head, this man is important to you.

But a sudden stiffening of anger was in him. He looked Porter Grimes in the eye and said what was on the top of his mind to say.

"If I have any politics," he began slowly, "it's in one plank. I favor *any* law that keeps any person or corporation from getting more than a legitimate share of this nation's wealth."

Porter Grimes's face grew cold. For a moment they stared at each other. Then the banker spoke, and his tone said he had no use for David Constable or any of his works.

"Young man," he said, "we believe out here in the conservative, tried, safe way. We've worked pretty hard to get rid of the poison of Bryanism and the Populist hysteria. That rot about hamstringing the railroads, which you seem to favor—and the things that go with it, like public ownership of utilities, trade unionism, and tax on incomes —is the rankest kind of socialism. Good day, sir!"

He rose. Dave and Tucker rose with him, and went out.

"Why in God's green earth did you do that?" cried Tucker. "You ruined everything!"

"Sorry if I caused you unnecessary trouble," said Dave shortly, "but that gent and I can never get along."

Tucker was silent and disapproving on the way back to their offices.

They separated at the *Clarion* shop and Dave went on to his own small place of business, his eyes on the ground, his thoughts not pleasant.

When he opened the door and entered, a visitor was there.

It was Judge Hutto. The tip of the old man's cane rested between his feet as he sat in one of Dave's chairs. His hands were on the curved handle of the stick, and his chin on his hands. He seemed asleep, with his bent back and hooded eyes, but Dave knew he was awake because at intervals he sucked on a burbling black pipe with a singularly offensive odor.

To Dave's polite greeting, the judge aroused himself sufficiently to bring out a sepulchral, "Good afternoon, young man," and relapsed into burbling on his pipe.

Dave wondered at the strange call. He seated himself at a table and pretended to work, but he was covertly watching the judge. Occasionally Dave had seen Judge Hutto walking on the street, his body so bent by arthritis that he was forced to peer up from under his white eyebrows to see ahead. His progress was a sort of three-legged locomotion, and his cane was no stiffer than his limbs—yet there was a certain jauntiness in the crippled figure. Judge Hutto managed a little swagger with his stick, he wore his hat at a defiant cock, and his gaze was so sternly questioning that all commiseration was discouraged.

The old man sat in the office and his pipe continued to gurgle—and to smell. Suddenly, the judge spoke.

"Young man—you getting acquainted with our village?"

"Why, yes, sir. I've met a lot of people."

"Who, may I inquire?"

Dave mentioned names. At that of Porter Grimes, Judge Hutto snorted.

"What's your opinion of Porter?" he asked.

Dave considered. "He's got views and personality," he said wrily, "even if the views are crooked and the personality gives you chilblains."

Judge Hutto's blue eyes opened. Then his face slowly cracked a little, remained cracked for the space of a second or so, and returned to its usual expression. It was what passed for a smile with the judge, and was one of the wonders of nature.

"So he read you out of the party?" said the old man, when Dave briefly recounted what had happened.

"I reckon."

"Well—you *could* throw in with us Democrats."

Dave shook his head.

"What are you, then?"

Dave laughed mirthlessly. "I hardly know what I am."

"Mugwump?"

"It's not my real nature."

"Constable," said the old man, struggling painfully to his feet, "you're just getting a smell of the everlasting battle. Money and political influence and power—against human rights. The smooth-handed men against the horny-handed men!"

Dave laughed a little at the explosion.

"I find you interesting," said Judge Hutto, "and that brings me to my errand here. I came to inquire, sir, if you'd favor us by having supper with the Huttos tonight."

This was a surprise, and a pleasant one.

That evening Dave met Mrs. Hutto—and was hardly prepared for her appearance. She was an iron-jawed female, half-a-head taller than her bent husband, with the look of a sergeant of Grenadier Guards, a parade-ground voice, and an imperious eye. But he grew to love Mrs. Hutto. If she had a harsh voice, she had a soft heart, and she was a famous cook. He almost forgot the unpleasantness with Porter Grimes before the evening was over. It was the beginning of a lasting friendship. Many a notable debate was Dave to hold in the time to come, with the judge, over chicken and dumplings at the Hutto table.

3.

Spring came on, raw and violent, with thundershowers and dust storms, interspersed—everytime the climate seemed utterly impossible —with days of such peaceful shining beauty that all the preceding days were forgiven.

Still Dave pored profitlessly over law books with no clients. Tucker, however, was making progress with the *Clarion*. He had a fresh and breezy editorial style, and an energetic nature.

4.

As Judge Hutto had said, the legal profession in Jericho was not notable for its lofty qualities.

Dave became acquainted with the county attorney, a waddling, fat-faced, fat-nosed man, with piggy-shrewd eyes and a nondescript mustache, whose name was Jasper Peddigrew. He was an indifferent lawyer, but considered himself a wit, and constantly interrupted his own sallies with queer, saw-edged laughter, made by drawing his breath gratingly back through his throat in a series of jerks. From the first, he patronized Dave offensively.

More entertaining, and unconsciously so, was a lawyer named

Ramseur Jackson, nicknamed "Ramrod," who, according to his own self-description, had "Alabama antecedents and a Virginia upbringing." He was a professional Southerner, pompous, portly, and goateed; much given to twisted stogies and black campaign hats.

"He's a man who should always be seen for the first time," Dave delightedly told Tucker. "You can't possibly rightly appreciate the Ramrod when you get to know him well."

But most exceptional of all Jericho's legal luminaries was a man of striking appearance Dave encountered one morning in the district court clerk's office. He was of middle height, very spare, erect and dignified, with black brows, iron-gray hair, and heavy-rimmed nose glasses. His pepper-and-salt suit, while threadbare, fitted him with distinction, and his shabby linen was spotless. About him hung a strong aroma of alcohol.

"So you're our new lawyer," said he, removing his glasses and looking Dave up and down.

"I am."

"And perhaps you think I should welcome you as a professional brother? If so, let me tell you outright that there are too damned many lawyers in Jericho already! And more coming in on every train. Why every shiftless ne'er-do-well thinks he can find himself a life of ease in the practice of law, is one of the great mysteries. Where are you from, sir?"

Dave was nettled by the deliberately insulting manner, but he answered as civilly as he knew how: "I came from St. Louis."

"Aha!" The other sprang on it. "St. Louis! And I suppose to a young man from a big city we look extremely rustic and naive? Very backward and uncivilized, no doubt."

"On the contrary, I find Jericho highly interesting."

"Ha! And what's interesting about us? Jericho's a damned ugly town. Don't attempt to deny it!"

"I'd rather say picturesque," said Dave, growing stubborn.

"Picturesque?" The pepper-and-salt man seemed determined to quarrel. "Drivel, sir! A town of false fronts. All the little, squalid, one-story buildings have false fronts to make them look like two-story structures; and the people have assumed false fronts, too. Never in my life have I encountered so many fourflushers."

"People have been friendly and accommodating to me," asserted Dave stoutly.

"Then, sir, you're damnably lucky!"

All at once Dave relaxed, and smiled. "I think I am. Luck's how you look at things. Back in Missouri, I once heard some small-town loafers arguing who was the luckiest man in their town. One of them finally summed it up." He paused, and deliberately fell into the whining drawl of a river-front Missourian. "'Ah reckon the luckiest is Link Lukins. Lookit whut he's got. Seven houn' dawgs. An' five fiddles. An' two bar'ls of white mule. An'—a deef an' dumb wife . . .'"

The other's black brows went up and he gave a clap of laughter.

"Gad, sir!" the pepper-and-salt man cried. "'A deef and dumb wife.' I shall treasure that!" Suddenly he thrust out his hand. "I am Jefferson Norman. Pleasure to make your acquaintance, sir. Should like to have you call at my house, at your convenience. Our establishment's small—a motherless daughter and I, that's all—but we'll welcome you, Julia and I."

Dave found himself liking the man in spite of the whiskey fumes.

"One final word of wisdom," said Norman. "How it happened, I don't know, but this city's entitled to some sort of distinction for the irredeemable knaves who constitute its legal profession."

"I've had some warning of that."

"Not one but's a scoundrel—including myself, sir. Bombastic, insufferable idiots, and most of us would die of a quinsy if we ever drew an honest breath—"

Dave smiled. "It sounds formidable, but I have a recourse."

"And that, sir?"

"I shall strive to be as great a villain as any of them!"

Again Jefferson Norman laughed. "And I make no doubt you will take care of yourself."

They shook hands and parted. That evening Dave learned more of his new acquaintance. He happened to mention the lawyer in Mrs. Dunham's hearing at the boardinghouse. Her immediate sneer was broadly evident.

"That soak? A disgrace to the town! And his child—just a baby —taking care of that old whiskey blotter——"

"He mentioned a daughter," said Dave. "How old is she?"

"Julia? Twelve or thirteen. Looks like a little old woman, and no wonder. They live in a shack on one of the back streets between here and the courthouse. Absolute paupers—with his bottle sucking."

"Too bad," said Dave.

"A person could feel sorrier for the girl—such wretched clothes—if she weren't so snippy. None of the other children will have a thing to do with her——"

"Poor youngster!" Dave was instantly sympathetic for the girl he had never seen.

"It's her own fault!" exclaimed Mrs. Dunham. "She's a little wildcat. Makes even the boys run when she's in one of her tantrums. If

Jericho wasn't so backward, the law would take her away from that old rum-soak. She might make a good hired girl—after her temper was broken. *I* could show them how to do it!"

5.

Once or twice in the weeks following, Dave saw Jefferson Norman in a rather objectionable state of intoxication. Mrs. Dunham had not exaggerated. Beyond doubt the man was an alcoholic—of the type that obtains a bottle and then locks himself in a room somewhere, to drink himself into sodden unconsciousness.

Yet in spite of this Dave found the man likeable. Sober, he was pleasant, even brilliant. He had no practice, yet he might have been a notable figure but for his weakness.

Late one evening Dave was walking home from the courthouse, knowing that supper was near and that Mrs. Dunham unfailingly visited her wrath on tardy boarders. To save time he cut across lots, through tumbleweeds and sunflowers and bull nettles, until, while hardly noticing it, he passed a small dwelling he had not before seen. It was surrounded by an unpainted picket fence, and had a single ragged box elder tree in front. His path led him under the branches of this tree. As he passed in their shade, a hard, dark object fell from above, almost striking him, and bounced on the grassless earth.

Dave stooped and picked it up, then glanced about with astonishment. He held in his hand a brier pipe—old, with a very smooth, worn finish, but apparently never smoked. His eyes went up to the branches from which had descended this extraordinary fruit.

In a large crotch he saw a thin, adolescent girl, crouching.

"Give it back to me," said the girl, half-defiantly, half-fearfully. "It's mine."

"This *pipe?*"

"Yes," she wheedled. "Please, you must give it back to me."

Awkwardly she began to scramble down, but her dress caught on a snag and revealed momentarily thin white thighs and a flash of some pale undergarment. At this she squatted again in the branches, huddling her skirts about her and glancing at him with embarrassed eyes.

"Leave it on the ground when you go . . . I'll get it then," she said.

With curiosity he studied the strange child. She looked just at the verge of adolescence, but her face was pinched and the buttresses of chin and cheekbone stood out in an unchildlike manner. Her hair was bleached nearly white by the sun and braided back so tightly it seemed to pull up her eyebrows. Neck, arms, and legs were scrawny; and the ill-fitting print dress she wore was so voluminous there was nothing to indicate either grace or charm in her unformed body. But she escaped utter plainness because of her eyes—beautifully shaped, violet blue eyes, with curving lashes of jet.

Dave said: "Very well. I'll put the pipe down here by the trunk of the tree. But first you must tell me what a girl like you is doing with a pipe. Do you smoke?"

"N-no. I only pretend. . . ."

"But why? Ladies don't smoke pipes."

"I pretend I'm a man."

Dave wondered at the hard, rebellious little voice.

"But—why a *man?*"

"Because that's what I wish I was. I'd give *anything* to be a man. I *hate* being a girl. Boys have all the fun, and they can do everything they want. Girls are—are *awful.* I despise them. I can run as fast as any boy my size, and I can jump as far. I can bat as well as any boy . . . but I can't throw quite as good. And there isn't a boy in this town *that isn't a-scairt of me in a fight!* I *ought* to be a boy. I *hate* the things girls do. And I hate *girls!* They're so horrid, and spiteful, and mean!"

"Now wait just a minute." Dave was smiling, but his breath was fairly taken away by this passionate tirade. "Girls grow up to be women, you know. And women—they're just the nicest people there are."

"That's what *you* say—because you're not one of them."

"A girl who doesn't want to be a woman is something new to me. What's your name, young lady?"

"It's Julia. Julia Norman."

"Ah!" Now he placed her—the daughter of his friend, the drunken lawyer. "I know your father," he said. "Here's your pipe."

He placed it on the ground and started away, but she called after him sharply:

"Stop!"

He turned.

"What have you got against my father?"

So unexpectedly fierce was the question that he came back and looked again up into the tree. Her face had paled and her eyes seemed almost black with some hidden emotion.

"I have nothing against your father. I admire Jefferson Norman."

"You *do?*" A surprising flash of beauty unveiled in her eyes. "You *admire* him? I—I'm sorry I was rude." She hesitated. Color came back into her face. "I . . . thought . . . you didn't like him." Now she showed a curious tremulous eagerness to make amends. "I talked the way I did . . . because some people don't like Father. That's why —why—I've whipped so many boys—they called him—things—" Her voice trailed off. Then her head went up and she spoke with a flare of anger. "Not one of them's fit to wipe his shoes!"

She paused. Her anger subsided.

"Leave my pipe and go on," she ended abruptly.

But he lingered. Something in the child caught at him.

"Tell me more about your father," he urged kindly.

She averted her thin face; her eyes no longer met his.

"There's nothing. Please leave the pipe . . . I can't come down until you leave. Please, Mr. Constable—"

"How do you know my name?" He was still more surprised.

"I've seen you."

He stared. There was something secret here, something baffling and intriguing. But further questions were useless. She had closed in on herself.

"Goodbye," he said, and walked away.

The child in the tree watched him go.

CHAPTER IV

1.

SUMMER came on with heat such as Dave never before had known: not the humid torpor of the Mississippi Valley, but dry, breathless heat, almost with a taste of the furnace in it.

Day after day the sun blazed intolerably, an angry ball of super-heated brass in the sky; and the plains flung back the glare like a burnished bowl of the same metal. The earth became dessicated. The roads were smothered fetlock-deep in powdery dust. Wheat fields which had been a promising, rich blue-green, yellowed and shriveled untimely.

Now for the first time Dave knew the universal dread that the wheat country feels when its great, staple, all-important crop is in jeopardy.

There was no escaping wheat in this wheat country. It was an all-pervading topic of concern and conversation. As the drouth grew longer, faces grew longer with it, as much in the town as on the farms. Times were good or bad as wheat went, and it was becoming evident that unless some miracle occurred this summer was going to end in a wholesale failure for the crop.

In the first days of June apprehension became almost dread certainty. And the farmers, having nothing they could do on their burning acres, began to appear in town, hanging about the store fronts in little sullen knots, or seeking what shade could be found among the small trees of the courthouse square.

Always they talked together, with hard faces and animal intensity in their eyes. They had a habit of dropping their voices, or of ceasing to speak altogether when someone not of their calling came near.

Men like Porter Grimes shook their heads at this. When the farmers were uneasy, politics was a chancy business.

Dave still had much time on his hands. He used it in making friends among these people. His office was right across from the courthouse, and it became a sort of hangout, where the farmers came for a drink of cool water from the bucket by the window, and to exchange a word.

One of them, in particular, interested Dave. He was a small, dark man, with a mahogany-brown skin, Indian-black eyes, and a long, shrewd nose. His name was Webb Pettis, he had a farm in the Bedestown district north of the river, and was an auctioneer on the side.

There was a quality of despair, a deep underlying resentment in him. One day he opened to Dave.

"Unless some kind of miracle happens, we're sunk this year," said Pettis. "There'll be hunger on the plains this winter. Plenty of farmers will be glad to get a half-starved jackrabbit, lean and stringy as whang leather, for a little meat in the pot."

Dave nodded, listening.

"It hadn't ought to be," said Pettis. "It wouldn't be, if we got our fair share of the price the world pays for wheat."

"Why don't you?" asked Dave.

"A flock of buzzards is always feedin' on our wheat all the way along. Commission men, elevator men, millers, bankers, railroads, speculators—by the time they get through, the farmer, who gambled a year of his life on the wheat, an' sweated, an' prayed, an' suffered with the wheat, gets mighty little. Enough, the big boys figger, to keep him goin'—no more. On a year like this, when the farmer will likely get no wheat at all, them facts looms up pretty important."

"Why don't you do something about it?"

"We did—once. When we had the Populist movement going, we had all the big money boys on the run. *There* was a movement! With Mary Elizabeth Lease yellin' at the farmers to 'raise less corn an' more hell,' an' with Sockless Jerry Simpson pullin' up his pants leg to show he had nary a sock on, an' then darin' the best of the Old Line speakers to meet him in an open debate, we brought a lot of wholesome rectitude in Kansas." Pettis paused. The light died out of his eyes. "But that's all over," he concluded bitterly.

"Where did it go?"

"Where it allus goes. Farm movements is short an' few to the stalk. There comes a time when the farmer gets his belly so lean that he leaves the plow handles an' goes to hittin' out. But it doesn't last long. Just as soon as he gets a bare taste of what prosperity might remotely be like, he forgets it all an' sags back."

The heat washed in from the open door like a wave. Sweat dripped from their temples. Pettis went over to Dave's water bucket, took another drink, and let the dipper slide back in again. There was silence.

Dave gazed at the farmer and his mind was filled with far thoughts.

"You've lost your momentum, Webb," he said unexpectedly. "You need to start it up again."

"How?" Pettis was immediately interested.

"Ever hear how the Grange started?" asked Dave. "It was a club

—purely social—at first. Speaking, and musicals, and spelling contests, and barn dances. But before it quit, the Grange was a power
that was heard clear back to Washington."

"Say—that's an idea!" said Webb. "A farmer's club—what would
you call it?"

"Oh, something simple—Farmer's Union, or Farm League. Or
anything like that. It ought to have the word farm in it, because it
ought to be open to all farmers."

Pettis was looking at Dave with a new kind of respect.

"After a while, when you get to know each other well, you'll find
you just naturally decide how you're all going to vote—and you'll be
a power."

Dave's ideas were forming as he talked. His enthusiasm came out
of the moment, but when he felt enthusiasm himself, he could com-
municate it. Pettis caught fire from his fire. In the week following,
Dave heard indirectly that Webb Pettis was busy organizing, in the
Bedestown district, a club called the Farmers' Co-operative Association.

2.

But then—right when it seemed the farm lands were ripe for this
idea he had given them—came a storm.

It was a storm the like of which Dave had never before seen in his
life. The day dawned bright and hot, with a saw-edge wind from the
southwest, so dry that his skin chapped and his lips felt as if they
were splitting. He had just stepped out of his office to get some
luncheon at noon, when he saw the cloud.

It was not a sky cloud. It seemed to roll along the surface of the
earth, higher than a great mountain, dun-colored and menacing, almost solid in appearance, with twisting sand-devils running before
its foot.

There was a thrill of fear in it; to him it appeared like an immense
roller which would crush everything under its ponderous weight, and
it was sweeping toward the town at a speed that brought added apprehension.

"Get indoors!" somebody yelped at him.

He stepped back into his office and closed the door and windows.
A tornado?

He had never beheld anything to resemble this. He waited, feeling
his pulse in his ears in the stuffy silence of his closed office.

Sudden darkness fell on the city as the sun disappeared—blotted out
by shredding streamers of yellow which now hung fairly above the
western roofs of the town. What light there was became ugly and
threatening—ochreous and garish.

All at once he caught a brief, terrifying glimpse of an immense brown wall rushing upon him. How could it have arrived so quickly, he wondered idly.

The storm struck.

One instant, the street outside Dave's window was clear as crystal; the next, it was smothered in a swirling blanket of dust. A wind smote the building, so heavy that it shook the structure violently. Dust came in through tiny interstices about the door and window, until Dave coughed with it. But almost at once he lost his fear. At least this storm was not a tornado. It was a dust storm—the greatest he had ever seen, but still a dust storm.

It was so dark now that he struck a match and lit a lamp. By the light he consulted his watch to time the storm. He went to his window and tried to see out. Choking dust clouds boiled so thickly he could see nothing, and it was as if night had descended.

Grains of sand, flung by the wind, made a sharp cutting sound against his window glass. A man caught out in this storm could virtually be flayed alive. Minute after minute the gale whipped and threshed, and the dust grew thicker, permeating his room until the flame in the lamp flickered and guttered.

Then almost in a breath the storm passed. One moment it was dark, the next it was light. He glanced again at his watch. Twenty-one minutes. Over his table, chairs, papers, floor, everything, lay dust in a thick coating.

A roar from outside sent him to the window again. A new diversion. Rain. On the heels of the dust the downpour came. It grew into a torrent, and a wind which was icy cold replaced the hot sirocco. He saw people outside, struggling across the street, soaked instantly to the skin by the driving sheets, their clothing clinging to their shivering bodies.

Yet they laughed. In spite of all discomfort they laughed. With joy and lightheartedness.

The miracle had happened. The wheat was saved.

3.

In the next days Dave saw how closely keyed to the wheat this country was. The whole mood of the people changed. Farmers who came to town with mud clinging to their spokes and spattering the bellies of their horses, were suddenly buoyant, joking and laughing. Bitterness was forgotten. Merchants extended new credit. Prosperity was back.

He did not see Webb Pettis.

The truth of the farmer's statement came over him with force. When prospects seemed bright, these people forgot their grievances, forgot the necessity of vigilance which is the eternal price of democracy.

There were seeds for pondering in this. The inconstancy, the instability of mankind in the mass became apparent to him. That was why leaders were needed; and why it was possible for selfish leaders to guide and coax the people into unhealthful paths.

He considered himself. He was too young for leadership, but he began to understand the attributes of leadership. A leader among men is one who does the thinking for other men. Where other men vacillate, he must be constant.

It is easier to be a politician than to be a leader. It is easier to manage men for their disadvantage than for their advantage. Even the true leader, honestly preoccupied with the good of the people, must on occasion use political trickery to obtain his ends. Since the American government is a political government, every leader must be a politician as well.

These thoughts brought him nowhere for the time being. He realized his own inadequacy, and turned to other things.

In the new atmosphere of prosperity as the harvest came on and the farmers began to be paid for their wheat, the water tower on the hill suddenly assumed a new significance to Jericho. A boom was on. In every direction the garish yellow of new pine frameworks rose to the rap of hammers and the brisk whine of saws.

The Commercial Club claimed the population had doubled in a year to two thousand and excitedly predicted ten thousand in five years. It seized the occasion to advocate a special bond election, to repair and put into operation the moribund water system.

"The *Clarion*'s got a prime issue to fight for," Tucker rejoiced.

"Congratulations," replied Dave lazily. "You won't have any opposition will you?"

"That's how little you know about it. Judge Hutto will fight it!"

"I didn't know the judge was such a dog in the manger."

"He's old-fashioned and stubborn. And he's the boss of the Democrats. It'll be old Hutto against the Commercial Club, and the *Clarion*'s going to the mat with him this time for progress and principle. Look out of that window."

Dave's gaze followed Tucker's gesture of disgust.

"A city of windmills!" exclaimed Tucker with loathing. "At least a score of them in view right from here. Advertises us as a hick town. Now, honestly, wouldn't you feel more civilized to turn on a faucet and have water?"

"Well—I don't think hot and cold water is the complete recipe for civilization. But I'm not against the water tower or progress. I'm going to hear what Judge Hutto has to say."

As Tucker promised, the *Clarion* conducted a stentorian campaign for the improvement bonds, but to everyone's surprise Judge Hutto declined to oppose them. The old judge was canny. He had not remained a political power in the leadership of a minority party these years because of making blunders.

He may or may not have arrived at his decision after a conversation with Dave Constable. Dave lounged over to the judge's office in the courthouse one morning, indulged in some anecdotes, talked half-humorously about politics in general, and departed. He had dropped a hint or two which gave the judge food for consideration.

Tucker was half-disappointed, and also inclined to crow.

"For once the old man swallowed his so-called principles," he told Dave. "He hates worse than mortal sin parting with a dollar."

"Some people are mighty superstitious about giving away their money."

"But this isn't his. It's the people's. He hoards it as if it were his own."

"Not a bad trait in a public man."

"It just hurts his ingrown conscience."

"You wrong him," said Dave. "It isn't conscience that bothers the judge. His conscience has had plenty of chance to make adjustments during his long life. It's one thing I like about him. Never trust a man with too hard and inflexible a conscience."

"How's that?" Tucker asked.

"Never mind." Dave laughed. "It's just a private idea of mine. All the great injustices of the world have been committed by men who were too sure they were right."

4.

When the Jericho Town Baseball Team climbed into Gotch McCurdy's picnic wagon, Dave felt almost silly. He wore a uniform—skull-fitting cap with long bill, wide-sleeved shirt, baggy knee-trousers, wool stockings, and spiked shoes. He was to pitch for Jericho, and this was Tucker's idea. Dave had not thought the time would ever again come when he would appear in public in this kind of garb.

The Jericho Town team was a new and improvised organization. It existed, in fact, for one day and one event—the dedication of the water tower.

This was Tucker's day of triumph. All of it was due to him. The

Clarion had been largely responsible for the triumph of the Commercial Club and the water bonds at the election. For the first time Tucker had made himself felt as a force in the community, and from now on he would be reckoned with. Because of this realization he made himself the heart of the committee appointed to arrange a proper celebration of the opening of the new water system.

While gangs of men swarmed around the old water tower, straightening it, calking its cracks, tightening its iron hoops, cleaning out the bat guano, and repainting, Tucker arranged with the committee a program of festivities. Pumping equipment was installed, and the *Clarion* announced that the Senior Senator from Kansas had consented to be the speaker of the day.

Today was the great occasion. Band music would precede the oration, a picnic on the prairie would follow it, and then would come the *pièce de résistance*—a baseball game, in which Jericho would meet a well-respected adversary, Dodge City. Considerable money was wagered on the game, chiefly on the size of the score by which Dodge City would beat Jericho's representatives, because nobody gave the home team much of a chance.

In the picnic wagon sat Dave and Tucker, Jud McManus, Charley Van Atta, and Chaucer Gatchell, all of Mrs. Dunham's boarding-house, with other members of the team. These five were the core. Tucker was the catcher and the captain.

Dave's statement that he had pitched for a semiprofessional team in St. Louis had been remembered. But it took days of withering and railing sarcasm before Constable agreed to take part.

After that there were three weeks of practice. The young men talked and dreamed baseball. They ran and sweated and caught and threw in the oven-hot sun. Together they washed off their mud and perspiration beneath a makeshift shower rigged in a barn—naked bodies gleaming in the chill downpour, shouts, laughter, horseplay, the stinging of each others' dripping flanks with the ends of wet towels, all the exhuberant, unconscious obscenities of vigorous young animals at play.

They could never quite get the smell of sweat out of them. Dave could sense it in the vehicle, above the other smells of horse perspiration and the sour, whiskey odor of McCurdy, the livery-stable man, who drove.

Three weeks ago nobody could have convinced Dave he would be doing this. He looked over at Tucker, at the alert bull-terrier features. As the picnic wagon went up the hill they could see the crowd around the base of the water tower and the faint strains of band music came to them.

. . . *He's a champion beyond compare* . . .

Tucker's nostrils flared. This was the atmosphere he loved. In every athlete a certain amount of exhibitionism is inherent, and he never had forgotten the roar of the crowds in his playing days at the University.

It had, however, taken a shrewd argument from him to win Dave.

"If you're going to be successful as a lawyer, you've got to be known in town," Tucker had said. "Think of it this way. One good ball game will get more people talking about you than winning a dozen lawsuits."

At the top of the hill they climbed out of the picnic wagon and joined the crowd.

"Band concert's about over," said Tucker. "Wonder how long the Senator will hold forth."

As J. Wilber Bratten, president of the Commercial Club introduced the Senator, Dave gazed at the crabbed old man who had for years dominated Kansas politics—a personage of medium height, heavy visaged, with long, wavy, iron-gray hair.

"*That* the Senator?" he asked.

"That's him," said Tucker. "Our great statesman from the bounding prairies—hayseed in his hair and gopher dust in his mouth."

"Get himself up like that all the time?"

"Always."

"He looks," said Dave, after studying the Senator a minute, "like something between the head gambler of a Cripple Creek casino and a member of the Chevy Chase hunt set—with a touch of the evangelist thrown in."

"Burning sunset on the painted desert," agreed Tucker.

The Senator fortified himself from a carafe of lemonade and launched into a thundering exordium. For a few minutes Dave listened intently. Then he perceived that the speech was no more than the usual collection of platitudes, and his attention wandered again to the figure of the speaker. It was a figure worthy of scrutiny. The Senator gave off the colors of the spectrum from his necktie, and though his frock coat and trousers were sober black, his embonpoint was encased in a fancy waistcoat of dazzling design.

"I begin to understand his secret," said Dave to Tucker at last. "I thought at first he was overdressed, but now I know why he does it."

"He just likes loud clothes."

"You're wrong. He knows his appearance uplifts his constituents like a strong shot in the arm."

"Maybe . . ."

"Out here things are inclined toward drabness. So when the Senator attends a wedding or a funeral—and he never misses one—those present receive a high-voltage thrill out of the spectacle he presents—

coupled with a proprietary pride in the knowledge that this gorgeous creature is *their* Senator."

Tucker grinned.

"He elevates the sovereign voter by merely shaking his hand," went on Dave. "And so—in spite of his stupidity, crassness, and venality—they keep sending him back to office."

Tucker gazed at his friend indulgently.

"I suppose," he chuckled, "you think you've now learned the golden secret of politics."

"Not quite. But I'm learning—and I don't quite like it."

The long speech ended. Mrs. Bratten, thinnish, blondish wife of the insurance man, cut a ribbon with a pair of engraved scissors. The band played again. And the crowd cheered as the pumphouse engines started with a loud coughing of exhausts.

The crowd began to break up. Some of the men and boys wandered about the tank, peering up at it. A few leaks dripped, but the engineer assured everyone that these would cease as the staves swelled.

Out on the prairie the women were busy preparing the basket picnic. Dave saw Mrs. Dunham's thick figure, and Belle beside her. Between them they lugged a heavy-laden basket toward the planks on wooden trestles which had been erected for tables. Belle looked youthful and almost slender beside her mother. He thought she gave him a faint smile.

5.

Standing together, Tucker and Dave watched the Dodge City team go out on the field to practice. The diamond was crudely laid out—low-growing clumps of prickly pear or Russian thistles decorated the outfield. The bases were homemade sandbags and the base lines had been accentuated by a mowing machine.

Nobody expected anything better. There was no grandstand; the spectators, having finished eating, stood in a wide V, the apex of which was behind the chicken-wire backstop.

A swart, wide man, with a blue-grained chin and eyebrows that met across the bridge of his nose, walked down the first base line in the blue uniform of the visiting team and began slowly heaving a ball to the Dodge City catcher.

"I've seen that guy play," said Tucker. "He's Al Steuber. Topeka—Western League. He's a ringer they've brought up. But he warms up slow. If we could get a few runs early, we might just trim those sodbusters. . . ."

He took Dave down the third base line to limber him up.

A small, dried-up man with a wide mustache, walked out on the field. Andy McAdam, the town drayman. He had been chosen to umpire the game because he loved baseball and because he could not be intimidated.

With the heat of the sun biting his back, Dave went slowly out to the mound.

"Take it easy—watch yourself!" barked Tucker after him.

Dave took his place on the mound, wabbled his fingers in the familiar loose, leathery clutch of the glove, and turned the new ball over and over in his hand.

He saw his teammates looking at him. His condition. That was their great worry. Dave had found that he could still pitch with fiery speed and that his fingers had not forgotten the cunning which makes a ball break sharply just before the batter swings at it. But when he grew weary he lost his ability to control the ball, and that could be fatal against a tough opponent.

He and Tucker were about all that Jericho had—a pitcher and a catcher. Of the others, Charley Van Atta, in the outfield, was a speedy runner but a weak hitter; Jud McManus, at first, was a good hitter but an erratic fielder; and Chaucer Gatchell, who played shortstop, was a fiery and eager player, but at times seemed to be all thumbs. These were the best of the Jericho players. Clearly it was incumbent on Dave to keep the enemy, as far as possible, from hitting the ball at all.

"Play ball!" shouted Andy McAdam.

The crowd tensed. Dave sensed curiosity and skepticism in the eyes fixed on him. Dave Constable, the people were saying. What does he know about pitching? Why doesn't Jericho get a real pitcher—like Dodge?

He grimly thought of a line: *They bet their red gold on your ruddy brawn.* . . .

Then he almost laughed to himself. *Butcher'd to make a Roman holiday.* That came next in there somewhere. He mustn't let himself take this so seriously. After all, a game . . . and he could not think of anything more purely American than this battle between unsung athletes on the sun-cured buffalo grass diamond.

Momentarily he was aware of faces. And there was Belle Dunham, the wind blowing her dress so that it outlined her plump body. . . .

The first Dodge City batter was at the plate, pawing the ground with the histrionic ferocity of the sport, and swinging his bat. Tucker crouched behind him, his eyes gleaming through the bars of his mask.

Dave thought: If I've just got control . . .

He wound his long body into a knot, a leg flailed high, and his body shot forward as his arm went through with the cunning last-instant wrist snap which gives the final degree of speed to the ball.

Cleanly white the ball cut the center of the plate and smacked viciously into Tucker's huge mitt. The batter almost dislocated his back with his fruitless swing.

"Stee-rike!" barked Andy behind Dave.

Tucker's encouraging scream rose above the sudden roar of the crowd as he threw the ball back.

Dave suddenly felt fine. Across his back the muscles were loose. His wrist was limber and strong. A feeling long forgotten took possession of him. This once had been much a part of his life.

He struck the man out. A great yell came from the onlookers.

It was good to be playing again. Down his spine, under the shirt, sweat was just beginning to trickle. Dave retired the side. The Dodge City players glanced at him with enhanced respect as they trotted out to the field. Rather impressive it had been—two strike-outs and a weak dribbling grounder, with the head of their batting order up.

"We've got to get ours early and often," Tucker was fiercely yapping at his men as the team went to bat.

Charley Van Atta, first up, waited and dodged and ducked until he got a walk. Jud McManus smacked a ringing single through short. Chaucer Gatchell hit. The enemy second baseman was on it, pounced, fumbled, threw—wide.

Bases full and none out.

Tucker swung three bats as he went to the plate. He discarded two of them and with the handle of the third carefully knocked the dirt out of his spikes. Then he pulled his cap low over his eyes, rapped the plate twice, and waited, his jaw bulged by a chew of tobacco.

Steuber pitched. Fiercely, Tucker slashed at the ball.

At the tingling crack of the bat he was off and an invisible force seemed to bring Dave to his feet.

He saw the white sphere cleave a low arc just over the second baseman's head, bite the sod, and leap on.

Tucker was a frantically scurrying figure around the base lines.

In the outfield two Dodge City men pursued the ball, got it, relayed it.

Tucker slid into third. A cloud of dust.

"Safe!" yelled Andy McAdam.

Three Jericho runners had scored.

Steuber, the Western League pitcher, was surprised and angry. He scowled at Tucker. Then he "bore down" as the phrase went. Tucker never got past third base. The next three batters went out in order.

"Three runs—better than I'd hoped," said Tucker as he came in to don his mask and chest protector. "From the ugly look on Steuber's face—our fun may be over——"

Out on the pitcher's mound Dave went to work. He pitched, using all the cunning and skill he had, working the corners of the plate carefully, trying to deny the foe a single good cut at the ball. Hotter and still hotter grew the afternoon. Sweat darkened his shirt on the back and at the armpits. Dust gathered in sticky, muddy grime on his face. He lost count, almost, of the innings. In a strange rhythm they succeeded each other. He sat on the bench, or took a turn at bat. And then he was pitching again.

In its first inning Jericho had played far over its head; a slump was inevitable. Somewhere along the line, in spite of Dave's grim steward-ship on the mound, runs began to appear on the scoreboard for the visitors. One, in the fourth inning, on Jud McManus's fumble and the first clean hit against Dave. Another, in the sixth, when Tucker dropped a third strike and later overthrew second trying to cut off a steal.

The thing Dave had dreaded began. The afternoon grew into a long weariness. The zest departed; his back muscles lost their suppleness. He began to allow bases on balls—not many, but too many.

At last he had the eighth inning behind him. But his long lack of training was telling. He came in from the mound and sat on the ground, nursing his strength. The Jericho team, impotent since that first inning against the murderous pitching of Steuber, failed miser-ably at bat.

Then he went slowly out for the beginning of the ninth, and he had never believed himself capable of such goneness. The score was still three to two in favor of Jericho. On the side lines he could hear the crowd imploring him, almost threatening him—to hold off the foe.

Jericho had not dreamed of really defeating Dodge City. But now, with the game so near an end and victory almost in sight, an hysterical excitement gripped the onlookers.

It was all up to Dave. From a hidden core in his being he sum-moned strength. Sweat stung his eyes. He whipped it angrily away with his sleeve.

Three batters to be retired.

The first struck out, biting foolishly on two wide curves, and then allowing Dave to ease a straight pitch past him for the third strike.

But now Dave knew the virtue was gone from his arm.

Almost helplessly he saw the next man hit a tingling single to right. He tightened his belt, pulled low the visor of his cap.

The next batter hit. Easy grounder. Easy for Chaucer Gatchell— no—he trapped the ball—dropped it. Too anxious for a double play. Too bad. Both runners safe.

A square, dark form came to the plate—Al Steuber, the professional.

All day he had been the most dangerous man in the Dodge City batting order. Dave read enmity in the narrow eyes under the black line of meeting brows.

If he could set down Steuber . . .

He saw Tucker's signal and heard Tucker's encouraging yell.

"Ball!" snapped Andy McAdam.

"Ball two-o-o!"

The Jericho infield swarmed around the little umpire. Jud Mc-Manus threatened. Chaucer Gatchell swore. Tucker Wedge pleaded. Through this storm Andy McAdam stood with almost rakish imperturbability. His hat was tilted back on his head at an extreme angle. His hands were in his pockets. He relished the tense atmosphere and his own invincible position as final arbiter.

Dave stood, resting, until the strident voices ceased and the men went back to their positions.

"Ball thre-e-e!"

Tucker hurled his catcher's mask on the ground and charged out furiously toward the umpire again. But Dave met him.

"Go back!" he said.

"That highway robber! It cut the corner just as clean——"

"Shut up and get behind that dish!"

Tucker looked at him. Nodded. Trotted obediently back.

It was Dave's crisis. He had a right to do with it as he wished.

One after another Dave slammed two strikes past Steuber.

Two and three.

He drew a deep breath. The crucial pitch.

He wriggled the ball in his glove. Wound up.

Delivered with everything in him.

Steuber took a stride forward and swung viciously.

When he heard the metallic ring of the bat against the ball, Dave knew it was all over. Charley Van Atta ran far back, but the white pellet sailed over his head. Trotting around the bases was little more than a formality for Steuber.

The game ended.

Dodge City, five; Jericho, three.

6.

The young men splashed and shouted under the shower, their white skin gleaming with clear drops of water, their hair glistening and wet.

Al Steuber came over to Dave, his nude torso shaggy with black hair.

"Nice game, Constable," he said gruffly.

"Thanks."

"With that fireball, why ain't you playin' for dough?"

"I'm a lawyer."

"You could do better pitchin' ball than chasin' ambulances."

Dave recognized a sincere compliment. But he was morose as he turned back to his dressing.

"What's the matter?" Tucker asked.

"I lost your game for you." Defeat still smarted in Dave.

Tucker laughed. "Are you kidding? You didn't lose it!"

"The hell I didn't. I grooved a fat one and he killed it."

Tucker slapped him affectionately on the shoulder with a wet hand. "We kicked that ball game away behind you, my friend. Felt like weeping for you all afternoon, holding those pirates off out there while we were booting our chances. What if Steuber did get hold of a lucky one? Do you know what? Nobody in town expected Dodge to beat us less than twenty runs, and most everybody doubted we'd even score. Why it's really a victory. You ought to hear what the crowd was saying. You're a hero, son, if you only knew it!"

"Cut it out!"

"I'm not joking. You did all the work and pretty near beat them, ringers and all. Everybody knows it. You just heard what Steuber said."

"A lot of guff." Dave still was not happy.

"Say," said Tucker looking at him closely. "You're on the verge of going stale. Know that? You need relaxation. Girls! That's the recipe. I don't think you've been out since you came to Jericho."

"I don't know any girls."

"*I* do. I know a little number—Trudy Marshall's the name. Schoolteacher in the winter, but, boy, no stick-in-the-mud in the good old summertime. She'll get a friend. We'll take 'em riding this evening."

Dave was dubious. "Who's the friend?"

"How should I know? And what does it matter, so long as she wears skirts? Trudy'll get somebody keen. Come on. It'll be good for what ails you."

Dave thought. "All right. I'll go you—once."

7.

A late moon slowly lifted itself, remote from the affairs of the world, as they drove their rented surrey to the drugstore.

Dave's stomach prickled with anticipation. He was eager, but almost timorous. The girls would be waiting there. He tried to picture in his mind what his girl would be like. He hoped she would be gay and friendly . . . and pretty. Especially he wanted her to be pretty. He felt a physical craving for the prettiness of this girl who was to be his for the evening.

Dave felt the excitement connected with women which young men know and which made him queasy with expectancy.

"There she is—there's Trudy!" exclaimed Tucker. "And there's—there's—good God almighty!"

The eagerness and the anticipation were washed clean out of Dave. It was Belle Dunham.

"God, I wouldn't have done *that* to you!" commiserated Tucker.

But it was too late to retreat. And it was very evident that Belle was as much surprised as they. . . .

With some constraint Tucker introduced Trudy, a small, dark, frolicsome person, inclined to giggle and constantly polishing her nose with her "shammy."

Dave said little. He gingerly took Belle's arm to help her into the surrey. The arm trembled.

"Match you for the back seat," suggested Tucker.

Dave glanced at Belle. "I'll drive."

Tucker did not argue. The advantages of a rear seat would be wasted, sitting with Belle Dunham.

As they rolled out of town, Dave holding the reins could think of nothing to say to Belle. She was as wordless as he. Stiffly circumspect, they sat gazing straight forward.

But in contrast Tucker, behind them, was ardently devoting himself to Trudy. In the front seat they were painfully aware of all that went on. Stirrings, gigglings, the preliminary fencings of a young man intent on taking liberties, and a young woman intent on making him earn them.

Tucker said something they did not catch.

"O-o-oh, Tucker!" Trudy giggled.

The voices grew lower, intimate. Fruitlessly Dave sought to make some casual remark to Belle.

Trudy's voice came, suddenly sharp with protest: "Tucker Wedge! No! You stop that!"

Dave felt Belle go rigid. But at once the voices on the rear seat ceased. In spite of himself, Dave could not avoid a quick glance behind. They were locked in a long kiss.

It seemed many minutes before the two in the rear seat stirred around again, rearranging themselves. Tucker spoke, venturing a commonplace or two. Finally he said:

"Hey, Dave—the water tower. Get a view from the hill in this moonlight——"

Dave turned the team up the road toward the dark, looming structure.

"The thing's still leaking," commented Tucker as they sat in the still darkness. Above the breathing of the horses and the occasional creak of harness, came a slow dripping.

"Let's get out and take a look," Tucker suddenly said.

"I'm not going to do it," said Trudy.

"Why not?"

"It isn't right." Virtuously.

"Yes it is."

"No."

"Yes."

"No."

It seemed this sort of thing would go on all evening. Tucker broke the impasse.

"Trudy Marshall, are you going to get out of here by yourself, or do I have to lift you out?"

"Tucker Wedge, you wouldn't dare!"

"Just watch!"

"You're a brute!"

"I am!"

"And a beast!"

"I am!"

"Then I'll get out."

Assuredly Trudy Marshall was no "stick-in-the-mud."

From Belle came a gasp of protest.

"Trudy—you're not *really* going to get out?"

"Of course." Trudy giggled.

"Don't you do it, Trudy!"

"Why not?"

"You mustn't!"

"Belle Dunham, don't be such a stick!"

Tucker helped Trudy out and Dave watched them walking over to the water tower. He felt more uncomfortable than ever, sitting alone in the surrey with Belle.

The horses stirred. He checked them, glad to be doing something. Anything.

The other couple disappeared—beyond the big tank. Envy came over Dave. If he had anyone in the world except Belle Dunham . . . Why wasn't she like Trudy—soft, pliant, persuadable?

From the corner of his eye he looked at her, stiff and silent. Yet for all her stiffness, he found her proximity subtly impelling. He began to wonder if he should not be doing something—wasn't it expected of him? Just to sit there was foolish and witless. After all *he* was the man. It was the male prerogative to make advances. . . .

"Want to get out?" he asked in a low voice.

"No!"

This was no half-teasing refusal like Trudy's. Belle's voice was tinged with suppressed emotion . . . terror.

He sat still. They strained their ears for sounds from the other couple. Once they heard Trudy's giggle. And again, briefly, Tucker's voice.

Then the night was still all about them, and the noises of the small prairie insects all that came to them, except for the water tower's slow *drip, drip*.

In spite of himself Dave could feel his blood slowly heating at his imaginings of what was transpiring beyond that tower.

He had momentarily seen the avid preoccupation of Tucker and Trudy with each other. The glimpse of them in each other's arms, mouths glued together, had a suggestion of violence in it, in spite of the immobility of their close-pressed bodies.

Anger compounded chiefly of disappointment came over him. Why was it ordained that he should draw a "stick"? Bell Dunham was unfair to him. Her primness and her repelling stiffness violated something in him. His anger made him take an unpremeditated action.

Tentatively he slid his left arm about the girl in the darkness. She was conscious, instantly, of the movement, and straightened upright, quivering.

"Don't!" She sounded queer, gasping.

Voice and action were prim. Impossibly prim. So prim that he felt like laughing. Only he didn't laugh. His arm tightened about her waist which was twisting . . . twisting to get away.

"Nobody's going to hurt you." His voice was strangely husky.

He leaned over her with dry-throated eagerness. His free hand forgot the reins, and captured her body. A sudden, soft resilience. The girl's breast. That completed the hot typhoon of his emotion.

She was warm, writhing, still resisting, but he drew her remorselessly to him. He heard her gasp—a throaty *Ah-h-h*—and then his mouth found her mouth, warm, shaking, and wet.

For a long moment they were fastened together, he a male curve of furious power, she seeming to collapse under his urgency. Then he drew back.

She half-rose. She was weeping. Her face, dim in the night, was twisted with a great terror, excited beyond all thinking.

"You—you leave me alone—you dirty—insulting—pig!" she wailed. Then suddenly she screamed loudly: "Trudy! Trudy Marshall! You come here this minute!"

Dave was contrite, not a little frightened. The girl was hysterical. He tried to soothe her, but she pulled far over from him, waiting in dumbly hunched hostility, tears running down her face.

Tucker and Trudy appeared from around the tower, hurrying.

"What happened? What's the matter?"

"I want to go *home!*"

"Now, Belle," protested Trudy with vexation. "Don't be like that."

"You get me home!" shrieked Belle. "You got me into this. Now you get me out!"

Trudy looked at her a moment. Then she glanced from one of the young men to the other, as if to say this was none of her fault. Dave was speechless with humiliation.

Soberly, Trudy climbed into the rear seat of the surrey.

"Better come back here, dear," she said softly. Weeping wildly, Belle complied, and began dampening, with her tears, the other girl's shirtwaist.

"What under the sun did you do?" whispered Tucker as he climbed in front with Dave.

"Not a thing—just kissed her."

"Is that *all?*"

"I told you I just kissed her!"

"Huh!"

In silence they drove back to the town. To Dave's relief, Belle seemed more composed as they let the girls out at the drugstore. She had repaired some of the ravages of her weeping with Trudy's "shammy."

"Some evening," Dave said as they walked back to the boarding-house from the livery stable.

"Sorry," apologized Tucker. "How was I to know?"

"You couldn't."

"Belle Dunham's worse than I thought."

"Well," defended Dave, "she didn't ask me to do it—she told me not to—guess she meant it——"

"It's that mother of hers. Belle's been dinned at so long about the perfidy of the masculine critter that merely being near a male man scares the poor girl witless."

Dave did not answer. In spite of the unpleasantness he was unable to shake off the warm memory of the girl's soft, struggling body. He was in an unhappy daze.

The boardinghouse was dark. That was a relief—both young men had half-feared to find grim Mrs. Dunham waiting up for them. At least Belle had said nothing to her mother.

They sneaked upstairs. Not until they were safe behind their own door was Dave able to tell what had occurred.

"What does she expect?" demanded Tucker indignantly.

But Dave felt better now. He could see a little of the humor of the evening.

CHAPTER V

1.

NEXT morning Dave went down to breakfast half-apprehensively; but Belle waited on him, as on the others, with no change of attitude or expression.

Midway of the meal Mrs. Dunham lumbered heavily in, as was her custom, to look over the room. Her eye wandered over Dave without any particular attention. He left the boardinghouse with relief.

That morning he learned that Tucker was right about the aftermath of the baseball game. Dave passed the McCurdy livery stable, and was hailed by a chorus of loud greetings from the stable loafers who never before had even noticed him. Farther on a couple of small boys halted and looked at him with respect; then turned and followed him for a block or so at a discreet distance. Several men spoke to him cordially, and at the door of his office he was stopped by Jasper Peddigrew, the county attorney, who was almost friendly in his oblique way. Later in the day he encountered the Reverend Matthias Widcomb and found even the man of God quite enthusiastic.

"I saw the contest yesterday," said the minister. "I would say your part in it was exemplary—most exemplary. You smote the Amalekites hip and thigh, brother."

The harsh visage carved itself into a smile and the preacher laughed heartily at his own biblical reference.

Dave was warmed by these public attentions. There was, however, one troublesome matter for his consideration, and he went back to his office, burying himself in the *Session Laws of Kansas* more to get his mind off that subject than to obtain any mental nutriment from this dry fare.

The troublesome subject was Belle Dunham. Dave discovered that the harder he tried to put her out of his mind, the more insistently she remained. He was not himself; his thoughts were not clear and manageable as before.

So, being unable to put her out of his thinking, he did the opposite and considered her deeply.

Certain inconsistencies in her behavior appeared as he thought over the events of the previous evening. She never had made scenes when other men attempted familiarities—so he had been told. Tucker himself had remarked that Belle had been "like a sack of suet" when he tried once to kiss her.

Her tears and histrionics had been reserved for Dave.

He wondered why, and gradually came to a conclusion not unflattering to himself: Belle behaved so wildly with him, because what he did, had a meaning for her that the actions of other young men did not have.

The implications of this were intriguing. In spite of an inward warning voice, he could not find those implications unpleasant. He was twenty-five. It is an age when the appeal of woman reaches its most imperious tide in man.

2.

Belle and Mrs. Dunham had just returned from church the following Sunday, when Dave heard the landlady calling him from the foot of the stairs.

"Mr. Constable!"

"Yes, Mrs. Dunham?"

"You're wanted at the door!"

He was surprised both at the summons, and at the indignation which was evident in her tone. But his surprise was still greater when he went to the door.

"Why, Julia!" he said.

In the past weeks Dave had seen Jefferson Norman occasionally, and once or twice he had encountered Julia.

He discovered that the child had a standing arrangement with the county clerk's office at the courthouse. When her father appeared there, intoxicated, someone got word to her, and she came to take him away.

It was pathetic to see them—and rather beautiful—the concern and loyalty of the little girl, and the affection, tinged with shame, of the man.

Even when he could hardly hold himself erect, Jefferson Norman treated his shabby daughter with gentle courtliness. Dave marveled how he could make her a bow so stately when he seemed almost ready to fall on his face. Julia could do anything she wished with her father, except make him give up liquor.

When he saw her at the front door—for Mrs. Dunham had left the child standing on the porch—he stepped out quickly with her. She had been crying.

"What is it?" he asked.

"Father," she said. "They've got him down at McCurdy's——"

Dave understood immediately. Julia had never before asked help in taking care of her father. This must be serious.

"Go on home," he said. "I'll fetch him."

She nodded wordlessly and departed, her thin legs winking in the bright sunlight.

Dave went to get his hat and considered what he had to do. He knew the McCurdy place.

There was a huge hayloft above, and stalls below with a central passage led into by double doors at each end. At the front was the tackroom for harness, and in the stalls nearest the street entrance stood a row of light buggies, a surrey or two, some carriages, a picnic wagon with seats running along the sides, and McCurdy's big, black hearse, which he rented out to all undertakers for funerals, complete with himself as driver in black silk hat and frock coat. The horses occupied the rear stalls. In a small lean-to at one side were the proprietor's office and sleeping quarters, in frequent use at night for gambling.

This was all quite usual. But the man who owned the livery barn was nothing usual.

Rufe J. McCurdy was reputedly the strongest man in Jericho, and proud of it—huge, beetle browed, generally wearing a few days' black stubble on his heavy jowl. He was somewhere near forty years old. In some long-past brawl his right ear had been so injured that it was twisted and crumpled in the ugly way known to the West as "gotch-eared." To this he owed his nickname, "Gotch."

Not a few persons in Jericho would have liked to get Gotch McCurdy out of town. He was disreputable, a fighter, and considered dangerous when drunk. Prohibition had produced in Kansas its own inevitable brand of lawlessness. The livery stable, it was whispered, was the center of bootlegging in Jericho.

McCurdy, furthermore, was a known woman chaser. Hardly a "cat wagon" came to town that he wasn't one of the first to it.

Cat wagons were a legacy of the reform wave which had swept the ordinary sporting houses out of Kansas. They were brothels on wheels—canvas-topped wagons, carrying a couple of diseased and slatternly prostitutes and a pimp. In furtive progression across the country they sometimes made stands down at the creek near the railroad bridge below Jericho, at a place where willows grew thickly enough to provide cover.

It was surprising how quickly a crowd of men and youths assembled, as an invisible intelligence ran through the town.

The jackdaw crowd would stand in a circle down in the willows, exchanging yokel witticisms with the tough, painted women who sat on camp chairs outside their wheeled establishment, wearing dirty wrappers and smoking cigarettes. Sooner or later a dare would be made by one of the men and taken up by one of the young fellows. Sheepishly reckless, a swaggering young Kansan would climb into the wagon with one of the "girls." What happened usually took no great time. The youth was back, greeted with half-jocular, wholly lewd, admiration. After that, the ice broken, the "girls" would be kept busy for hours. . . .

But when Gotch McCurdy was in the crowd, no preliminary maneuvering was necessary. He preferred being first. It was little wonder that the respectable people of Jericho would have felt safer with the stableman out of town.

Yet he had strange contradictory traits. Although he was said to be mean with animals and was known to have killed a fractious mule by beating in its head with a stick of stovewood, he was, when not drunk, kind to children, and frequently allowed the town boys to borrow his two greyhounds to hunt jackrabbits.

He was the only man in Jericho who could lift over his head an iron ball weighing one hundred pounds, which stood in a corner of his stable. The ball possessed no handholds and this was a real feat of strength. He admired strength, though he had no tolerance for anything decent; and the nearest he ever came to being converted was when a traveling evangelist named Dow, a man as big as Gotch himself, put up that iron ball as easily as Gotch had ever done. McCurdy, thereafter, attended a revival service or two; but he managed, in spite of his respect for the evangelist's biceps, to remain successfully unregenerate.

Thus far Gotch McCurdy had been convicted of no crime; but bootlegging was ascribed to him, and some said worse.

There was a story of old Riley Buskin, a rancher living south of Jericho, who returned to his place late one night after a lodge meeting and saw somebody busy among the hay bales in his meadow. The rancher was too old and feeble to deal with a thief, so he rode to town for help. At one time Gotch had worked for him. Buskin knew the liveryman was afraid of nothing, so he galloped directly to the red livery barn.

Gotch was not there. The rancher returned to his home. On the way he encountered a hay wagon loaded with bales. He was morally sure they were his bales. But the driver was Gotch McCurdy; and so black was his glare that for months afterward old Buskin feared to say anything about the episode.

Dave put on his hat and started walking rapidly toward the livery barn, several blocks away, wondering what he should do.

On a Sunday, Gotch certainly would be drinking. The usual shiftless, rough crowd would be hanging around the barn. Interference might meet with ugly resentment.

3.

Dave was correct in his prediction to himself about the crowd. A dozen or fifteen men were there; loafers, looking for any diversion. A taint of bad whiskey was in the air.

Several of the men spoke to Dave as he came up. They all knew who he was, since the Dodge City baseball game, and in their greetings was a certain friendliness and respect.

He looked around for Gotch. At first there was no sign of him; but almost at once he appeared at the door. When he saw Dave, he scowled.

"What you want?" he growled.

"Have you seen anything of Jeff Norman?"

"What's it to you?" The man was half-intoxicated and dangerously truculent. But Dave confronted him with an unquailing eye.

"Mind if I look around?" he said quietly.

"What the triple-plated hell do you mean?" demanded McCurdy, taking a threatening step forward.

The crowd fell back, except for one man. He stood to one side and Dave now marked him for the first time—a hulking Irishman named Mullikin, as drunk and threatening as McCurdy.

"Don't take nothin' off of him, Gotch!" said Mullikin. "If he gets smart, bust him!"

It was ugly—the ring of disreputable loafers, the brute at the door, the other sneering to one side.

But Dave did not retreat. Instead he walked straight forward. His eyes had grown coldly bleak and he did not deviate from the line he had taken toward the door.

Gotch's face grew black as he barred the way.

"Stand aside!" Dave said.

They were almost of the same height, but compared to the wide-shouldered, thick-muscled stableman, Dave seemed slight and almost weak. For a tense moment their spirits clashed fiercely.

Then the crowd saw an amazing thing. Gotch moved. He glared as if he would enjoy killing the young man, but he moved—to one side. Dave walked past, without glancing at him, into the "office."

As he entered he heard a great laugh, a hoarse bellow of derision behind him. At first it puzzled him; then he realized it was Mullikin, the Irishman, deriding McCurdy for being thrust aside.

Dave paid no attention. He saw Jeff Norman, sodden drunk, lying on the cot among dirty gray quilts. A couple of loafers pushed inside the door to stare.

"Hello, Mr. Norman," said Dave. "I came to get you."

"Ah. Constable, isn't it?" said Norman. "Good of you. But don't desire to leave now. Sleepy . . ."

"Julia asked me, sir. She is quite concerned over you."

The blear eyes opened. "Julia?" A slight frown appeared. "Well. I suppose . . . come at once. I . . . dislike to keep her waiting."

Dave took him by the arm to help him rise from the filthy pallet. He stood weaving, hardly able to stand erect.

In that instant they heard the sudden rising snarl of male animals in rage. The loafers at the door disappeared, their attention turning to the excitement without.

Dave let Jeff Norman sit again on the cot. His mouth closed grimly, and the cold look came back to his eyes as he stepped to the door, expecting anything. There he halted.

This new fury was not directed at him. The giants, McCurdy and Mullikin, stood confronting each other, bristling and roaring their anger.

The Irishman had laughed when Dave faced Gotch down. On him McCurdy now turned with the wrath of a beast. Mullikin was not daunted. There was no reason to be. Between the two men there seemed almost nothing, in size or strength, to choose.

The Irishman was a great, muscle-bound section foreman, bullying a gang of meek Mexican track-laborers on work days, and roistering on week ends. Men said he did not know his own strength. Between him and Gotch a smouldering enmity existed, based on a primitive, inescapable question—which of them was the better man.

As Dave stepped from the door, Mullikin, drunker even than Gotch, stood snarling while McCurdy cursed him with every bitter obscenity to which he could lay his tongue.

Suddenly Mullikin moved. A sixteen-pound iron crowbar leaned against the stable wall. The Irishman seized it, and whirling it above his head with both hands, rushed murderously at Gotch.

In that moment the air was charged with death. The section fore-man's face had an insane, bloodless look. He lashed the ponderous weapon through the air like a switch. A blow from it would spatter McCurdy's brains like the contents of an egg.

Gotch did not move. As Mullikin rushed forward, swinging the iron club, the liveryman's great, hairy hands snatched at it—grasped it, held it.

Now began a contest so savage that it held the spectators hypno-tized with its fury. One above the other, the giants locked their fists, each throwing every ounce of his mighty strength in the effort to force back his foe or wrest away the bar, each grimly determined not to yield.

They were settling at last an issue long delayed. Nobody moved to interfere.

To Dave they seemed to form a tableau—a terrible, almost dream-like tableau. No motion was detectable at first. As if their feet were rooted deeply into the ground, the two adversaries stood in silent, tremendous struggle.

Dave heard the hoarse breathing of their effort. Their backs bent like huge strung bows, their heads sank between their shoulders, their muscles seemed almost to crack with the stress on them, as the men glared into each other's eyes.

First Mullikin pushed McCurdy back. Only slightly. Their immense feet thudded on the ground. It was Mullikin who gave way for a struggling step or two, now. The crowbar remained exactly in the position it had been—upraised between the two men, the objective of the struggle, the sudden symbol of their rivalry and hate.

Sweat dripped. The crowd remained fixed in breathless fascination.

Then as the feet trampled back and forth and the men gasped with the terrible force of their contest, the crowbar changed its position slightly. Almost imperceptibly—a fraction of an inch, no more.

Another shift. Another. So gradually at first that the spectators hardly could see it, the movement of the bar grew.

A great sigh came from the crowd. Gotch McCurdy was gaining the upper hand. Slowly he was forcing the Irishman back, twisting the crowbar over his head.

With infinite deliberation the process continued, as if it were some planned move executed with almost glacial slowness.

The Irishman's face grew haggard. He staggered backward, his face running wet with sweat.

A devil's look was in Gotch's eye, and on Mullikin's face were hate and desperation. Back went the Irishman, the crowbar bent farther backward over him.

Neither spoke. The only sound was the continued labor of their breathing, the trampling of their feet, the drip of their sweat on the baked earth.

Suddenly, with numbing quickness, the end came.

A hitch-rack stood before the stable. Gotch forced Mullikin with brutal inexorability until the railroader's thick back bent over the crossbar of the rack.

Backward, backward Mullikin bent.

All at once he uttered a long, whimpering moan. He was down. Flat on the ground. He lay twisting, agony in his face.

Gotch wrested free the crowbar and whirled it over his head like a black-browed fiend.

"McCurdy!"

At the shout, the giant hesitated.

"Put down that bar!"

The shout and command had come from Dave. Gotch turned on him a strange, blank, sightless stare. For a moment he stood, while the crowd shrank back, not sure what new violence he might inflict.

Then he shook his head as if to clear it. Slowly he placed the crowbar against the wall, and stepped back from his fallen foe.

Dave walked forward to the prostrate man. With the imminent violence removed, the crowd now surged about. But, with a suddenly enhanced respect, the men gave Dave room.

Mullikin looked up at the curious, downturned faces, and the gray pallor of a great sickness was upon him.

"Get me out—of here," he gasped beseechingly to Dave. "It felt —like I busted—something inside——"

Deep in his vast torso soft wet tissues had been ruptured when Gotch bent him back over the hitch-rack. Instinct told the man that his injury was mortal.

"Get him on the cot. Somebody go for Doc Patterson."

They hurried to obey the authority in Dave's voice.

Jefferson Norman appeared, swaying at the door. They pushed him aside as half a dozen men carried Mullikin in.

Outside, Gotch McCurdy glared around him. Nobody moved or spoke. Lowering his head like an angry bull, he turned and tramped back into the stable.

The loafers remained, gaping at the door. Dave did what he could to ease the suffering of the man on the cot.

Fifteen minutes later Dr. Patterson arrived to take charge.

"H'm. H'm," he said. "Pulse very rapid. May be a major blood vessel rupture. Get him out of this filthy place to his home immediately."

Dave remembered now the errand which had brought him here. "Come on, Mr. Norman," he said. "Your daughter's waiting."

With acceptance almost pathetically childish, the iron-gray lawyer allowed himself to be led away from the sobered stable crowd.

4.

Mullikin was dead next morning. Dr. Patterson did everything that could be done for him, but an internal hemorrhage is a hard thing to stop. The Irishman had died in agony.

It was Tucker who brought this news to Dave.

"That's the finish for Mr. Gotch McCurdy," he said with satisfaction. "He can't wriggle out of this one. Public feeling's pretty strong. He'll go to the pen this time—it's been yawning for him long enough, God knows."

"McCurdy's not guilty of any crime," said Dave. "I saw what happened."

"Well," Tucker was grim, "after what that desperado has done in the past, it doesn't make a whole lot of difference. People are good and tired of him and his ways."

"You can't send a man to prison because you're tired of him."

"It's been done."

Dave recognized this as an expression of a solid segment of Jericho public opinion. Tucker was intimately acquainted with the way the businessmen and the prominent people felt, at least. Dave did not feel like arguing.

"A good lawyer could acquit McCurdy," was all he said.

"And who'll McCurdy get? Jasper Peddigrew, as county attorney, is no bargain as a prosecutor, but with people feeling the way they do, no reputable member of the bar will take that livery-stable bum's case."

Dave shrugged. Tucker departed, and he returned to his work. He dismissed the matter.

He was hardly surprised, though he did not welcome it, when he heard his name spoken from the door that afternoon.

"Lawyer Constable?"

He turned from his desk. It was Gotch McCurdy, huge and sullen, who stood there. The man appeared more brutal than ever with his coarse chin-stubble and his small black eyes glittering evilly.

"Hello, McCurdy."

Gotch spat tobacco juice villainously at Dave's spittoon, and spoke without bothering to wipe the trickle of dark slime that ran down from the corner of his mouth into the thicket on his chin.

"Guess you know I'm in trouble," he said.

"I guess I do."

"It was Mullikin's fault. But they're goin' to arrest me."

"How do you know?"

"Mebbe I got a pipeline."

Dave found himself disliking the man.

"Sit down," he said.

Gotch took a chair that creaked under his weight.

"McCurdy," said Dave directly, "you're forever in trouble. What's the matter with you?"

"Folks is ag'in me."

"No such thing. You're against other people."

The black eyes glittered dangerously. Dave looked into them un-flinchingly. Surprisingly, the black eyes fell.

"A man's death is a mighty serious matter," said Dave with less severity.

"We was drinkin'. He laughed . . . well, you know about that. But I never done nothin'—mebbe cussed a little. He come at me with that granny bar——" he hesitated, frowning more deeply than ever. "*You* seen it all. I come to get you to be my lawyer."

"McCurdy, you'd better get another lawyer."

"I want you."

"Why me?" Dave was seeking a way out.

"Because you wasn't afeared of me. The man that handles this case is goin' to have to have guts."

Dave considered that a moment. Then he spoke:

"McCurdy, I'll help you. As you say, this case may take guts. If it weren't for that I'd refuse. But I'll accept it now." He paused, and spoke even more seriously. "But there's no good beating around the bush. People are down on you—and it's your own fault. I'm not going to preach to you, but I don't want you making things any worse for yourself—at least not until after this trial. So I'm giving you some orders. If you don't obey them, I'll withdraw immediately from your case."

Nobody had ever before talked like that to Gotch McCurdy. He could have broken Dave in two with his hands. But he said:

"What are them orders?"

"Stay off liquor. Try doing a little work. If there's any booze on your premises, get rid of it. Understand?"

Gotch listened humbly. "Just as you say, Mr. Constable," said he, so meekly it sounded almost ludicrous. "Do . . . what you can for me, will you?"

He rose and lumbered out.

CHAPTER VI

1.

DAVE found a letter awaiting him at the boardinghouse that evening.

My Dear Constable:

This is at once a note of gratitude and farewell. In the unhappy condition you found me Sunday there was a particularly regrettable circumstance—I failed to impart to you a bit of news we owe you as a friend of this little family.

Julia and I are leaving Jericho. When you receive this we will be gone. I dislike farewells, which is my reason for choosing this method of apprising you.

One of life's vagaries confronts me. I had supposed all the family money long since dissipated, but unexpectedly I discover that a distant cousin, residing in Delaware, died and left her small estate to us, her only living relatives.

I might say that I was, in a manner, celebrating this unlooked-for event when Julia asked you to seek me. Naturally it did not occur to the child to tell you any of this.

Again my thanks for your many kindnesses. Be assured of our good wishes.

Your most obedient and sincere friend,

JEFFERSON NORMAN.

There was no mailing address. Well—perhaps he would hear from them later.

He started upstairs, the letter in his hand, when he saw Belle hurrying down. He paused and made room for her to pass.

"Good evening, Belle——" he began. He had hardly spoken to her since the evening of the water tower.

But she ignored his greeting and went running down, holding her skirts up at the sides. He saw that her color was high. Her eyes were lowered and she seemed agitated.

He stared after her as she disappeared into the dining-room, before continuing up to his bedchamber.

The singular occurrence still puzzled him as he opened the door, but he forgot about it at once at the sight of an even more singular spectacle which presented itself within.

Tucker stood in the middle of the room, clad only in a suit of knit underwear, very baggy at the knees and seat, and a pair of box-toed, yellow button-shoes. His eye was wild, and he clutched frantically to himself a coat and pillow.

"Where is she?" he demanded.

"She?"

"Belle Dunham! Did you see her?"

"She went downstairs."

"I caught her—Dave, I caught her just now. Hiding! In there!" Almost hysterically he pointed a quivering finger at an open door in the end of the room.

The chamber occupied by the friends was an example of Mrs. Dunham's grasping habits. It was none too large to begin with, but the landlady had stolen even a part of its already meager space, by having an end of the room partitioned off for a storage closet. A door opened into the storeroom, which always was kept locked except when the mistress of the house was obtaining linen or bed clothing. Dave saw the door open now, but at first he could not grasp Tucker's meaning.

"That fat, prying heifer was in there *hiding!*" repeated Tucker with a high, strident note in his voice.

"Calm yourself down, Tucker—what——"

"Calm? Calm down?" Tucker's tones were those of Lear, finding himself by all the world betrayed. "I come home—start to change my clothes before supper. I'd just taken off—every damned thing—except my union suit. And I've only Providence to thank *that* wasn't off too—in another two seconds I'd have been naked as a jaybird——"

"Yes?" A light was beginning to come into Dave's eye.

"I hung my pants on the doorknob—the knob of *that* door——" Tucker darted a glance at it as if it were a creature of living treachery.

"It's been locked before—always locked——"

"Yes, yes," prompted Dave.

"*This* time it . . . came open——"

"Go on!"

"And I—I found myself looking right at her, and she at *me*—like this—*this*——"

His voice died in a wail of violated modesty.

The utter absurdity of the tale destroyed every semblance of self-control in Dave. He fell on the bed and laughed aloud.

Tucker stared at him morosely for a moment. Tight-lipped, he began dressing.

"Any humor you see in this—" he said, at last, with chilling dignity.

It brought Dave out of his mirth. "Oh, come Tucker!" he protested. "After all——"

Tucker glared. As majestically as a short man could, he dressed and departed, slamming the door after him.

Dave sat up on the bed. The matter did not seem so funny now. He realized he had wounded his roommate's feelings and he was sorry.

Deeply contrite he followed Tucker downstairs and made conciliatory overtures. But the coolness remained throughout the meal.

Tucker went to a meeting that night—the monthly business session of the Commercial Club. Dave returned to his office and worked late on the Gotch McCurdy case.

He expected Tucker to be in bed when he got home, but the room was empty. It was long after midnight before his roommate returned.

2.

They dressed silently in the morning, the constraint still on them. At last Dave said:

"Meeting lasted pretty late last night, didn't it?"

"Not very." Tucker was short.

Dave bit his lip.

"Tucker," he said, apologizing frankly, "I'm not going to let you hold a grouch against me. I'm going to say it now—that was a stinking mean thing to laugh at you—and I'm sorry——"

He stopped awkwardly. Both of them were frightened before the possibility of a display of sentiment.

"Well—" said Tucker at last. He stopped, drew a long breath. "Say, Dave—I was an ass——"

"I was the ass," said Dave, gruffly.

Tucker frowned terrifically and kicked the floor. "I guess that's what we both are—just a couple of asses."

Neither of them saw anything funny in this solemn declaration. They shook hands, and quickly dropped the grip, because both were moved and in terror of showing it.

To change this dangerous subject, Tucker said:

"Reason I was so late last night—I had a sort of a date after the meeting. Trudy Marshall."

"She back here?" Trudy had gone away to teach in September.

"Just for a day. Some kind of teachers' convention."

"Tucker."

"Yeah?"

"Gotch McCurdy asked me to take his case."

"The hell you say!" Tucker was immediately interested. "What did you tell him?"

"I took the case."

Tucker stared at Dave. "Good God!" His voice contained annoyance and disapproval "Didn't I tell you how folks felt about that bum?"

"I had to take it."

"But why? Why do you always have to go right in the teeth of the whole town?"

"Tucker, McCurdy's not guilty of those charges."

"What if he isn't—do you owe him anything? He's a thug, and an outlaw if I ever saw one. Let him fight his own battles—he'd certainly never do anything for *you!*"

"Perhaps not."

"Don't you see, Dave? I want you to do all right for yourself. This —this—it'll only make things harder——"

"I'm sorry. But it's what I've got to do."

Silently they went down to breakfast together.

3.

Dave could not keep his eyes off Belle Dunham as she waited on the table that morning. In the back of his mind, speculation seethed concerning Tucker's encounter with her.

The girl seemed unconscious of both his glances and his thoughts. Deliberately and unruffled, she went about her duties. None of the young men at the table was ever entirely oblivious of the presence of Belle. She was twenty-three, of the type which ripens early. Though a connoisseur of women might have said that her richly contoured figure would become gross and flabby in a few years, Dave was provided with no such insight. He knew only that when she passed near him, or he caught the light scent she wore, he experienced a disturbing sensation.

His mind kept reverting, in spite of his efforts to prevent it, to that night by the water tower; and he remembered the feel of the girl in his arms, the softness of her hair, and the taste of her mouth. Even her stormy weeping was a part of a swelling tide of emotion, which now seemed to possess a strange meaning.

He realized this thinking was not good. He was certain, also, he was not in love. But some great and exciting urgency was on him, overriding caution, driving him in spite of himself.

A night or so later he overtook Belle, walking languidly as usual, as he came from his office. It did not occur to him then that the apparently casual encounter might not have been wholly accidental. His pulse quickened as he called to her.

In a manner oddly unsurprised, the girl came about and allowed him to reach her side. For a moment they walked together in silence.

He suddenly found he had things to say to her, yet his tongue seemed paralyzed.

"Belle," he blurted at length, "are—you angry with me?"

"Why should I be?"

It caught him by surprise. "Why—because of what—happened that night——"

He stopped, realizing that he was stammering an accusation against himself.

She considered. "I guess—a man can't help it—when he gets to feeling a certain way——"

This seemed to him real forbearance.

"I was afraid you'd not understand," he told her eagerly. "I—I really didn't realize what I was doing. It certainly will never happen again."

"Then . . . I'm not mad."

Her calmness astonished him, made him almost uneasy. He found that the girl filled him suddenly with strange and bewildering thoughts and yearnings.

"Belle——"

"Yes?"

Almost as if he had nothing to do with their formation or utterance, the words came:

"There's a dance at the pavilion tomorrow—will you——"

She glanced at him with quick alarm.

"I—couldn't."

"Oh."

He was dashed. But almost immediately she changed her mind.

"I—guess I could—if ma didn't know——"

"Did you say anything about——"

"Of course not! But ma—says you're a *rounder*. . . ." Again the quick glance as she used the disreputable word.

"What do *you* think, Belle?"

"Oh, I don't think that."

He was warmed by this assurance. "That's all that counts with me," he told her. "Will you go?"

She hesitated.

"If I could meet you—away from the house—maybe——"

With a curious feeling that he was watching someone else doing all this, he found himself making arrangements. The girl agreed readily to his plan.

When she parted from him at the door of the boardinghouse, he felt an exhilarating sensation of achievement.

4.

Next morning, as he made his way through the courthouse corridors, Dave experienced the strongest misgivings.

A crowd was hanging around the halls—and long before time to open court. He could not but feel this was an ill omen.

A preliminary hearing in a Kansas criminal court is for the purpose of determining, not the guilt or innocence of the prisoner at the bar, but whether it is worth the expense and effort for the state to conduct a jury trial, with its elaborate and costly processes. Normally, therefore, since such a hearing is quickly finished, it attracts small attention.

But the preliminary hearing of Gotch McCurdy had drawn a large gallery. Dave did not like it. Public sentiment sometimes asserts itself in a courtroom, and even a responsible judge has been known to be swayed by it.

Dave knew his case thoroughly. He had a definite theory on which he intended to make his defense. But he had hardly bargained on a hostile crowd in the courtroom—and here were the idle and curious of Jericho, always the worst element to contend against. He went into the courtroom, took his place at the counsel table and began to arrange his papers before him, while the curious craned from the seats behind.

Jasper Peddigrew, the county attorney, waited until the last moment before the opening of court, then waddled in. He was quite secure in his mind about this hearing, and as his cunning little eyes sized up the crowd and decided it was an occasion to gain notice, he began making continuous conversation with his assistant, with the deputies, with the court clerk, and with acquaintances in the first rows of seats. He interrupted his conversation only with his own peculiar, saw-edged laughter, which was largely at his own sallies. Except for a slight nod when he first entered, he paid no attention to Dave.

Judge Hutto's bent figure and white thatch appeared at the high desk. A deputy sheriff led Gotch McCurdy in.

Dave had half-expected a demonstration when the stableman entered the courtroom, but public animosity, if any existed, was restrained. Some of Peddigrew's assurance disappeared at this. He had expected more active support from the onlookers. But he had overlooked the fact, as had everyone else, that several days had intervened since the death of Mullikin, indignation had cooled, and a good many people in the community had begun to remember that Mullikin himself had a reputation as unfragrant as McCurdy's. Some had a well-developed feeling that two public nuisances had met at McCurdy's stable that Sunday, and in the elimination of one by the other, a sort of wry justice had been worked.

Not at this, however, but at the new young lawyer's manner of conducting his case, Peddigrew and his staff experienced a really painful surprise.

David Constable stood up before the court with a disarming, disheveled look, a lock of hair twisting across his forehead. He appeared limber, easy going, young; and he spoke with a half-embarrassed grin, seeming deferential to judge and opposing counsel to an uncalled for degree. Many in the courtroom, particularly women onlookers, sympathized with the young man—he seemed hardly fitted to combat the ponderous odds against him.

But as the state called witness after witness, it was noticed that Dave's cross-examinations were shrewd, and as purposeful as a steel chisel. He had an odd, humorous manner which was ingratiating, and he made several slight stumbling errors in procedure. But old Judge Hutto on his high bench knew even sooner than did Jasper Peddigrew that the "slips" the attorney for the defense made were in unimportant particulars when no great issue was involved; and that when a really vital point was being made, or a recalcitrant witness was to be driven into a corner, Constable moved with a sure, remorseless skill.

Peddigrew had not taken the trouble to make a thorough preparation, expecting to have the prisoner bound over without difficulty. By midmorning he was floundering. Constable was turning his own witnesses against him.

Time and again, under cross-examination, persons put on the stand by Peddigrew made damaging admissions that it was Mullikin who really had assaulted McCurdy.

Peddigrew became impatient, angry.

At last he was forced to a thundering impeachment of one of the state's witnesses—a farmer, Will Mawson, whom Dave had beguiled into saying that the Irishman had tried to kill McCurdy.

Peddigrew had his own methods. He believed in bullying and a loud voice in the courtroom.

"Were you drinking that Sunday?" he bellowed, waddling threateningly toward the witness.

"Well—mebbe—I had a few drinks—" said Mawson, badly confused and frightened.

"You were drunk!" trumpeted Peddigrew. "Your honor, this man is disqualified by his own testimony. I move his evidence be stricken——"

"I object!"

Dave's voice cut so sharply that the crowd sat forward.

He turned to Judge Hutto.

"I should like to ask the honorable county attorney in just what stage of drunkenness his witness was——"

"That's irrelevant!" shouted Peddigrew. "Any fool knows that a man's drunk or he isn't!"

Smoothly, almost pityingly, Dave's voice came.

"I'm sorry to hear Mr. Peddigrew in these words qualify himself as a fool. Because every *wise* man is aware of no less than five classic stages in drunkenness."

His manner had caught the courtroom, and as he made a masterly pause, it was observable that Judge Hutto, the sheriff, the prisoner at the bar, the spectators, even Jasper Peddigrew himself, listened intently. Slowly, on his fingers, Dave counted off the five stages of drunkenness:

"*Jocose . . . Morose . . . Bellicose . . . Lachrymose . . .* and *Comatose . . .*"

In the courtroom hung a moment of surprised silence, followed by a yell of laughter. Jasper Peddigrew glowered. But Judge Hutto chortled even as he rapped for order. It took minutes to restore decorum. And the courtroom audience still was joyously whispering the "five stages" over, as Judge Hutto upheld Dave's sudden motion to quash the indictment against McCurdy, for lack of evidence.

It was a very neat piece of legal swordsmanship. Gotch was free —and without having had a single witness called to testify in his defense.

Judge Hutto himself offered congratulations.

Others praised Dave. He felt a warm glow. The "Five Stages" became a saying on Jericho's streets. The *Clarion* published them, with a lively account of the proceedings, and other newspapers picked them up. The witticism grew statewide—passed over the borders of Kansas. As far away as St. Louis, or El Paso, men were quoting Dave's adjectives.

". . . Saw Gil Blake last night—looked perilous near the fourth stage—lachrymose. . . ."

". . . An' Jed Freeland hadn't no more'n reached jocose, when Sil Grovetree hit him. O' course he skipped clear over to bellicose right now, an' flattened Sil, who reached comatose quick an' expeditious. . . ."

It was the beginning of a reputation for courtroom humor which was to follow Dave.

These things, of course, Dave did not yet know. He went back to his office, and was shortly waited upon by Gotch McCurdy.

"You done mebbe better for me than I had comin'," said the stable-man, grudgingly, and with a half-frown.

"Depends on how you act from now on."

"Anyway, thanks."

"Stay out of trouble."

"Do my best."

"Come around and see me once in a while."

"I will."

"You and I may be good for each other, Gotch."

"Don't know how much good it does *you*——"

"Leave that to me."

"Sure."

David Constable was not really superstitious. But he was later able to date the beginnings of his career from the preliminary hearing of Gotch McCurdy. Toward the man he grew to feel a curious attach-ment, partly of sentiment, partly of interest, partly of half-humorous loyalty and sympathy. In after years Dave's enemies would make much of the strange friendship thus begun, and at times even his friends would fail to understand it. The lawyer that day appointed himself in some degree a guardian and counsel to the clumsy giant. And to the time of McCurdy's death Dave always secretly felt that Gotch was to him a talisman of good luck.

5.

Night shut down over the world, and Dave drove his hired buggy up the street. The sharp shadows and blinding lights of day were gone. Houses were soft gray, uncertain masses, shot with spots of brightness where lamps gleamed in windows. Trees loomed in dim shapelessness.

His heart still was big in him with the day's triumph. He was eager to reach the cottonwood grove on T Street, where Belle had promised to meet him.

About this adventure was a suggestion of furtiveness and risk. It was obvious that Belle feared her mother. Her agitation when he proposed the rendezvous, showing how much it cost her to overcome her fear and surrender to his plan, quickened in him a pleasant sen-sation of power. She was afraid to come out with him; yet she could not resist coming. That was the way it seemed to him. He liked the feeling.

There ahead were the cottonwoods, a dark adumbration against the night sky. He peered eagerly into the gloom. At first he saw no sign of her. He began suddenly to fear she had not come after all. Perhaps at the last moment she had decided against it. Or her mother had intercepted her. Disappointment clutched at him with sharp fingers.

Something moved. A great relief flooded over him. It was Belle's figure. He pulled up the horse, and leaned over to give her a hand into the buggy. Her fingers clutched at his, damp in the chill autumn evening.

As the horse got under way again, the girl arranged herself in the seat, smoothing her skirts, folding her hands in her lap. They emerged from the full murk of the cottonwoods and he had a good look at her under the stars. To him in the intimacy of night she seemed suddenly more handsome than he had ever before known her; highlights sparkled in her eyes.

Very demure, she sat well over on her own side of the buggy, and he touched the horse into a smart trot with the whip.

The Jericho pavilion, which was their intended destination, was an open-air dance platform of the crudest type, built of lumber, a mile beyond the city limits. It was so placed as to avoid interference from the strait-laced element which, in Kansas, listed Seven Deadly Sins quite different from those denominated by the early Church Fathers. The Kansas Seven were: dancing, cards, the theater, nonattendance at church, tobacco, drinking, and profanity. To the peculiar mental bent, the chief zest of which is the regulation of the lives of others, not even theft, murder, or adultery seemed somehow so important as these seven sins.

A sudden, uneasy thought occurred to Dave.

"You're sure your mother doesn't know where you are?"

"She thinks I've gone out with some other girls. She doesn't—even think—I like you."

His heart thumped at this admission from her.

"What if she found out you were with me?"

"It would be—awful."

He did some more thinking.

"There's going to be a crowd at the pavilion. What about all those people—don't you think someone might tell her they saw you?"

"Oh—do you think . . . ?" Her voice contained real fear.

A bold idea came to him.

"What if we skip the pavilion altogether?"

"Where would we go?"

"Oh—we could just drive around. And talk. Nobody would see us. Belle—there's something I want to ask you anyway."

She gave him a quick sidewise glance.

At a side road he turned the horse. She said nothing, though she again looked at him. On the hard earth the horse's hoofs said *clop-clop,* and a loose spoke rattled in the left rear wheel. But between the two on the seat there was a long silence.

"I won my case—the McCurdy case—today," said Dave at last.

"I heard."

"It was a good case to win."

"I imagine."

"Belle, I discovered something today."

"What is it?"

"Before I get through I'm going to make people respect me as a lawyer."

"That's nice."

"Maybe—some day—I'll even be a *big* lawyer."

"That's nice too."

It was disappointing, but he went on, trying to capture from her a spark of genuine response.

"But there's something more."

"Is there?"

The buggy was two or three miles out on the prairie. A distant farmhouse showed a gleaming spot of light at a window, where some woman toiled late in her kitchen. Dave pulled the horse to a stop, and the wise animal, accustomed to the incomprehensible vagaries of human couples after dark, slacked off resignedly on three legs, and hung his head.

Belle sat up straighter and drew her breath in sharply.

"I think we ought to go back."

"But I want to talk." He tried to make out her face. In the darkness her eyes seemed wide, her lips parted, her breathing almost stopped.

"I want to talk—about something I've never done much talking about," he said. "I—I thought that you might understand."

"I—I'll try." She sounded frightened.

In him was the great, instinctive wish of every young man, to express hopes and aspirations, to voice ideals, for the sympathetic ears of a woman. Dave began to talk, not looking at the girl, his eyes on the distant farmhouse with the lighted window.

"The world's coming to something new," he said. "Up to now it hasn't been a very good world for—well, the ordinary man. Think what happens when there's a war. The little man's the one they send out on the battlefield to leave his rotting corpse among the weeds. The big man—with wealth and power—doesn't even risk his money. Did you ever think of that, Belle?"

"N-no."

"Today our great rich American families are living at Newport and on Fifth Avenue in magnificence not equaled by the Emperors of Rome. And at the same time—in mining towns and loom towns and steel towns and packing-house towns and on the farms from one ocean to another—the very places where all the wealth is created to support the luxury of Newport and Fifth Avenue—men and women live in hovels, barely eking out an existence."

His eager eyes sought hers in the darkness, but he could not read her thoughts. Her silence dampened his enthusiasm, but he tried again.

"This is the new thing: People have begun to question something that's been admitted and nurtured for ages as a law of nature—the unassailable sacredness of the right of property. Until very recently every law, and every court, and every government, have indomitably maintained that property rights were paramount over every other sort of right. Most of them still do, but now some men are questioning it. Belle—*I* question it. I *more* than question it; I challenge it! Money rights are not more sacred than human rights."

He was carried away, his eyes alight.

"Belle—I wanted to tell you this. I'm going into politics. Because this is going to be the battleground of my generation. And I believe, as much as I believe in anything in the world, in the justice of that battle."

It was the first time he had expressed the thought to anyone.

For a moment Dave experienced an immense gratification in having merely spoken these beliefs of his aloud. Toward the girl beside him he felt a sudden warmth of gratitude, merely because she had listened. He turned to her, the burning fire still in him. Her face, with its blowy blonde hair and its wide cheekbones seemed somehow almost apathetic in the night—but he craved expression of some kind from her.

"What do you think, Belle? Don't you think I should?"

"Why—I suppose—so——"

Almost fiercely he insisted, hoping that she might pour out to him some magical enthusiasm, add fire to his fire, help him in the crystallizing of a credo for his life.

"Tell me, Belle," he almost pleaded. "Isn't it a man's *duty*—if he believes as I do—to throw himself into a fight of that kind? Tell me!"

But she drew back, half-timorously.

"If that's what you want—I think it's all right," she said. "But—it's nothing to get so—excited over——"

Numbingly he knew in that moment that Belle Dunham had not the slightest understanding of anything he had been saying to her. The disappointment was bitter. Then he began to blame himself. Why should she, after all, be interested? Girls knew nothing of politics. Theirs was a different world. He had been talking wildly, like a fool, about something infinitely remote from her.

"I guess this—all this—is a little boring to you," he apologized.

"Oh, no. I like hearing you talk——"

She hitched over closer to him. Her reply was unsatisfactory. She liked hearing him talk—as if the sound of his voice were the main consideration. Concerning the ideas which meant so much to him, she had no feelings, one way or another.

But by her little act of coming physically nearer to him on the buggy seat, she sponged away all his disappointment with a new sensation. By that move she had invested the situation with sudden intimacy.

"This is the first time we've ever been alone—really alone—" she breathed.

The words seemed to him to possess strangely subtle implications, and his high thoughts faded. Her nearness and the fact that she was female and young suddenly transcended all other matters in his mind. A burning came in his stomach, and his arms ached for her. All at once she had become a different Belle—one who did not fear him. Her thigh pressed softly against his and her shoulder nestled on him.

He put his arms about her. There was no struggle. The intoxication of her body, the soft rise and fall of her breast against him, swept every other sensation out of him.

As if she could no longer wait, she began kissing *him*—suddenly, eagerly, hungrily. Her lips, heavy and moist, clung to his mouth; her hips half-turned on the seat, and her whole body seemed fused with his.

They had to pause for breath. And she was not weeping.

Belle did not even take herself out of his arms. Her face was close to his. As if she had plumbed him, and knew her power over him, she asked a question which seemed to express her understanding of something profoundly secret in him.

"I thought you wanted to *talk*." She laughed lightly.

She suffered herself to be drawn to him again, to be kissed, to join him in mounting excitement.

The moon climbed high and the Milky Way flourished all across the great night sky. Far away, on the prairie, the lone lamp in the farmhouse winked out. The family over there at last had gone to rest. In stately circles, of which the man and the girl in the buggy were hardly conscious, time passed. The horse, wearied of long standing, tugged at the reins until he got his head down; then cropped with quick snatches at the tall grass by the roadside.

Later, much later, she said: "What were you going to ask me?"

He sat up, suddenly remembering.

"It was—was——"

He stopped, at a loss. For the first time he released her.

"What?" she prompted, with breathless anticipation.

He said: "Why were you up in our room—the other evening when Tucker found you?"

She seemed disappointed, for some reason, and he regretted the question.

"You needn't tell me."

But she spoke quite honestly. "I had no business there."

"Why?"

"Because—I came to take something."

He regarded her with amazement. Her face turned away, her voice low.

"You came to—*what?*" he asked.

"To take something that didn't belong to me. I wanted it—a little bit of a thing—that tie pin you wear sometimes. I wanted it . . ."

"But why?"

"Oh, Dave—because it was *yours*. I—I—was afraid to ask for it. . . ."

"Belle!" He was almost numbed. "If you wanted it, I'd be glad for you to have it. Why, Belle, I'd give you almost anything I've got——"

A wild jubilation and something like humbleness battled in him.

He tried to take her to him again. But the spell was broken. She resisted now.

"No. It's late—awfully late. We must get home——"

All at once he realized that they had been sitting in the prairie night for hours. . . .

6.

At Belle's suggestion, he let her out some distance from the house and took the buggy to McCurdy's barn. He walked back, thinking about the girl and the night.

But as he reached the porch steps of Mrs. Dunham's, he stopped.

Within the dark shadows of the porch he made out a thick figure. Mrs. Dunham. Waiting for him, grimly, obdurately silent.

He heard a snuffle. Still farther back in the dimness sat Belle, weeping, in a chair. They had awaited him outside.

As he hesitated at the steps, Mrs. Dunham harshly scraped her throat.

"If you have any explanation, Mr. Constable, I'd thank you for it."

He swallowed, dumb.

"I'm listening, Mr. Constable!"

"Mrs. Dunham, I beg of you——"

"Don't beg of *me*, you—hyena!" The woman's voice rose, strenuous with passion.

He sought again to quiet her. "Please, Mrs. Dunham——"

But she would not be silenced. "Belle's told me the whole thing!" she cried in strident triumph. "There she is—sitting over there—the fat, lazy, strumpet! I got the whole dirty story out of her! And let me tell you here and now, mister, that if anything happens—after this——"

"Mrs. Dunham!" came his shocked voice. "Why, nothing's going to happen—nothing bad *did* happen——"

"That's what *you* say! *I'll* wait and see! And if it does—I'll prosecute you to the limit of the law. There's a bastardy law in this state. I'll send you to the pen—I'll ruin you as you've ruined my daughter! I'll show you that no smooth libertine can take advantage of a silly, foolish, disobedient girl without paying for it!"

From Belle came a loud whimper. Dave was helpless and utterly humiliated, his ears hot in the darkness. He knew the loud voice was waking the roomers above. Routed, he plunged past the old woman into the dark hallway, but her furious denunciation pursued him:

"You're not sleeping under this roof, you damned rake! Take your things and get out!" Evidently she turned on her daughter, for Dave could hear her: "You—Belle Dunham—you get to bed! I'll deal with you in the morning. Oh, what have I done to deserve this—that a child of mine should turn out to be an ungrateful, prideless, deceitful hussy! Get in there!" Belle seemed to have fled, for again the beldame's strident lungs screeched up the stair. "Young man! I'm staying right here until you've taken your filthy presence out of my house!"

Stirrings were audible in all the upper-hall bedrooms. Mrs. Dunham's tenants were awake and listening. Dave found Tucker sitting up in bed.

"Holy Moses—what happened?"

"Nothing!" snapped Dave.

"She can't put you out in the middle of the night, you know. State law——"

"I wouldn't stay here another hour for all of Jericho! Help me get some things together, will you?"

With his suitcases Dave stumbled down the stairs, past the implacable figure of Mrs. Dunham.

She snarled something at him, triumphantly, but he went out without answering.

A block away he glanced back. Belle's bedroom light was still burning. She would be flat on her bed, weeping. . . .

7.

Two weeks, completely intolerable.

The story was all over town next day. Dave found himself, somewhat to his surprise, not so much blamed, as the object of raillery which had in it an element of rakish admiration. But he suffered cruel embarrassment just the same.

He thought of Belle, and what she must be undergoing, his hate for the brutal old woman who was her mother grew with his concern and pity for the girl.

Temporarily he took a room at the Apex House. There came a day when he received a telephone call. It was followed by a secretly arranged meeting with Belle—an interview painful with her weeping.

She could not stand it, she told him. Her life was hellish, unbearable. Her mother's endless contempt . . . everyone staring at her as if she were something unclean. He had to do something. She sobbed more loudly. If this went on much longer, she would kill herself. . . .

There came the moment when Dave said to Tucker: "You're the first I'm telling. Belle Dunham and I were married last night."

"Married?" Tucker almost shrieked, his face flushing with emotion. "God almighty, Dave! Oh, hell, *why* did you do a crazy thing like *that?*"

"She was losing her mind," said Dave. "After what happened everyone thought . . . well, it was up to me."

"But don't you *see?* Mrs. Dunham just used that incident to club you into marrying that worthless, fat frump——"

"Tucker, you don't seem to understand that you're discussing my wife."

Tucker gulped. "Forget what I said," he muttered after a moment.

Dave was touched. "My life won't change much," he said.

"A man can't help being changed by marriage," said Tucker morbidly.

"Well, let's not borrow trouble." Dave suddenly grinned. "Do you know that you haven't even congratulated me yet?"

And Tucker belatedly offered his good wishes.

CHAPTER VII

1.

WHEN he was away from his new home, Dave sometimes found it the oddest sort of sensation to think that he was married at all. Events had taken place with such bewildering speed, that sometimes in retrospect he had the queer feeling that he had been through a dream, or that all this had happened to someone else.

When he was home with Belle, however, his marriage was real enough.

In the first days physical sensation crowded out all other thoughts. The first time he saw his wife nude, he was shaken by his eagerness, curiosity and desire. She stood before him, half-shrinking, and the blood pounded heatedly in his ears. In those first nights his passion was a tempest, undiminished, almost slakeless. . . .

But the wonder and novelty and joy passed sooner than there was any need. Belle, he discovered, had little to return for his passion.

At first he believed that he himself must be at fault. But afterward he came to realize that a woman may, if she desires, counterfeit warmth to snare a man into marriage, without feeling it deeply. After that he lost a part of the humble gratitude he had felt toward her for merely allowing herself to be his. Not all, however. At least he did have a woman of his own; and this was to him a mighty and mysterious possession.

At the very first, Belle really tried to be amiable and pleasant, and they had some good times together. But even in those first days, he noticed a kind of slackness in her that disturbed him.

They rented a house—a small, square cottage with a brick chimney at the exact peak of its hip roof, and four monotonously similar rooms. It was humble and meagerly furnished, because Dave could afford no better; but for a while Belle seemed to take pleasure in it, as a child is happy with a new toy. She made some efforts to dainty it up, but the mood did not last. The woman possessed no powers of extended concentration and little imagination. Within a few weeks she had grown bored with keeping house.

It was not that she was ignorant of housework, or that the work she had to do was an ordeal—since the house was very small. Her long training under her mother's martinet eye had equipped her with all the knowledge and techniques necessary; but there is an important difference between knowing how a thing is done, and having an interest in doing it.

Belle was indolent not only in body, but in feeling. An indication of her attitude was that she never used any term of endearment for her husband. She called him "Dave," nothing more. None of the love names women use occurred to her.

Once a week a motion picture was shown in a vacant store building not far from the courthouse square, the admission fee being ten cents. Belle never missed a picture. This was, perhaps, her greatest single enthusiasm. To Dave the blotchy, jerky movies of the day were an ordeal after the first novelty wore off, because their paucity of ideas offended him. But to Belle it was heaven to sit in the darkened building and watch the gyrating figures on the screen.

A travel-lecture series came to town and he tried to interest her in it. But at the first of the series, when she discovered there were no stereopticon slides, she went to sleep and refused to attend any of the others.

On Sundays she regularly attended church with her mother. Dave did not accompany her, because he could not abide Mrs. Dunham.

Otherwise they spent their time at home. Left to herself, Belle's methods of occupying her time were in a manner revealing. She spent long hours eating candy, which she loved, and trimming and buffing her fingernails. She liked fancywork—nothing very creative, but simple crocheting in which she could follow directions illustrated with pictures in some magazine. This kept her hands busy while allowing her mind to remain blank.

She read the Montgomery Ward mail-order catalogue. He had tried reading to her, but she went to sleep over *Lorna Doone*. The catalogue, however, never failed to stimulate her. Evening after evening she hurried through the dishes, arranged herself in a comfortable position by the table lamp, and page by page went through the myriad items listed and pictured in the thick soft-paper book. Occasionally she might send off for some trifle; but her object was not to buy. She seemed to be perfectly happy when merely studying the pictures, reading the descriptive advertising, and comparing the prices with those for similar articles in Jericho stores. When she discovered that she could save a few cents by purchasing a certain teakettle through the mail-order house instead of at the store, she announced it as if she had just discovered a new planet in the solar system. She had no intention of purchasing the kettle, but the knowledge that she was able to make this saving afforded her a feeling of cleverness which gave her satisfaction.

About this there was something childish and almost pathetic. Belle *was* childish—that was it, Dave decided. So long as her routine was undisturbed she had a certain placid good nature; but when Dave, seeing that she was living only a fractional life, tried with all good intentions to bring her out of it, he discovered that his effort only aroused resentment in her. She did not wish to be disturbed. It was irksome to exert herself. And when she had resentment about anything, she flailed out, like a child, at the person nearest. Dave, of course, was that person.

It shocked him when he discovered that she had one fault much more grievous than languor—a violent, illogical, almost dangerous, furze-fire temper. She displayed with growing frequency as the months passed, a tendency to fly into incomprehensible rages over inconsequentials which left him gasping and angered. And with this she revealed a curious bent for twisting any argument until he found himself in the wrong.

"Look, honey," he once said, trying to turn off a growing quarrel with humor, "you're a born prosecuting attorney. With you in office, the state would never lose a case. For keeping the defense off balance and discovering a variety of causes for action, there isn't an equal to you in all Kansas."

But his amusement only further aroused her fury.

"Don't you compare *me* to anything like a lawyer. You—you shyster!"

"Belle!"

Her rage had reached the blubbering stage. "Oh, ma *told* me what I was letting myself in for. Why did I have to marry a jackleg lawyer? Why did I *do* it?"

He was numbed by the sneer, the savage wish to hurt.

But later, after some hard thinking, he came slowly to an understanding of some of the causes of this abusive and stormy cast of mind.

Behind all of it stood the figure of Mrs. Dunham.

Throughout her life Belle had been accustomed to being told exactly what to do. Each act of hers, day after day, was dictated by the domineering old woman who was her mother. Belle came to follow the orders unthinkingly—her mind wandering, perhaps, but her hands or feet still performing the duties prescribed for them.

Her marriage to Dave was almost the first thing she had ever done on her own initiative.

It does not require brilliance in a woman to catch a man. Dave had been easy to catch, because Belle was without any real competition. He had little contact with other girls, because in a town like Jericho couples paired off; and when he came to town Belle was almost the only young woman who did not have some kind of an attachment. Propinquity was her further ally. The little tricks and stratagems she employed were such that naturally occurred, and she used them almost unconsciously. Effect followed cause with almost unbelievable simplicity.

To Belle, marriage was something a girl undertook because it was somehow expected of her. She entered into it without thinking through or understanding all the implications of it.

Marriage meant separation from her mother. But she had become so accustomed to that overpowering personality, that before long she found she could not well get along without it. Her initiative had never been developed. It is said that men who have been long in prison sometimes do not know how to conduct themselves when the restraints are removed. Perhaps something similar to this affected Belle.

Most girls would soon have adjusted themselves; but Belle's mental inertia was basic. When her life with Dave began to expand out of the ordinary, trouble followed.

It was relatively late that Dave understood her ingrown fear of association with other women. Her boardinghouse background, her lack of education, above all her mother's treatment of her as a girl, had convinced her that others of her sex looked down on her. She was terrified of the ordeal of meeting even the wives of Dave's acquaintances.

She had, during their first weeks together, infrequent bursts of candor, and gradually, through these confessions, Dave grew to have some comprehension of how it was with her.

"You wouldn't expect so much of me," Belle once whimpered, "if you knew how I had to do when I was a girl."

"How, Belle?"

"Ma never let me do like other girls—she was always comparing them to me—running me down. . . ."

This blame of her mother was a form of self-excuse growing out of Belle's own weakness. He listened.

Mrs. Dunham, it appeared, must have hated her daughter and set out viciously to destroy whatever confidence the girl had with ugly disparagements. She sneered at Belle, because she lacked the fine carriage of such a girl, or the pretty hair of another, or the good schoolmarks, the industry, the smooth skin, or various accomplishments of still others.

And when at last—and quite naturally—the child grew awkward and unsure, and began to slink and hang back, the old woman took to dragging her out and flagellating her with sarcasm in public. Belle grew to fear other women because her mother succeeded in convincing her of her own inferiority.

Yet in spite of all this, Belle allowed no one to say a word against Mrs. Dunham. When Dave once or twice ventured a mild criticism, he was met with a rage so flaming that he was careful to avoid the subject afterward.

He knew now that Belle missed her mother. She was homesick for the familiar tyranny. So long had her life been controlled by matriarchal ukase that Belle was confused in an existence without it. And this was at the bottom of their trouble.

Yet in spite of everything, Dave and Belle might have worked out at least a tolerable existence together, had they been left alone.

2.

From the day of the Gotch McCurdy case, when he taught Jasper Peddigrew that neat lesson in courtroom tactics, Dave had been sensible of an altered attitude in the county attorney.

At first Peddigrew had sulked. But he no longer snubbed the younger lawyer. Dave was treated with respect, if the respect was tinged with dislike.

Then came another change.

November approached and all attention was on the fall elections. Peddigrew was again a candidate for his office, and worried over his chances against a Democratic opponent, Ramseur Jackson.

Jackson was the professional Southerner with "Alabama antecedents and Virginia upbringing," with whom Dave had early become acquainted. The man interested Dave because of his imposing manner, compounded of a glaring gray eye, a bristling mustache and goatee, and a "presence," which is to say, a potbelly. He was unhandicapped by any sense of humor, and gifted with a single-minded and undeviating admiration of himself. Also he was a heavy drinker, and most people thought he had small chance to defeat Peddigrew who had the support of Porter Grimes's Republican organization.

Jackson, however, believed profoundly not only in his own qualifications but in his prospects. And Peddigrew, who knew his first-term record had not been sensational, was afraid.

He stopped Dave one morning in the courthouse, with an extended hand and a cordial smile.

"Ah, Constable!" he said. He massaged Dave's hand.

He asked with solicitude about Dave's health, how he was getting along, how Mrs. Constable was enjoying her new home, and finally brought the subject around to politics.

"Are you taking any part in the campaign?" he asked.

Dave smiled. "No. Porter Grimes considers my political views heretical."

"Bosh!" Peddigrew exclaimed. "All bosh. It don't make any difference what a man's theories are, I always say, so long as he's a good, sound Republican. You're that. Sound." He paused to let this compliment sink in. "We're not fighting the tariff battle out here, I always say," he added.

"So Porter's talked to you about me?"

"Nothing derogatory. He thinks highly of your abilities, quite highly. Of course he disagrees somewhat with you in a few particulars. But it wouldn't make any difference to *me* in any case. I admire a man who stands on his own feet. I do so myself." Dave knew the man to be a sycophant, and perhaps his expression betrayed his thought. "Within the limits of party loyalty," Peddigrew added, as if realizing his last statement needed qualification.

Dave waited to see where all this led.

"I understand you're acquainted up around the Bedestown district," the county attorney continued after a moment.

"Some."

"Those farmers think well of you, Constable. One of them in particular, who is named—ah—Pettis, I believe——"

"Webb Pettis. Yes, we're friends."

"He has influence in the northern part of the county."

"So I understand."

"A word dropped to him——"

"Might help you?"

Peddigrew laughed his disagreeable saw-edged laugh with a trace of uneasiness. "Well, I like to watch those little corners in a campaign. No telling what this wild man from Dixie might do——"

Dave grinned.

It was diverting to watch the strange transmutations politics can make.

3.

The day after the election Dave told Belle: "I can have the job of assistant county attorney if I want it."

"You can? How do you know?"

"Jasper Peddigrew believes I did him a favor. I spoke to a friend in the northern part of the county and the farmers up there voted for Jasper, defeating Ramseur Jackson."

"You're going to take the job, of course?"

Dave shook his head. "I think not."

She stared at him. "I don't see why. After all it was a pretty big favor you did him."

"I didn't intend it as a favor. The reason I talked to Webb Pettis was that I was convinced that Jackson, loaded with whiskey as he always is, would be a worse county attorney than Peddigrew, who is usually sober if he is a pompous ass."

"What does the assistant job pay?"

"One hundred and twenty-five dollars a month."

"You're not such a fool as to turn *that* down?"

"Why, honey," he said, "it would be easy to take it, but should I? If I tie myself up to a political appointment like this it will delay me two years in getting started with my profession. Time enough later on for entering politics."

All she could think about was the salary. "You're not making enough progress to worry over, I should think!"

"I'm beginning to get some cases, Belle."

"Beginning! That's just it. At this rate it'll take you years—and I'm wearing rags—and living in a house I'm ashamed to be seen coming out of. Just because you're too—too stuck on yourself—and too pig-headed—to take a decent job when it's offered to you."

She began to weep.

Next day he took the job in Jasper Peddigrew's office.

4.

Three days later Belle said: "Ma's selling the boardinghouse."

"That so?" said Dave.

"She's too old to go on working."

"I suppose she is."

"She's got to give it up—she can't slave like this forever."

Her laboring of this point gave Dave a twinge of uneasiness.

"What—is she planning to do?" he asked.

She hesitated, and it seemed as if her glance at him contained a hint of nervousness. At last she said:

"She's going to live with us."

He was thunderstruck. *"Here . . . ?"*

But she knew now how to handle him. She hackled up and screamed angrily at him. "And why shouldn't she live here?"

His thoughts were not pleasant. But he dreaded an explosion from Belle. At last he said: "Well—if it will make you any happier——"

"I'm not suggesting it to make *me* any happier!"

"In that case——"

"It'll only mean extra work—*loads* of extra work——"

"Then I certainly don't think you ought to do it, Belle."

"She's got to live *somewhere,* doesn't she? I'm all she has—her only living flesh and blood. Do you expect me to let her sleep in the street?"

"Of course not. If you want her, honey, it's all right. She can help you around the house."

But she would not accept that. "Help? Shows how little you know! It will just mean extra things—extra washing, cooking, cleaning—as if I haven't more than enough already to keep two women busy."

"Belle," he said, "if your mother has sold the boardinghouse, she has some money of her own. Isn't there some other way——"

"Oh, I know!" she burst out at him, her eyes beginning to redden with tears. "You don't *like* my mother—you never *did* like her. You've always felt superior to her—superior to me. Yes, you have! Well, at least she never asked anybody to help her! She's got her pride—and so have I!"

"Now, Belle, I meant no criticism of your mother——"

"If you *amounted* to anything—perhaps I could help her out. But no! We have to live like shanty Irish—and you won't even let me offer my own mother a room in my house. She'll have to keep going until she drops—that's what you want—isn't it?"

Her face was mottled and she was sniffling with rage. Yet he had a sensation of wry amusement as he saw how she had, in a curious crabwise manner, contrived to place the blame of all this unpleasantness on him.

At the end of the week, Mrs. Dunham moved into his home—bag, baggage, goitre, and all.

He detested the woman. But when she became a part of his household against his wishes, he made shift to be polite.

For her part, she at first made quite evident efforts to be as pleasant as it was in her to be; perhaps because she was not yet entirely sure of her ground.

Belle also was on her best behavior. To impress her mother, she went far out of her way to play the devoted and happy wife.

Dave began to think that women are prone to utter things irresponsibly, without meaning them. He remembered Belle's violent statements now as a surge of desperate spirits which bereft her of judgment. In her new lazy amiability he was able to forgive his wife much.

The unnatural peace prevailed for a week or more. Then, one day, Belle and her mother had a violent quarrel. Dave heard only the tail end of it, and it left him marveling at the vehemence with which the women assailed each other. Afterward he marveled even more at how they seemed to forget everything that had been said. The cutting remarks and the outrageous insults seemed not to rankle. They resumed an even tenor.

But a great change had taken place. From that hour a new order of things set in—an order already in effect and acknowledged. Mrs. Dunham had reasserted her instinct and habit of command. The one furious outburst at her daughter put Belle effectively in her old, subservient place. Henceforth, the old woman took charge of the household. Dave helplessly watched this, saw his wife meekly accede, and he could not interfere because she accepted the new status without rebellion, almost gratefully.

He hated it. Dictatorial, loud-mouthed, hypocritical, and opinionated, Mrs. Dunham seemed to him like her own goitre—an unpleasant excrescence.

But sometimes the saving grace of humor came to his assistance. He was able to find amusement even in his mother-in-law.

There was, for instance, her greedy appetite for food. Against this she balanced an affectation of benevolent concern for "unfortunates" —although she was careful to include in this category only persons far enough removed from her to make it quite safe to worry about them while avoiding any direct exertion toward alleviating their condition.

The Chinese people, whom she believed always to be suffering from famine, were a favorite subject of her solicitude.

"My conscience hurts me so over the poor Chinese whenever I see a bit of food left over on my plate," she would say.

She did not try to explain how her devouring of a particular mouthful of food could be of any earthly benefit to the Chinese, starving or otherwise. But it gave her an excuse whereby she consumed many a tidbit with self-approval, which otherwise she might have been forced, through sheer shame of gluttony, to leave on her plate.

The starving Chinese, Dave noted, were to Mrs. Dunham a blessed sacrament of self-indulgence.

Like many who lack real affection for any human being, the old woman lavished exaggerated regard on pets.

She moved into Dave's house with a small menagerie—six goldfish in a large bowl, garnished with pottery castles and water plants; two canaries, named "Melba" and "Tetrazzini," although they sang little, preferring to sit like puffed yellow balls of feathers on their perches, with an occasional peevish chirp; and, finally, Girlie, the plethoric pug.

Girlie, overfat, snobbish, and ill tempered, was Mrs. Dunham's favorite. Dave could see why. The animal fawned on the woman, and Mrs. Dunham loved being toadied to—even by a dog. She talked baby talk to the disgusting little beast, and waited on her as she never would have waited on a child. Girlie scorned table scraps. The only food for her dainty taste was liver, fried to just the right degree of rareness. Mrs. Dunham waited on Girlie, but for all her endearments

she never allowed the dog one bit of real freedom. Girlie went outdoors only for certain necessary functioning, night and morning—and
then on a leash, under Mrs. Dunham's personal supervision.

5.

As a relief from the objectionable situation in his home, Dave
plunged with immense energy into the work of the county attorney's
office.

Jasper Peddigrew was a politician, and a bad lawyer. He was bum-
bling and large spoken, but very soon Dave discovered that, if the
county attorney's office were to discharge its duties with any success,
it was up to himself to make it do so. Peddigrew proved quite willing to let Dave take over the work.

The new assistant, therefore, prepared all cases, questioned witnesses
and defendants, drew up informations, conducted preliminary hearings, issued warrants, and in general did the lion's share of work in
all trials, although in really important cases Peddigrew, of course,
made a habit of putting in an appearance and delivering one of the
arguments. On such occasions it was worth something to hear him
address the jury. He tossed his arms, roared, and stamped. He
reached deep into the lexicon for glittering phrases, and what he
lacked in logic and substance he more than made up in lung power.

It was the cool eliciting of evidence by David Constable that won
the cases for the state, but Jasper Peddigrew managed to take to himself most of the credit.

Among those who thoroughly understood where the real strength
lay in the county attorney's office was Judge Hutto. On one occasion
the judge remarked publicly that when Dave Constable chose to take
anything seriously he was a pretty deadly piece of legal ordnance—
tough on a witness who tried to steer away from the truth, and
possessed of an amazing command of precedent, parallel, and previous
decisions. Other lawyers grew at first to respect, then to fear Dave as
an antagonist, but Judge Hutto became, in a manner, his advisor and
patron.

"Young man," the judge said one day, "I'm keeping an eye on you.
You've a kind of genius for law—a shame you didn't devote yourself
to a profession more respectable."

"I'm astonished to hear you say that, judge," said Dave.

"The law, sir, is a scurrilous trade. A lawyer forever must carry
his conscience in his pocket. Forever he must curry favor. Forever
he must represent himself for what he isn't. Examine, young man,
the examples near you—the august representatives of your profession.
What are they? Typhoons of words, seas of buncombe, asses in lions'

skins! They are examples, sir, of a profession dedicated to twisting
and pulling the law—which originally may have had a pure purpose
—into an even fouler vehicle of obscurement and injustice than it already is!"

"Judge, I'm sorry to hear you in this vein. I agree with you that
men have abused the law, but it remains the most important corner-
stone of civilization. Some day I hope what you call its obscurement
and injustice will be cleared. I have even dreamed I might help in a
small way toward that goal——"

"You refer to politics?"

"Yes, sir."

"I'd feared it." The judge shook his white head gloomily. "Once it
bites a man, the virus is in him forever. Forget it, Dave. Its honors
are empty, its rewards paltry, its demands immense, its pitfalls bot-
tomless."

"In a democracy, politics is in a measure a duty——"

"I see that I'm wasting my breath. You're a dreamer, Dave—
questing forever for rainbows and mirages and human justice. It will
remain in you—such is the tenacity of the incorrigible romantic. And
some day it will break your heart."

A strange bitter gentleness was in the judge.

6.

The months passed slowly and became years.

North of the river in the upper part of the county a new organization slowly grew among the farmers, with a little, Indian-eyed auctioneer at its head—Webb Pettis. The organization was known as the
Farmers' Co-operative Association, and its influence began to be felt
in politics.

When Porter Grimes discovered that David Constable had been a
prime mover in this organization, he said openly that he "gave up"
on the assistant county attorney. There was no chance of making a
real member of "the team" out of the young upstart now. A trouble-
maker—Grimes shook his head sadly. He hinted that he had given
Dave much opportunity, and that Constable had displayed no proper
gratitude.

Dave did not take the trouble to offer a rebuttal to Grimes. He
found that he could not discuss his own theories of politics even with
his friend Tucker, who by now was an important cogwheel in the
Grimes organization. In the first months after his marriage, he had
seen Tucker frequently. But they grew apart. Dave had given up
his evenings away from home, and Tucker was a gay bachelor, playing poker and sometimes becoming slightly exhilarated on Kansas

bootleg whiskey. His right to take a drink whenever he wanted it he defended strenuously as a personal privilege; and because of his growing importance, none of the authorities ever interfered with him in this, in spite of the state prohibition law. This was a rebellion on Tucker's part against the strict tenets of the Republican party, but it was forgivable since otherwise he conformed most rigidly.

Porter Grimes grew more powerful each year in land, in wheat, in cattle, in connections with railroads, packing houses, and public utilities. He was wealthy already; some day he would be tremendously so. His interest in politics, the value of which he understood as did few men, was no idle hobby.

As for Dave, although he had been virtually "read out of the party" for his activities among the farmers, he began to discover unexpected strengths. He had more friends among the Democrats than he did among the Republicans, although he still considered himself a good Republican.

At the end of his second term as assistant in Jasper Peddigrew's office, the strength of Dave's alliances with political forces not strictly regular was demonstrated when the Republican county convention was maneuvered into a surprising turn by Webb Pettis and Andy McAdam. It nominated David Constable for county attorney—an act of utter insubordination against the expressed instructions of Porter Grimes.

Grimes did not forgive this. It was a sore matter, also, for Peddigrew, who felt that his subordinate had failed in loyalty. At this Dave smiled.

"A county attorney should be honest, intelligent, and efficient," he said, "but not necessarily permanent."

Although Porter Grimes gave him none of the party-machine support, Dave was easily elected. Grimes bitterly asserted that Dave had received more Democratic than Republican votes, and he was not wholly easy in his own mind when he said it. He knew an insurgent power had been born in the county, with which he must some day deal. Men were saying that David Constable had a way with the voters, and he might go far.

To all this Dave said nothing. A leader, he conceived, becomes so through his own will, but also through fortune and circumstances. He was beginning to taste a high ambition for the future, but was content for the present to do the work assigned him as well as he could—and this included no public insistence on liberal beliefs. His office had a defined duty—the prosecution and punishment of crime. Time for the theory of government later.

So time passed. When Dave went into office as Peddigrew's assistant, Theodore Roosevelt was in the White House, talking radical and acting conservative; the Panama Canal was much discussed as a coming project; muckrakers were lambasting the trusts; the British were concluding an imperialistic little war against the Boers in South Africa; Mark Hanna was still running the Republican party; and Bryan was still digesting the Populism the Democratic party had swallowed.

By the time Dave was well into his second and last term as county attorney, the fat reactionary William Howard Taft was in the White House; Theodore Roosevelt was regretting ever having stepped out for him; the Panama Canal was well along to completion; the trusts had made a great comeback; trade unionism was growing, but Populism was forgotten; a schism had been bred in Congress between the Standpatters and the Progressives; and across the sea Kaiser Wilhelm, in military boots and a *pickelhaube* was rattling his sword as a preliminary to a world disaster few yet could foresee.

Jericho had changed with the world. It had acquired paved streets, a brick and stone business section, an "exclusive" residential district on Water Tower Hill, bona fide police and fire departments, and a population of six thousand. The old wooden water tower had been replaced by a metal standpipe, painted the color of aluminum. Jericho was prosperous and growing.

Tucker Wedge had grown with it. He had converted the *Clarion* from a weekly into a lively daily newspaper; had paid off its debts; and had financed for it a new two-story building, faced with glazed white tile. Over the front entrance was a motto, which he had borrowed from another newspaper, although few in Jericho knew it:

O, JUSTICE, WHEN EXPELLED FROM OTHER HABITATIONS,
MAKE THIS THY DWELLING PLACE.

Tucker's reputation as an editor now rivaled even that of William Allen White and the famed Emporia *Gazette,* although for different reasons. White was the spokesman for whatever liberal thought existed in the state at that period; Wedge was a sounding board of the solid conservative sentiment. They were friends and sometimes carried on good-humored, even witty, exchanges with each other in their respective newspaper columns.

The *Clarion,* in fact, was known well outside the state. Its weightier editorials, particularly those disapproving new economic and political trends, were sometimes quoted in the big conservative dailies of the East, and paragraphs from it began to find their way into *The Literary Digest*.

When Tucker visited Wichita, Topeka, or Kansas City, his brethren in the publishing business made much of him; he was sought after as a banquet speaker, and entertained in the homes of notables. In spite

of the way their lives had diverged, however, he and Dave retained
their old regard. The *Clarion* never turned against Constable, for all
his insurgency. And it was taken for granted that if Dave ever announced for Congress, as many expected he would do, Tucker would
support him.

But in Dave's own home, matters had not developed for the better.
A few months after he took his political job he was able to move his
family to a more substantial two-story house which he at first rented,
then purchased. It was not on Water Tower Hill, where the homes
of the socially elite now clustered, but in a less pretentious neighborhood near the business center, where Belle and her mother felt more
comfortable. Here they made some acquaintances among the neighbors, but neither of them made any real friends.

Each year Belle became more like her mother. Time had dealt
badly with her. She grew fleshy, and complained of ill health. She
and Mrs. Dunham seemed to enjoy quarreling; but they invariably
made common cause against Dave.

Mrs. Dunham, these days, seemed to regard him with silent triumph. He knew he was merely tolerated in his own house, and he
had long since lost any warmth toward Belle. He felt sorry for her,
but her own nature prevented this from becoming sympathy.

Dave had given over trying to do anything with his wife. Always
she could defeat him in any emotional crisis, because she possessed
the audacity to create—or perhaps lacked the perception to see—situations which had no answer save in tragedy; so that, because he had
the responsibility for her, he drew back each time to protect her from
her own extremes.

He could never forgive her for forcing that virago, her mother, on
him. And still less for aping her mother so that now there was little
to choose between them in unpleasantness. But his pride prevented
his discussing this with anyone.

He slept in his own room, alone, now, and he devoted himself
single-mindedly to his work and his politics.

He was lonely and alone. He regarded other married couples and
wondered if all men shared the same fate in marriage. Certainly there
were frequent manifestations of hate between man and wife in the
legal actions which passed through the courthouse.

Yet something in him rejected any complete cynicism. Somehow,
somewhere, there was balm, and strength, and understanding in the
life together of men and women.

On that summer evening when Tucker brought home a new wife,
he pondered greatly on all this. For good or ill this was an event of
great moment. He hoped that Tucker had found in a woman what
he had not found.

CHAPTER I

1.

ALGERIA WEDGE.

Algeria Westcott Wedge.

She tried the name over and over, with different inflections, as she arranged her hair.

Wedge—the sound of it was plebeian, she had to admit. A carpenter's tool of some kind, wasn't it?

Westcott was more euphonious. Yet her first husband, Hale Westcott, for all his aristocratic name, had been the dullest man Algeria had ever known—immersed in wholesale groceries and tedious figures, and falling to sleep right in the face of company when the talk turned on any interesting subject.

Algeria's doing of her hair was high art. She began by parting it slightly to the left, drew the heavy masses skillfully into a high soft roll on each side, and then twisted the length of it behind into a thick, shining coil at the base of her shapely head, where she pinned it. She had seen Maude Adams wear her hair thus—when the actress was touring the nation in *What Every Woman Knows*.

Algeria made a little face at herself in the mirror of the hotel dressing-table. No matter what she did with her hair, she could never resemble Maude Adams.

She envied women like Maude Adams hungrily. Not that she had stage ambitions. Women who succeeded in other walks of life were equally enviable. She hunted their names out in the newspapers, and read everything about them. Mrs. Alfred Gwynne Vanderbilt, giving horse shows and ruling Newport with an iron hand; Pavlowa, dancing like a snowflake; Elsie de Wolfe, creating talk with her new trends in interior decoration; Edith Wharton, writing famous novels; Mrs. O. H. P. Belmont, that dowdy old frump, filling the eyes of tens of thousands as she grimly led a Suffrage parade down Fifth Avenue; even a certain Mrs. Henry White of New York, who recently had achieved celebrity through doing nothing more than merely allowing herself to be painted by the great John Singer Sargent.

All of these women possessed something Algeria greedily coveted —distinction.

In this town of Jericho, she reflected, her lot was far more likely to be the opposite—oblivion.

In the few days she had been in the city on the plains, she had studied Jericho with painstaking minuteness. Her list of acquaintances was already growing rapidly. From the women she had expected a certain initial hostility—after marrying Tucker Wedge "right under their noses"—and in this she had not been entirely disappointed. But it was not difficult to deal with them, and it suited her purposes to make friends. Already, Jericho dowagers were telling one another that Mrs. Wedge was not so bad as might have been feared—rather sweet and unassuming in fact, a person who might fit into things after all.

But the women of Jericho had hardly gauged Algeria correctly. Her gentleness was merely lulling them, for she regarded Jericho as a battlefield . . . another battlefield. All arenas which Algeria entered became battlefields. She had fought all her life long. From the day she put on long dresses—and before—life had all been conflict to her. She was objective enough toward herself to recognize that this was due to her own nature. There was not in Algeria Wedge one static fibre.

Gazing at herself in the mirror, she thought with nervous discontent that under circumstances only slightly different, she might have been notable like those others. In her had long been building a vast ambition—an ambition perplexing even to herself, because she could not, superbly articulate as she was, put it exactly into words. She wanted something: but she was not sure exactly what it was.

The indefinableness was involved in the very fact of her womanhood. Men have simpler goals and outlooks. A woman is circumscribed—by herself. Her aspirations remain vague, necessarily clouded, as a corollary of the accident that made her a female creature.

At one time Algeria had been rebellious over this: she had shocked her friends in Peoria with her bitterness.

"You have a man's mind, Algeria," a woman once said to her, intending it as a compliment.

"A man's mind—in a woman's body. I can think of nothing more tragic," she had replied.

"Then stop trying to think like a man," she was told.

On this smug assumption she turned with fury. "Why does nature

make a woman a Body, primarily—and not a Mind? A body . . .
what for?" She sneered. "To bear and suckle children? Animal
functions!"

"Algeria!" Female voices were horrified.

"I don't care! I'll never admit that breeding and child culture are
the final ends and aims of life!"

"Algeria Westcott," her listeners bleated in panic, "if you're going
to talk that way, we're not going to listen."

"Very well." She was grimly amused. "Sex may be all right, and
motherhood enough—for *you*. But neither of them fulfills *me*."

Afterwards the women told each other nervously, "Never take Algeria seriously. You know how she is . . . she just does that to see
how we react. . . ."

They forgave, but they never quite forgot.

2.

That was years ago, however, and she was much wiser now.

Time had taught her that the question could not be simplified.
She had learned to respect and even admire women who were able to
wear their womanhood like a beautiful gown.

Algeria understood herself now far better than in those early rebellious years—so well that she had ceased repining. She had made an
important discovery: there are compensations in being a woman. Society is so organized that women escape certain responsibilities and
gain certain advantages. A good mind—even in a woman's body—
may achieve important things.

That desire for achievement was in Algeria, like avarice. She
wished to be admired, envied, looked up to, but it went deeper than
that. What she really craved was power—genuine power. It was in-
born in her. And a hunger for recognition obtained by her own
accomplishments. She had only contempt for those who based their
claims solely on being appurtenances connected with a fortune, or a
name, or a position in the social register.

Over the years she had sedulously surveyed every possible avenue
by which a woman might reach the kind of recognition she desired.
Literature occurred to her early—women had attained immense fame
by writing. She attempted it, but quickly discovered that she had
neither the talent, nor the willingness to subject herself to the kind
of drudgery it entailed.

She took up the study of music, but her gifts for it were small also.
Next she doggedly attended art classes and splashed her smock liber-
ally with paint, but never achieved anything approaching a successful
painting. When an amateur theatrical was held in Peoria, Algeria

was certain to be seen, struggling with a role; but though she did as well as any of her fellow-amateurs, and received the usual flattering press notices in the Peoria papers, she knew how great was the gulf between her abilities and those of an even moderately capable professional actress, let alone the women she admired most—Maude Adams and Julia Marlowe.

So by degrees it came to her that since none of these careers was feasible for her, she must contrive one of another kind.

Unlike some women, Algeria was always able to view herself with complete detachment. She recognized and took account of her own shortcomings as remorselessly as does a superior general, when he estimates the weaknesses of his various divisions in matching his army against a respected adversary. This knowledge of her deficiencies was one of her major sources of strength.

To begin with, she was under no illusions as to her looks—she was not, and never had been, pretty. As an adolescent, in the little circle of her friends at the academy, she was almost the least attractive. In those days, when the cultivation of physical charms seemed the dominating fascination to young femininity, some of the other girls had been inclined to feel faintly sorry for her, even to give her patronizing suggestions toward "improving herself," which made her boil inwardly, although from the very beginning she had known how to keep her face carefully and casually sweet.

The years, she thought, looking into the mirror, had not improved her much, for all the care she had given herself. Not that she was ugly. She was just ordinary, she told herself.

Because she wanted money and leisure, she had married Hale Westcott, thirty years her senior, and, as referred to by the Peoria papers, a "merchant prince." After marriage she "kept herself up," allowing herself to grow neither gaunt as did some of her friends, nor fat as did others. Now, widowed and suddenly wedded again, she realized that she could not for many more years hold back the lines on her face, the sag in her chin line, the inertness of figure which comes remorselessly with maturity. She was two years older than Tucker, who was thirty-five—a fact she was careful to admit neither to him nor anyone else. At her age, those two discrepant years loomed direfully.

As she finished pinning up her hair, she studied the gray streaks in it. This she did not so much mind—gray was not fashionable, but her original way of doing her hair was one of her charms, which she enhanced by subtly hinting that she had been "prematurely gray" since youth—which gave her, she discovered, an oddly exciting interest to some men.

Pitilessly studying herself, she decided that her nose was too flat, her mouth too wide, her brows too heavy. Because she had early known the pang which came with the realization that she would never be pretty—and courageously accepted it—she had, since girlhood, cultivated the compensating qualities of vivacity, audacious speech, and a superb manner which carried off remarks that sometimes left people gasping.

Charm became her specialty. She studied its every facet. When she encountered a woman who possessed that most elusive quality, she analyzed her as remorselessly as a biologist dissects a butterfly under the microscope. If the study revealed her subject as possessing something beyond mere physical magnetism, she examined that thing with a view to making it a part of herself.

Taste in clothes was fundamental and essential; and Algeria's taste was beautiful and impeccable. Her wardrobe was not extravagant, but every article in it was the fruit of intelligent discrimination, and she knew how to wear with an air, whatever she put on.

But many women wore beautiful clothes. She sought less common and obvious superiorities. One of her early thrills was the discovery in herself of a gift for conversation. Sometimes she was able to hold silent a whole group of chattering girls her own age—because she so interested them in what she was saying that they forgot their own talk. This was a major triumph. It was a trait to be improved.

To talk well, she became an avid reader, a tireless inquirer into many matters. In the early stages she was in danger of becoming something of a bore because she conversed too much and was too obviously proud of her newly acquired erudition.

But it was integral in her to sense and quickly understand attitudes and feelings in others. Too much talk, however brilliant, creates prejudices against one—particularly, Algeria thought, if one is a woman.

She changed her viewpoint and studied to be selective. Usually people seemed to respond most quickly to the novel and the smart in conversation; and with this diagnosis, her course was clarified. To acquire a grasp of subjects that were correct and profitable in social intercourse was the trick.

With this progression in understanding, it became manifest to Algeria that real knowledge of a subject was of less value than being able to speak as if one knew it. She turned her considerable talents to acquiring phraseologies—a magnificent short cut, and one which, while the mastering of it was relatively easy to her, provided her with immediate and unassailable advantages.

She liked music, but had no talent for it: so she hunted for and mastered musical terms and phrases until she could recite them so glibly and with such authority that all women in Peoria acceded to her in musical discussions. She schooled herself in a surface apprecia-

tion of painting, how to distinguish true vogue from that which is
simply amusing, together with a grasp of the queer jargon of art. She
disciplined herself into maintaining a skimming acquaintance, at least,
with important current books, and through theatrical magazines kept
informed so that she could discuss important plays and actors.

These weapons proved surprisingly adequate. She became a sort of
oracle and critic, with a conceded position. It was easy to fall into a
familiar cognoscent vein on almost any smart subject. Having once
created her impression, she was careful never to pursue the matter too
far, lest she bore her listener. Divert and titillate—but never fatigue or
sate.

Such were the shock troops which Algeria Wedge marshalled for
her campaign against the walls of Jericho.

3.

The cramped pettiness of the field was the chief defect. Algeria
had taken dullness for granted in Jericho, and she hoped to meet it
in some degree with resources of her own. But a "city"—as it ridiculously persisted in calling itself—with a population of only six thousand, and set in the midst of a country so illimitable, so flat, and so
sparsely inhabited, offered distressing limitations. To become the
First Woman in Jericho was a distinction too trivial to be worth the
effort.

The day after her arrival, Algeria had been taken on a tour by
Tucker and his friend David Constable. She found Constable, on
this excursion, engaging and humorous.

"It doesn't take more than two looks to see all there is to Jericho,"
he told her. "But you're going to live here——"

She had thought Peoria provincial, but Peoria seemed in retrospect
the apogee of sophistication, of mellowness, of elegance, compared
with this.

Yet after her first sinking sensation, she resolutely set out to discover somewhat of interest. From the top of Water Tower Hill, Dave
pointed out the two rival business centers, Jerrytown and Jugtown.

"Of course the Commercial Club doesn't even admit they exist,"
interpolated Tucker. "Bad for the town."

"But why *are* they?" she asked. And when they told her of the
county-seat war, for the first time she was all interest. Conflict never
failed to stimulate Algeria.

"So!" she said, gazing at the sprawling streets and the dwellings
below. "That little, tawdry-looking place once had its moment of
fire and glory."

"Not much glory, I'm afraid," said Tucker. "And, darling, people wouldn't like your references to Jericho——"

"The *Clarion*'s in the Jerrytown part, I see." Algeria was probing shrewdly, as usual, for essentials.

"Of course. In general, Jerrytown's the substantial section. You might say it's the Republican section. A lot of Democrats live in Jugtown."

"A lot of Democrats—in Kansas?"

"It's a hangover from the old cattle days. Have to fight them like thunder at election—except Dave, when he's running."

She turned archly to Dave.

"Don't tell me *you're* a Democrat!"

"Not exactly." He grinned.

"Dave's a kind of an Ishmaelite," said her husband. "What's that Kipling thing? *The Cat That Walked by Himself.* That's Dave." He chuckled at his friend. "Dave's listed as a Republican, but he's got some fairly odd political notions——"

"The only odd thing about me is that I've any ideas at all," said Dave.

But after he left them at their hotel, Algeria reverted to the subject.

"Dave would have been a Populist, I believe, if he'd been early enough," said Tucker, answering her question. "He's pretty near a Socialist, some folks say, right now——"

"No!"

"At least his ideas are pretty—advanced. If that's the word. But he's a natural politician, smarter than a whip."

"That slow-moving string bean?" She laughed. Suddenly she was interested. Pieces were falling into their places and it pleased her.

"Don't you let his lazy drawl fool you. Dave Constable's being talked about for Congress right now. Of course the *Clarion* will support him—even if we don't quite agree with him."

"You think a very great deal of Dave, don't you?" Her voice had an odd inflection.

"More than anyone in the world—except you, darling. And—wild notions or not—the people trust him."

"Because he's honest?"

"More than honest. He's honorable. There's a difference. The honest man lives up to the letter; the honorable man to the spirit."

"But those radical ideas——"

"They've never scared me. Actually, they're harder on him than anyone else. For instance, Porter Grimes insists he's dangerous, so the Republican organization's always bucking him——"

"Yet he stays in office?"

"Sure. The farmers eat out of his hand."

"But what are some of his wild ideas?"

"Oh—for one thing, he thinks public utilities ought to be publicly owned——"

"That *is* socialistic!"

Tucker laughed. "Dave talks, I sometimes believe, just to get people like you and me excited."

4.

All this had taken place that morning. Algeria was now preparing to go to dinner—at the Constables. She was looking forward to this evening.

She wondered about Mrs. Constable. All women know ways of appraising a man through his wife. Algeria's long habit of assaying feminine character made her judgments well-nigh flawless. She heard a knock at the dressing-room door.

"About ready, dear?" It was Tucker.

"All ready," she called brightly. "Just putting on my hat."

She emerged and for a moment basked in the adoration in her husband's eyes. Her waist was corseted very small, and in her high-heeled slippers her feet looked tiny. Her gloves were smart, and the cunningly draped dress brought out her figure well. The large hat with its two white ostrich plumes was a rich background for her magnificently heaped hair. She was satisfied with what she saw in Tucker's eyes, but when he came impulsively to her, she would not let him kiss her.

"Don't, don't! I mustn't be mussed."

He drew back, disappointed at finding her most unreachable when she was most enticing.

"How far is it?" she asked.

"Not far. We'll take the Hudson."

"Let's start. I'm eager to know these friends of yours, dear——"

It immensely delighted him.

5.

The house was white, of two stories, with some good elms about it; but it possessed the ugliness of the tortured Victorian architecture—gingerbread scrollwork, bay windows, and thin, over-turned porch posts.

Dave drew them in at the door with a smile, and presented the two women who stood behind him.

"This is Mrs. Constable—Mrs. Wedge. And this is her mother, Mrs. Dunham."

Algeria exchanged with them the long, speculative glance which women reserve for one another. Every detail of costume, every trait of feature, something perhaps of the soul beneath, is taken in by that single, indescribably frank, curious and estimating, yet utterly expressionless, contemplation.

Belle Dunham—some years younger than I am, thought the visitor. Fleshy. No excuse for a woman to let herself go like that. Probably lazy and stupid. Her hair's a fright. The rat shows right through her pompadour. Yet—she might have been rather pretty at one time. . . .

Mrs. Dunham's corpulence dwarfed even her overplump daughter. Her eyes, because of her goitre, protruded slightly back of her glasses. Algeria dismissed her, mentally, as impossible. An ingrown tyrant.

Belle conducted her guest off to divest herself of hat and gloves, and Algeria's eyes were busy. Furniture, decorations, carpeting, and arrangement of the rooms, she saw, were heavy, without taste or originality. The woman who kept this house lacked imagination.

"How are you liking Jericho?" asked Belle, as Algeria removed her hatpins before a mirror.

"It's diverting." The hidden meaning—Algeria's secret amusement —passed lightly over Belle's unsubtle head.

"That's a pretty hat," said the hostess next, trying to assume leadership. "But you'll find it rather impractical out here. Guess you don't have much wind back East."

A hot wind had been blowing all day and Algeria hated it, but she smiled. "We have occasional winds 'back East,' as you call it."

"Well—it's East from here." Belle still fenced.

"Yet New York people refer to Peoria as 'out West.' Have you ever been in New York, Mrs. Constable?"

"No. I—" It was *touché,* decidedly. Belle had never been out of Kansas.

"Do you know—neither have I," confided Algeria surprisingly. "Some day we must go there together."

The speech and the smile that went with it had their effect. Belle, seeking awkwardly to forestall a foe, found Algeria quite willing to be friendly; and also that there was no way of getting past her guard. Under a truce they joined the men in the parlor.

The dining-room table was set and a smell of roast chicken issued from the kitchen.

"I guess we're ready," said Belle.

"Let's go in then," said Dave, grinning amiably. "Hope you don't mind just a country supper at a country lawyer's. And I hope you don't mind our informality. We haven't any servants—nobody out here does, much. Don't need them," he went on, oblivious of the wreck he was making of his wife's pride, "when Belle and her mother can cook like they do. Nothing like running a boardinghouse to teach you how——"

"David!" Belle flushed with angry embarrassment.

"There's no disgrace to a boardinghouse," he protested.

But Algeria saw that his wife was furious. During the entire meal Belle sat, almost glowering, eagerly intent on opportunities to dig at her husband. An anecdote by Tucker reminded her shrilly of some absent-minded blunder of Dave's; and another from Dave himself brought forth a scathing reference to a social contretemps of which he had been guilty.

Dave paid no attention; but the little byplay was in such bad taste that Algeria was glad when they finished at the table and returned to the parlor.

6.

"I want to hear something more about Jerrytown and Jugtown," she said, taking up the first topic she could think of in order to escape Belle and Mrs. Dunham.

Dave smiled. "What do you want to hear?"

"Is it really such a cleavage?"

"Right down the line." He nodded. "Even the churches——"

"Oh," she said, "I never saw a small town that wasn't full of church fights."

"This is different," Tucker told her.

"Different and funnier," added Dave.

"Tell me," she begged.

Dave and Tucker smiled at each other.

"You tell it better than I," Tucker said.

Dave looked at Algeria. "Tucker's newspaper likes to refer to Jericho as *'a city of churches,'*" he began. "We boast about a good many houses of worship, including the little, off-brand religions that struggle for existence in what you might call the outer perimeter of things ecclesiastical. But the two big churches are the First, and the Community."

"And one's Jerrytown, and the other's Jugtown?"

"Exactly. The First Church is the brick structure with the square tower and the atrocious 'art glass' windows you saw four blocks south of the courthouse. It ministers to the souls of the substantial citizens of Jerrytown. The Community Church, eight blocks west, is a frame edifice on pseudo-colonial lines. It's the religious center for Jugtown."

"But the rivalry?"

"Cuts clear through—down to the janitors. The First Church is denominational; the Community Church calls itself interdenomina-

tional. The First goes in for Latin in the pulpit; the Community—
but that's a story."

She found herself smiling at him with amusement.

"The pastor of the First Church," he went on, "is the Reverend
Matthias Widcomb, who's long on labored Latin and self-conscious
literary quotations. A good man, Dr. Widcomb, but a bit tedious.
When he first came here, he simply bowled them over."

"By being tedious?"

He grinned. "Jericho, which in ordinary matters has, I fear, only
a slight leaning toward classical learning, profoundly admires it in
one place—the pulpit. On his first Sunday in the church Dr. Widcomb paralyzed his congregation by finishing his prayer thus: 'Thou,
O Lord, are the *ne plus ultra* of our aspirations, and the *ultima thule*
of our expectations. Amen.'"

"Oh, *no!*" she laughed. "Not clichés even in Latin!"

"You may consider them clichés, but the church-goers of this town
agreed that a parson who could throw Latin like that, catch-as-catch-
can, could write his own ticket with the Jericho faithful."

"And so the First Church went one up, I suppose?"

He nodded. "But the Community Church called soon thereafter a
young English clergyman, with the high-falutin' name of Harry Fortescue Questor. He lacked diplomacy and always managed to have a
church fight going on like a gang of alley cats on a back fence. But
he kept his job because of the quality of his preaching which, in its
way, was fully as astonishing as Dr. Widcomb's."

"Greek or Sanskrit, I suppose, instead of Latin?"

"No. It was his pulpit style. He'd go along in a dull, pedestrian
vein, like any ordinary preacher—then right in the middle of this drab
performance, he'd suddenly take off into perfectly astonishing flights
of rhetoric."

"How odd!"

"Wasn't it? Jericho, which knows fine language when it hears it,
conceded the reverend gentleman had extraordinary gifts, and sat on
the edges of the pews waiting for his pyrotechnic displays."

"So the Community Church went one up?"

"Until Judge Marty Hutto heard him."

"Who is Judge Hutto?"

"A friend of Tucker's and mine, a great reader, and a sort of a
freethinker. After listening to Harry Fortescue Questor, he confided
to a friend that he'd always admired that particular passage, and never
heard it better rendered. And when the friend inquired where the
passage was from, Judge Hutto told him."

"And where was it?" she asked, eyes alight with eagerness.

"Of all places, from Robert G. Ingersoll."

She laughed, and he joined her.

"Jericho finds it difficult to approve of someone who, like Judge Hutto, reads Ingersoll even casually," he concluded. "It wouldn't stomach a minister who quoted the great atheist from the pulpit, and even sawed off the quotations as his own. Our divine moved to other fields."

Algeria found herself highly entertained. But the talk switched abruptly.

"They're cutting wheat already south of Cow Creek," remarked Tucker.

"And prices will be lower than last year," said Constable. "Seventy-nine cents today at Wichita."

"Three straight years since there were decent prices for wheat." Tucker puffed his cigar. "What's the reason?"

"Same as always. Too much wheat land. The farmer's profits attacked from a score of different quarters." Dave spoke earnestly. "The game's to keep down the prices to the very lowest level at which wheat can be grown and the farmer escape actual starvation—so he'll grow it again. *That's* the beautiful theory behind our economics today. And what the Kansas wheat farmer suffers, producers of crops and every other raw material are suffering everywhere else."

Algeria leaned forward. "Why do you say that?"

Dave gave her a quizzical glance. "You may as well know that your husband and I don't agree on the matter—although to me it's as obvious as a pair of spats at an Anti-Horsethief picnic."

"I want to know what *you* think," she smiled.

Dave rubbed his chin and shot a keen look at her. Then he puffed a moment at his pipe.

"The biggest thing wrong with this country today—and it's going to get worse until something's done about it—is that sacred institution known as the Corporation. The big business corporations have this nation by the throat."

"I've always been taught the corporations developed the country, produced goods cheaply, raised living standards, brought wealth to America." Algeria shrewdly drew him on.

"What I will say may sound heretical to you, in that case. But here's a bit of history to illustrate: When the Constitution was created, ten amendments were added, the fifth of which forbade the Federal government to deprive any person of life, liberty, or property without due process of law." He saw her nod. "It was intended to refer to human beings, you see—but the corporations already were at work. Chief Justice John Marshall, a great and terrible old man, interpreted the amendment so as to define a corporation as an 'individual' or 'person,' which was what the corporations were after. Years later, after the

Civil War, the fifteenth amendment was added. Remember it? It was specifically designed to protect the newly enfranchised Negroes from interference by *state* governments. But its framers, headed by Roscoe Conkling, were largely corporation lawyers. They used, with the utmost care, wording which fell into John Marshall's interpretation."

Dave twinkled over at Algeria, sitting rapt there, her eyes on him.

"To this day that amendment has never been able to protect the *Negroes,* for whom it was intended. But it has repeatedly been invoked —by Roscoe Conkling himself, and others—as a protective bulwark for the *corporations*——"

"You mean Congress deliberately——"

"I've noticed this about Congressmen, Mrs. Wedge. They may be honest—but ordinarily they're not fanatical about it."

"But—well—please go on——"

"So the corporation," continued Dave, "once legally constituted—and you can get a charter for almost nothing in Deleware or New Jersey or West Virginia—has today all the privileges of a citizen—with none of a citizen's liabilities. It is, in effect, a huge, predatory, and *immortal* being, out-living men, forever growing and expanding, through devices like mergers, and interlocking directorates, and holding companies. A Frankenstein monster the country has builded. Nobody, under the present laws, can curb it. And its rapacity is such that it will not curb itself."

Algeria watched his mobile face, with the eyes gleaming and the expressive mouth. For the moment, only he and she were in the room, as far as he was concerned. He gestured with his pipe.

"I foresee a day when the United States might be ruled by an oligarchy of great holding companies, with the people no better than serfs —if we don't somehow manage to rule the corporations first."

"But how?" The man's fire thrilled her, but even then she was conscious of a cool and detached curiosity in the back of her mind.

"There is a neutral land in law, wherein the courts deny, to both state and federal government, power—and it is inhabited chiefly by the large corporations. That neutral land must be abolished. All the corporations, trusts, and companies which hold a direct influence over the lives of the great bulk of the population—the public utilities, electric, gas, water, and transportation, *including* the railroads—should be owned by the people."

It was what Tucker had told her—and it contravened her whole background of beliefs.

"But you'd destroy private enterprise!" she expostulated. "It's— socialism, isn't it?"

"Private enterprise? Socialism? They're nothing but shibboleths. I do not fear words. As for the first, the great corporations are themselves eliminating private enterprise about as fast as it can be done—in favor of monopolistic practices. As for the second—do you know they cried 'socialism' a couple of generations back when free public schools for children were established? And before that they made the same outcry against governmental operation of the postal system. Tags that somebody hangs on to a truth mean nothing."

All at once he stopped. His infectious grin returned and he lit his pipe again. The intense earnestness departed from his face.

"Forgive me," he said. "When I get heated up, I become so voluble I seem to forget my punctuation—ignore commas, throw in a semicolon only when I have to pause for breath, and never arrive at a period unless somebody up and throttles me."

But though they spoke of light matters after that, she watched him and thought of what he had said. As she departed at the end of the evening, he shook her warmly by the hand.

"Good night. I hope I didn't talk too much. You're a very stimulating person—do you know that, Mrs. Wedge?"

She laughed and gave his fingers a little squeeze.

"I was *very* interested—and I'm going to call *you* Dave!"

"Then I'll call you Algeria. Thank you."

She found herself liking him.

On the way back to the hotel she said to Tucker: "Dave is everything you say. But those dreadful women!"

"Ticked 'em the first minute you saw them!" he cried triumphantly. "Knew you would. We have to put up with them on account of Dave. Magnificent, isn't he? Almost makes you believe! What a shame—his family life. But he can never say I didn't warn him——"

He broke off suddenly.

"What about it?" she urged.

He shook his head. "It's Dave's cross to bear—not ours."

7.

It was almost the first thing Tucker had ever refused her. She did not like it as she prepared for bed, though she understood his loyalty. David Constable's mind was of the first quality, he had humor, and she admired his integrity. He was the sort of man who could be counted on as a friend.

But Algeria knew his weakness now.

David Constable would never take an unfair advantage of an enemy. That was it.

He had spoiled the two selfish women in his household. He was kindly, trusting, sincere. Altogether he was admirable and strongly appealing. Yet even as she recognized these things, Algeria Wedge coldly began making plans to cut through the living bonds which held this man and her husband together.

It is no light matter to destroy a thing so delicate and precious as a deep friendship, and of this she was fully aware. But first things came first, and her reasons were of the best.

In these days Algeria felt a great and growing confidence in herself. She knew now that she had full ascendancy over Tucker, who regarded her with a mixture of awe and adoration. His allegiance was important. She could afford to share it with no one.

And this was no mere blind female desire to dominate a man, she told herself. Tucker's future would be greater and more certain in her hands than otherwise. This she sincerely felt.

At the same time, she realized she must act with great care. It is fatal for a woman ever to permit a man to suspect that she is attempting to order his affairs for him.

Algeria thought. . . . What a curious thing male vanity is! But I've seen too many women, infinitely superior to their husbands in intelligence and ability, who lost whatever influence they may have had, because they did not take that vanity of men into consideration. Tucker, poor dear, this is going to be for your own good. But you must never know. . . .

Thinking back to David Constable, she was sure that in all Jericho he was the one person she really respected—and perhaps really feared. Their first contact—before they had even seen each other yet—was through that gibing telegram. When she read it, she had experienced a thrill of uneasiness. Now she believed he had had no malicious intention, but she also wondered just how far he saw into her.

Once or twice that evening his glance had held in it something oddly speculative. . . .

She hardened her decision. To break a strong friendship is cruel, and it is not the easiest of accomplishments. But Algeria knew how she would go about it. Those women were the key. She had watched them narrowly, and she knew they had no love for the man who supported them.

Belle Dunham, that boor, she thought. Afraid of me, afraid of anyone who doesn't share her boorishness. So eager all evening to pick little flaws in her husband. Small soul and small mind in a gross body. She is so lacking in graces and ideas that her only means of asserting herself is in those awkward efforts to ridicule a man she knows is far superior to her. *Some* day . . . I may show her what *real* ridicule feels like. . . .

Algeria completed her toilet and wrapped a beautiful sleek negligee about her.

She smiled. There was grim humor in her situation. She despised

Belle Constable, yet the woman was her greatest discovery in Jericho. Momentarily Algeria was almost grateful to her.

She laughed a little to herself as she emerged from the dressing-room. Tucker, in yellow pajamas, lay propped on an elbow in bed, gazing at her with pleased wonder.

"Happy, darling?" he asked.

She let him kiss her and then turned out the light.

"Yes," she whispered, smiling in the darkness. "Happy. Things are going to work out . . . wonderfully."

CHAPTER II

1.

IT was a day typical of the high plains summer—hot and dusty, with a southwest gale that was almost a palpable wall against which one could lean.

In the *Clarion* building, a block down from the Jericho courthouse, beyond the Apex House, the heat was accentuated by a cosmic untidiness, for although the structure was only two years old, it already had acquired the grimy appearance which all newspaper habitations, sooner or later, seem to present.

Tucker Wedge perspired freely in his shirt sleeves as he worked in the inner sanctum of the *Clarion*. His private office opened on the city room, where Clarence Snead, the managing editor, kept a martinet eye on the small staff.

Two desks were in Tucker's cubicle: one with a flat top, covered always with heaps of dingy exchanges; the other with a roll top, stuffed forever with the heterogeny of an editor's accumulation. Tucker sat between the desks, on a swivel chair, usually laboring at the roll-top desk, where he maintained a sort of clearing amidst the litter, for a writing space.

He was writing at this moment, using a fountain pen, for he had never learned to use a typewriter. His thoughts came more smoothly with ink, which flowed into a chirography that was clear, energetic, and aggressive, like himself; and which the compositors never had any difficulty in deciphering.

Tucker's balding head bent absorbedly over his work. When he was writing, he was happy. At the moment he was well launched on an editorial, and he felt several varieties of satisfaction—the consciousness of a generous act for a friend, the pride of moulding the public mind, the adventurousness of something more than a little daring.

The editorial concerned David Constable. It was an editorial which Tucker had himself proposed to Dave, as part of his rush of high spirits after he brought Algeria home as his wife. It was an editorial that might conceivably put Dave into Congress.

Tucker read the first sentences:

Once in a blue moon there appears before the public a figure which cuts across ordinary party barriers—a man whose fitness for office and devotion to the cause of the people combine to make him acceptable to all who are interested in intelligent, able, and honest government. Jericho can pride herself that she has produced such a man at this time.

While he has by no means confirmed or even taken notice of the repeated rumors that he will be a candidate for Congress, the name of David Constable is on every tongue. Here is a citizen of whom the Short Grass can well be proud. His record as a public official is the best testimony as to his character. Although nominally a Republican, he is acceptable to all except the most hide-bound Democrats. In the final analysis he is a fine citizen first, a party man very much second.

David Constable is a plain man who wears ordinary galluses to hold up his britches, and is proud of it. His record as county attorney has been exemplary. He understands the needs and desires of Kansas as do few men, now or ever. *The Clarion,* should David Constable see fit to announce his interest in the office of Representative in Congress from this district, would have no hesitancy in espousing his cause. . . .

Tucker experienced a glow. There would be sharp outcries of anguish mingled with anger when this editorial appeared—particularly from the Republican district committee and Porter Grimes. But Tucker, who almost invariably hewed closely to the "regular" party line, felt a swashbuckling recklessness as he considered that it did no harm occasionally to display a little independence. His endorsement of David Constable, by now stamped as an "insurgent," would certainly bring Tucker considerable publicity—statewide at least, perhaps even national—as a man who placed public good above mere party regularity. Also Dave deserved the office, if he wanted it. This editorial was a fruit of their long friendship.

He resumed writing. So filled was he with the pleasure of his own fluency that he did not at first look up when someone entered his office —until there was a little feminine exclamation. At that he jumped to his feet.

"Algeria!" he cried. He was delighted to see her. She permitted him to kiss her, but lightly. Her summer dress was fluffy and her new hat quite fragile. She carried a sunshade and she looked hot and not very happy.

"How can you bear to work in such a pig pen?" she asked, looking distastefully around. He drew her a chair and she seated herself gingerly; with good reason, too, for the dainty fabric of her gown risked defilement from the touch of anything in this office. Wherever a newspaper lives, it somehow manages to smirch all its surroundings with its ink, and litter all its floors and premises with its soiled, offcast paper.

"Pig pen?" protested Tucker mildly. "It's just like all newspaper offices——"

"How can you stand this heat?" she interrupted.

"It *is* pretty bad this afternoon." He was regretful, not because of his own discomfort, but because the heat annoyed his lady.

"I thought I'd perish at Clarissa Grimes's garden tea. A garden tea. In Kansas. On such a day."

"Clarissa's gone to a lot of work on her garden——"

"In Clarissa's case, I'd prefer no flowers at all. Honestly!" she raised a fastidious brow. "She's one of those cute *young* things—baby face and all gushing and giggles. First she *insisted* on taking us on a tour, posing at each and every plant until we sighed for a desert with never a spear of vegetation. Then she dragged us through her house, and talked endlessly, tiresomely about her antique furniture. Oh, dear——"

"You're worn out, my poor darling. Didn't you meet anyone amusing?"

"Amusing? In Jericho?" She closed her eyes in utter weariness as she peeled the gloves from her damp hands. "I've spent literally hours, just *forcing* myself to be civil to that horde of bores and frumps. Old Mrs. Hutto—and Lillian Bratten—and Sara Cox—and Mrs. Widcomb —and Henrietta Farthing."

She checked them off, as an epidemiologist might name a series of malignant plagues.

"It's dull for you, I know," said Tucker regretfully, almost pleadingly. He was beginning to wonder uncomfortably how much longer this wife of his would put up with exile in these hinterlands. It worried him more than he would have admitted.

2.

Tucker watched her with concern as she sat wearily back, laid her head back with closed eyes, and sighed in the heat.

"Tucker," she said, "isn't there *anything*—to make life a little more worth living——"

He did not know how to answer. For a moment she remained silent, then she sighed and sat up.

"What are you writing?"

"An editorial."

"Oh." She glanced over at his desk. "Is that it? Let me read it——"

He handed her the sheet of paper quite obediently. Holding it at a distance as if its nearer presence might smirch her fragile finery, she glanced at it.

Suddenly she read something aloud. ". . . A figure which cuts across ordinary party barriers." Then she frowned slightly.

"Tucker, who is this about?"

"Dave Constable, darling."

"What's it for?"

"That editorial," he said complacently, "puts the *Clarion* squarely behind Dave for Congress."

"Oh."

With new disfavor she returned her gaze to the paper, reading the fragment of writing through. One other line struck her.

". . . A plain man, who wears ordinary galluses to hold up his britches and is proud of it. . . ."

She read it aloud with relish that was almost malicious.

"A qualification for Congress?" she asked, looking over at him. "How else should his—ah—britches be held up?"

"It's—it's just a way of saying he's a—man of the people."

Tucker flushed. Algeria had made the phrase sound silly . . . and it had seemed so homely and good in the writing.

"I see," she said, but her tone implied she did not see at all. He began to wonder if there were something foolish about the whole thing. Algeria's eyes ran over the page again, quite without compassion. The glow had departed from Tucker. She seemed to be convicting him of writing that which was both puerile and vapid. After a moment she lowered the page.

"Why do you want to send David Constable to Congress?"

He smiled feebly. "He's the best man for the job——"

"And that awful vulgarian, Belle Constable—in Washington for no reason at all—except friendship?"

"Why, it's more than that."

"So," she said. "This is how you leaders of the public do things."

All at once she sat up. In her eyes grew some hidden speculation. The lassitude was all gone now. Her face was lit by an inspiration. *Washington.* It had suddenly come over her—why, it was the solution of her own problem. The nation's capital suddenly became a region of beckoning promise. Bitterly had she begun to regret the step which had brought her to Jericho's barrenness. Now she saw the way out. Washington . . . she savored the thought with eagerness. For the moment, however, she did not reveal her thoughts.

Tucker was staring at his wife somewhat miserably. He believed her to be still sneering at his way of writing and it hurt him.

"Guess it wasn't very inspired," he admitted. "Somehow I can't get started today—maybe the heat, as you suggest."

Already she was off on a new line. "Oh, darling—you mustn't feel badly! There's no hurry, is there? It's months before the campaign anyway. Wouldn't it be a little premature—just at this time—in any event?"

He was delighted at the belief that she was thinking with him after all, and this convinced him of her wisdom.

"You're right!" he agreed. "Since I didn't get a good scald on it—I'll hold it up a few days."

"Then take me home," she said. "It's getting late, and I've people coming this evening. What an ordeal in this heat! Oh, dear!"

She began picking up her things, and he rose, charmed that she had asked him to do her this service. Of all her victories in Jericho, Algeria's greatest was the complete enthrallment of the editor of the *Daily Clarion*.

3.

"Oh, how I dread this!"

Belle had come downstairs, dressed self-consciously in her finest, and wearing her Christian martyr face.

Dave awaited her at the door. Mrs. Tucker Wedge was giving a Sunday Afternoon, and they were among the invited guests.

In Jericho, the Wedge Sunday Afternoons were well-recognized events by now. This was due entirely to Algeria. Nobody ever before had thought of a Sunday Afternoon, and nobody could have possibly conducted an occasion as she did.

Hitherto Jericho women had confined themselves to dinners, or perhaps teas, when they entertained. Occasionally, to be sure, there were evening affairs at which someone "executed" at the piano, or sang, or gave "readings." Card playing was not favored. No nice woman drank—and the men only in the uttermost secrecy.

Usually Jericho avoided formality, and thus people succeeded in having a fairly agreeable time together. Men could sit out on the porch in summer; shoes off, their sock feet on the railing, smoking cigars and telling stories. Women could gather within, to exchange scandal, baby troubles, and household ideas.

But Algeria Wedge had made this whole pattern antiquated and gauche. Her first Sunday Afternoon caught Jericho quite by surprise. People came—not a regret was sent—as much from curiosity as any other motive. They observed a whole new order, already installed and working.

Mrs. Wedge served no heavy repast. Instead there were paper-thin sandwiches, beautifully moulded salad, light cake on a magnificent cut-glass stand, and tea or coffee.

With cups and small plates balanced precariously, the guests stood about, or found seats, and made shift to emulate the graceful self-possession of their hostess. Thus, in one afternoon, Algeria by sheer force of personality, succeeded for a time in raising the entire intellectual level of Jericho. From group to group she passed, imparting something to each conversation, a touch of gayety here, a flavor of sophistication there; stimulating and at the same time conveying—to every woman who had even the slightest thought of attempting to rival her—a feeling of helpless misery.

No hackneyed conversation was permitted. If Algeria detected the slightest indication that her guests were relapsing into familiar Kansas topics like the wheat crop, dress patterns, or common scandal, she swooped gracefully on that group and introduced something more felicitous. If scandal was desired, she impelled them to a discussion of Lillian Russell's affairs; if clothing, the newest from Paris; if politics, the feud between the White House and Oyster Bay; if music or art, Caruso's latest success with the Metropolitan, or Boldini's current portrait.

The "atmosphere" she thus created was an achievement of the first quality, and a tribute to the hidden force of the lady who performed the minor miracle.

After that first success the Sunday Afternoons came once each month. Algeria always invited the Constables. And Belle Constable invariably felt completely lost when she went. So each time she went through the same routine of balking and wailing and repining before they set out. This was wearying to Dave.

"You'll enjoy yourself when you get there," he said patiently.

"Enjoy myself! You don't know what it is, being a woman. Having that awful snob look down on you, and laugh at you behind your back."

Dave did not relish seeing his wife standing ill at ease with that pathetic smile frozen on her face, left completely out of the conversation; but he supposed these affairs had to be gone through.

"She makes me feel like *dirt*," Belle moaned. "She's *horrible*——"

He knew his wife was completely unable to take care of herself, and the knowledge left him with a feeling of helplessness.

Dave gave in: "Very well, we'll not go."

But Belle was terrified by the mere suggestion. All at once it appeared that she could not stay away. She was possessed by a vague dread of what people might say. Through it all she made her husband feel her irritation, her inadequacy, her hatefulness.

Tucker had purchased the Hudspeth house, a large stone residence of nondescript architecture, with a history.

Cassius Hudspeth—"Cash" Hudspeth to Jericho—was a pioneer who had tried out many lines of business, all with great absence of success. He had attempted real estate, farm implement sales, insurance, a racket store, even a private loan company. They all expired; and at seventy he was considered an eccentric failure—eccentric because he had a Harvard education and read the Greek and Latin classics in the original.

In his seventieth year he obtained, by some accident, a recipe for an ointment from an old druggist friend. It contained a little camphor, a touch of wintergreen, and plenty of unguent, and Cash Hudspeth began manufacturing it in his basement.

To his surprise, the ointment sold so well in its little white porcelain jar, that presently he was able to begin advertising "Camphorolium" in the newspapers—as a peerless remedy for sunburn, insect bites, skin irritation, swellings, bruises, contusions, sprains, infections, pimples, and itching piles. The demand increased rapidly, as is the way with nostrums which take hold with the public. Cash Hudspeth was able to quit his other activities and devote all his time to his product. One day a national drug manufacturing concern bought him out—at a figure that made him the richest man in Jericho next to Porter Grimes.

So he built himself a mansion of stone, and being a lover of classical erudition, he caused the Latin word for "greeting" to be carved on a granite block above his door.

That was an error. The Latin word is *Salve*. But since he was the only classicist in Jericho, everyone persisted in giving it the wrong pronunciation. Cash Hudspeth vainly spent his last years trying to teach people that the word was pronounced in two syllables—*sal-vay*. But the connection with his business was too apparent: Jericho persisted in pronouncing it plain *salve,* under the impression it was an advertisement for the ointment he sold in the little porcelain jars. He died, embittered over the obtuseness of the town, and instead of endowing a park or library in Jericho, he left his money to a religious seminary in the East.

When Algeria Wedge moved into the house, her first act was to have a stonemason cut the inscription off. Dave could see the scar of the chisel fresh above the door as he came up the porch steps with Belle.

Algeria greeted them with effusiveness. The large drawing-room was well filled with people, most of them with cups and plates. Two women sat, stiffly self-conscious, at opposite ends of a table, pouring coffee or tea, and their hostess took Dave and Belle to the table to get them sandwiches.

Dave stayed close to his wife. He had made up his mind to listen for slurs and cutting remarks, to see if Belle imagined a covert antagonism on the part of Algeria, or if it actually existed. At the end of a few minutes he was only puzzled.

He heard Algeria tell Belle how *well* she looked, and wondered why his wife winced.

He heard Algeria compliment Belle on the workmanship on her new dress, and ask her if she had made it herself. Belle grew red.

He heard Algeria begin animatedly to describe an heirloom table she had just obtained and then interrupt herself to say, with a curiously flat voice, that she had forgotten—Belle wasn't much interested in that sort of thing, was she?

He found time in all this to wonder at his own male obtuseness. Something was going on, but the remarks he had heard seemed so innocent it was hard for him to read into them the malice Belle seemed to find. He could feel the atmosphere tingle but the play was too fast for him. He was not able to follow it, and the secret women's world in which it took place was shrouded from him so that only briefly did he see the glitter of the knife-edged words.

He frowned slightly, but at the moment Tucker came past and bore him off to the library, ostensibly to show him a new set of books, really to offer him a taste of bourbon.

When they returned to the drawing-room, Dave looked over at Belle. He saw that she was floundering, attempting to maintain self-control, unable to parry the other woman's smiling probing.

He still marveled secretly. This attack was so adroitly feline. It seemed to consist of inflections and hints, always with the smile of apparent goodwill and friendship. But it was evident that his wife was having a bad time.

He stepped to her rescue.

Porter Grimes had the floor, denouncing the new Farmers' Co-operative Association movement, which had been experimenting recently at group buying and selling for the farmers.

"It's contrary to American principles," Grimes was saying. "It's a blow at legitimate business. It's socialistic. Kansas will never stand for it——"

"Why?"

The room stilled suddenly. Porter Grimes did not relish thus being challenged. His brows were half knit as he turned, but when he saw who had asked the question, his expression changed into his curious half-face smile.

"Ah," he said, almost with a sneer. "It's my friend Constable."

There was a slight titter. Grimes had managed to say it in a way that implied many things—the eccentricity, irresponsibility, disreputability, even, of his questioner. He turned his back on Dave and prepared to resume his lecture. But Dave interrupted again.

"Answer my question, Porter," he said, smiling. "Why is it that a group of farmers, doing business together, violates any American principles? And if they do, what are the principles they violate?"

Porter Grimes looked back at him, his face stiffening.

"It's an attack on the whole profit system," he said slowly. "And that's the foundation of America. Without the profit system, what would this country be? A howling wilderness."

"Without the producer," Dave said, "there would be no profit system. I don't know what made business so sacred in America that it
can't be entered into without the password and countersign—but I do
know that the middleman, of whom you speak with such profound
respect, Porter, produces nothing and he'll have no profits at all if he
doesn't quit throttling the men who do produce for him. From that
standpoint you ought to be throwing up your hat for the Farmers'
Co-op, instead of calling it socialistic. You remind me of Milt Brewer's
snake."

When Dave Constable told a story, people were impelled to listen.
Men from other parts of the room came drifting over to him. Women
followed. Algeria, glancing about, suddenly realized that for the first
time that evening she had ceased being the center of everything. It
was almost amusing—she smiled secretly to herself and joined the
listeners.

Dave's story was a foolish, drawling anecdote, and he told it in a
whimsical manner. A friend of his, Milt Brewer, loved to fish, back
in Tennessee, along the Mississippi River. He fished with a jug of
corn-squeezings along, and whether the fish bit or not, the fishing
was always good for Milt. On one occasion, he found a prostrate tree
beside the bank, stepped over it, seated himself, and had just cast his
bobber into the water, when he observed, to his intense disgust, a
cottonmouth water moccasin, deadly as a rattlesnake, coiled up right
between his feet, looking at first one leg, then the other, and trying
to make up its mind which to bite first.

"Milt didn't dare to move either leg," Dave said sadly. "He knew
if he did, that would make up the snake's mind. So he sat still and
thought."

Dave illustrated the pensive attitude and expression.

Presently Milt Brewer bethought himself of a knife he carried, a
knife with a spring blade which would open with the pressing of a
button. He got out the knife, pressed the button, and opened the
blade, still holding his fishing pole in the other hand.

Now, Dave explained, it became Milt's problem to spear the ugly
arrow-shaped head of the snake just right—one blow was all he had,
and if he didn't nail the serpent to the ground with that blow, his
finish was at hand.

Dave went through an elaborate pantomime, as Milt Brewer made
the most careful calculations, poised himself for the blow.

"At this moment," said Dave, "a catfish attached itself to Milt's
hook and began thrashing around, further complicating matters. Milt
couldn't let go of the rod for fear he'd lose the fish, but the jerking
pole upset his aim."

With inimitable skill he portrayed the scene so that everyone, even

Algeria, could fairly see the man on the log, the jerking pole, the open knife, and the deadly reptile coiled between his feet, looking at first one leg, then the other, with dripping fangs ready to sink into the one finally selected.

All at once Milt Brewer struck. He was true to the hairsbreadth. The snake's head was pinned to the earth.

To a person, the listeners breathed deep with relief.

"And that moccasin snake coiled its body right up Milt's leg," said Dave. "He jumped backward off that log so fast he left his pants sitting on it. Friends of mine remind me of that snake—which couldn't make up its mind until too late." Algeria found herself joining the laugh with hearty enjoyment.

Dave smiled about him; and for all her own slight irritation, Algeria was impressed by the manner in which the faces of her guests had relaxed with pleasure at his magical, homely drawl. At the same time she observed that, for the time being at least, the roomful of people, with the exception perhaps of Porter Grimes and herself, belonged entirely to Dave.

How easily he had brought this Jericho gathering back to earth. She was too wise to make any further effort to restore her "atmosphere." For this one occasion she permitted her guests, with ease and relief in their faces, to relapse unconsciously into their familiar inconsequentialities.

As the guests were departing later, she gave Dave's hand an extra squeeze.

"You were our bright star," she told him.

His eyes smiled into hers. "You're quite a girl, Algeria."

She wondered a little about that, afterward. But out of her hidden duel with him, and out of Tucker's editorial which she had intercepted, a decision was crystallized. David Constable would never get to Washington—if she could prevent it. She would go there herself. She would put Tucker into Congress, somehow.

Jericho, she thought purringly, would have its importance to her after all. As a stepping-stone.

The first move was made. Whether they realized it or not, a split was begun between Tucker and Dave. With clever handling it would become a chasm. It was Belle Dunham whom Algeria was using to make and widen the split. Subtle disparagement, hinted ridicule, veiled disdain were the weapons. It was easy to talk over Belle's head, to make the woman squirm. Easy and a little cruel. But necessary. Belle would take her feelings out on the only person she could—her husband. Algeria knew that Belle Constable was working on Dave already. As surely as if she had heard them, she knew they had quarreled on the subject. Sooner or later, whether he wished it or not,

Dave would be forced to take some sort of cognizance of Belle's accusations. When he did, Algeria would make her next move.

She thought of Dave's last smiling look and word. Did he suspect what was taking place?

The thought brought a momentary chill; then she felt all right again. Even if he did suspect, he would make no mention of it to Tucker. She had studied him, she was sure of it. He had a code by which he lived: it was a weakness through which she would defeat him.

4.

In the summer night the air made no movement, and the heat pressed down like a sticky blanket. From the far horizon came a faint flicker of lightning: its momentary reflections briefly diminished the gloom in the bedroom, bringing out soft highlights on the dark polished wood of the dresser.

Nothing would come of that heat lightning. It was another of the frauds of the country—seeming to promise coolness and rain, never making good its promise.

To Belle, in her hot bed, life seemed made up of false heat lightnings. She stared, in her discomfort, at the dark shadow of the ceiling. In the next room, floor boards creaked and sagged under the weight of her mother, who was retiring. Belle heard the bed springs squeal, and Mrs. Dunham's gusty sigh. The old woman would have finished her invariable, meaningless ritual of reading her chapter of the Bible. Presently she would snore.

Belle closed her eyes, trying to capture sleep before the snoring began. But she could not sleep. Her body twitched. If only a breeze would start up . . .

In tiny droplets perspiration welled and trickled across her skin, under her armpits, on her forehead, beneath her breasts.

Just my luck, Belle was thinking. Just my luck, to have That Woman come here . . .

Belle believed in bad luck. She believed she was an especial victim, an objective of misfortune. It was a thought which at times gave her something resembling satisfaction; her mediocrity was relieved by Fate's selection of her for its worst.

The more she thought about this, the more bitter she became. She decided she would have it out with Dave in the morning. No longer would she stand for being snubbed and patronized by That Woman. No longer would she allow Algeria to make her "feel like trash." It was deliberate and wicked purposefulness, Algeria's treatment of her. Belle knew it. Yet the question kept recurring, *Why?* Why does she have it in for me?

For Belle it was much easier to feel than to think. As she groped vaguely for causes and reasons, the trail always seemed to lead back to Dave.

Dave did not sleep with her. He had his own room. This had been so since a year after her mother came to live with them. It happened after a quarrel. He took his personal belongings and moved into the small room at the back of the upstairs hall, where with his books, his pipes, and his papers, he spent most of the time when he was in the house.

Secretly, Belle felt that his preference for a room by himself reflected on her. Of course she let no one, not even her mother, guess this feeling. She was at some pains to impress on Dave himself, that the arrangement pleased her . . . she almost overstressed it at times.

Down the street a dog was barking. Monotonous, rasping sound. Why didn't someone take a stick to that dog? It made Belle so nervous she felt like screaming. She clenched her fists to control herself.

Before she was married . . . she began to think how matters had been with her then. She had not been exactly satisfied with life. She hated the boardinghouse. Her mother was domineering, forever finding fault, ready to prick any momentary hopeful illusions Belle might have concerning herself.

For a reason Belle never understood, Mrs. Dunham hated men; and she spent much time telling her daughter that men were selfish, untrustworthy, bestial. The young men at the boardinghouse, deviling Belle, gave circumstance to her mother's iteration. They seemed to have one thing only on their minds.

Thinking back on her own marriage, Belle still was somewhat amazed. It was her first and only rebellion against her mother.

Often enough she had speculated on marriage; and as a girl there had been times when the prospect of it seemed most desirable. To be her own mistress, out from under the matriarchal tyranny, was a dream of bliss.

She had deliberately set out to make David Constable marry her. It had not been difficult. And the accomplishment had given her a temporary sensation of great triumph.

But marriage had been her most profound disappointment. The physical experience was something you became accustomed to. She was filled with dull wonder at Dave's early ecstasies, because she felt none of them. Later her attitude resembled contempt.

At first she worried about pregnancy, but nothing happened. Later she was examined by Dr. Patterson, who told her something Latin. The sense of it was that for her to have a child was, for some reason, a practical impossibility. This was relief rather than disappointment, because Belle had no cravings for motherhood. It also made her relations with her husband even more repugnant.

She had expected much from marriage. To be married would be to have the world open to her, she thought—but the world had not accepted her any more than before.

In the end she discovered that she had become so accustomed to her mother's domination that she could not get along without it. So Mrs. Dunham came into her household, and Belle almost thankfully returned to an acceptance of her mother's ideas, her mother's thinking, her mother's decisions.

Her mother hated Dave.

Dave . . . Dave . . . Dave . . .

Everything came back to Dave.

He had brought about the changes in her life. She associated her unhappiness with everything he represented—sex, and masculinity, and the law, and this house.

Above all, she hated him for leaving her alone, to lie by herself, as if she were not good enough for his bed.

5.

Belle sat suddenly up in the dark room. Then she rose, put on a wrapper and went down the hall. A thin bar of light below Dave's door showed he still was working. She opened the door.

His face, half-blocked out in shadow, turned toward her with surprise. In his hand was a thick book, and behind his ear a pencil. He was making notes on a pad of paper.

Slowly he rose to his feet.

A tempest of emotion seemed suddenly to be choking within her for expression. Words came in short snatches; her voice was strangled:

"We've got—something—to settle!"

In his face came a tired look. He had been through things which started like this before. . . .

"What is it, Belle?"

"Don't you *ever*—ask *me* to go to that Wedge house again!"

He studied her wearily. Tucker's friendship meant much to him; he saw ahead a whole phantasmagoria of trouble.

"God knows I've tried to make a go!" she went on with a kind of wild, desperate violence. "But it's impossible! You *won't* see my side. You won't do *anything!* If you think I'm going to keep on being made a laughing-stock, you're crazy! I'll—I'll—" Her eyes quested around the room. The desk drawer was open and she saw the handle of the .32-calibre revolver he kept there. "I'll *kill* myself first!"

He caught the direction of her gaze and pushed the drawer shut.

Sometimes he really worried about Belle, her rages were so furious. It seemed possible that she might actually do something . . . insane.

Heavy steps came down the hall. Mrs. Dunham. She stood just outside the door, her fat arms folded above the great puddings of her breasts which bulged her yellow wrapper. Her hair was in two scanty gray braids; and her face was strangely shrunken above the goitre, because her false teeth still were in the water tumbler on her dresser and she had not put on her glasses.

Wordlessly she buttressed her daughter's anger.

In him also grew anger—but not at the sobbing hysterical woman in his room, nor at her mother outside his door. Dave's anger grew hot at Algeria Wedge.

It was she who had used her superior mind and address and position to wound and humiliate Belle. And he, like Belle herself, could not understand why. Belle had never given Algeria any offense. The reverse, rather. She had shown Algeria hospitality, in her own fashion —although at Dave's insistence. He wondered if women simply embarked into blind, unreasonable hatreds as they seemed sometimes to embark into blind, unreasonable loves.

But this thought was discarded as soon as conceived. Algeria was far too well balanced for sheer extravagant emotionalism without good reason. He burned at the thought of his helplessness before her treatment of his wife. A man could not afford to notice a thing like that. In this lay the devilishness of it.

He made an effort to soothe Belle.

But her sobbing continued. It was not in her to surrender an emotional spasm, once it was started. Rage was a rich sensation, to be prolonged.

At last he surrendered: "All right, Belle. I agree with you. We'll not go to the Wedges' again—now or ever."

When at last she had wearied herself into retiring to her bedroom, he sank into his chair, his mind numb.

He wondered if somewhere, anywhere, there was an answer to this intolerable situation which seemed slowly to be driving him mad. Long ago he had accepted the fact that Belle had no love for him; no feeling whatever. But his sense of responsibility toward her remained. He had married her, and he felt he must see her through.

Perhaps, it suddenly occurred to him, she needed someone she *could* love. Children sometimes made the difference between happiness and bitterness in women. Was Belle starved for a child . . . ?

CHAPTER III

1.

THE woman had been dead at least ten hours.

"Perhaps longer," said Dr. Rister, the coroner. *"Rigor mortis . . ."*

Dr. Rister was a big, slovenly man with a dull, marblelike eye and heavy sagging lines in his face. He had failed as a practicing physician. That was why he was the coroner.

The upstairs room in the old brick flat-building was mean, with stained wallpaper, peeling badly, and a torn carpet. Dave glanced toward the rumpled bed, and Dr. Rister pulled back the dirty sheet.

The woman was perhaps thirty-five, but the sagging hollows in her cheeks made her seem older. Her lips had fallen apart. Between them, uneven teeth showed, dingy and yellow.

Dave was thankful that someone had closed the eyes. No matter how many times he viewed cadavers in his official capacity, he never had been able to get over an instinctive shrinking. A human corpse is piteous and yet somehow repelling. Few men enjoy the contemplation of their own inevitable dissolution.

"Cause of death?" he asked.

"She was sick a long time, the other roomers say. Malnutrition, pernicious anemia, a malignancy perhaps. Decide that at the post-mortem."

"You'll sign the death certificate?"

"Certainly. No need for a jury. Any capable physician——"

Dave turned away. Rister was not a capable physician, but this case was so simple that a layman would know that an investigation was needless.

The air in the room was close. He walked over to the window and pulled aside the flimsy, rotting curtains. Although the September morning already was warm, the sash was down. He raised it.

"Relatives?" he asked, as the fresh air came in.

At the open door half a dozen women crowded, peering. All of them lived in this upstairs rabbit warren, which never was free from the smell of coal smoke and the snort of switch engines in the nearby freight yards. Two were Mexicans—track-laborers' wives. The others were nondescript.

"She had a little girl," said one of the women. She pronounced it "gairl." Dave glanced at her. Unclean hair and a shawl. She appeared to be Irish.

"How old?" he asked.

"Noine."

"Where is the child?"

"I got her down to my room. Missis Meader an' me wurruked togither in the laundthry. That's whin she was strong enough, God rest her soul, an' may the souls of all the faithful departed through the maircy of God, rist in peace."

"Mrs. Meader?"

"Her." The woman indicated the lump on the bed. "The little gairl's called Edie."

"I'll take a look at her."

Crowding women and children, smelling of uncleanness, made way for him as he followed the woman with the shawl down the filthy hall. Another miserable room. He glanced at the cracked mirror of the bureau, the small stove, the plain chairs. On a rusty iron bed a child lay, curled up.

"Asleep, sad little craycher," said the woman. "Turrible—the child right thayer—settin' besoide her dead mamma. How long, the saints only know . . . body was cold when we got to it——"

"Who discovered it?"

"Guess I was the furrust. Got to wonderin' about not seein' Edie. Missis Meader had been porely a long time but the little gairl played in the hall. We'd run in wid a dish at avenin', some of us. Them Mex women down the hall was rale good hearted, though the messes they'd cook—Holy Mother forgive 'em—would turn a body's stummick. If it hadn't been for all of us—white an' Mex—I don't know how the pore craycher would've got along these last weeks at all, at all."

"Tell me how you discovered the death."

"I listened to the door. A coupla times. I *thought* I heard snufflin'. Turned out it was little Edie, cryin'. So I called some of the others —Missis Rucker, an' Missis Chacon, an' Missis Martinez. At furrust Edie wouldn't let us in. But finally she done it. Then . . . we seen."

Dave looked down at the child. Thin, sleeping kitten. Stains of tears on her face. The long childish lashes made dark shadows against her cheeks, suggesting pain.

"What's goin' to come of her?" asked the woman. "The Blessed Saints know I can't take care of her, much as I'd loike——"

Voices wakened the child. She opened immense brown eyes and looked up, dazed by sleep.

"Hello." Dave smiled.

She did not smile back. Her eyes were too big for her face, and behind them was unutterable woe. A child had felt its world ripped away from under its feet. . . .

She was not pretty, but something in the pinched, pathetic little features tugged at him.

"Let's see how you look, Edie," he said, with deep kindness. He stooped and picked her up. The tiny arms went about his neck. At that submissive, pathetic gesture of acceptance, pity filled him. She was still in her nightgown.

"Her face needs washing, Mrs.——"

"Kinny." The woman took the girl and carried her over to a washbowl and pitcher at the window. "I'll clane her up. Haven't railly had toime yet. What you goin' to do wid her, mister?"

"Take her to my home for the present."

"Glory be to all the saints! I'll make haste. If ye'll be so good as to turn yer back, I'll have her dressed in no toime. Come, me darlin'. Hear what the gintleman said? We got to make ye purty."

Dave stepped into the hall and watched while two men carried a sheet-covered stretcher down the stairs. Below, the inevitable crowd of morbidly curious gathered about the hearse.

2.

The world changed for Edie. Before there had been in it two—her mother and herself. Now there were four.

In the first days she was almost perfectly dumb, hiding away in the room she had been given upstairs, coming down to eat with her eyes on the floor, never speaking unless spoken to, almost like one who had lost her wits. Sometimes sudden noises startled her, and she shook all over, the spasms of a creature quite benumbed.

When she was offered food, she ate it, without seeming to savor it. She did not play or amuse herself.

There were times when she cried, burying her face in her arms, in long and violent fits; when it seemed that her pain was more than she could bear, and nobody could comfort her. But she would check herself when she could, stifle her sobs, and afterwards sit, with wet eyelashes and lips, trying to overcome her hiccups.

Time passed without being counted; and at last she seemed to recover from the savage part of her anguish, and gradually to notice things about her.

The three in the house with her each treated her differently. She remembered the day she came.

Dave stood with her before the door. There were two women, staring with unfriendly faces.

"This is Edie," said Dave.

Edie stood trembling in her ragged clothes.

"I want you to take care of her a few days," Dave said. "Until I can find her a permanent place——"

She felt him pushing her into the house. She shook again with the spasm of fear and reaction.

"Has the cat got her tongue?" asked the older woman. Mrs. Dunham. Her voice was sharp and hostile.

Dave took two steps toward them and there was in his face something neither Belle nor her mother had ever seen there before.

"Understand this," he said. "She needs kindness as badly as any creature I ever saw in my life."

"We ain't got enough to do already——" began Mrs. Dunham, and then stopped.

Belle had done the utterly astonishing. She went down on her knees beside Edie, and put her arms about the child.

"Poor—little—baby!" she crooned.

Edie felt the arms about her, and suffered herself to be led upstairs.

Days passed like a dream. Gradually she began to feel a sense of belonging to this place, although she did not forget what had been said about staying only a few days, and wondered vaguely when she would be sent away. She came to dread the time she would be taken off, clinging as do all children, instinctively to the accustomed, in preference to the unknown.

Dave was big and kind, seeking to understand her, a friend and protector. Belle, after at first making much over her, lost interest and became indifferent. Mrs. Dunham never liked her, and Edie secretly returned the dislike.

A schedule now came into existence, to which she became accustomed. First, there was getting up in the morning. She would hear them call her, and their voices seemed to drag her up out of the immeasurable comfort of sleep. Sleep had a color—green. Deep, dark, infinitely soft, warm, velvet green. This was sleep. She was happy and at peace; and she fought against being dragged out of it. She tried to ignore the voices and felt herself sink down once more into the softness and comfort.

But her name was sure to be called again. Now she knew she must part with sleep. The voices were impatient, irritable. It was day, and she dressed quickly and hurried downstairs.

Mrs. Dunham always scolded her at breakfast: first, because she had no appetite, and second, because her hair was untidy.

After that, there was school.

Edie was in the third grade, and carried her lunch in a little tin pail. The girls ate their lunch in the girls' cloakroom, most of them wriggling and giggling together. Edie ate in a corner alone.

After school she returned directly home with her books and empty lunch pail, because there were duties to perform. She helped put on the supper things. When the evening meal was over, her especial task came—washing the supper dishes. This had been arranged for her by Mrs. Dunham, who believed that everyone should have a routine of labor to perform in the household.

At first Edie had only the supper dishes to do. But later Belle and her mother occasionally forgot or neglected to do the noonday dishes. So Edie washed them also. This experiment was such a success for the women that presently it was a settled arrangement, arrived at without Edie's consent, that the day's accumulation of dirty china, silverware, pots and pans, should await her in the kitchen sink after supper.

Edie washed the dishes without complaint, until the last one was soaped and cleansed in hot water, and polished with a towel, and put in its proper place. Sometimes she was almost nauseated by the grease-scummed water and the garbage smell, but still she made no protest.

When the dishes were finished, she studied her books. This was done in the dining-room, where the family usually sat because the women did not want to get the sitting-room untidy. The big dining-table was a convenient place on which to arrange the books and papers, and when Dave was home in the evening it was fine, for he often helped her.

He would sit beside her and show her the mistakes without scolding, and sometimes he would stroke her head, or let her lean against his shoulder. When he showed her the mistakes she did not make them again, for she had a quick, avid little intelligence, though she was very timid.

Sometimes after lessons, Dave told stories before she went to bed. They were funny stories, and when he told them she laughed dutifully, because it pleased him. Otherwise in those first days she never laughed.

These were the best times. The worst times were when she awoke in the night and thought of her mother. She remembered her mother as a wistful pair of eyes; and as kisses, soft and often repeated in anguish —kisses given as if trying to impress forever the feeling of a pair of lips against Edie's cheek. Otherwise Edie could hardly picture her mother any more, save for one thing.

Sometimes when she awoke at night she would close her eyes tightly and almost by will power make her mother come back to her through a remembered song. She would *think* the song in her mind, the refrain running silently with the words:

> Sleep, little one, and be good,
> The birds are all in the wood;
> They fly in the wood
> 　From tree to tree,
> And soon they will bring
> 　Sweet sleep to thee.
> Sleep, little one, and be good.

It was her mother's song; and it was the only thing Edie had of her mother's. There was no other keepsake. The song was to her a tangible thing: she treasured it and brought it out of her memory when she could. She would never forget it.

3.

In the weeks that followed Dave kept his tongue and watched.

From the moment when Edie's arms stole about his neck, his heart opened to the child, and the feeling for her grew day by day. Her face never failed to light when she saw him. Sometimes, when she met him outdoors, with the restraints absent, she was almost boisterous in greeting him.

It was understood between them that this sort of thing would not do in the house. Edie and Dave were in a certain degree conspirators. They had jokes together on the sly, and after a time they knew a way of laughing heartily without a sound being heard.

Dave had watched the sudden movement which sent Belle to her knees when first Edie came—human, impulsive, warm. That moment of her self-forgetfulness created in him hope. Perhaps the child in the house *might* change her.

Week after week he put off sending Edie away. The old woman was the problem. Freed of her mother's influence, Dave thought that he might bring Belle to a new interest in life, through having something about which to mould her own life.

When Belle showed indications of warming to the child, his hope grew. It relapsed when she sank back into her loose indifference.

With what resources he had, he strove quietly to develop in his wife some self-determination. He sought to win her with gifts. He praised her lavishly for inconsequential things she did.

Mrs. Dunham, grimly sardonic, watched as if she knew that when the time came she could assert herself and put to nothing whatever he had patiently built up.

Nevertheless, he continued to hope. One day he thought . . .

Edie let herself into the house quietly when she came from school. She paused in the hall and listened. There were voices in the dining-room.

"I *have* been looking for a place," she heard Dave say.

"You haven't tried very hard." It was Mrs. Dunham's voice.

"Ma's been pretty much put out lately." That was Belle. "She's wondering just how much longer we'll be saddled——"

Now Edie knew it was herself who was being discussed.

"The child's really not much trouble," said Dave.

"Trouble! Of course she's trouble," Belle said.

"Edie tries to be helpful, Belle."

"She's clumsy as a cow!" broke in Mrs. Dunham. "And it isn't that we haven't tried to teach her. If I've shown her once, I've shown her a hundred times. But she still knocks over everything she comes near. And you can't get a thing out of her. *I* don't think she's very bright."

"It looks to me," said Dave, ignoring the last remark, "as if she does a lot of work around here."

"You don't know what work is! At her age I was doing *real* work, not just washing a few dishes. And when Belle was nine, she was helping out like a grown woman. A boardinghouse is no *joke* for work!"

"Edie's small for her age, and she doesn't look strong."

"She's strong enough! Stringy and stubborn. You can't *kill* that type!"

A moment's pause. Dave spoke again.

"Belle, now it's come up, I want to ask you something."

"What is it?" Belle sounded suspicious.

"I'd like to adopt Edie."

In the silence that followed, Edie, listening in the hall, felt her heart in her throat. Almost instantly it fell.

"Are you crazy?" burst out Mrs. Dunham. *"Adopt* her? Why——"

"Mrs. Dunham, I didn't ask you. I asked Belle."

"It seems to me I have something to say about it! I do half the work around here. And there's enough for a dozen already, without having that young-un permanently to take care of——"

"Belle, what do you say?"

Edie waited breathlessly.

"Tell him, Belle," said Mrs. Dunham with acrid triumph. "Tell him just how badly you want to have the care and responsibility of somebody else's brat. Tell him whether or not you want to lead your own life."

"It would mean so much to the child," said Dave.

Belle's voice came suddenly. "No!"

"Consider, Belle——"

"No!"

"You heard her!" cried Mrs. Dunham. "You think you're the sharp one, don't you? Thought we'd go soft? Well, Mr. Nice-and-Easy Constable, it isn't as simple as you think. Is it, Belle?"

"No," said Belle. "I'm tired of being imposed on." She seemed to gather strength from her mother, working up her anger. "What do you take me for? I'm serving notice on you right now—that girl leaves here!"

"To go where?" asked Dave.

"Anywhere! What do I care? The state has a place for that kind, hasn't it?"

Edie let herself out of the hall door again, so quietly that they did not hear her.

After a moment she came in, with a good deal of noise this time so she would be certain to be heard.

The talk had snapped off short.

She went upstairs.

CHAPTER IV

1.

ALGERIA WEDGE paused a moment before the door and looked at the legend on the frosted pane:

PORTER GRIMES
President

Then she turned the knob and entered. In the anteroom of the private office, a young woman sat at a desk, gazing at her inquiringly through heavy horn-rimmed glasses. She was a dark, earnest young woman, about thirty, with a muddy complexion. Rather plain and humorless. Algeria knew who she was: Kay Middlekauf. For a time she had been secretary of the Commercial Club. She sang in the choir of the First Church. Efficient type, but quite dull.

"Is Mr. Grimes in?" asked Algeria.

"May I ask your business?"

Algeria's eyebrows lifted at this officiousness.

"Kindly tell him that Mrs. Tucker Wedge wishes to speak with him."

Miss Middlekauf sat still for a moment, hesitating.

"Well?" asked Algeria. She had a superb way of speaking, and something about her caused Miss Middlekauf to rise and go into the bank president's office.

She returned in a moment, with half-resentful coldness. She did not relish being brushed aside in this manner—particularly by a woman. But she was well trained.

"Please go in, Mrs. Wedge."

2.

Porter Grimes opened all his mail himself. Even envelopes that evidently contained only useless advertising matter were brought to his desk with the others by Miss Middlekauf.

In opening the mail, he used a thin-bladed knife shaped like a scimitar, with a mother-of-pearl handle. It had been given him by a friend who had purchased it from an Arab in Jerusalem, while touring the Holy Land. Porter Grimes made it a point to explain the history of this memento to visitors in his office. He had cultivated a reverent manner in the telling, and was able to create quite a strong impression of deep religious conviction in his listeners.

The opening of the envelopes was neat and efficient as was everything he did. Each was slit with a single, smooth motion, and placed in a careful pile. Not until all were cut did he look at any of the contents.

The first perusal was swift. Useless trash went into the large wicker wastebasket. Personal communications were placed in one stack; business letters in another; political mail in a third. After the sorting, he read financial and business first, then political, and personal last of all. By the time he called in Miss Middlekauf for dictation, he already had framed every reply—save for a few he answered in his own hand.

It illustrated his whole character, this ritual of the morning's mail. Porter Grimes lived under a basic belief; or, perhaps better, a basic instinct.

Concealment.

His was the nature of a hermit crab, craving a hard and impervious shell about him.

There was in him a fundamental distaste for intimate contacts, and a fundamental distrust of other men. To Porter Grimes it had never occurred to analyze these feelings of his. Had anyone suggested to him the hermit crab parallel, he would have been violently offended. He was a successful man, and considered himself strong and self-reliant. Actually his strength was ruthlessness and his self-reliance consisted of a suspicion of the motives of others, based on a knowledge of his own.

Nevertheless the hermit crab comparison was apt. As that creature seeks the heavy convoluted shell of the whelk in which to conceal its sickly, soft body so that only its eyes and claws are without, the banker surrounded himself with as many protective barricades as he could, to invest him with a feeling of security.

The chill impersonality of the bank was a protection in itself. But Porter Grimes liked walls and barriers of stone and steel. All the teller's windows had metal bars. In front of the cashier's desk was a low wall, over which that official could survey the foyer and keep borrowers at a distance. But the real inner citadel was Porter Grimes's private office. The frosted glass pane which bore his name was impervious to vision, and Miss Middlekauf was instructed to take the name and learn the business of every visitor before admitting him to the final Holy of Holies where sat Porter Grimes himself.

Even in his home this scheme of defenses was carried out. In front of his property stood an arborvitae hedge ten feet high, through which nobody, passing on the street outside, could see. Two ironwork gates guarded the driveway entrance. These were rarely closed, because Jericho felt that a closed gate to one's front yard was neither friendly nor neighborly. Porter Grimes had no particular wish to be either; but he was careful to avoid, where possible, offending local habits of mind. His house was the largest in Jericho, with solid red brick walls and a slate roof—almost like a fortress. Its windows were shrouded by heavy drapes.

Intense reserve characterized his personal habits. One of the things in which he took pride was that few could tell what was in his mind. He never played poker, since he considered any kind of a gamble not only foolish, but immoral. Porter Grimes believed only in the sure thing. Yet he would have made an excellent poker player, because of the iron control of his features. His smile has been alluded to: his face went only halfway with it, dividing in two in the middle, so to speak, the lips and mouth giving the impression of cordiality, while the eyes remained cold, probing, suspicious.

Not even Clarissa, his wife, knew what he was thinking. Toward her he maintained a cold gravity, treating her like a child. In reality she was quite childish. Clarissa was Grimes's third wife. He had buried the first and second. This one he had taken only two years before.

She was twenty-five—too young and flighty to suit him—but he had slowly made her conform to him. Once or twice, at first, she attempted foolish rebellions—even ran away to her mother. But Porter Grimes waited with patience. He knew the way of handling that. Since the old lady was herself on allowance from him, it did not take her long to send her daughter packing back. And though Clarissa wept and shut herself up in her room after these revolts, her husband treated her, as he would any other subordinate, with a mixture of such frigidly tinged courtesy and superiority that she had given up at last. By now her flightiness had all departed, and also a good deal of her youngness. She was quite submissive and obedient. In a word she had become the kind of a wife he wanted, shadowy, silent, a pale adumbration of himself.

Whenever he could do so, Porter Grimes used anonymity in his transactions; it was another case of hermit crab concealment. Through it he carried on many devious affairs—nobody but he knew what they all were. That was one reason for his opening his mail himself.

He was a big man; recognized as such all over Kansas. Yet his beginnings had been right here in Jericho. Beside the bank, the Jericho telephone company, both principal grain elevators, three lumberyards, the Cox Department Store, two realty companies, and small businessmen and farmers whose numbers only his private records could show, there were many from outlying parts of the state who took orders from the big man behind the opaque glass door.

Porter Grimes knew how to give orders because he had schooled himself in taking them. He did not relish a remark attributed to David Constable, but there was some force in it:

"Porter knows how to make the best use of the short end of the stick. When somebody bigger forces him to take it, he doesn't complain but does as well as he can with it. That's why he's so expert at giving the short end of the stick to weaker men—and making them like it."

It was true he had taken the "short end of the stick" from certain railroads, certain electric companies, and certain political bosses. In every case he served faithfully and eventually with profit. His confidential services for the railroads gave him valuable appointments as right-of-way agent for routes being surveyed. He helped obtain electric "franchises" not only in Jericho but other towns, taking over municipal systems for the big utilities—sometimes skating on very thin ice politically—yet using such discretion that he was hardly known in the process. For this he did not go unrewarded. As for the political bosses —he comfortably felt that nobody in Kansas could longer give him orders; his growth had placed him among the top leaders of the party.

Porter Grimes had just finished his ceremonial with the morning mail when Miss Middlekauf announced Mrs. Tucker Wedge.

3.

The banker rose when Algeria entered. Of course they knew one another socially, but this was the first time she had ever been in his office.

He surmised that she was seeking a contribution to some cause or charity. Had she been anyone else, he would have had Miss Middlekauf attend to it. But she was the wife of the owner of Jericho's only newspaper, and Porter Grimes was a very careful politician.

Besides, Algeria intrigued him. In his brief conversations with her, he had felt in her something above and beyond most women.

She accepted the seat he offered, and listened to the inevitable to-what-am-I-indebted-for-the-pleasure-of-this-visit speech. It was a conversational cliché that presumably had to be endured whenever one talked to a man. When he finished, she said directly:

"You may be surprised at my reason for coming, Mr. Grimes."

"Any call so charming is always a delightful surprise——"

The man actually was going off on another labored compliment. She hastened to truncate it.

"What would you say, if I told you I am here because . . . I think you may be in a little trouble?"

In mid-speech the banker forgot what he was saying. He stared at her for a moment, open mouthed, then sat down slowly.

"Ah—just what do you mean, Mrs. Wedge?"

Again it flashed through his mind that this was the wife of the publisher of a rather powerful little newspaper. In spite of himself his mind travelled back along his own trail. It was a fairly long trail, and difficult to hunt out.

"Political trouble, I mean," she said.

He experienced immediate relief. He was able now to summon an indulgent chuckle, beginning to feel more sure of himself.

"Now, what would a beautiful lady know about politics?"

Her eyes crinkled at him in a surprising smile. There was mirth in the eyes, but something warmly, intimately more. Only a woman can admit a man to the kind of pleasant intimacy which her gray smiling eyes now gave to him. He warmed, in spite of his cold nature.

"I know this much," she said. "You're head of the party in western Kansas. Some day you may head it in the whole state. But you won't —if a certain thing happens next election."

"Ah! And what is it you suppose would do such damage?"

"The winning by David Constable of a seat in Congress."

For a moment they regarded each other, summing each other up. The unscrupulous man gazed with genuine respect on the unflinching woman.

But he was still the hermit crab. "I've always considered Dave Constable a very able young man."

"Indeed he is," she agreed brightly. "Able enough, if he should be elected, to take over the control of the party."

The bold thrust forced his admiration. He returned her smile in his curious divided manner.

"And if this is true—you have some suggestion?"

"Another candidate—of equal ability and popularity—but with, let us say, a little more regular party loyalty."

"Who is your man?"

"Tucker Wedge."

The cards were on the table.

Porter Grimes belonged to a generation of men with very easy consciences when the itch for acquisition was involved. He lived in an era of railroad and public utilities combinations, in which politics played an important part. He knew all the moves, and how to use the tools at hand.

Here, however, was a new experience. The woman across his desk was unlike any political phenomenon with which he had ever dealt.

She sat there, in her soft brown autumn coat, a veil catching her graceful plumed hat under her firm little chin. About her was not one masculine trait. She was slender, charming, challenging—perhaps not quite so pretty as Clarissa. But compared to Clarissa, Algeria seemed somehow rare and daring.

It was femininity which sat opposite Porter Grimes. But it talked with the speech of a hard, realistic man.

The hermit crab, in complete admiration of this extraordinary creature, almost came out of his shell.

"Why do you believe your husband could beat Constable, Mrs. Wedge, and why do you think he'd be more acceptable to the regulars of the Republican party?"

She began to tell him.

In the next half-hour Porter Grimes found himself speaking with an openness almost without precedent in his life. He listened as Algeria outlined her plans, and grew sure that not only did she fully understand his language, but that she could be depended on to control her husband.

Her knowledge of the basic problems of politics astounded him. Unlike his political prototypes of the large cities, Porter Grimes enjoyed none of the advantages offered by the saloon, the poolroom, the bawdy house, the labor union hall, or the gambling rendezvous, as centers of political power. Instead he worked through churches, temperance organizations, and civic booster groups, improvising his own methods. He made a god of substantiality, and cultivated the odor of sanctity. But at the end he arrived at the same goal other political bosses arrived at—power, for whatever uses he wished to devote it.

All these things he heard Algeria outline to him, and he listened with a smile of profound admiration.

She knew even that he made a habit of secret benefactions. In all Jericho there was no church to which he did not in some manner contribute.

"And every contribution," she smiled, "is an investment—you're buying stock, so to speak, in vote-producing organizations."

By the end of her visit, he and Algeria Wedge had arrived at a very complete understanding. Porter Grimes saw her to the door, respecting her more than any woman he had ever known. A steely fibre was in her that appealed strongly to something in himself.

4.

There were times when Algeria had trouble defining her own feeling toward her husband. She was fond of Tucker, and she felt he had high abilities in his own field. Furthermore, she was loyal to him.

Yet she could not conceal a knowledge that she was his superior in maturity of thought and vision.

Tucker did not even know yet what she was planning for him. And she could not tell him, directly. She would have to bring him to it through his own thinking, so he would feel the idea was his own.

A perturbing index of Tucker's nature was the manner in which he remained a sort of perpetual college undergraduate. He still lived in the glory of his fraternity days at Kansas University. The gaudy little bit of pearl-encrusted enamel with its gilt chain was always displayed at the correct place on his vest. Religiously he attended alumni banquets and "rushed" various pimply faced youths as prospective "material" for his Greek-letter organization.

This was juvenile, but it was a part of Tucker. He was a confirmed "joiner"—always with the crowd, a great Commercial Club man, a handshaker, a backslapper, deriving enormous pleasure from gatherings—gregarious to the last degree.

Sometimes this was very wearying to Algeria, but she never blamed her husband for it—any more than one blames a child for having adenoids. Her attitude toward him was protective, indulgent. She observed how he relished small honors—his election as president of the Kansas Editorial Association; every time large papers noticed his editorials; when committees called on him to insure his backing for some project. Tucker swelled to these gestures.

So she humored him, sat with him at an endless succession of speaker's tables, rose and smiled to countless introductions by toastmasters who singularly lacked originality. Now at last she was beginning to see the good of it.

After dinner that evening, she said to Tucker:

"I was at the bank today, and spoke to Mr. Grimes."

"You were?"

"He was very agreeable. We discussed you."

"That so?" Tucker was pleased. "What did Porter have to say?"

"Oh—nice generalities. He interests me."

"Why?"

"He seems more than an ordinary banker."

"He *is* more. He's perhaps the most important man in western Kansas."

Algeria knew this better than he did, but it suited her to have him tell it to her; and she feigned surprise.

"Is he so powerful? That little bank seems hardly——"

"Porter's bank is a lot bigger than its building. Look at the deposits. Besides, he's more than banking."

Tucker expanded. He dwelt on Porter Grimes's wide interests—land, wheat, livestock, insurance, railroads, packing—practically everything that went out of or came into Kansas. And particularly, and above all, how Grimes was the Republican czar of half a state.

"That sober-sides?" She gave him no inkling that all he had recited was hardly more than a surface scratching of the full knowledge she herself already possessed.

"Your sober-sides is also pretty various-sided."

"Then that makes what he said all the more interesting."

"What did he say?"

"Why—let me think—he said he thought you could be the next Congressman if you wanted to be."

"Porter said that?" He was almost stunned.

"He said—I'm sure these are his words—that you're the best-qualified man in the district—for the honor and responsibility."

The idea was brand new to Tucker. "He believes that, does he?" He began to think out loud. "Of course—it's ridiculous. I have no political ambitions——"

"Why not?" she asked, almost sharply. "I'd think going to Congress would be simply wonderful. And if anybody's entitled to it—it's more than due you!"

He was charmed by her partisanship. But he still was not accustomed to the thought.

"I couldn't think of it. The *Clarion* needs me. Besides, I haven't the slightest notion I could get it——"

"If Porter Grimes wanted you?"

"In that case—" He hesitated. "If he were really serious—I suppose——"

"He *is* serious. Believe me!"

He glanced at her queerly. With increasing zest she watched him, seeing the fascination of this new idea growing in him. The lure of politics is insidious and tantalizing, and Tucker, through his newspaper work, had been close enough to it to feel some of the immense attraction.

"It's crazy!" he burst out, almost angrily. "I've got no business in politics. And there's Dave Constable——"

"Has he ever announced?"

"N-no."

"Are you sure he's going to run?"

"Well—not really——"

"Is it right for him to expect you to hold off while he makes up his mind? That's like a dog in the manger—it's not like Dave Constable!"

"No, of course. Dave's no dog in the manger."

"If the situations were reversed, you wouldn't be."

"Certainly not."

This was dangerous. The one thing she feared, the thing she must get around, was this deep-set loyalty and affection for David Constable. Already the thought of it had begun to cool him toward her suggestion.

She shifted ground suddenly.

"Of course, darling, I was only asking. I don't know a thing about politics. It's rather messy, isn't it? You look tired."

"Why—it's been rather a hard day at the office." He was grateful for her concern. This new thing confused him.

Algeria crossed over to him and perched herself on the arm of his easy chair. On either side of his head she placed a hand, and drew it back against her breast. Her palms were smooth and scented . . . she began softly stroking his temples, his brow.

He closed his eyes to the luxury of it. But he was not sleeping: he was thinking. Drowsily thinking, half-mesmerized by the trickling power from her fingers.

The hands did not falter in their steady caresses. Ideas began to arrange and sort themselves in his mind. To please the woman who was caressing him became the aim of all existence. She would like being the wife of a member in Congress. An insidious thought. If he accomplished this for her, it also meant immense triumphs for himself. The great arena of the nation and the world . . . high adventure and a share in the making of history . . . a name made imperishable . . . mighty accomplishments to lay at the feet of Algeria . . . he was still thinking these things when he went to bed.

He was still thinking them when he arose next morning.

5.

At breakfast Algeria made no reference to the previous night's conversation. It was as if the whole subject were washed clean from her mind.

But she did not miss her husband's deep preoccupation. She knew her seed had been planted and would become a great tree. This was no great surprise, for she understood Tucker profoundly—better than any other person on earth understood him. Better than he understood himself. His weaknesses and strengths were as clearly seen to her as were her own weaknesses and strengths. His innate vanity, properly directed, might become a source of great power.

Algeria was sure now of her ability to handle him. There is a type of flattery to which physically undersized men are often susceptible. She had shrewdly discovered that because Tucker was of inferior stature, he secretly hungered to be recognized as a "big man" in matters beyond the physical.

In the next days she deftly played on this desire. At one time she suggested subtly that he had large capabilities, too large to be circumscribed in a field so small as Jericho. At another she mentioned his writing, his public speaking, or the acclaim he had enjoyed here or there. She encouraged him in a book he was considering—a novel. She told him that regardless of its success the publication of a book under his authorship would enhance his prestige.

All the time she carefully avoided any mention of politics or of Congress. Her whole plan was to hold before him a picture of the desirability of recognition above and beyond any he might hope for as a country editor, which would be so fascinating that his own mind would form for him the determination and the plan by which that recognition might best be achieved. As she built in him this secretly growing ambition, she one day made a carefully prepared move in another direction.

One of the difficulties with Tucker was that he possessed scruples. Politics is a game in which scruples are only a weakness. Algeria had admiration for men like Porter Grimes. They did what the instincts and morality of their times dictated. No false ideals among them. There were Porter Grimeses all over Kansas, all over the nation. Among them existed a freemasonry. To each other they rigorously kept their word, although to nobody else. Together, they formed a subtle, interlocking, invisible empire. A man taken up by them had unlimited prospects, provided he played according to their rules. And scruples were an article of merchandise for which none of them had the slightest use.

Tucker must be educated gradually into strict realism in his thinking. And a sense of obligation to a man like David Constable was most unrealistic, from the standpoint of Algeria.

Constable was winding up his final term as county attorney, and the stream of laudatory articles concerning him in the *Clarion* set Algeria's teeth on edge. He was an excellent county attorney, she conceded—perhaps the very best in Kansas. But this merely created an added problem. It is far more difficult to deal with a highly capable and honest adversary in politics than with one who may be stupid or venal.

So, a few evenings after their talk about Congress, and while she knew the idea was boiling in his head, mounting and becoming more and more obsessing, she began an oblique attack on David Constable, this time shamelessly using women's weapons.

"Have you heard from the Constables lately?" she asked.

"No. Come to think about it, I haven't seen Dave in days."

"Tucker—I've been wondering something . . ."

"What?"

"Do you think Dave dislikes me?"

"Why no." He was surprised. "Why do you ask?"

"Because—it's so strange—the way they've treated me. I always ask them to our affairs. They never come."

"After all," he laughed, "it's no penitentiary offense to stay away from one of your little soirées."

"Perhaps not. But Tucker——"

"What, dear?"

"Rudeness—to something kindly meant——"

He glanced over sharply; there was a slight tremor in her voice. It was pure histrionics. To some men it might have rung false. But Algeria knew her husband.

"It isn't Dave's fault, darling, I'm sure——"

"It is! It can't *help* be. He must *know!*"

"We've been friends too long. Why, we were fellow inebriates and gambling partners for years——"

"And you haven't seen him in days?"

"That's true." Tucker thought uneasily. It did seem strange . . . Dave had not been around. . . .

"Doesn't that mean something? Oh, Tucker——"

Her voice told him how painfully she was stabbed. His anger grew. Nobody—not Dave Constable's wife, nor Dave himself—could do this to Algeria.

6.

Now Algeria sat down and did some thinking.

One thing Tucker had said remained in her mind. *Fellow inebriates and gambling partners.*

It brought to the foreground a certain disquieting fact.

In some manner David Constable had succeeded in placing himself in a category separate from most politicians in Kansas. He did what others would not dare. It was that ungodly humor of his, she supposed. Even the reputation of being something of a "free liver" did not seem to handicap him.

But the same immunity would not be enjoyed by Tucker. Algeria had made a close study of the Kansas temperament and it had brought her to some cynical conclusions.

Kansas was an abode of many Pharisees who thanked God that they were not as other men. They condemned sin more loudly and constantly than it was condemned anywhere else, but they had their own category of sins. Certain sins were blacker than others.

The very blackest, from a political standpoint, was to be a "wet" in this state of prohibition protestation. It came ahead of fornication or fraud. Every man in politics felt it necessary to bugle afar his adherence to the state dry laws. What happened when someone was known—as Tucker was all too well known—to have small regard for prohibition, and to drink his liquor defiantly, as a personal privilege?

You may have boon companions in Kansas, who will join you in drinking and gambling and sometimes in affairs of a primrose tinge; but it is a curious truth that those same friends will, on election day, go to the polls and vote against you for it.

As she considered this discouraging thought, a sudden inspiration came to Algeria. Her thinking reached farther into the Kansas mind. And she arrived at a magnificent conclusion.

Kansas loved a man without blame and without blemish, of pure and spotless character—true. But—here came Algeria's flash of genius —Kansas loved one thing even more: a sinner who has been saved, a brand from the burning.

This conclusion offered her a solution stunningly simple.

At once Algeria began preparing her plans. And in the carrying out of them she displayed such skill that her part never was suspected.

CHAPTER V

1.

SOMETIMES Tucker Wedge grew slightly weary of Clarence Snead. Clarence was a little man with white hair—snowy white, it had been so since he was thirty—and a face as red as a turkey's wattle.

His head jutted forward and his nose, from which his overbite caused his mouth and chin to recede, jutted out from between his eyes just where his forehead sloped backward.

David Constable once had said: "Clarence has a profile like a snapping turtle"

It was a pretty fair description. Even Clarence's eyes, with their drooping lids and slow glitter, had a sort of snapping turtle look.

Clarence bore the title of Managing Editor of the *Clarion*. It was Tucker's private joke that whenever his editorial employees asked for an increase in wages, he could always satisfy them by giving them, instead, a new title. The *Clarion* had possibly more "editors," than any other newspaper in the country: city editor, county editor, sports editor, society editor, church editor, market editor, club editor, telegraph editor, courthouse editor, even Y.M.C.A. editor—some members of the staff combined two or three such titles, and proudly signed them beneath their signatures when carrying on correspondence. Managing Editor was the loftiest title of all, next to Editor-in-Chief, which Tucker reserved for himself.

Clarence Snead was Managing Editor: It was a distinction he allowed nobody to forget. He was one of the countless mediocrities who fill the newspaper offices of the land; the faithful "old employees" with never a rebellious thought—or an original one—who labor on America's daily journals for pittance wages, living and dying in obscurity, but clutching to themselves the pitiful small rags of the editorial "titles" they may possess. Clarence supervised the news columns of the *Clarion*. He also contributed editorials. In this last he took great pride.

Like many long-suffering people, he had one enormous grievance. He kept it to himself for a long time, and nobody suspected it; but it indicated something of the kind of a man he was. Clarence lived in a constant state of suppressed fury over the fact that nobody had ever asked him to be a pallbearer at a funeral.

For some obscure reason, election as a pallbearer meant to him recognition of his position. He was never asked to officiate in the capacity, however, simply because nobody ever thought of it—he was such a drab little background figure.

So it happened that when funerals of prominent persons were held, and the lists of active pallbearers and honorary pallbearers were published in the *Clarion,* Clarence invariably read them through, down to last name, and then went into a corner to sulk for the rest of the day.

Tucker was honestly surprised when, one day, Clarence took this trouble to him. With some acerbity the white-haired little man—who had cultivated a certain stiff, dry dignity—told his employer that he was tired of being discriminated against in the matter of pallbearing nominations. It appeared to him, he said, that there was a deliberate effort to cheat him of due recognition. After all, he pointed out with self-conscious deprecation, though he *did* write under the anonymity of the editorial page—he cleared his throat significantly—he was certain he did not overstate matters when he said he was in a *small* way, at least, a moulder of public opinion. It seemed only fair that recognition be given his *position,* if not to himself as an individual.

Tucker made an effort to soothe him; but Clarence refused to be soothed. He boxed the compass around Tucker's desk for a full half-hour, outlining his grievances. Sometimes, he said darkly, he almost thought a sinister influence was at work against him. He would mention no names, but it was becoming evident that there were *certain prominent citizens* who gave lip-service to the *Clarion,* but in whom the *full loyalty* they proclaimed might be open to serious question. . . .

When Clarence concluded this lengthy complaint, Tucker hoped fervently that the next funeral would discover on its list of pallbearers a place for his subordinate.

2.

As it chanced, the very next funeral was that of old Brad Tillett, one of the *Clarion*'s own compositors. Brad had worked for the paper a long time, and he received a sort of office funeral. His wife chose six men from the mechanical department as active pallbearers. Then, because the *Clarion* was a clubby sort of an organization—and perhaps prompted by Tucker himself—she announced that the honorary pallbearers would consist of the entire *Clarion* staff.

Tucker thought this a rather neat solution, and hoped it would satisfy Clarence. But the next day the Managing Editor came around, his face redder than ever and accentuated by his snow-white hair, obviously suffering from painful emotion. He told Tucker that this— *this*—was the finish. A direct slap in the face. The very idea of including *everybody* as honorary pallbearers was completely humiliating. For a conscientious man, who asked very little, God knew, to thus find himself lumped, yes *lumped,* in an anonymous mob—when all he wanted, surely, was very little to expect—exceeded the bounds to which patience should be required to go, even with the most long-suffering.

At this point he gave Tucker a look which more than implied that he felt the publisher himself might have a finger in this conspiracy.

Tucker mentally sighed and considered uncomfortably how often this sore subject was likely to come up again. It was one of the crosses to be borne in getting out a newspaper. You had to deal with newspaper people. And they were all crazy, or they would not be in it.

Clarence, of course, was more trying than most newspaper people —even more than Hallie Wooster, the slatternly society editor with the voice like a slate-pencil squeak, who was forever waxing indignant over slights, fancied or real. Clarence employed the very tactics that a nagging wife uses. He refused to be driven off; and Tucker, who always tried to treat his employees with courtesy, was never able to summon the courage to order him about his business. Clarence remained in the editor's room. His indignation increased. He poured forth torrents of words. His eyes flashed and his teeth glittered over matters totally petty and unimportant. Inwardly groaning, Tucker knew himself to be henpecked in his own office.

An idea suddenly came to him.

"Clarence," he said, "I'm sorry about the pallbearing business. But I'm glad you came in, because there's something highly important I want to talk to you about."

Clarence paused in midspeech and his eye on Tucker became slightly uneasy.

"The committee from the Jericho Church Federation has just been here," Tucker explained. "It's about the revival services—the Bancroft revival——"

"Oh, yes, sir. They start next Sunday. We've had several little items about them from time to time."

"That's just it. *Little* items."

"As much as we usually carry in advance of a revival."

"Between ourselves, Clarence, I'm afraid the *Clarion*'s not done nearly well enough by revival movements in the past. We of the newspaper profession have an inclination to be a trifle worldly."

"If I may say so, I'm glad to hear this from you, sir. I've at times felt myself we were a trifle cavalier in our treatment of evangelistic services——"

"This revival stacks up to me," said Tucker, "as a genuine community effort, a really important movement, in which a great many of our readers will be interested. My wife, for instance, sets great store by it. Now you, I understand, are a churchman yourself——"

"Well, yes I am," said Clarence, who was a deacon in one of the smaller churches of Jericho. "And I fully agree——"

"I'm glad you agree, because here's what I want to do. The *Clarion's* going into this Bancroft revival in a big way. We're going to organize a regular news bureau to handle the thing—not only meetings, but personalities, arrangements, activities, side features, conversions—the whole story, big-city way."

"Splendid, sir!"

"I want the Bancroft meetings handled as a revival never was handled before. And—" Tucker paused impressively, "I want you to take charge of the bureau. You'll have no other responsibility during the continuation of the meetings. You'll have two persons under your direct orders as assistants. Will you do it?"

"Why, certainly, sir."

"I want you to represent the *Clarion*—to *be* the *Clarion,* Clarence —working hand in glove with the leaders of the revival, sitting on committees and doing everything you can to further the cause. We'll manage, somehow, to get out the paper while you're on this assignment." Tucker slapped Clarence bluffly on the shoulder. "We may limp, but we'll do our best until you're ready to return to the helm. And we'll devote each day not less than a full page of space to the Bancroft revival. A monumental job is what we want to do. The *Clarion* depends on you, Clarence!"

For once, Clarence saw himself the very center of important affairs. He would sit in the press section, just below the pulpit, and people—countless people—could not fail to see him. He would hear himself referred to by name from the rostrum—revival speakers never failed to lavish praise on the press. His heart grew big.

"I accept the assignment," he said, masking his exaltation under a look of demure, undeviating loyalty. "I'll try to do the greatest job for you, Tucker, a man can do——"

"It will be worth it." Tucker spoke with deliberate, slow emphasis. "It wouldn't surprise me, Clarence, if something pretty important came out of these Bancroft meetings. . . ."

3.

To little Clarence Snead, whatever in his life preceded or followed the Bancroft Revival Services was forever pallid in comparison. The meetings came in October, becoming at once the great focal interest of all Jericho—prime subject of talk on the streets, in homes and stores, even at such places as McCurdy's O.K. Livery. And in the very center of this mighty stream of discussion, happily swam Clarence.

The Reverend Saul Bancroft arrived in town, and presented a soul-satisfying spectacle. The evangelist was a great, bull-like man—massive, moving slowly, with head half-lowered as though ready to charge. His hair was long and iron gray, and he wore bushy gray sideburns. Heavy bags hung under his eyes—black eyes that seemed inflamed—and his eyebrows were twin forests of bristling black hair.

His most notable trait was his voice—startlingly deep, a double bass, which he used at times with terrifying effect. It was a bull's bellow when he wished, a bellow to be softened at will. That voice, tremendously effective—particularly on his woman listeners—gave him a strangely subtle change of pace in his preaching, when he chose to substitute the sweetest of yearning tones for his vast roaring.

For Clarence was reserved the seat of glory in the tabernacle tent. He sat nearest the evangelist's great figure. From his press table at the foot of the pulpit, he watched the flickerings of lightning in Dr. Bancroft's heavy-lidded eyes, glimpsed the way his tongue formed the words of fire and power that launched from his thick mobile lips. The rough wooden rostrum quivered and shook under the revivalist's tread right before Clarence's nose, as if a male elephant were trampling there.

Every strategy meeting was attended by Clarence. He was elected secretary for the revival—a compliment to the *Clarion,* which, however, he accepted as a personal tribute—and was privy to all statistical details: the amount of the collections, how many house meetings were held, what pastors contributed of their time and effort, the number testifying at the experience meetings, above all the total of conversions.

Dr. Bancroft began his series of sermons in the familiar manner —by blackguarding the city for its sinful condition. Clarence was amazed to learn what a den of iniquity Jericho was—and he wondered how Dr. Bancroft had been able to discover the existence of such conditions in so short a time. Heaven, it appeared, was a relatively unimportant place compared to Hell—and the evangelist condemned the vast majority of the citizens of Jericho to the latter place. According to his telling, the best business streets of the town were lined with "Blind Tigers," and "Jezebels and Harlots" brazenly plied their trade on every corner of the most respectable neighborhoods.

Clarence asked himself how he had overlooked all this evil, but then he joined the rest of the congregation in the acceptance of all statements, and in indignation that such conditions should exist, as well as in determination to do his part to end the sway of the devil.

Having established his premise, Dr. Bancroft was fully launched. Clarence recorded every sermon. A stenographer took down for him each night a verbatim transcript of the inspired words. Sometimes these puzzled Clarence. Read in cold print, they sounded incoherent and meaningless. But somehow, when Saul Bancroft was up there shouting, his words possessed conviction and meaning and emotional validity. Clarence was vaguely disturbed. He said nothing to anybody, but quietly edited the sermons so their sentences would at least parse and make sense.

In spite of these slight waverings, his assignment was a continuous joy and pride. On several occasions Tucker praised Clarence, and as he had promised, the *Clarion* devoted each day a full page to the revival, its sermon, its accomplishments. Clarence sometimes found time to wonder at this sudden new interest in things religious on the part of his employer.

4.

The final night of the revival came. Conversions had been quite numerous, but Dr. Bancroft professed himself downcast, disappointed, heartbroken. He berated himself for not having "carried the spirit more strongly to the people."

This was the preparation—the "build-up" for the final climax. To reach a certain goal—three hundred, five hundred souls saved—became suddenly a civic effort for Jericho. The American instinct for competition was appealed to—the thing became a contest, almost a game. Pressure was brought on likely "brands" to be saved from the "burning."

But what the evangelist needed, what the revival needed, was a bellwether—some significant figure whose appearance before the altar on the climax night would precipitate the last burst of emotion, and carry the revival with it to triumphant statistical culmination.

On that final night the circus tent which served as a tabernacle was jammed to capacity. The united choirs of the churches outdid themselves. The evangelist plunged into his last sermon.

Never before had Saul Bancroft spoken with such fire, such immense fervor. As the sermon came to its thundering conclusion, Clarence almost wished he were not of the saved—so that he could offer himself to the evangelist, to swell the total. He even seriously examined himself. Perhaps he *did* need a new start, an access of religious fire . . . but no, for a deacon of the church to go forward and confess himself a sinner would cause too many questions. He sadly decided against the impulse.

A short prayer concluded the sermon. And now the bull voice in the pulpit offered the period of opportunity for conversion. Saul Bancroft's tones sank to a soft, hushed petition:

"Come—oh, won't you come? . . . Come . . . just take my hand and God will enter your heart. . . . Come before it's too late. . . . Come, please come. . . ."

Drops of sweat gleamed on his massive features. He stood far forward at the edge of the rostrum so that the blunt toes of his immense shoes almost touched Clarence's nose. In muted voices the choir repeated ceaselessly a hymn:

Almost persuaded, Christ to receive . . .

Clarence wrestled with an almost hysterical impulse to rise and shout. *Why* didn't they come? Were they going to disappoint Dr. Bancroft after all? How could they let this revival fail—after all the effort, all the prayers, all the beautiful articles he had written in the *Clarion*? Why, oh why, didn't somebody start the thing going?

A few persons rose and hurried furtively forward. Clarence glanced at them almost with anger. Such a pitiful, niggardly handful . . .

Dr. Bancroft was pleading like a humble beggar:

"*Won't* you come forward? . . . Tomorrow may be too late. Will the choir render just one more stanza of that sweet, blessed hymn? . . . Oh, my brothers and sisters, come——"

Clarence felt like weeping; tears, in fact, did smart in his eyes.

Then he heard behind him a gasp, a great rising sigh of amazement and exaltation. By the feeling in the back of his neck Clarence knew . . . the great moment was upon them.

He turned and looked: and his throat almost closed his breath off in his excitement and his sudden rush of emotion.

Far back, almost at the door on the center aisle, a short, strong figure had arisen.

Tucker Wedge.

His balding head gleamed under the lights and an invisible magnet seemed to draw every eye in the tabernacle to him.

At his first move, excited little exchanges ran back and forth among the deacons and ushers hovering at the rear. A moment Tucker stood silently, as if making a momentous decision. That heartbeat of immobility dramatized his action to the last pitch of excitement. Dr. Bancroft had seen him, and Tucker had the satisfaction of knowing that from the moment he rose the evangelist had eyes for nobody but him.

Face rigid, head high, he started up the aisle. Behind him on the sawdust passageway tramped hurrying feet. Fingers clutched at his elbows. He realized that he had become the head of a comet—the ushers and deacons and dignitaries were massing behind him, bearing him triumphantly forward.

A mighty wave of sound filled the tabernacle tent. Other persons were on their feet, countless others. Feminine sobs sounded and men mopped their eyes and blew their noses with emotion.

Tucker Wedge, the magnificent conquest of this revival, swept majestically forward into the white-lighted focus of delirious excitement.

To little, white-thatched Clarence Snead, huddled in the press seat below the pulpit, it was a supreme moment. Like a worshiping small gnome, he gazed at his adored, his heroic employer, who was coming forward, taking the hand of the revivalist, leading Jericho on the path to glory.

5.

Hours later, wrung out by his emotions so that he could hardly speak, Clarence found himself back in the *Clarion* office. It was late— past midnight—but he wanted to write this epochal story while it still burned in him, while he yet possessed that divine feeling.

As he sat at his typewriter, alone in the city room, trying to think how to approach his tremendous subject, the door opened. Once more the light of adoration leaped into Clarence's eyes. It was Tucker Wedge accompanied by his wife.

Clarence rose as they entered, standing reverently on his feet.

"You here, Clarence?" said Tucker in surprise. "Pretty late to be working, isn't it? We've been out to a friend's house. Stopped by on our way home for the exchanges. . . ."

"Tucker—Mr. Wedge—" began Clarence, and stopped, choked by his feeling. "That was—was the most magnificent thing I—I ever witnessed in—my whole life—" He stammered, came to a full halt, too overcome to finish.

Tucker gazed at him curiously. On the lips of Algeria seemed to hover the faintest hint of a smile.

"How—how can I possibly write a thing like that—do it justice?" Clarence tried again.

Tucker's face grew kindly. Genuine devotion can always be recognized.

He cleared his throat. Then he said something that was to be repeated afterward—to become a part of the legend of Tucker Wedge, the man of the people, who refused to take even himself seriously.

"Clarence," he said, "write it up just as if—it were a dogfight."

He passed out with Algeria, leaving Clarence standing humbly, gazing after them.

CHAPTER VI

1.

DECEMBER came, and the first cold weather.

Sometimes in the morning the window panes had on them thick frost forests—tiny ice trees and ferns and shrubs, complete with branches and leaves, stamped there by the frigid night.

Edie still lived at the Constables'. A place had not yet been found for her, but it was understood she should leave as soon as Dave had made the proper arrangements. Meantime she continued with her school and with her household tasks.

In the mornings she would get out of bed when called and dress very quickly, shivering and hurrying; then bolt downstairs with teeth chattering to the warmth below.

One morning she heard Belle and her mother arguing.

Mrs. Dunham said: "Algeria's *Catholic*."

"No, Ma, she's Episcopal."

"What's the difference? Altars and robes and candles! It's nothing but a branch of the Catholics."

"Anyway, she and Tucker are joining the First Church, Sunday."

"Wouldn't you know it!" said the old woman bitterly. "Wouldn't you just know it—the dirty, stuck-up snobs."

The announcement that the Wedges were to affiliate with the First Church really surprised nobody, since it was perfectly logical. The First Church was the largest church in Jericho, and represented the most important denomination. It had the most prominent people. The head of its board of trustees was Porter Grimes himself.

But in spite of the fact that everyone believed the Wedges would do exactly as they did, there were varied attitudes expressed when it was definitely known they were going to do it. The Reverend Matthias Widcomb, good man, was almost tremulously gratified. To have the thing settled was a relief and a blessing.

There was a subtle purring of satisfaction among the large houses on Water Tower Hill. But elsewhere, particularly in the congregation of the Community Church, which had held a lingering hope, Mrs. Dunham's view was echoed in countless variations.

All this was incomprehensible to Edie. She went into the kitchen for her breakfast. Oatmeal and milk; she loathed it.

But Mrs. Dunham saw her listless play with the spoon and turned on her savagely as usual.

"Edie! Now you eat that—every bite of it! And hurry up. What's the matter—isn't it good enough for you? Get that silly look off your face! You'd think it was poison. Now I'm going to stand right over you until you get every bite of that down."

2.

Mrs. Dunham was the archenemy.

She watched continually for chances to inflict her malice on Edie, although Edie diligently did the work assigned her and tried to keep out of the old woman's way as much as possible.

Edie had just discovered the joy of reading. It came to her all of a sudden—she cared nothing about reading one day; the next it seemed she was living her life for it.

It happened when Dave brought her home a book—different from schoolbooks where you mark with a pencil how far you are to take next day. It had a green cover and its title was *Five Little Peppers and How They Grew*.

Edie thought at first it was concerned with plants, but she began dutifully to read it, because Dave had given it to her—and straightway she was transported into a new world. The book was not about pepper plants, or any other botany. It was about people—children. For the first time Edie lived a life of joy through the printed page. Almost in one breathless sweep she read the book, and then started over at the beginning to read it through again.

But so much unadulterated pleasure did not escape Mrs. Dunham's eye. Almost at once the old woman began to object to Edie's reading. She asserted that the child was "wasting too much time on that trash." She said that Edie was "injuring her eyes and interfering with her schoolwork." Most damning of all was her charge that "Edie's got so she isn't a bit of use around the house."

Dave had to intervene to prevent the taking away of the book, and even so there was a rigorous limiting of Edie's "reading time"—a half-hour each night, "if she got her homework done," and an hour on Sunday afternoons.

Edie began to hurry home and work hard to finish her tasks, in order to enjoy the precious half-hour with the Little Peppers. It was surprising how rarely she succeeded in completing everything in time. Somehow the work was arranged in such a manner, or delays and obstacles so intervened, that Edie with despairing anguish, saw herself cheated night after night. This also she owed to Mrs. Dunham, and she had no appeal.

Out of this came Edie's sin.

In Dave's room, among the law volumes, she one day discovered a worn copy of *Cumnock's Choice Readings,* and seized on it as a wonderful prize. Some of the selections she thought incredibly grand—"Spartacus to the Gladiators," and "King Robert of Sicily," and others.

Knowing that the book, if discovered, would be taken from her, she resorted to deceit. When she was alone in the kitchen after supper, doing the mountain of dishes, she would prop *Cumnock* on the table and snatch passages from its open pages while she worked.

One evening Mrs. Dunham stole into the kitchen and caught her with the book before her. At the old woman's exclamation of mingled triumph and wrath, Edie jumped with such painful surprise that she dropped and smashed a dish.

That completed the sin.

Edie was punished for "acting lies," by being deprived of all reading for a week, and put to bed early each night.

She accepted all this with the patient resignation of children, which is as pathetic as it is astonishing. Long ago she had become so accustomed, that it meant almost nothing to her, to being accused of endless wickedness, and hearing herself called "liar," and "sneak," and "lazy no-good."

3.

One day there was a new kind of sin.

Edie came home from school, stole around to the rear of the house, let herself in at the back door, and crept up to her room.

This sin she hardly knew how to contemplate.

Gradually she had made friends with one or two of the other little girls at school—timid explorations at first, becoming a tentative working relationship. She now had playmates at recess, and someone with whom to eat sandwiches in the cloakroom at noon. Also, at times, they walked home together after school.

Most often Edie walked home with the Horst girl, Wilma—plump and giggly, a year older than Edie, the daughter of a baker who lived a block down the street. Wilma had a proud way of walking and a trick of switching her skirt-tail, which she had copied from her mother.

On this afternoon as they walked home, swinging their book straps, Wilma imparted information.

"My sister Georgianna is going to get married."

"When?"

"Next June. *I'm* going to be flower girl."

Edie's eyes grew round at this unimagined glory.

"Can I come and see you, Wilma?"

" 'Course not! This is a *private* wedding. Family an' friends only."
Wilma turned up her small freckled nose.

"Well—when *you* get married, will you invite me? I'm your friend."

"Maybe. I'll see. I may not get married."

"Oh, sure you will, Wilma!"

Wilma shook her head.

"Why not?"

It had never occurred to Edie that a girl would not marry. It was a
thing that happened—like school, or losing your milk teeth.

Wilma looked superior. "I ain't goin' to have any man doing *that*
to me!"

Edie's eyes grew wider. "Doing what?"

"Don't you know?"

"No."

"You don't know *anything,* do you?"

"Wilma—please tell me."

"You'd *like* to know, wouldn't you?"

"Yes—please! *What* do they do to you?"

Wilma's skirt-tail switched more importantly. "I don't think, if you
don't know, I'd ought to tell you."

"Oh, yes! Pretty please! I'll *die* if you don't!"

Wilma considered. "Well," she said, "will you promise never to tell?
Not *anyone?*"

"Promise!"

"Cross your heart and hope to die?"

"Cross my heart and hope to die!"

"Swelp you?"

"Swelp me!"

Wilma drew a deep breath, proud of being able to impart such
knowledge to an acolyte.

"Lean your head over."

Edie obliged.

Wilma put her fat little lips close to Edie's ear and whispered to her
the thing that men do to women.

Edie pulled away and looked at Wilma, her eyes filled with horror.

"Oh!" she cried. Her sexless little mind failed to grasp any meaning
or logic in what she had heard. "Oh, what do they want to do *that*
for?"

Wilma could not have told her. To cover this lack of an explanation,
she began shrieking with wild laughter.

Edie stared, unbelieving: this was too terrible to accept.

"*Why?*" she insisted.

"Because that's the way men *are!*" Wilma said.

"*All* men?"

"All the men in the world!"

"Not my Uncle Dave!" Edie was reaching for a straw.

"Yes he is, too!"

"He isn't!"

"He is! All men are!"

Sudden fury flamed in Edie. "Wilma Horst, you take that back, or I'll—I'll scratch your eyes out!"

"You don't dast!"

"I do too dast!"

They flew at each other like a pair of little cats, but Wilma had nothing to match Edie's outraged ferocity. In a moment she was flying down the street, howling. Edie hurried home, emptied now of all emotion.

A short time later, Belle and her mother received Mrs. Horst, who marched over with Wilma. The girl had some scratches on her cheek, eyes red with weeping, and a garbled story.

Edie had wanted to "talk nasty." Wilma, virtuously refusing to listen, had been assailed. That was the version.

Edie was hunted to her room, confronted, adjudged guilty, sentenced.

Mrs. Horst, departing, paused for a final salvo: "How old did you say the child is—nine? Rather *precocious,* I'd think. If I were you, Mrs. Constable, I'd be glad she wasn't my *own.*"

It was almost laughable, except that Belle had no sense of humor, how exactly alike mother and daughter switched their skirt-tails in indignant rectitude as they walked away.

This time Edie got the whip. She abided it as well as she could, crying only when the keenest lash of it bit her legs. No supper, no reading, no nothing. She was put to bed at once; and she was told that this was the end. She would go to an orphan asylum in the morning.

An hour later, Dave, coming home from the office, heard the shocking tale repeated with vindictive triumph by Mrs. Dunham.

He listened, his face growing stern.

"I don't believe it!" he exclaimed flatly.

"She scratched the Horst girl like an alley cat," said Belle.

"Probably a good thing. Where's Edie?"

"We put her to bed."

"When Mrs. Horst was making her accusations, did you bother to ask Edie's side of the story?"

Mrs. Dunham volunteered: "It wasn't necessary. Her guilt showed right in her face."

"But what did she say?"

"She got sullen as usual. She wouldn't say anything."

Dave drew a deep breath. "Have you ever heard of the principle of justice—that the accused is presumed innocent until *proved* guilty? No, of course not! Yours is a court of conviction, not of justice."

He looked at them grimly and went upstairs.

In questioning the child, he felt an extreme delicacy. This was a woman's task, surely. But since the truth had to be found, he did it.

It took him half an hour.

He discovered that Edie refused to talk because she had taken a childhood oath not to tell.

He ascertained that it was Wilma who had brought up the discussion.

He learned how Edie, in her loyal innocence, had championed himself.

At the end, Edie having been assured that neither she nor life was as wicked as she thought, Dave returned downstairs.

The women sat in the dining room, with half-questioning defiance.

"Get her some supper," he ordered.

When they did not move, he shouted with such anger that for once they were brought out of their seats, hurrying to obey.

He calmed himself.

"Edie told me the whole story," he said. "If there's one thing I know, it is that she does not know how to lie. It was childish in the first place—children talking about what they did not understand." He described briefly what had happened.

He started upstairs to bring Edie down to supper, but turned once more.

His mouth was white about the lips, and by this the women knew he still was very angry.

"The poor little thing needs a mother," he said. "Not an executioner."

4.

The first snow came that night, not heavy, but slick and gritty on the sidewalks, and bringing a sharper breath of winter.

Next evening Edie brought home a note. It was from the school principal, a man with an undertaker smile, to whom Jericho gave the courtesy title of "Professor." He wrote:

Dear Mr. and Mrs. Constable:

I take pleasure in informing you that Edie has made the highest average marks in her grade during this term. Her behavior also has been excellent. In recognition of this fine record, we have chosen her as one of four children, to participate as individuals, in the Christmas Program. She is to recite, her selection being: Second Chapter of the Gospel of St. Luke, 1st to 21st verses, inclusive. I am sure this honor to Edie will be a source of satisfaction to you.

Respectfully,

HERBERT A. CHALLEN, *Principal*.

Edie was amazed by her enhanced status when she brought home the note. Belle looked at her with new eyes. Even Mrs. Dunham seemed to soften. Dave was filled with pride.

"Is that Horst girl on the program?" was Belle's first question.

"She's in the chorus."

"What's the chorus?"

"That's where the whole grade sings folksongs."

"*All* of you? But that fat little snip isn't going to be on the program 'as an individual'?"

Belle rose, a flash of triumph in her face.

She was beginning to savor an immensely sweet victory. She would meet Mrs. Horst, and already she planned her attack.

. . . How are you, Mrs. Horst? Beautiful winter day—Christmas is almost here, and a body'd hardly know it, would they? Edie's *so* looking forward to her vacation. She's earned it, dear little thing. She's got a part *as an individual,* you know, on the Christmas program. Because she led her grade. But then—I suppose Wilma is on the program too, isn't she? . . .

With relish Belle envisaged how Mrs. Horst would stiffen, and try to pass the question off. But Belle would not permit her to do so. They would know—both of them—what she was driving at. And the knowledge would rankle as bitterly in Mrs. Horst's full bosom as it would be sweet in Belle's.

Edie, finding herself for the first time in favor, was slightly bewildered. But although the program was two weeks away, she set out to "learn her piece." She memorized rapidly, and in almost no time had it, from beginning to end. Dave took time to show her how properly to express the beautiful lines of the Nativity story.

He was enormously pleased, particularly by Belle's attitude. Once more he had hope. It was for this he had been patiently waiting. In the months past he had forced himself times without number to sit silently, even when he felt that Edie was being treated with outright injustice, because he wished to avoid arousing further vindictive spite against her. Once or twice he had intervened for her, but in general he tried to keep his hands off, in the hope that Belle eventually would come around to an acceptance of the child. Now it began to seem that the hope might be fulfilled.

For to Belle this was a supreme event. She was to sit in the school auditorium, in a place reserved for parents "or guardians" of children who had star parts in the program. She planned a new dress, because many eyes would be upon her. For the first time she considered herself in the light of a mother—a child's mother received the lion's share of glory for the child's achievements. She did some discreet boasting. The encounter with Mrs. Horst occurred, and it was satisfactorily similar to what Belle had imagined, for Mrs. Horst, not having been informed by Wilma of Edie's achievement, was entirely unprepared to meet the situation. Belle left that field in complete triumph as her rival retreated in fuming disorder.

Edie was hardly able to believe her own happiness. Delightful plans were being discussed as preparations for Christmas were made. In addition to the Christmas tree and the hanging of stockings, there was to be a Bran Pie.

This last was Dave's idea, a remembrance of his boyhood home in Tennessee, and he described its amusing workings. Presents are placed in a wash tub and entirely covered with bran. With a roasting fork one stirs in the bran until a gift is brought out. The name on the gift is read, the lucky receiver gets the next turn with the fork, and so it goes around. Sometimes the fork brings up no more than a note, but that adds to the excitement. *Look under the pillow on your bed.* One races upstairs—no telling what is there, probably something too bulky for the bran tub. And when the whole tub is emptied of presents, the bran is carried out, and one may sit down and enjoy the treasures in exquisite leisure. Edie was sure she would be unable to wait for Christmas to come.

The Friday night before Christmas, the night of the program, another light snow was falling, mixed with sleet. Dave drove the Chalmers car anyway, although progress was precarious. One hardly knew how to stop the car; it was as likely as not to whirl end for end and coast, when the brakes were put on. By keeping the speed slow, however, he did not have much trouble in reaching school, although there had been one or two accidents already in town that evening.

A crowd of children and their families was converging on the school. Little girls were all sprigged and ribboned and freshly frocked. Little boys, temporarily, were scrubbed and combed.

As Dave parked the car and they prepared to get out, Belle leaned forward, filled with important news. She said: "Dave—why not tell her now?"

He nodded, too pleased to speak.

Belle put her hand on Edie's shoulder.

"Edie, we're going to adopt you," she said. "We decided last night, and the papers will be signed tomorrow. You're to be our own daughter!"

Speechless, Edie sat for a moment, groping, feeling, trying to grasp this immense fact.

"Aren't you going to say anything?" asked Belle in a voice of disappointment, after a moment.

"I—I can't talk—it's—it's——"

Tears suddenly blinded Edie. She put her arms around Belle. Then she hugged Dave's arm passionately.

"I wo-won't cry," she said. "It's j-just too wonderful!"

Dave was touched. Belle felt a warm glow. It was a happy moment. A good moment.

Edie left them when they reached the school building, going around to where the children were to gather. Dave ushered Belle and her mother into the auditorium. They squeezed into seats designed for small bodies, and looked about.

Here and there teachers sat stiffly, in their best. Belle noticed several acquaintances, including Mrs. Horst, who refused to meet her eye. She preened herself.

A tall, black-clad figure mounted the steps to the stage on which stood a piano, a table, and two or three chairs. It was Professor Challen, lean, gray-haired, with a flabby handshake and that undertaker's smile. The children filed in, scrupulously correct for once in deportment. Dr. Widcomb gave the invocation. A schoolteacher went to the piano while the audience rose to sing "America."

A freckled little girl pounded amateurishly at the piano. The "chorus" sang something faintly Elizabethan in mood. An uncomfortably overdressed small boy sawed a violin.

Professor Challen stood up and said:

"Our next number is the Christmas story—recited by—ah—Edie Meader."

The great moment for Belle. The great moment for Dave. They sat forward, proud and eager, for once together, for once in passionate accord, listening as one creature.

Professor Challen assumed his best undertaker's smile. The audience grew silent. Little Edie was up there before them all, in a white dress, her big eyes brilliant in the lights.

And it came to pass in those days that there went out a decree from Caesar Augustus . . .

The little voice was clear. Edie was remembering all the inflections Dave had taught her.

Belle sighed. The little voice went on, and on.

Suddenly it stopped. Belle sat rigidly up. What had happened? Edie stood up there, looking . . . looking . . .

Saying nothing.

5.

Edie had forgotten.

Right in the middle of the Nativity story she halted, gulped and could no longer go on.

The undertaker's smile on Professor Challen's face did not alter. The crowd sat tense and silent.

Still Edie stood there, rooted.

A murmur gradually grew: She's forgot. She's forgot her piece. She don't know what to say. She's made a failure of it. Poor little thing, poor little fool . . . little idiot . . .

Stricken, terrified, Edie stood by the table with the big poinsettias. She had known the piece. She had memorized it over and over. Hundreds of times. She had been afraid of something like this; it had paralyzed her with fear when she was in bed sometimes. But never for one moment had she dreamed it could be as horrible as it really was.

The faces out there, the sea of faces, merged and swirled and swayed before her. Dreadful faces. Horrible faces. They were watching her . . . expecting . . . expecting. . . .

And she could not give them what they expected.

One moment before it had gone so smoothly, so effortlessly. She had felt a little ecstasy in the way it came from her lips:

And there were in the same country shepherds abiding in the field, keeping watch over their flock by night. And, lo, the angel of the Lord came upon them, and the glory of the Lord shone round about them: and they were sore afraid. And the angel said unto them—said unto them—said . . .

And then it stopped coming. It just stopped. The next word . . . it was lost in a void, the black void of Edie's terror. The next word would not come. It was gone forever.

She stood before them and time dragged on lead-weighted feet. The great clock above the stage ticked slowly, remorselessly, and the whispered voices out in front grew silent again. The child made a movement. Maybe she was going to begin, maybe she would remember, maybe she was going to go on after all. . . .

Edie didn't. Her frightened eyes grew wider, searching the faces. Where was Dave? Where was Belle? Where were they? She could not find them. Suddenly somebody leaned over beside her. It was Professor Challen.

Whisper in her ear:

"You may take your seat now, Edie."

With mouth twisted and face pale, Edie walked slowly off the stage, back to her seat, and heard the loud clapping of the crowd.

The crowd was sympathetic, but she did not know that. The applause sounded only derisive.

She shrank in herself. Everything seemed hazy.

Between her hands she twisted her handkerchief. She bit her lips—they wanted to quiver so.

Dimly she lived through it as the program dragged to its end. Deeper and deeper her ignominy and her offense sank into her. How would she ever face them . . . Dave—and Belle—and Mrs. Dunham?

The last song was sung. Proud parents pushed forward to claim their offspring. Edie stole away to one side, and out of a door into the hall.

Even yet she was unable fully to understand the thing that had happened to her.

She wanted to get away.

Get away as far as possible. Nothing in her nightmares had been as fearful as this living nightmare.

A grown-up or two stopped her and spoke.

"Very good, Edie. . . . You did very well. . . . Except for forgetting a little, you did as well as any of the other children. . . ."

She hardly heard them. She hoped to escape from the schoolhouse and hide herself.

Someone called her.

Belle. Dave, behind his wife, looked very worried. He had seen Belle's face, and he knew Belle.

There had been a moment when she was confronted by Mrs. Horst, a suddenly smug and triumphant Mrs. Horst. That had completed the damage already started.

Belle's face was mottled. Her rage, over which she had no control, was threatening to burst into a fantastic explosion. She was trembling with the excess of her fury.

Dave wanted to reach Edie; to take her away and comfort her. But Belle would have her say first.

"I told you!" The bitter words came from her almost in triumph. "I told you! If you'd listened to me—this awful thing wouldn't have happened. Oh—to have it happen like this. To *me!* What have I done——"

"Belle!" Dave was urgent, pleading. "Now, now, it wasn't so bad!"

"*Bad?*" Her voice was like a whiplash as she turned on him. "It's the worst thing that ever happened! Why did you have to go bragging to people? Why didn't you keep your big mouth shut? I can't look anybody in the face—anybody ever again!"

She was close, very close, to hysterical tears. But she held them back. Instead she turned with hate on the shrinking, tortured child.

"*You . . . little . . . idiot.*" The words came with cruelty, without pity, with remorseless slowness. "You little, half-witted idiot! If you think—for one single part of an instant—that I'll *ever* sign that adoption paper now, you can get it out of your head—*right now!*"

"Belle!" Almost fear in Dave's voice.

"Shut up!" she snarled. Again she turned on Edie, beside herself. "You little beast—you've humiliated me as I was never humiliated before. I sat there—expecting you to redeem yourself for everything you haven't done this year. *I* sat there—and you stood up on that platform like a drooling imbecile, with your mouth open, struck dumb! God, why did this have to happen to me? Oh, God!"

Edie did not answer. There was nothing she could say. Farther and farther back into the hall she retreated.

All at once, with a wild little sob, she turned and ran out into the snow through an open door.

"Edie!" Dave called after her. He leaped forward. "Edie!"

He ran out on the schoolporch. She was gone.

Down on the street in front, he heard the blare of an automobile horn, a dreadful, sickening crash, shouts; lights came to a stop, people were rushing.

He ran.

They were lifting Edie out from under the wheels.

With her eyes so filled with tears, as she ran out into the street, she hardly saw the glare of the headlights, and she did not hear the sudden scream of the braked-down tires until darkness came. . . .

6.

Even after the funeral Dave hardly spoke.

When they returned to the house from laying Edie in the grave, and the last unctuous words had been said by the neighbors, and they were alone at last in the house, the three of them, he turned a white face on Belle.

She shrank from him.

He made no move toward her. He said nothing.

But she saw his eyes.

At last she was frightened.

She began to sob, as he turned and went slowly up the stairs.

CHAPTER VII

1.

ON Saturday night, Dave went downtown for his week-end shave. The barbershop was a luxury he could afford to indulge himself in when he chose now; but habit still clung strongly from his less prosperous years, and on weekday mornings he still scraped his own chin with a straightedge razor, crouching forward at the badly lit mirror in the bathroom.

The Saturday night shave was a rather general tradition in Jericho —a man who got his twice over, against the grain, could go until Monday without bothering with his whiskers again, or so it was usually felt.

This provided the excuse. But Dave's real purpose was different. Jericho's business section always was thronged on Saturday nights. His visit to the barbershop gave him the opportunity to see friends and engage in conversation which he was otherwise denied during his busy week.

Winter had passed. Long since the wild geese had gone north in their high, trumpeting arrows. As Dave walked with long, slow steps through this darkening evening in late March, he felt the velvet balm of spring.

It was still as if he had suffered a great sickness. After Edie's death, through January and February he scarcely spoke to or noticed the women in his house. As much as possible he worked away from home, and when he could not do so, closed himself in his own room.

But Belle, who had watched him at first with fear, gradually grew more confident, as she assured herself that he contemplated no violence. At last she and her mother resumed their normal tenor, even forgetting the unwonted civility with which they had treated him in those first weeks after Edie's death.

This he hardly noticed. His responsibility for them was a load he somehow had been ordained to carry, and he continued to bear it. But he seemed numbed to them.

The thought of divorce had come to him, particularly at first when his grief and rage were at their deepest. But divorce in that day was yet a heavy matter, a not very reputable undertaking, a scandalous thing really. He thought of it as an extreme resort from which he shrank.

He was unhappy, more so than he had ever been; but he had become well accustomed to unhappiness. He wondered if anyone was happy when married. Knowing how "appearances" were kept up by his own household, he sometimes believed that all marriage was a stylized mask, bearing the design of a pleasant smile, but hiding behind it the death's head of misery.

He remembered Thoreau's words: *The mass of men lead lives of quiet desperation.* And he thought grimly that the philosopher must have been thinking of married men.

There was yet another reason why, for the present at least, he put aside the extremity of divorce. This was politics. For a man in politics, the divorce court came near to being an execution block. Just now, David Constable had important matters to consider, and an important decision to make which bore on politics strongly.

Insistently it had been coming—in swift little eddies at first, but lately in a sweep almost like a current—the wish of many men that he stand for Congress. Out over the district he knew that, without any authorization from him, the Farmers' Co-operatives had been quietly circulating petitions to place his name on the ballot. Here in Jericho he was asked almost daily what he intended to do. It was popular pressure, genuine popular pressure, to which he must give attention openly soon.

On Main Street someone hailed him, and he turned aside to where Andy McAdam and Timberline Wilson, cronies, stood smoking in lazy content, their backs comfortably against Andy's dray, which stood at the curb.

"Ye announced yet, jedge?" asked Andy.

Dave grinned at the impudent question, and puffed his pipe.

"Somethin' ought to be done about the *Clarion* an' its loony 'vice crusade,'" Andy continued, with a certain argumentative positiveness, as if he had made this statement several times, to others.

"It's hurtin' the town," said Timberline. His real name was Henry, and he was agent of the Wells Fargo—a paunchy, middle-aged man in baggy pants, whose nickname derived from the way his hair grew only part of the way up his skull, then stopped suddenly like the timberline on a bald mountain.

Dave settled his back against the dray beside them.

"I'm interested to know there are two schools of thought on sin in Jericho," he said.

He straightened up suddenly, and the other two looked as he gravely lifted his hat to a car that drove by.

Algeria Wedge was one of the few women in Jericho who could drive a car. She sat very straight in the big red Hudson, her chin lifted high. That was because she was small and had to stretch her neck to see over the wheel; but it gave her the appearance of haughtiness. She did not appear to notice Dave's uplifted hat. But Tucker, who sat beside her, nodded although he did not smile.

Dave's lips straightened into a line for a moment. Then he smiled slightly.

"Tucker appears to be a little late getting away from the office," he remarked pleasantly.

"An' Mrs. Wedge appears to be in a hurry," added Andy.

"She was busy with her driving," said Dave. "Boys, I owe a barber down the street a quarter."

2.

Dave walked on.

Andy had just brought up a matter which had been much in the consideration of all Jericho during recent weeks. The *Clarion* had taken to crusading against "vice"—which meant, in Kansas, liquor. That, in turn, meant politics. Liquor was the familiar Kansas whipping boy; and a breast-beating about liquor conditions was an almost inevitable preliminary to a newspaper attack on some public official charged with law enforcement. In this case Dave was all too well aware who that public official was to be.

The *Clarion* crusade had come as an aftermath of the Bancroft revival, and might therefore have been put down to a change of heart by Tucker Wedge due to his conversion. But there was something more than mere concern over a little bootlegging in the *Clarion*'s altered policy.

Dave hardly knew how the attacks had begun. In the first weeks after Edie was killed, he had been too obsessed with his pain to notice much of what the newspaper said or to be concerned by what was behind it. He heard then, as he heard increasingly now, that Tucker had ambitions for Congress. This at first did not bother him. If Tucker wanted to go to Congress, he could come to Dave and say so. They would make an arrangement—they always had been able to adjust everything.

But Tucker had made no overtures; Tucker avoided him.

Meantime the *Clarion*'s clamor increased.

Dave was not thin skinned, but the hostility of the constant barrage, with its hints, its innuendos, never coming out in the open, grew a little wearing.

Like hysterical women it is the nature of newspapers to overdo things. The *Clarion*, seeking to substantiate its excitement over "conditions" in Jericho—where little liquor really was sold, and where crime was at a minimum—made statements so fantastic as to be laughable. Except that so stated, and re-stated, by the only newspaper in town, many persons were beginning to believe those statements.

The *Clarion* baldly asserted that prohibition was a "farce" in Jericho; that no effort was being made to enforce the statutes; that there was a "pay-off" from a "bootleg ring."

All this pointed to David Constable, as the official directly responsible for law enforcement. A good many men in Jericho were betting that a direct attack, by name, was only a short time off.

And this was a situation which nobody would have deemed possible a few months before, when the friendship of Tucker Wedge and David Constable was a Short Grass proverb. Dave himself could not understand how it was possible now.

"Hi-ya, Dave."

He stopped. It was Webb Pettis, the Bedestown-district farmer and auctioneer. Dave was glad to see him; they were the best of friends.

"Thought you might like to know," said Pettis, his Indian eyes gleaming, "that if ye ever get your mind made up, we're ready in the north. Ye'll get a full endorsement from the Co-ops, an' the petitions'll be in good shape. When ye goin' to announce?"

Dave laid his hand on the auctioneer's shoulder. "Too early, Webb."

"Don't see why."

"I want to see what—some other people are going to do."

He did not let Webb know either how the Christmas tragedy had altered him, taking the zest from his planning; or how a friend's defection had given a flavor of bitter gall to everything.

Webb thought he understood. "If Tucker Wedge announces, Porter Grimes will swing the district convention for him."

"What of it?"

"So ye ought to announce quick—head him off."

"It wouldn't do any good. Grimes would never back me. If I should run, Webb—mind, I say *if*—it would have to be as an independent."

Webb drew a deep breath. "An' ye'd run off with it!" he exclaimed. "Dave, ye gotta let us help ye. The farmers are for ye a thousand per cent——"

Dave shook his head. "Not yet."

Webb hesitated. Then, unwillingly, he said: "Jest as ye say, Dave." He thought a moment. "One thing, though, I been wantin' to tell ye. Get the *Clarion* off ye somehow."

"By going on a lot of liquor raids?"

"It's practically sure-fire politics in Kansas."

Dave's gaze contained amusement. "Am I really hearing Webb Pettis advise me to start breaking into people's homes, stick my nose into their basements, investigate their mail and baggage shipments—to get a few votes?"

"Others has done it."

"I can't. There's a principle here that's too big."

"I don't see no principle, Dave."

"In the first place, no matter what he does, a county attorney is an open target—if a newspaper wants to make him so, as appears to be the desire of our local representative of the great free press. But aside from that, a county attorney, if he has any sense of responsibility, has to exercise a certain amount of discretion where sentiment is broadly divided on a law."

"I don't quite get it," said Pettis.

"Prohibition's not backed by a unanimous sentiment—like the laws against theft, murder, fraud, and so on."

"But it's on the statute books."

"Sure, and there used to be a law on the statute books condemning women to be burned as witches. And another fining a man if he kissed his wife on Sunday. But prohibition was adopted in Kansas by a vote of only ninety-two thousand to eighty-four thousand. A nine to eight vote margin is a pretty narrow majority, Webb."

"But——"

"Enforcement of the wishes and demands of a majority on a substantial minority is one of the injustices with which man has been cursed since the beginning of history. Every religious persecution, every intolerance, every suppression of minority peoples, has partaken of this. Fanaticism never led to justice."

Pettis gave him a straight look. "I got to respect you for that, Dave."

"I'm going to keep basic rights—which the fanatics forget—in mind. There's very little liquor sold in Jericho. No blind tigers. Mighty small drinking. When I catch a bootlegger, I punish him. But I draw the line at snooping into private homes."

3.

A candy-striped barber pole stood beside the door, and David Constable turned into the shop, removed his hat, coat and collar, and got into a chair.

Will Pipkin, the head barber, always shaved Dave. Will was a genial foul-mouthed man, who obtained at least as much social enjoyment as financial return from his vocation. It was restful to hear him talk when the warm towel was over one's face. Beside, Will's flavorful monologue never failed to put one well abreast of all information and gossip in the town.

"When you announcin' for Congress, Dave?" began the barber as he put on the hot towel after lathering.

There it was again. The same insistent question.

"What's the hurry?" asked Dave in a muffled voice.

"Because I can't do nothing for Tucker Wedge an' that apple-butter mouth of his."

"Apple-butter mouth?" asked Dave as the towel was removed.

"It's just an old saying." The barber put on a new fluff of lather. "That's a mouth cut so far back on the sides that the tongue can't lick all of it, an' there'll always be some apple butter left sticking in the corners."

Dave chuckled. Tucker *did* have rather a wide mouth.

"Lots of your friends are plenty sore over what Wedge has been sayin' in his two-bit paper," said Pipkin.

"A man's entitled to his convictions."

"You're long-sufferin' or plain crazy. He's tryin' to kill you, so you can't run. Him in Congress! He don't look no part of a Congressman —too damned sawed-off."

"It would take something more than short legs to make me vote against a man," was all Dave said.

Pipkin began to shave. Dave did not wish to talk. All he wanted was to rest. He enjoyed the comfort of the chair, the crispness of the starched neck cloth, the light touch of the barber's fingers on his chin, the soft clatter of the brush stirring the lather in the mug, the clean, straight pull of the razor on his face.

His mind turned inward; voices in the shop faded away. Even Will Pipkin's talk receded. Behind his closed eyelids he saw again the cold stare of the man in the red car—the cold stare, and the cold nod, and the cold profile of the man's wife as they swept past.

Something in him rebelled against admitting that the Tucker Wedge, with whom he had lived and sported and worked these years, was the man who had just given him that chill glance. Yet it had to be faced —something had gone terribly wrong.

He felt the injustice, the sense of having been traitorously abandoned, of having been attacked without warning from a quarter he least expected. Anger burned in his stomach. Then for a moment he wrestled anew with doubt. His mind was crowded with reasons—his professional necessity, the zest that was gone from his life—why should he give up politics.

But after that came once more the hard stillness of his own volition. He saw things clearly now.

He could not afford to let the world know his resentment against Tucker. Above everything he must preserve his good spirits, his easygoing ways. In politics it is the conception the people have of a man that elects or defeats him, and Dave's popularity was erected on the conception of his good humor and tolerance. He would have to deal with Tucker Wedge, and with all those for whom Tucker Wedge stood. In doing so he must let time tell its own story, and be ready.

Pipkin finished shaving, and raised Dave to a sitting position. The lawyer now realized that the barber had been talking all the time, although Dave had not in ten minutes replied to him. One remark, however, somehow lingered.

"You said something about a new lawyer in town?" Dave asked.

"Yeah." Pipkin appeared surprised. "A *woman* lawyer!"

"Humph!" Dave had encountered a few woman lawyers. There was nothing about them that he liked.

"What's her name?" he asked.

"Ain't heard. I understand she's in Judge Hutto's office."

Dave grunted. "Didn't think the judge would stand for a she-lawyer."

He felt the starched cloth taken away and got out of the chair. By the time he paid Pipkin he had already forgotten the topic of the female invasion of his profession.

He had something more important to consider. At last he was beginning to make up his mind concerning Congress and Tucker Wedge.

4.

In the pitch darkness of night, he came up suddenly in bed, listening.

Something had jarred him out of profound slumber. He lay wondering. Gradually, he realized—an explosion of some sort. The echoes still seemed to whisper in the night-trapped streets.

He switched on a light. Two o'clock, his watch said. Two o'clock in the morning and black as the inside of a gun barrel.

The stillness was broken again. *Boom . . . boom . . . boom.*

Any lingering sleep fled suddenly. Gun shots—shotguns.

All at once a spiteful crackle of sharper reports. Revolver. Somewhere near the center of town.

Dave vaulted out of bed, dressing rapidly. Feet pounded the sidewalk outside. Belle and her mother were at their doors as he came into the hall, tossing querulous questions.

"What was it?"

"Somebody shooting, Ma."

"Outlaws? We'll be murdered—in our beds——"

Dave hitched his suspenders over his shoulders and started down the stairs.

Belle, her face swollen from slumber, one cheek covered with a faint tracery of pinkish lines where the pillow had wrinkled, compressed her lips with obstinate disapproval.

"What do you think you're going to do?"

"I'm going to see what happened."

"And leave us?"

"Nobody's going to want *you*," he said nastily.

The remark had the effect he desired. They forgot their panic in anger.

Still buttoning his shirt he went down the steps and out on the porch, standing listening in the chill night. Voices shouted distantly. He could not make out what they said.

A telephone rang suddenly and insistently in the house. He went in quickly, but Belle was before him.

"Yes? Mr. Constable? Yes? What happened? Yes, he's right here——"

Sullenly she handed him the receiver. People always insisted on talking to Dave . . .

"Dave, this is Jake," said the voice on the phone. Jacob Gurney, the old sheriff. "It's Porter Grimes's bank—safe's blown. You'd better get on over——"

5.

There were five banks in Jericho. Out of all these the bandits would *have* to pick Porter Grimes's.

That was Dave's thought as he left his car in front of the building and walked toward the door.

In the darkness a crowd milled about on the sidewalk, kept back by a young policeman who recognized Dave and let him in.

Jake Gurney eagerly clutched him by the arm. The sheriff was an old-time character—a little man with a set of store teeth, which he wore in his pocket most of the time. Just now his mouth looked caved-in and his chin jutted curiously. Dave could hardly understand what he said.

"Had n'aum'ble. S'mbuddy s'd went suth."

"Oklahoma?"

Jake mumbled incomprehensibly.

"Put in your teeth!" said Dave impatiently.

The sheriff looked astonished. He reached into his pants pocket and took out the ugly dentures with the unnatural orange gums. He hated wearing the plates because they did not fit him, and in the present excitement he had clean forgotten them. When he put them in his mouth he hissed a good deal, but at least he could be understood.

"Take a look in there," he said.

Dave entered the vault. The door of the safe hung twisted on its hinges. Papers and ledgers lay scattered about and broken glass crunched underfoot.

"Reckon it was one of them Oklahoma gangs," whistled Gurney. "Mebbe Al Spencer."

"Could be anybody." Al Spencer was a celebrated bank bandit of the Oklahoma hills, but Dave disliked the habit which law officers had of ascribing every crime committed to some publicized figure. "Anyone see them?" he added.

"Mrs. Walston an' Helen Schroeder at the telephone office."

"Where are they now?"

"Took Mrs. Walston home. Had high-sterricks."

"The Schroeder girl?"

"Still at the office."

"I'm going over. When Porter Grimes gets down, bring him to the courthouse."

The telephone office was only half a block up the street, a small frame building, full of people. A repair man had arrived and was working on the long-distance cables.

"Them guys knew all about telephones," he told Dave. "Traced out an' cut every out-of-town wire."

A big German girl, with pimples on her cheeks and light-brown hair done in a greasy pompadour, sat chewing gum with nervous concentration. She was just getting over her scare and beginning to feel her importance. Dave pushed through the crowd, and when she understood who he was, Helen Schroeder paid attention to no one else.

Ja, she saw the men. Two only came into the telephone office. One was a big, rough-talking man, the other a square, sawed-off man. They wore masks—handkerchiefs with eye holes cut out—and carried double-barrel shotguns. *Ja,* they threatened her and Mrs. Walston. And Mrs. Walston with her bad heart. The bandits made them sit over by the waiting-room. The big, rough-talking one began cutting the cables. The square, sawed-off one never said anything, but stood guard. After the other one finished cutting the cables, he went out. The explosion come a little later. *B-r-r-r-oom!* Somebody outside the door called, and the square-set man pointed his shotgun at them and said he would kill them if they moved. Mrs. Walston like to fainted. Helen didn't feel so good herself. The man went out. They heard a motor car and some shooting. That was all.

6.

Porter Grimes arrived at the courthouse almost as soon as Dave did. The banker was furious, pounding the table, demanding action.

"I want those bandits found and my money recovered, or I'll make things so everlastingly hot around here you'll never forget it!" he shouted.

Dave regarded him curiously. He had never seen Grimes display any kind of emotion before.

"What's the loss?" he asked when the banker cooled down.

"Around ten thousand. Mostly greenbacks." Grimes grew more calm, became specific. "We can give you the serial numbers of some. They took about seven hundred dollars in gold. But all the silver—two thousand dollars and more—was left."

Dave nodded. "Too heavy to carry. Old hands. No local amateurs in this holdup."

Grimes shot him a glance of suspicion. "Why are you so sure?"

"Professional bank bandits never fool with local men. Too dangerous."

Grimes sneered. "Just don't overlook any suspects because they happen to be acquaintances," he said.

"Just what do you mean?" asked Dave, angered.

"I want action. That's what I mean!"

Grimes stamped out.

He left Dave with something to think about. Coming just at this time the robbery of Grimes's bank was embarrassing. Already he could see a threat behind the banker's remarks.

Porter Grimes never thought of anything without weighing it in terms of politics. He so weighed this major crime which had been dumped into Dave's lap. If the county attorney failed to arrive at a solution for it, there would be serious political consequences, Dave felt certain.

By sunup, he had finished talking to everyone who had a version of the robbery. Not much was gained. A blue touring car had been seen—a dark blue Marmon. Some thought it took the road south.

The buff stone courthouse looked gaunt in the early sun, and Dave was jaded as he talked to Jake Gurney again.

"The bandits had shotguns?" he asked.

"Yeh. Broke into Downey's Hardware to get some shells. After the safe was blowed, they shot down all four streets at the bank corner." The old man munched on his loose teeth. "Just banged away in the dark, not shooting at nothing, but trying to scare folks."

"Anyone hurt?"

"Nope. Some roofs got peppered. Everybody was awake but with them guns going, nobody wasn't doing nothing."

"Where were you?"

"I crawled out of a back window in my quarters here at the courthouse, and got down into a culvert. But before I could get unlimbered, they was gone."

"Then you didn't fire those revolver shots I heard?"

"No. Don't know where they come from. The bandits, I guess."

Dave dismissed the sheriff and sent out for a sandwich and a cup of coffee.

Almost at once the sheriff was back.

"Gotch McCurdy's around town bragging he fired that revolver," he said excitedly.

"Bring him in," ordered Dave.

The coffee and sandwich had arrived, and he had just finished the meager breakfast, when Gotch was ushered in.

"What do you want with me?" The big man scowled, ugly as ever.

"Just want to know what you know about the robbery, Gotch. You shot that revolver?"

"Yep. The blast woke me up. I think I hit one of them bandits."

This was news.

"Why do you think that?"

"I'll show ye where they washed him up."

They went in Dave's car—Gotch, Jake Gurney, Clarence Snead of the *Clarion,* and Dave. Gotch indicated blood, splashed on a horse trough near the railroad station, and traces elsewhere in the trampled mire. He glanced about with a look of triumph.

But as they turned back to the car, a woman came from a small yellow house across the street.

"Are you Mr. Constable?" She was old, with yellow parchment skin and faded blue eyes. A shawl was over her head.

"I am, madam."

"I thought you was. I seen you at one of them trials."

"What can I do for you?"

"You lookin' at that blood by the trough?"

"Yeh," said Gurney. "It's where one of them bandits washed up after bein' shot."

"Bandit nothin'," said the old woman with scorn. "That ain't bandit blood. It's chicken blood."

"How do you know?"

"Kilt a chicken there myself, yestiddy afternoon."

She walked around the horse trough, peering and pointing. Now they noticed, for the first time, feathers. Gray, and bloodstained, and muddy.

"Just a chicken after all," said the sheriff. "What you got to say, Gotch?"

"I seen the blood an' figgered it was man blood," growled Gotch. "I kin make a mistake like anybody else, can't I?"

He stared at them bitterly, then walked away with a great swing to his shoulders.

An unreasonably ridiculous anticlimax, this. Clarence Snead of the *Clarion* was right there to see it.

The *Clarion* took full advantage of the incident that afternoon. Dave and Jake Gurney were represented as a pair of bungling and stupid amateur sleuths, rushing about on low-comedy false clues. The story as carried by the paper ended as follows:

The discovery by our local Hawkshaws of indubitable blood on the town horse trough, was a fitting climax to the day of remarkable activities. Unfortunately, it was pointed out by an old lady living in the vicinity that the blood was not the gore of a bandit, but chicken blood—she herself having sacrificed the fowl there.

Jericho can only hope that when its brilliant upholders of the law get around to making an arrest they will capture something more important than a Dominicker rooster.

Dave laughed with the rest of the town. The joke was on him, certainly. But he felt a growing anxiety, and already he could sense further complications.

CHAPTER VIII

1.

FROM the very moment it happened, Dave knew that Gotch Mc-Curdy's even casual connection with the case was awkward. Some of Dave's friends had long warned him that McCurdy was doing him no good; but he invariably defended the stableman, with his perverse loyalty to the curious, half-protecting relationship he had always maintained toward Gotch.

"A dog with a bad name gets blamed for a lot he never does," Dave would say.

Yet the rumor had grown insistently greater in the past few months that Gotch McCurdy was the biggest bootlegger in Jericho. If this were really true, Dave had no evidence of it. Had he possessed the evidence —and he had twice taken the trouble to investigate the matter—he would have had McCurdy jailed as quickly as any man in Jericho.

The liveryman drank heavily; that was indisputable. He was quarrelsome, and had been in a fist fight or two. But for him Dave felt a sympathetic pity. The new age of automobiles had all but closed down his livery business, and the big man grew more sullen and down-at-heels every day, refusing to go into garage work, in spite of Dave's suggestion.

"Guess you don't hardly know how it is to find yourself left out by people's changing ways," he said gazing at Dave bleakly. "Horses— that's my life. Horses is flesh and blood and hunger and thirst; and when you're by yourself in the stable at night, you never get lonesome because you can hear the horses chawing their hay, or stompin' in their stalls, or whickering. Horses smells good—even horse manure smells natural, like it was meant. But what about them gasoline buggies? There's no more company in an automobile than there is in a barb-wire fence; an' the stink of burnin' gasoline makes me sick at the belly."

A surprising bit of sentiment, that, for Gotch McCurdy. He swore and blustered and spat, directly after uttering it, in sheer disgust at himself for allowing such a weakness to show; but it had revealed a glimpse of his secret heart, and after that Dave would not have turned against Gotch, even though he was quite sure that some day McCurdy might become a weapon for his enemies to use against him.

When Gotch made his brief, stupid intervention in the bank robbery case, Dave felt that there was misfortune in it.

He said nothing about it, however, to Gotch or anybody else, but threw himself with all his energy into the baffling, tantalizing, apparently bootless task of trying to trace the robbers.

Nobody knew the labor of the next weeks through which Dave Constable persisted. As he had expected, Jake Gurney, the sheriff, was utterly incompetent. He gazed helplessly at Dave, and sucked on his loose plate, and it was then that Dave took charge—as he had known all along he would have to take charge.

The bandits who had robbed the bank in Jericho were not local men; of this Dave was certain. He acted on the theory, and in the days that followed his assumption of the responsibility of the hunt for the criminals, he became a slave driver in both his own and the sheriff's offices.

The long distance telephone became an inspired extension of his thoughts and words. Police chiefs and sheriffs in distant cities like Denver, Kansas City, and Tulsa became very familiar with the voice of the Jericho county attorney, as he ran up the tolls unsparingly.

He furnished to all police bureaus the most reliable descriptions he could obtain; received and transmitted tips to places where they might bear fruit in action; made shrewd deductions which galvanized the search, now here, now there. Far across the state and neighboring states ran the ripples of his thought. Every town in Kansas, large and small, was combed thoroughly. Whenever the search flagged, David Constable spurred it. Constantly alert, forever whipping the hunt to a faster tempo, he succeeded in making the Jericho bank bandits the objects of the most intense and widespread search the Southwest had seen in years.

His own dogged will and desperate energy were responsible for all this. But the clues on which he worked were so few, the territory into which the robbers had disappeared so wide, that although his ceaseless day and night effort made him haggard and worn, he grew more deeply pessimistic each day over the prospects of success in his tracking of the raiders on Porter Grimes's bank. And each day the *Clarion's* sneers at the paucity of the results he had obtained grew broader.

2.

Dave expected the *Clarion* editorial; but it came on a bad day.

Three weeks had passed since the robbery, and the April wheat fields were blue-green with promise.

He had slept badly. One of the prairie night storms swept across the town sometime before morning with a sudden thunderous and spectacular electrical display, and he had wakened to close the windows of the house.

Storms seemed to affect Belle's humor. Though he avoided her as much as possible, he had been unable that morning to escape an unpleasant passage—ridiculous and childish but leaving him stinging with irritation. He flung out of the house and went to his office where his desk was stacked high with work.

Many persons were waiting to see him. Caxton Cully, his horse-faced, spectacled secretary, brought in the mail unsmiling. Dave closed the office door, looked over correspondence briefly, and consulted his day's calendar. Three informations to dictate, a warrant, two briefs to review, other matters of a routine nature; these could wait. He decided to see the people in the reception room at once.

One by one, Cully ushered them in. The usual complaints. Neighbors who harbored night-barking dogs. A spite fence which had been built. Threats had been made against someone. A short, dark man with a rough nose and immense mustache insisted on pulling his chair close to Dave and whispering, with foully unpleasant breath, that he would tell—for a consideration—where someone had hidden a load of liquor. Dave informed him that the county had no money to pay for such information and urged upon him the duty of telling anyway; but the fellow shook his head. He evidently believed his information was worth money somewhere, and departed with a spiteful scowl over his shoulder.

A bulky woman in a grease-spotted dress and an ugly old hat told him with a German accent that she wanted her husband—her ex-husband—arrested for sending her last month's alimony, thirty dollars, in pennies, buried in a bucket of axle grease. She poked toward Dave a crumpled paper. He read:

CLARA. I THINKING YOU HAVE LOTS FUN MIT THIS BUCKET. HOPING YOU WORK AS HARD FINDING YOUR MONEY AS I MAKING IT. AUGUST.

Another time Dave might have been amused at the spiteful little incident. Today he only ushered the woman wearily out, referring her to the judge of the district court for relief.

Cully entered and stood with the door ajar.

"Lady to see you."

"Who is it?"

"She says she's an attorney."

Dave's patience suddenly frayed. "That *she-lawyer?*"

Cully hurriedly closed the door. For a moment the two men stared at each other. Then Dave grinned apologetically.

"Reckon she heard me, Cully? Sorry—I've certainly got no reason to yell at you. But I have no use for women lawyers. They complicate and mess up the profession—trifling minded, and use unfair tricks. I suppose—I'll have to see her. I'll ring the bell when I'm ready."

Cully laid the afternoon *Clarion* on the desk and retired.

Mechanically Dave opened the paper and glanced over it. All at once his face grew rigid with concentration. On the front page of the paper was a two-column boxed editorial:

Time to Face the Facts.

For months crime has been on the upgrowth in Jericho. The existence of a bootleg ring long has been well known, and gambling brazenly continues in the city limits. *The Clarion* repeatedly has called attention to these conditions, and has been ignored.

Now, however, the community faces something more serious. A major crime—an unsolved major crime—confronts Jericho.

The robbery of the Jericho National Bank is a threat and challenge to the peace and safety of every man, woman, and child in the city. From the first the public has demanded without a dissenting voice, that the culprits be found and punished. Yet what has been done?

Weeks have passed, and not one move has been made to run the criminals to earth. The tight little ring of county officials, feeling safe in their sinecure positions, has not stirred. It has, indeed, laughed at demands of the citizens for action.

The bandits showed such blatant temerity, such unequaled coolness, in their robbery of the bank here, that it is no wonder the exploit has aroused comment. Nor is it to be wondered that more and more people are beginning to wonder if there was not a sense of sureness, a feeling that the usual dangers had been eliminated, which made these criminals feel free to take their time, terrorize the town, and make off with $10,000 in cash.

An insistent rumor is heard today that the bank raiders had a direct actual connection right in Jericho—a connection which would give them a pipeline direct to the county attorney's office. There is more than idle gossip to this report.

An unpleasant duty faces *The Clarion,* but one from which it can no longer shrink. It is necessary to place the blame for the lethargy, the inefficiency, if not the outright venality and indifference with which this case has been handled, where it belongs.

David Constable, county attorney of Blair County, is the man upon whom this blame should rest. David Constable has failed to act. David Constable has allowed inefficiency, corruption, and personal favoritism too long to guide the conduct of his office.

How long are the people of Jericho going to endure the cynical refusal of this man to carry out the mandatory duties of his office? How long will the people submit to his inefficiency, his betrayal of the public trust?

For eight years David Constable has lived at the public trough. It is time he be discontinued as a beneficiary of the tax payer's money.

The Clarion speaks the thoughts of every honest and law-respecting citizen when it demands a clean-up at the courthouse. That clean-up must begin at the very top—in the office, so badly mishandled, of county attorney.

David Constable must go!

3.

Dave read it over twice, and sat gazing, far away, out of the window. He had not dreamed Tucker would go quite *this* far.

He rose and paced back and forth, the newspaper clutched in his fist, his face haggard, scarcely seeing the room about him.

This was a blow below the belt. Tucker knew how Dave had been laboring, the impossible odds confronting him. Such an editorial as the *Clarion* spewed forth on its front page was indecent, dishonest.

He seated himself again, and thought for a long time. Now he realized the inevitability of the public feeling to which the editorial referred.

All over town, it seemed, whispers had started that Gotch McCurdy was "one of the bandits." The stableman, the public believed, was just the kind of a person who would possess the nerve to assist the bandits in their robbery, then remain behind in Jericho to face down the townspeople.

Gotch was the pipeline direct to the county attorney's office, to which the *Clarion* referred. Poor Gotch. Forever in trouble. Now he had Dave in trouble with him.

Dave swore to himself, a rare thing for him.

All at once he remembered the visitor outside and buzzed the bell on his desk. Cully came.

"Is that woman still out there?"

"No sir. She left about four-thirty."

Surprised, Dave glanced at his watch. He had been sitting, alone in his office, more than an hour.

"I'm sorry—I forgot about her," he said.

"Anything else, sir?"

"No. Go on home."

"Goodnight, sir."

"Goodnight, Cully."

4.

Resentment came next day—the full feeling of having been greatly wronged. War now was openly declared, a war not of Dave's choosing, forced on him against every desire.

The bitterness of this feud was deeper than ordinary bitterness, because it ended forever an old friendship. Anger burned slowly in the pit of Dave's stomach.

But anger which is visible in the sight of many people is one thing, and anger which is contained within oneself alone is another. Not even Cully knew how the *Clarion* editorial had wounded Dave.

During the day after the appearance of the attack, many came to Dave, to express their anger at Tucker Wedge and his newspaper. Tucker's editorial had clarified Dave's position. He had been raised up as an antagonist in an evil feud. Men love antagonists. Instinctively they draw around, form a circle, and give the antagonists room for the fair play of their fighting qualities. By the very act of becoming antagonists, whether they are roosters, or dogs, or small boys in fisticuffs, or political enemies, they are lifted above all mediocrity in the public eye.

Since David Constable had been singled out by the *Clarion,* the organ of the Old Guard, of Porter Grimes and his machine, quite unintentionally he had been made a symbol of the opposition—the Insurgents. Overnight, in Jericho, the words and movements of Dave became more significant. Toward him turned the eyes of many men.

The *Clarion,* as usual, was unable to keep from overdoing and overstating. Had it allowed that first editorial to stand, it would have been in a strong position. But for a week editorial followed editorial, shouting for action against the bank robbers, extolling the righteousness of the paper's cause, assailing David Constable, demanding that he resign from office.

This kind of thing vitiates itself. People presently ceased reading the editorials. Dave remained good humored throughout the attack. Eventually the public forgot about the charges, the flurry was over, and he was allowed quietly to go ahead with his patient campaign to capture the Jericho National Bank robbers.

5.

The invitation was in Algeria's own crisp hand, and Dave read it with astonishment.

Mr. and Mrs. David Constable . . . cordially invited to . . . reception at the home of Mr. and Mrs. Tucker Wedge, to meet the Honorable William Jennings Bryan . . . Tuesday, April 12th. From 3 to 5 o'clock. R.S.V.P.

It seemed sheer impertinence at first. Then he knew that the manner and occasion gave it a certain grace. This would be Algeria's idea. No one else would think of a gesture like this.

Much had been said in the *Clarion* recently about the impending visit of the Great Commoner, who was to lecture at the Doric Opera

House, as an event of the Chautauqua series. Bryon, as everyone knew, was building toward a fourth try for the presidency. The Chautauqua platform was a sounding board made as if by special design for his particular type of histrionics. From one end of America to the other he was thundering for temperance and religion—with the shadow of politics always behind. The "Crown of Thorns and Cross of Gold" speech was still the era's most famous oratorical effort. Farmers and workingmen continued to crowd to see the Free Silver champion.

Again Dave read the invitation over.

Behind its lines he seemed to see Algeria, with her face tilted in that inimitable way of hers, saying to him with her smile: Come on, David —let's forget all our differences for an afternoon. . . .

Well . . . Bryan was a famous man who three times had been the presidential candidate of a great party. Dave was curious about him; his viewpoints seemed so puzzlingly contradictory to a man who could judge him only by the newspaper accounts.

The coming of a personage so eminent was an overpowering event for Jericho. Algeria's alertness in snatching the distinction of entertaining him right out from under the very fingers of various earnest persons of Bryan's own party—to say nothing of a laboriously organized reception committee which got its invitation in too late—was another proof of her remarkable qualities.

The fact that the Wedges were important Republicans gave the gesture a flavor of tolerant broadmindedness which would appeal to even the Republicans of the Short Grass country; and Tucker Wedge, as publisher of the *Clarion,* was in some sort a quasi-official representative of the city; while certainly Algeria was far better fitted than anyone else to play hostess to Bryan.

Dave found it amusing to picture the disappointment which the Democratic reception committee had swallowed, and the unhappiness with which it obtained what satisfaction it could out of arranging an elaborate meeting for its hero at the train, and such political conferences later as he would agree to hold.

Dave decided: I'll drop in. Just long enough to pay my respects.

6.

He arrived at the Wedge home on the afternoon of the Bryan reception, late and alone.

"We've been missing you, Dave!" cried Algeria as she greeted him. He had occasion again to admire her fine eyes, bright, just now, with apparently sincere joy at seeing him. "Everybody's so rushed these days . . . but when things quiet down a bit, we *must* see more of each other. Old friends are *best* friends after all. . . ."

Nobody could do this as Algeria did it. She gave him no indication that she even was aware of a rift between her husband and him; no hint that she had so much as read the *Clarion*'s bitter editorials. And when she saw that Belle was not with him, she did not embarrass him by inquiring about his wife.

Instead, she took him impulsively by the hand and pulled him toward a group which surrounded Bryan.

"Tucker—Dave's here!" she said.

The room stilled momentarily. It was the first time Tucker Wedge and David Constable had met since the former had attacked the latter. In the moment of stillness the two men looked into each other's eyes, and each face was devoid of expression.

Then Dave thrust out his hand and smiled.

"Howdy, Tucker," he said.

"Good to see you, Dave." But Tucker's smile was no more than what he gave to any stranger in his house. He turned toward the guest of honor.

"Mr. Bryan, I have the honor of presenting David Constable, our county attorney."

Tension in the room disappeared. Everyone began talking again.

Dave saw before him a broad, balding man with immense Roman features, hair shaggy and long at the back of his huge head, and a mouth as wide as a saucer. Mr. Bryan was attired in the alpaca coat and string tie he had made his hallmarks. In his hand was a plate heaped high with sandwiches, of which he ate greedily. From this congenial occupation he took time to extend to Dave a free hand, somewhat smeared with butter and bread crumbs.

"Delighted, Mr. Constable." Bryan spoke with the practiced orotundity of the magniloquent public man. "Once had ambitions to be a county attorney myself." He waited expectantly for the titter at the quaint notion that he had ever had aspirations so humble, got it from the group about, and continued. "I always take off my hat to a county attorney. Nearly always the chief repository of legal knowledge in his community. Has to be—forced on him, whether he likes it or not."

Another titter. Bryan took advantage of it to shovel an entire nut-bread sandwich into his capacious maw. Food was an obvious passion to him. He chewed noisily, smacking his lips.

"Always delighted to meet a Democrat holding public office," he went on. "Little difficult to do—know that from personal experience."

He leered around expectantly, and got his giggle.

"But I'm not a Democrat—I'm a Republican," said Dave.

Bryan looked annoyed. "I seem to have been misinformed. Well, I suppose you Old Guards have this state in a strangle hold."

"I doubt that the Old Guards do." Dave glanced at Tucker, who looked away.

"Ah. You're a Progressive?"

"Call it that."

"Perhaps that explains the impression I garnered from a remark dropped by—I should judge the opposite wing of your party—" Bryan glanced over toward Porter Grimes who was conversing with Jasper Peddigrew.

"I could understand how you might," smiled Dave.

"Humph. I've been informed that Kansas is the bulwark of stand-pattism; a barnacle state, willing to encrust itself on outmoded reactionism, while the tides of time and progress sweep by."

"Then you've listened to a gorgeous piece of brass-bound mendacity, sir," said Dave warmly. "Kansas is naturally liberal in her outlook. Of course, we always have those with us who would try to crush that liberalism. But so do other states. Watch the Progressives. There's a big movement growing in Kansas."

"Well," Bryan twinkled, "any kind of a split in the Grand Old Party is good." He engulfed another entire sandwich, this time of chicken salad and white bread.

Algeria swept down upon them with J. Wilber Bratten in tow. The insurance man—whom Dave considered an egregious bore, a fountain of words, and given to self-adulation—pumped Bryan's hand, his thick-lensed spectacles gleaming with eager cordiality.

"Ah," he said loudly. "A privilege, I'm sure. Don't belong to your party, Mr. Bryan—but we've got interests in common. Uplift work and handling crowds. Never saw you in action, but I heard you're a master." His teeth glittered and his heavy face was alight with enthusiasm. Bryan opened his mouth, but J. Wilber gave him no chance to speak.

"We've got different methods of doing the same thing," he said breezily. "*I* handle people by the miracle of song. I'm Number One Tail-twister of the Jericho Commercial Club." He gave a noisy laugh. "Perhaps you've heard of our quartet?" Obviously Bryan had not. "Luncheon singing's the soul and essence of any club, I always say. Look at me—in demand in neighboring towns whenever the local leaders want to arouse civic life—and always glad to go."

"Very worthy 'm sure," mumbled Bryan, seeking refuge in a lettuce-and-olive sandwich.

"Really makes no difference *what* they sing—or whether they sing good or bad—just so they sing, I always say. If you're going to cut out anything on the program, I say cut out the speeches. Nobody learns anything from those windjammers anyway."

Bryan's eye grew slightly glassy, but J. Wilber rushed ahead, oblivious of the fact that he was treading on the tender toes of one who prided himself on being the world's foremost exponent of the derided art of after-dinner speaking.

Algeria, hovering uneasily in the background, went at last for Lillian Bratten. In a moment the insurance man's thin, colorless wife was at his elbow. She clutched his sleeve and spoke in an imperative whisper.

"What's that—uh—" J. Wilber leaned over. He glanced in startled fashion at Bryan, as he listened.

"Uh—hope I haven't bored you—" he began.

"My husband sometimes forgets himself in his enthusiasm," said Mrs. Bratten sweetly.

She led J. Wilber away.

From under his long-tailed coat Bryan pulled a black silk handkerchief and wiped his forehead. His eye fell on Dave.

"Who is that glittering-eyed fanatic?" he whispered hoarsely. "I didn't catch his name."

"J. Wilber Bratten—our most prominent underwriter and most extravagant town booster."

But Algeria was with them again, smiling.

"Tucker's not taking very good care of you, Mr. Bryan. Here are some more of our people who desire the honor of meeting you."

Dave found himself excluded. He walked over to the table where stood the teacups and sandwiches. As he accepted a plate and a cup from a woman who seemed to be presiding, he glanced about the room.

Algeria's taste was everywhere evident. She had kept old, mellow heirloom furniture instead of using the current atrocities from Grand Rapids. The high-ceilinged walls were covered with soft blue wallpaper which blended well with the dull green of a colonial figured rug. Blue draperies brocaded with a gold design softened the high windows. Above the mantel hung a great Adam mirror, its gold frame harmonizing with the gold frames of the few paintings on the walls, and the impressive gold chandelier.

His gaze followed Algeria's quick figure crossing the room until she came to a girl sitting on a rose-colored sofa.

All at once Dave stopped looking anywhere else.

Youth in a white silk dress. Slim curved body above, fluffy fullness below. Honey hair under a straight-brimmed little hat with snowy birdwings sweeping upward. Only a beautiful woman would dare wear that hat. On her it was wonderful.

He knew he was staring. He began to sip his tea, furious at himself because he could not keep from stealing glances.

Who was she, sitting so supple and straight, smiling at Algeria?

She did not glance his way; yet he was sure she was conscious of him. He had a strange awareness that she was thinking of him at this very moment . . . as he was thinking of her.

Without real volition, almost as if magnetized, he found himself drifting over toward the rose-colored sofa. Algeria saw him, rose, and swept him toward them with a smiling glance.

"Do come over, Dave," she said. "This is someone else I want you to meet——"

He acknowledged the introduction without catching her name. He was too busy, standing before the seated girl, in appreciating her—the whiteness of her bosom in the low-cut dress, the roundness of her throat. Above all her eyes. They were set wide apart under clear dark brows; and they were violet blue.

"But I *know* Mr. Constable," the girl said. "And I'm glad to see him again—at last."

"Again—at last?" Assuredly this was not one of his brighter moments.

"I was in your office two hours one day last week——"

His awful soul clutched him in horror.

"You—*can't* be——"

" 'That she-lawyer'? I'm afraid it's so."

Laughter lurking in violet depths completed his rout. He fumbled and stumbled. And she was inclined to be merciful.

"You needn't apologize—at all. I knew you were busy." Her voice was like the C-string of a harp, a rich, sustaining chord.

Algeria saw a tardily arriving guest and left them.

"Please try me again——" Dave began lamely, and stopped. All at once he realized he had not understood her name when Algeria was presenting him. He mentally cursed himself, then threw himself on her mercy.

"You know—I'm very stupid about a thing like this—but I didn't understand your name——"

She seemed surprised. Then she laughed.

"Of course you'd not remember me. I'm Julia Norman."

He stared. "Julia . . . *Norman?*"

"Are you surprised?" Mirth crinkled in her eyes again.

He was more than surprised. He was stunned.

She read his thoughts. "You're saying to yourself, can this be that spindle-shanked little wildcat that used to roost up trees and pretend she was a man? Aren't you, now?"

She laughed, and then they were laughing together. She made room for him on the sofa, and he was delighted to sit beside her.

"I discarded that old brier pipe years ago," she informed him.

"And ceased wishing you were a man?"

"And ceased wishing I were a man."

"All men should be glad of that."

Her eyes changed, an expression he could not read. He wondered if this badinage was in good taste. This was Jeff Norman's daughter. Grown up, true, into a woman. But still she must think of him as of an immensely older generation.

"Your father—he's well, I hope?"

She shook her blonde head. "He is dead. Five years ago."

"I'm sorry—I didn't know——"

"How could you? Please don't feel sorry."

She spoke with matter-of-fact calmness as of something long acknowledged.

He said: "Julia——"

For some reason she delicately half-colored.

"Julia—will you believe me, if I tell you—that seeing you is the best thing that has happened to me on this day——"

He halted, aghast. What had come over him? But she was back in the bantering mood.

"Perhaps, then, you'll remember me next time I come to see you!"

"You must come again."

"I may."

"Soon?"

"You might be surprised."

"Jeff Norman was my friend."

"I know." She was more subdued. "He spoke of you—often."

"I want to know what's happened to his daughter."

Her eyes rose charmingly to his and she said something unexpected.

"If you want to—I think it's your right to know."

Before he could digest this, Algeria was back with two elderly dowagers to meet Julia. Dave rose, and stepped aside.

People were leaving. Almost reluctantly he followed.

He hardly heard the orotund phrases of William Jennings Bryan as he shook hands. "Crown of Thorns and Cross of Gold" words. Bryan could not avoid mounting a figurative rostrum even when he was no more than acknowledging the departure of guests at a reception.

7.

There were, in the *Clarion* next day, three articles of interest to Dave.

On Page One was an account of the Bryan meeting of the night before, including a verbatim report of the great man's speech—which, analyzed in cold type, appealed to Dave as little more than bombast and Bible.

On the Editorial Page was an announcement. Tucker Wedge was

a formal candidate for the Republican nomination for Congress. With the announcement was a well and pleasantly written little editorial, by Tucker himself, the final paragraph of which said:

We suppose that we should bow to custom by saying that our decision was brought about through overwhelming demand on the part of the public. But every reader of *The Clarion* would know that was the old malarky. We are running for Congress simply because we should like very much to be a Congressman. But in addition to the pure, out-and-out American feeling that it would be the greatest honor in the world to sit in this Nation's legislature, we hope and pray that the people of this district will believe us when we say, with all sincerity, that if we do go to Congress, it will be humbly, realizing we don't know everything and very eager to learn. And that we'll everlastingly remember that we represent a section of this Star Spangled land that likes to call a man by his front name and doesn't give a hang whether he's rich or poor, fat or thin, tall or short, so long as he is honest, tries with the best that's in him to bring home the bacon for his constituents, and never for one moment forgets that he's a native son of this blessed prairie people.

It was the kind of editorial at which Tucker excelled. It struck the homespun note, and the sincere note, and the note of objectivity—in short, the kind of editorial that would appeal to western Kansas.

The third story that interested Dave was on the Society page. It was a description of the Bryan reception at the Wedge home, with a complete list of all guests present. Dave was surprised at his own almost schoolboy feeling of pleasure when he read, at the very bottom of the list, two names in accidental juxtaposition: Miss Julia Norman and Mr. David Constable.

CHAPTER IX

1.

SUMMER, the season of fecundity, of preoccupation with the business of preparing the world against the sterile winter season to follow, is never a time for idleness and introspection. Like all other men in the wheatlands, Dave found his mental vision narrowing with the approach of harvest.

The farmers lived in the moment, forgetful of time, not knowing how they possibly could find the hours they needed to accomplish all the work that had to be done. In the buffalo grass pastures, meadow larks hid their eggs cunningly in small nests. Spring calves, having frolicked until they began to grow too heavy for such infantile sport, very quickly became sedate young heifers. The vivid blue-green of the wheat fields turned yellow-green, then the color of burnished brass.

Machines, with spidery reels slowly whirling, stalked through the tall ripe grain leaving crisp, severe swaths shorn behind; and men gathered the straw from the headers into bargelike wagons and stacked it in neat-rounded yellow mounds. Already the smudge of coal smoke here and there told where thresher engines were at work. The grain elevators in the towns began to fill their great bins with a reddish sea of wheat which presently would overflow all containers—if the railroads, as usual, failed to send to the country a sufficient number of freight cars to draw off this sudden spate.

The heat of summer was exhausting. When men could, they sought shade and avoided overmuch exertion. Even the cattle stood with their heads hidden under each others' bodies, in search of coolness and to escape the flies. Fragrant, warm, saturated with sunlight, the summer pervaded everything.

Dave alone, in almost all of Jericho, never lowered the high pitch of his effort. Sitting in his shirt sleeves with his office window wide open to the brassy breeze from the yellowing wheat fields, he worked in those days with unremitting patience, but with a growing feeling of hopelessness. His thoughts were solemn and grim. The three outlaws who had invaded his town and torn open the bank became symbols of an evil which had come to him. He had never seen them but he fixed upon them a personal enmity. They had robbed Porter Grimes, yet it a curious manner they were of Porter Grimes—the hook of their malicious act deep in Dave's flesh. If he caught the bandits, he took from Grimes, from Tucker Wedge, from the political organization they controlled, a part of the power they had to use against him.

He possessed only a few small bits of knowledge on which to work. These seemed slim enough; but they were all he had, and even they could not be brought to bear as yet.

He was like a man with only a small load to his weapon, who must place his missile carefully or be deprived of all its force. A certain development must occur before he could use even the small inklings he had gathered.

The weeks had passed without any information concerning a certain blue Marmon car. Dave had ascertained, very quickly after the robbery, that such a car had been stolen in Garden City, not so far from Jericho as distance was reckoned in that country—and only a day before Grimes's bank was raided.

Dave had sent a complete description of that car to every police department and sheriff's office in his five-state area, and now he sat and chafed at the inefficiency of peace officers everywhere, the inertia which could not discover a car so well documented after all these weeks. He had to wait for the recovery of that car, for it would tell him where next to move.

One day, just at the end of harvest, he received a long distance telephone call—from Tulsa.

"They just found your car—that Marmon you been looking for," said the voice at the other end of the wire.

"Where?"

"In the Arkansas River a few miles below here. Had to scrape off the mud three inches deep before we could check the engine numbers or even see what color it was. But it's that Garden City car all right—blue Marmon and the engine numbers checks."

"So that's why the car didn't turn up before."

"Yeh. The thieves drove it off the bank to get rid of it."

"I'm coming down on the next train," said Dave.

It was an overnight ride to Tulsa. He was given a brief handshake by a bushy-browed Oklahoman, with shoulders like a wall and a chin that was blue even immediately after a clean shave. Riley Reternik, police chief at Tulsa. He was without uniform and wore a wide cowboy hat.

"Glad to meet you at last," said Reternik. "I got so dad-blamed familiar with yore voice on the phone, I feel like I've knowed you for years."

Reternik conducted a police department that was a buttress against the outlawry which surged up from the broken Indian country south and east; and the crime which brewed in the sprawling oil fields around. His men were not the ordinary municipal policeman. They were sunburned and taciturn, with something of the frontier about them.

"You got any leads?" Reternik asked Dave.

"A slim one. Let me see your criminal identification cards."

It took quite a while. But at last Dave showed a card to Reternik:

BUD BENTON, alias Bill Benton, Bob Hendryx. S.P. 18329. SEX: M. RACE: W. HEIGHT: 6 ft. WEIGHT: 191. AGE: 29. EYES: Br. HAIR: Blk. SCARS and MARKS of IDENTIFICATION: Mole left cheek, Tattoo of snake inside left forearm, scar of old knife cut upper part of rt. shoulder. OCCUPATION: Tool-dresser and trouble shooter. RECORD: Arr. susp. burg. Muskogee, Sept. 2, 1905. Released. Arr. att. hwy. rb., Aug. 19, 1906. Convicted. Served 6 mo. Co. jail, Sapulpa. Arr. susp. burg. Vinita State Bank, at Tulsa, May 11, 1908. Conv. complicity. Sentenced 1 to 10 yrs. hrd lbr. penitentiary. Paroled May 12, 1909, good behavior.

"Trouble shooter," said Dave, pointing at the line giving the occupations of the man. "What kind?"

The police chief checked. "Used to be a telephone maintenance man before he come to the oil fields," he said.

"That's what I've been looking for." Dave told Reternik the Schroeder girl's story of the man who cut the outgoing cables at the telephone building the night of the robbery. "He knew everything about telephone systems," he added. "And this description answers to what she said of his general build."

Riley Reternik tapped the card on his desk and studied.

"I ain't surprised," he said at last. "We know Benton. He trains with the Childress brothers, Pat and Jim. Troublemakers, all of 'em. Liquor runners. Car thieves. But we ain't had nothing on them. They hang around High-low—an oil dump west of here. This is what I been waiting for. We'll take care of the whole outfit right now."

Dave glanced with a faint sensation of surprise at the blue-jowled officer. There had been a curious edge of deadliness in his voice. They went out together.

Tulsa, in the white heat of magical growth due to the oil which was being pumped up in viscous floods from the bowels of its earth was still in the process of becoming accustomed to the tempo of its new life. It had been a sleepy little Indian trading post. Then it had grown used to the sight of skeletonic oil derricks multiplying on every hill, and the familiar blighted appearance as the petroleum killed the grass, and the stinking odor of sludge pools which sometimes added crooked pillars of inky smoke to the sky as they were burned out. Tulsa had seen its population soar almost astronomically, had seen tall buildings shoot up, and had observed mansions in the nabob district, erected by newly created oil millionaires who still wore cowboy boots and insisted on a brass cuspidor in the middle of a five thousand dollar Persian rug.

But about Tulsa, the country still had not fully shaken off the frontier ways. And to this wildness was added a new element—the oil field criminality. Small mushroom towns sprang up among the derricks, and the residents of those towns were not all oil workers. Some of them were bootleggers, harlots, gamblers, highjackers, a shifty, sinister element.

One of the scrofulous little shanty hamlets thus born was High-low, which obtained its title when the ownership of its site changed hands during a game of Seven-up, in which the winner displayed an indisputable high and low for the winning points. In High-low's jerry-built shacks was hatched enough evil to cover all Oklahoma.

2.

The ambush took Dave by surprise, although he was a part of it. Not until the last moment did he realize the silent, ferocious plan of it. The Tulsa officers did not believe in taking bank robbers alive.

The heat was fierce and the men sweated. Riley Reternik's chin was blacker than ever, and his eyes gleamed from slits between the lids. Faces were grim, pitiless. In the posse, manhunters gulped whiskey and cursed in undertones.

The Childress brothers and Benton had a habit of driving each morning to High-low, from the Childress farm where they all stayed. Just beyond a sharp bend in the winding country road through the blackjacks, the cars of the posse had been drawn up so that they formed a barricade which could not be passed.

Dave felt himself swept along on a tide of acidulous blood lust; something he had set in motion and could not stop.

It came—the sound for which they had waited. A motor car, cut-out open, made a loud, ugly noise as it approached them, stilling the birds and destroying the quiet of the blackjack woods. Somebody said:

"It's them—that stripped-down Apperson Jackrabbit them Childresses drive. They allus go with the cut-out off. Get ready."

The concealed posse saw the car swing around the corner. Three men in it. Dave saw their bodies tense with surprise, turning to swift dread. The driver pulled up, began frantically to back around in the narrow road.

"Kill that engine and get out!" shouted a voice.

"Jesus, Pat—it's a trap!" screamed one of the men in the Apperson.

The car seesawed, snorted, roared, with dust rising in a dense cloud about it.

In the woods burst a sudden crescendo of sound. Shotguns—rifles. Gray powder smoke hung heavy among the trees.

The car coughed convulsively and stopped. The driver crouched over the wheel as if to protect it with his body. He was dead. Beside him, another man flung himself back, then lay with his neck dangling loose as if it were disjointed, the blood running from the mouth and nose of his hanging head.

The third man leaped out of the car. But he took only two or three wavering steps before he went down.

3.

Dave still felt ill as he took the train for Jericho.

Reternik accompanied him to the station.

"We done that job good," he said with satisfaction. "Pat Childress an' Benton was cut damn near in two by the buckshot. Lucky that Jim Childress hung on long enough to make a confession. That clears yore bank robbery, don't it?" He leered. "Down here in Oklahoma we believe in doing things right."

Dave remembered the confession of a man with a shattered chest.

"We . . . robbed the bank in Jericho. Why in hell . . . did you have to keep the case so hot? We . . . would have got away. . . ." He lay silent a moment, his eyes closed. Then. "Never heard . . . of no little ol' country bank robbin' . . . where so much stink was raised. . . . No, it was our job. Nobody helped us." Another silence. Then: "Jest our luck . . . to pick out of all the country a bank where we was as good as dead from the start. . . ."

Afterward, Reternik said: "That was a compliment to you, if you want to look at it that way. You certainly are a bearcat, Mr. Constable. Pleasure to work with you."

So it was ended. Dave could feel no triumph. It had been a ghastly, unpleasant experience, and he still chilled to the cold deadliness of the Oklahoma manhunters.

Three men dead . . . Dave hoped Porter Grimes would be satisfied with this bloodletting. He himself was very weary.

When he reached Jericho, the next day, the *Clarion* already had published the story of the killing of the bank bandits. The story was only slightly colored—just enough to leave some of the people still with a sneaking feeling that perhaps after all there *was* some local connection with those robbers. . . .

4.

It was night, the harvest was over, and the killing of the Jericho bank bandits had ceased to be a topic of conversation.

Dave drove north along the road which crossed the river toward the Bedestown district. He was alone in the car, on his way to speak at a meeting of the Farmers' Co-operative Association. The invitation had come from Webb Pettis the week before.

At first Dave had demurred, but Pettis urged.

"Jest tell 'em what you've said before—to me an' a lot of other folks, Dave," he said. "This state's due for a bang-up big fight. It's going to stretch all the way from the mouth of the Kaw to the headwaters of the Smoky Hill. The farmers have got a dim idea of what they want, but they need somebody to put the feeling into words. We think you're that man."

Dave accepted, because the Farmers' Co-operative Association had become an important place in which to speak certain things that needed saying. Webb Pettis was right about the battle that was coming. It was time that the lists were drawn for it.

The car topped a low rise and Japanese lanterns made spots of frail light in the grove ahead. A nicker of horses in the night—farmers' teams tethered at the roadsides.

Trees huddled about a white frame schoolhouse, the Bedestown school, which stood on the site of an early-day boom town which had flowered briefly and died, leaving only the grassed-over depressions of old cellars. The Japanese lanterns and the movement of people gave the dark grove a country fair atmosphere. As he swung the car around to a stop, voices greeted Dave.

Webb Pettis, with his snapping black eyes, came into the circle of light.

"Dave, howdy!"

From the schoolhouse came a thin sound. Violin strings scraping.

"Young folks limberin' up," said Webb as he led Dave toward the building. "Little heel-shakin' before the program."

They entered. Windows and doors of the schoolhouse were wide open, and the interior was brilliant with lights. Bedestown was a "liberal" district and permitted dancing. A few Catholic parish schools did so, but most of the regular districts in Kansas were too strait-laced. Bedestown was intransigent because its district was populated chiefly by descendants of a freer old-time cattle population which cared little for bluenose injunctions.

Benches had been cleared from the floor, and two fiddles and a harmonica were "tuning up" on the teacher's platform. Older people sat comfortably talking around the walls. On the floor young couples already had begun to take their places.

"Nobody much up here from town," said Pettis, lingering, "but here's a young lady. Mebbe you know her."

"Why—of course—" said Dave.

It was Julia Norman.

"We got Miss Norman to come up an' give some elocutions," explained Pettis.

"So you're a reader," said Dave to the girl. He felt a slight sensation of disappointment. Every second woman in his acquaintance, it seemed to him, had a little repertoire of overarch, or overemotional "selections" which she would "render" at the slightest excuse, and on any occasion.

Her eyes crinkled at him. "I'm afraid I'm bad at it."

He instantly forgave her for being a reader.

"I began it in school," she went on. "It was a way to earn money. I needed money."

He looked at her with a curiously welcome fellow feeling.

"Why—I played baseball for the same reason."

They both smiled.

"I'm callin' the figgers for the dance," said Webb Pettis. "Care to try a turn, Dave? Folks'd take it real kindly."

"Webb, I haven't danced a step in years——"

Beside him, Julia spoke: "Maybe—we could try it together."

"Do you know the square dances?"

"Some of them."

"Well," he said, and stopped. Suddenly he wanted very much to dance with her. "You don't know what you're letting yourself in for, but if you're game—I should be, too. Come on."

They started out on the floor. He was suddenly delighted by the way her yellow hair shone in the light, and the grace of her figure in a long lemon-colored gown with a froth of lace at the throat. Her eyes seemed remarkably brilliant, and there was a thrill in the touch of her fingers on his arm.

Sober farmfolk around the walls nodded their approval when they saw Dave Constable in the figure. Julia saw him nodding and speaking to acquaintances. It seemed that he knew almost everyone, and everyone seemed to think well of him.

From the platform, Webb Pettis cast about a masterful eye, and waved to the musicians. With a preliminary *zum-zum-zum* of fiddle strings, they broke into a lively tune, full of quavers and runs. Dancers on the floor commenced tapping toes; girls smiled challengingly at young men who swayed across from them. All at once Webb broke into a high-pitched nasal singsong:

> Hark ye partners,
> Rights the same.

Dave bowed to Julia and she bowed back gaily, making bright eyes at him.

> Balance ye all.

With a speed almost ferocious the young men leaped at their partners. Dave, not fully sure of himself, advanced somewhat less violently
on Julia. He saw strong-bodied girls swung about in mad gyrations,
and found himself with Julia in the circle of his arm. She was laughing, and making up for his lack of verve, swung him, whether he
would or not. Then they were out to answer for the nasal overtone of:

> First lady to the right;
> Swing the man that stole the sheep,
> Now the one that hauled it home,
> Now the one that ate the meat,
> Now the one that gnawed the bones.

A sudden intense pleasure came over him at the lightheartedness of
the whole thing. He grinned at the quaint doggerel.

He reflected that he was fourth in the row of men—which, in the
remarkable transaction of the sheep being described by Webb, meant
that he came out with no more than the bones of the pilfered carcass.
But he seized, swung, and passed on the young women who came flying down the line, until Julia herself came whirling, and went back to
her place, flushed and excited.

> First gent, swing yer opp'site pardner,
> Then yer turtle dove.
> Again yer opp'site pardner,
> An' now yer true love.

The outlandish words gave him secret, almost guilty enjoyment.
Yer turtle dove . . . yer true love . . .

He glanced across at Julia, wondering how she felt about accepting
even for a brief tenuous moment this role thrust on her by the figure
caller. She was smiling deliciously back at him.

> Come to yer pardner once an' a half
> Yaller hammer right an' jaybird left,
> Meet yer pardner an' all chaw hay,
> Ye know where an' I don't care,
> Seat yer pardner in the old arm chair.

The number was ended. Julia left the floor with him, chatting
brightly and gaily. He was lightheadedly happy.

"Thank you," he told her. "You were wonderful."

"You're not going to stop?" Actually, she seemed disappointed.

He smiled. Dancing with Julia was too heady and dangerous.

"A dozen young men are looking at you. If I want to escape lynch-
ing, I'd better let them have their turn."

Then she let him lead her to a seat, where as soon as he stepped aside she was surrounded by young farmers. Dave watched her a moment, as she laughingly replied to their importunities. She glanced at him, half-questioning, as she was led out on the floor by a long-legged young dandy in a yellow silk shirt and wide-ruffled fancy sleeve holders.

To his amazement he momentarily hated that youth in the silk shirt as he watched the girl give herself over to her new partner. To rid himself of the feeling, he stepped outside where the older men talked their everlasting politics.

5.

The music came to an end, and benches were pulled back on the floor. Dave looked around the schoolroom and saw Julia with a youth on either side. When she caught his eye she detached herself and came over.

"Where do we sit?" she asked.

He was ridiculously happy at this gesture of loyalty. She had chosen to return to him when there were many younger men eager for her company.

"Why—most anywhere," he said. "I suppose rather close up front— where we won't have too much trouble reaching the platform."

They found seats a row or two back from the rostrum. Webb Pettis, as president of the Association, took a chair behind the teacher's desk and introduced an apple-faced woman who sang in a tremulous voice something lugubrious which ended:

> One held a lock of thin gray hair,
>   One held a lock of brown,
> Saying good night to the old Stars and Stripes,
>   Just as the sun went down.

A very sunburned young farmer read the secretary-treasurer's report. Then Webb Pettis said:

"We got a treat for ye, folks. When ye see the young lady I'm goin' to introduce to ye, ye'll agree that if she's as nice to listen to as she is to look at, we're in fer somethin' plenty good an' splendid. Miss Julia Norman, of Jericho."

Julia fluttered forward, and Dave heard whispered comments.

"A stunner."

"You tellin' me?"

"She's a lawyer."

"With that face an' shape? Yore kiddin'!"

Julia turned toward them and began—the scene from *Les Miserables* in which Jean Valjean wrestles with his conscience, then confesses to save an innocent man from being sent to prison.

At first Dave listened with interest; then with surprise; and finally with complete delight. When she first told him she "read" it had seemed such a hackneyed accomplishment—but this was nothing like the ordinary parlor monologue. The girl had training and dramatic talent; her voice was magnificent—not too deep to be feminine, but rich enough for power.

She reached her climax: "Gentlemen of the jury, release the accused. Your Honor, order my arrest. He is not the man you seek; it is I! I am Jean Valjean!"

Dave joined the storm of applause and there was something personal in his pride at her triumph.

She gave as an encore something light: "The Subscription List." Irish dialect. He had heard it before, though never so well done.

The tremolo-voiced woman was singing a second number: "Wait For Me, Kitty, My Own," as Julia returned to Dave with a smile that was a question.

"You were magnificent," he whispered.

She whispered back: "You needn't say things like that!"

"I wouldn't say it if it wasn't true."

"Then, thank you."

They turned their attention to the platform, in the knowledge that many eyes were upon them.

Webb Pettis was saying:

"The gent who talks next needs no introduction. An' I think I speak the sentiments of most everybody here present when I say we hope somebody as downright, an' honest, an' strong for the folks that works for a livin', as Dave Constable is, will go to Congress next election."

Dave found himself on the platform, receiving their sincere applause. He began in humorous vein.

"Mighty nice of the Colonel to call a lawyer like me honest. I remember another auctioneer that wasn't as polite. A certain attorney in Jericho—we won't mention any names—was questioning this particular Colonel in a livestock suit. He couldn't shake the testimony, so, I'm sorry to say, turned to sarcasm—an unfortunate habit of the profession."

A friendly laugh from the crowd.

" 'They call you Colonel,' says this barrister, kind of sneering. 'What regiment were you colonel in?'

" 'You might call it the cow brigade,' drawls the colonel.

" 'I want a serious answer!' raps the lawyer.

" 'Well, then,' explains the auctioneer, 'it's this way. The Colonel in front of my name's like the Honorable in front of yours—it doesn't mean a thing!' "

The farmers, delighted by this anecdotal victory of one of their own class, guffawed with relish.

Dave saw Julia, three rows down, laughing beside the cackling Webb Pettis.

He wondered suddenly how she felt on the issues he was going to discuss, and all at once it became to him important that he make his case to Julia Norman. He began to speak—and it was to her. The audience, listening intently, did not know that David Constable was talking to the girl in the third row, almost as if they were alone in the schoolhouse together. What he was saying, the farmers wanted greatly to hear. They drank it in.

He had a gift for vivid phrase. He named a politician prominent in Kansas. "If he didn't button his pants in front, you couldn't tell whether he was coming or going." He named another. "He doesn't drink. He doesn't gamble. He doesn't even go to church. You might say he has no vices of any kind. Kansas expects a man to be himself as long as his strength holds out—still, such as they are, I don't think his peculiarities qualify him for public office."

The crowd cheered him on. "Golly," chuckled Webb Pettis, "how that Dave kin peel them four-flushers."

Julia scarcely heard what he said. She was looking at the strong face of the man on the platform, the steady gray eyes, the rebellious curl of sandy hair on his forehead, almost as if she were seeing them for the first time.

Dave was putting into words something that these people long had felt but which they had been too inarticulate to state for themselves— the case against unrestrained capitalism, political oligarchy, corrupt control.

"Sycophantic, boot-licking menials of this oligarchy of wealth scuttle to our legislative halls to pass laws and more laws to further bind the common people, so their overlords can heap up more and yet more of the wealth, which is our common heritage, for themselves. We face a gigantic system, a settled and soulless machinery. This, my friends, is worse than bank robbery, worse than predatory outlawry. It is crime organized with the cynical and bloodless purpose of looting all wealth from the one to whom it belongs—him that creates it!"

At that the farmers were out of their seats, howling applause.

Then Dave began, running boldly the gamut of social reforms he deemed needful—and they were without exception the things which had become the target of the utmost savagery from the spokesmen of the order then existing.

He called for a tax on large incomes, to force wealth to bear its commensurate share of government costs; for public ownership of utilities which affect the daily weal of many people; for the curbing of injunctions against strikers, recognition of unions, and arbitration of labor disputes; for regulation of banks, stock issues, and gigantic corporations, partnerships, and trusts; for a limit on speculation; for equitable regulation of transportation, storage, and handling rates on farm products; for government insurance of bank deposits; for a means of security for old age; and finally, for the popular election of Senators, to deprive political machines of their most deadly source of power.

It was bold, daring doctrine. Men like Porter Grimes, hearing that speech, would have grown purple with anger; and the newspapers would have called his proposals radical, demagogic, or chimerical. But the farmers were with Dave to a man.

Julia Norman, sitting beside Webb Pettis in the third row, heard a great clap of applause. Dave was leaving the platform and the enthusiasm of the crowd threw itself at him. The farmers were standing —whistling and shouting.

But as he came down the floor his eyes were on Julia.

He noticed that she was not applauding. She was sitting still, gazing at him as if in surprise or wonder.

6.

Yet she waited for him at the door when the meeting broke up, and spoke to him.

"Mr. Constable—I'm a mendicant."

"Oh? What are you a mendicant about?"

She seemed a little embarrassed. "To tell the truth, I need a lift to Jericho. You're going back tonight?"

"Why, sure——"

"The Pettises brought me out, but it means a long ride to town and back for them. Would it be *too* improper if——"

He laughed.

"Of course not. It will give us a chance to catch up on things since you left Jericho . . ."

They said goodbye to the Bedestown people, and drove for some time, silently, over the dark road southward.

At last Dave said: "You didn't think much of my speech."

"Why do you think that?"

"I couldn't help noticing—you didn't applaud."

"Didn't I? . . . I didn't realize it. I was thinking so hard—about what you said."

"Then you didn't disagree with me completely?"

"You put into words for me tonight something I've been trying to say for myself a long time——"

"Julia."

"Yes."

"I'm going to tell you something that may sound—well—odd."

"What is it?"

"I knew how everybody else in that schoolhouse felt, but I didn't know what you thought about these things. So I—sort of addressed my remarks—just to you——"

She turned and he could feel her studying him in the dark. Then her profile was to him again. She did not answer.

For two miles the road slid back under the car's headlights.

He was regretting what he had said. The constraint was his fault. He tried again, changing the subject.

"If you'll let me say so—you're an object of great interest—even curiosity—to me. I'd never have dreamed that you'd become a lawyer —and a very good one——"

"How do you know I'm a good lawyer?"

"Judge Hutto. He confessed to me that he had more than half a doubt when you wrote asking for a place in his office——"

"Because I'm a woman?"

"Chiefly. But now he swears by you."

"It's very nice of him." She said it moodily, he thought.

"He says you have a nice feeling for abstruse legal points. And he wishes you'd change your determination to stick to briefing. The judge believes you'd be highly successful as a jury lawyer."

"I don't think it's time for women to appear in the courtroom—yet."

"Yet?"

"A conclusion resulting from hard experience."

"How? Tell me."

"If you wish. When father and I went back to Wilmington to claim the estate his cousin left us, we found it wasn't much. Not enough to live on. He tried to establish a law practice, but it didn't work. He died two years later. Pneumonia—in his weakened condition it was fatal."

"So that was how——"

"He was an unhappy man," she mused. "I think he was glad to pass on. In his life there was one supremely bitter disappointment."

"His failure?"

"No. His daughter."

"You?" He was surprised.

"You know of his great concept of the law," she said, "its sacred function as a bulwark for the common man against the encroachments of government, wealth, or power of any other kind." Her eyes went to him. "I've seen him weep in shame at his weakness. The lawyer blood ran far back in his family—some of the Normans were great lawyers."

She paused.

"So his greatest bitterness concerned me. I was a girl. I think it was the only thing that marred his perfect love—he had so greatly wanted a son to take up the heritage."

"No son could have given him the affection you did."

"A daughter's love was not enough."

He shook his head, serious in his sympathy.

"I should have been a boy," she said.

"We've disagreed on that before."

Now she gave him a fleeting smile in the dimness.

"Go on," he urged.

"There was a little money after the funeral. I decided to go to school and study law. I thought in some manner I could justify him by doing that." Another pause. "I didn't know what I was undertaking."

"You found it so difficult?"

Almost passionately she turned to him. "You fight against entrenched power. But you do not know how it is to beat yourself against entrenched tradition. The law didn't want me—I was a woman."

"There are women lawyers. Mary Elizabeth Lease is one——"

"Only a few. The way is hard. I think the school years were the unhappiest of my life."

Dave remembered his own prejudice when he heard that a "she-lawyer" was in Jericho. It seemed strange now, so completely had he accepted Julia in her status. Then he thought: What if she'd been homely, or dowdy, with bad teeth, or ungainly?

Aloud he said: "I begin to think my sex is brutally selfish and blind."

She shook her head. "I have no resentments against men. There are perhaps natural reasons for this whole way of thinking—the customs of the race. You suffer when you break a custom, even if it's a custom based on conditions which have changed."

"And when did you arrive at this highly magnanimous conclusion toward men?"

She smiled. "Maybe it's because I simply can't help liking men. And then, to be truthful, men haven't been any worse than women. There is a certain class of women which considers it immoral if not criminal for another woman to make any departure from the established ritual of life."

"So you were lonely."

She nodded. "Yes. Forever the outsider."

"Julia—with your beauty—an outsider?"

"If I was at first accepted, people turned against me when they found I was a law student. It placed me in the category of intellectual women. Prejudice was sharp, so school was a sterile, drab experience. That's when I reached my conclusion."

"About courtroom practice?"

"Most women lawyers call themselves feminists, but they're really masculinists. Consciously or unconsciously they want to be the counterparts of men. They believe—as the law schools teach—that the law contains a complete set of principles from which the correct answers can be drawn, if one is sufficiently logical."

"And you think otherwise?"

"I've watched great lawyers in action. And they're not entirely dogmatic, entirely doctrinaire. They know that legal principles are the result of the race's instinctive preferences and inarticulate convictions. And that though sound thinking is logical, the logic has a basis that's flexible. That is where women lawyers made their mistake. They failed to take advantage of the strongest weapon they had—intuitive tact."

"That's a penetrating judgment, Julia!"

"You needn't laugh. Because women in law had already succeeded in building up a prejudice against themselves, I made up my mind for the present to be seen rarely and never heard in the courtrooms."

They fell silent again. In all this she had been careful to keep the conversation correct and not too intimate. But a woman's words are one thing, her being is another. Nothing Julia could have said or left unsaid would have kept her near presence to the man in the car from being impelling, mysterious, intriguing. She seemed to realize this, and sat, almost frightened.

The car surmounted a small rise in the road and suddenly the lights of Jericho lay before them.

Relief came over him at the nearness of the town and with it the tension between them seemed to depart. He relaxed. Now that Jericho was just ahead with its promise of safety from emotion, he talked more easily.

"Whether you know it or not, Julia, a real miracle's happened to you."

She laughed, a little nervously. "I'm like Topsy—just growed."

"Something more. When I first saw you—you were——"

"An ugly little tree cat?"

"No such thing. A child who'd been hurt. You were fighting a battle —I knew what it was——"

"You—really did . . . ?"

"You were defending your father—from everyone—including yourself——"

"I—perhaps I was," she admitted. She glanced at him and there was something like gratitude in the look.

After a moment he went on. "You've given me a new viewpoint on woman's problem in law. But there's something more to it. Please remember—there are many good lawyers. The market's glutted with them. But you're a woman as well as a lawyer. A very wonderful woman."

He waited. Her head was lowered.

"If you—think that—I'm pleased," she said, almost in a whisper. "A woman is—well, a woman. It's nice to be told that you're a success at it."

And then they were in the town.

CHAPTER X

1.

THE deep-lined visage of the Reverend Matthias Widcomb was solemn enough ordinarily. But today its expression was even gloomier than usual.

The good man sat behind the heavy Mission desk in his study. In his hand was a sheet of paper. A bit of paper with some scratchings from a graphite pencil on it. Yet what power it had to take all the peacefulness out of the day.

Dr. Widcomb had said to his wife, Eugenia, that very morning, that for once, thank Heaven, affairs seemed to be running smoothly in the parish. The pledges from the Every Member Canvass were sufficient to assure finances for the coming year. The burden of the choir, grievous to some parsons, was capably lifted from his shoulders by J. Wilber Bratten. Other matters were as capably handled by Porter Grimes, or Mrs. Tucker Wedge—real pillars of strength in any church.

At present he faced routine duties only. There were the sick. Old Mrs. Apworth, after a lingering illness which had been a sore trial to the minister—the old woman insisted on daily spiritual comfort chiefly because it enabled her to argue with him—had finally passed away. Others who were ill were less contentious. He made his rounds conscientiously and strove to turn the thoughts of these to a consideration of the Hereafter. Sometimes he felt that his exhortations along this line were not received with the gratitude he could have wished, but he continued the labor with a rigid sense of duty. Aside from this, and the preparation of the morrow's Sabbath sermon, he had thought the period ahead fairly clear.

As he glanced again at the letter in his hand, the minister's dark features grew even more sombre. It really was most trying. The letter was printed in pencil, and its words were not only mysterious, but conducive to apprehension. At the top of the page was a biblical quotation:

PROVERBS V, 18-22

Let thy fountain be blessed; And rejoice in the wife of thy youth.
As a loving hind and a pleasant doe, Let her breasts satisfy thee at all times;
And be thou ravished always with her love.

For why shouldest thou, my son, be ravished with a strange woman, And
   embrace the bosom of a foreigner?
For the ways of man are before the eyes of Jehovah; And he maketh level
   all his paths.
His own iniquities shall take the wicked, And he shall be holden with the
   cords of his sin.

All this was very baffling. But that below it, was more so. It was a
message, in that same painfully printed hand, directly to the minister
himself:

Rev. Widcomb:
   Watch in the church Monday evenings after dusk and behold that which
should not take place in the House of God. Is to Dives permitted that
which is denied Lazarus? How great is a sin committed before the Altar
of Jehovah?

No signature. It might have been written by a crank. Some Bible
fanatic. Every parish has one or more of them, and sometimes they are
a grievous cross for the minister. Dr. Widcomb was tempted to throw
it in the wastebasket, but two sentences held him. *His own iniquities
shall take the wicked, And he shall be holden with the cords of his sin
. . . Is to Dives permitted that which is denied Lazarus?*
   Sin, the rich man, and the beggar. It made Matthias Widcomb's
head ache; but he refrained from casting away the letter. His first impulse had been to take the thing to Eugenia. But an instinct of discretion stayed him. He knew Eugenia's weakness. Talk.
   A sharp edge of irritation lay in the fact that he was thus left alone
with the problem. Again he studied the letter; now he began to feel
that he must heed it.
   The time element was annoying. Monday evening, after dusk. The
parish knew that Monday was the minister's day off. He had a standing joke that the parson was the only man in town who worked seven
days in the week; but in reality he succeeded in managing a certain
leisure for himself. Each day he had his nap—for a parson's mind
must be refreshed. And on Mondays he refrained as far as possible
from all parish duties. Yet this note specifically named Monday.
   The more he thought, the less he liked it. Matthias Widcomb was
not altogether a fool. *Dives.* The man of wealth. Who? The first
thought, naturally, was of Porter Grimes, who was the richest man in
the congregation. But others were comfortable in this world's goods.
Matthias shrugged impatiently. He must not even think of suspecting
any person until he *knew.* There must be witnesses, and they must be
men whom nobody could designate as *Dives.*
   The film of momentary rage and bafflement still clouded his mind

as he turned to the composition of his sermon. He already had decided on the text. Psalms 8:4. *What is man, that thou art mindful of him?*

2.

In the darkness a hand fumbled at the brass knob of the church door and then inserted a key in the lock.

The man let himself into the building and closed the door softly behind him.

In spite of himself he shivered slightly as he passed through the dark cavern formed by the overhanging balcony and entered the long, dim rectangle of the auditorium. Always he felt, on these occasions, that first, premonitory shiver.

At the farther end of the main aisle in which he stood, with its careful, regular rows of dark oak pews on either side, he dimly made out the pulpit and the gilded organ-pipes behind it. The windows of the church were blobs of pale grayness which failed utterly to illuminate the cavernous interior. He did not switch on a light. Almost tiptoeing, he went down the aisle in the darkness, hesitated before the rostrum, and mounted to the choir loft behind the pulpit.

In the silent gloom the church seemed almost a living thing, breathing in long, deep, regular sighs. His cursed imagination. A sensation of danger, always; yet he could think of no place safer. The very smell of the building, musty and deserted and biblical, was almost a guarantee of safety.

The man began to fiddle with some sheet music, although he could see nothing more than pallid oblongs which the pages made in the dimness. By his attitude and this characteristic action, one watching him even in the darkness might have recognized the figure of J. Wilber Bratten. It was his position as choirmaster which enabled him to carry a key to the door of this church.

The inescapable feeling of peril never failed to make J. Wilber queasy with uneasiness; for in spite of his six feet of stature and his bull throat, he was a timid man. But with the fear was always another sensation. The fear seemed, really, to invest this adventure with a certain added zest. It was the whole combination of circumstances surrounding this act which made of it something especially sensuous and thrilling.

To J. Wilber Bratten everything else in life was deadly monotony. Even making money had grown tiresome. Lillian was monotonous, and the two children. Music—even that became monotonous at times.

The man believed he had a "way" with people. His insurance office ran smoothly, and it was flattering to have his employees fawn on him and call him "boss." The Commercial Club ran smoothly, chiefly because of him. He could not imagine the Commercial Club continuing its existence very long without his activities as "tail-twister," and "pep-per-upper."

The First Church choir also ran smoothly. Jealousy was quite sub-merged in it. He drilled his choristers like slaves—he was an autocrat, conscious of their deference, and worthy of it.

The First Church choir was a one-man affair. J. Wilber had made it and he maintained it. Sometimes when he stood up to sing he saw Lil-lian's face with its peculiar dumb-animal adoration, clear back at the rear of the church where she always sat. He wished Lillian were not so inclined to sit back. . . .

The thought of his wife carried him to another woman.

Kay Middlekauf was in the soprano section. She had a sweet, light voice; nothing brilliant, but she supported J. Wilber well in duets.

He had done a lot for Kay. She was not very pretty with those horn-rimmed glasses, and she never had been popular. When she went to Kansas University she was not invited to join a sorority. Bratten got her the job of secretary to the Commercial Club, from which she went to a better position as secretary to Porter Grimes.

J. Wilber had never heard that Kay had gone out with a man . . . he believed she was completely in love with him. So unreservedly did she put herself in his hands, so unquestioningly did she obey him, that in this alone lay deep satisfaction.

He heard a slight noise at the church door.

Self-consciously he turned his attention again to the dim sheet music in his hands. He heard Kay Middlekauf feeling her way forward to-ward him.

She never failed in these trysts. It was part of her sense of obligation to him, but more, too. She was as starved for sensation as he. Never before had she had a man. . . .

Her shadowy form took shape in the aisle. She progressed, touching with her fingertips the oaken backs of the pews on her right. J. Wilber, in the choir loft, drew himself up, his back against the organ console, waiting with mounting excitement.

Her face, a dim oval now, turned up to him as she ascended the two sets of steps. Her voice, a breathless whisper:

"*Wilber* . . ."

Long ago they had abandoned coy preliminaries.

He seized her masterfully, and began to kiss her hungrily on her throat, beneath the chin.

She clung to him, breathing heavily.

"Are you sure . . . it's all right. . . ."

A vague, throaty whisper. Invariably she asked the question; and it underlined the abjectness of her terror, making the very fact of her coming to him a more compelling sacrifice.

"Certainly," he whispered curtly. "I've told you over and over that nobody ever comes near here on Monday nights."

"But . . . it always seems so *awful*. . . ."

"If you feel that way——"

"Oh, no, Wilber . . . no." Now her fear that he might abandon her was greater than the other terror. "I'll not ask any more. . . ."

It was as if some force outside of them drove them together. In his arms he bent her back; they sank together on the rug behind the pulpit.

3.

When the electric lights flashed on their ghastly illumination, neither the man nor the woman at first understood what had happened. Neither conceived, in that initial moment, the full immensity of the disaster.

Not until the minister and his two trustees came solemnly down from the gallery, their feet on the stairs like the tramp of doom, did Kay, dragged to her feet by J. Wilber, cover her face with her hands.

Then she fled; running, stumbling, gasping in terror, out into the night, slamming behind her the great door.

J. Wilber did not flee. He stood, jaw hanging, and stared at the three, grim, approaching figures, blowing hard and scared.

"How can we credit our eyes, Brother Bratten?" said the preacher after a long time.

J. Wilber's mouth was wry and drawn. "I can't explain . . . I couldn't help it. . . ."

Nothing more was said.

He passed out of the church, his head hanging like a dog, sick unto death.

4.

Before morning, Kay Middlekauf was gone. She caught the midnight train for Lawrence. Nobody ever saw her in Jericho again.

And before gossip was even started, J. Wilber Bratten was gone, too. To Denver.

The three men who had seen the shocking desecration at the very altar of the church swore each other to secrecy. But human nature can stand pressure only to a limit.

Before the day ended, the story was all over Jericho.

5.

Kay Middlekauf and J. Wilber Bratten were the subject of all talk in Jericho the week following. On Thursday David Constable encountered Julia Norman on the street.

"Hello," she said.

"Hello."

"Are you going my way?"

"To the courthouse."

"Well—you can walk with me for a block."

It pleased him that she enjoyed his company.

Insensibly they slowed their pace, so as not to use up the block too quickly.

Odd in what ways women take possession of men's imaginations. She walked along beside him, gay, challenging, to all appearances the self-possessed woman of the world. Of a sudden, as he turned his head, he missed her. Glancing back he saw her almost pressed against a store-window, her head tilted in the irresistibly graceful attitude of feminine interest and curiosity.

Returning to her he found her completely immersed in the contemplation of some tiny figurines, exactly like a child, wide eyed before a toy.

"Look," she said. "Mr. Pickwick."

It was a laughable little four-inch pottery figurine in the window. Flat hat, spectacles, a long green coat stretching over a jovial fat belly, gaiters, a shawl over the arm, a cane in the hand, and a handbag. The plump, high-colored little face wore a look of ineffable good humor.

"Oh, the shawl and gaiters!" Julia cried. "Mr. Pickwick—just arriving at the Blue Lion, Muggleton!"

He did not answer. She glanced at him.

"Don't you agree?"

"I don't know."

"You mean—no, you can't—you surely *are* a *Pickwick Papers* reader?"

He shook his head. "I've never read them."

"Then you must do so at once. Oh, how I envy you—reading them for the first time. I've a copy and I'll lend it to you. It's dog eared and old and very precious, but I'll let *you* borrow it."

"Thank you."

"I—if it weren't so crazy, I'd go in and buy that little Mr. Pickwick right now."

"What would you use it for?"

"I don't know."

"Then it wouldn't be of much use to you."

"That's just it! Every woman has a craving in her sometimes to have things that are no use at all. Just frivolous, and—and—funny and useless——"

They walked on. Her transitions, from complexity to simplicity, from maturity to childhood, from seriousness to frivolity, were as natural and unconscious to her as breathing.

In the block they walked, Julia seemed happily unconcerned, natural, accustomed to his presence.

But he was intensely conscious of her.

He found himself measuring himself against her. And immediately tried to crush out the thought. He was married. And if he had not been . . . there was the disparity in their ages.

Something she said suddenly riveted his attention.

"Whom do you suppose I got a letter from today?"

"I can't imagine."

"Kay Middlekauf."

"You did? Poor Kay. It must be terrible for her."

"I suppose so."

He was startled at her near indifference.

"You don't think it was pretty bad?"

"I feel very sorry for Kay," she said.

"Yes, it was hard on her."

"She *took* it hard."

He thought he understood. "The disgrace?"

"No."

"Then what was it?"

"Losing Bratten."

"Oh!" This view astounded Dave.

"When a girl like Kay goes for a man, she goes pretty completely."

"So it appears." He was dry.

She glanced at him. "You're thinking—about the church part of it—" She gave a little fastidious grimace. "That was revolting, I'll admit. But it wasn't Kay's choosing. She was in love with him."

"How do you know?"

"She roomed right below me in the apartment house. That was why she wrote to me."

"Oh, yes. The letter. Did she have anything to say?"

"It was brief and pathetic. Some little possessions left behind—she asked me to send them. She hoped that the 'horrible thing that happened' wouldn't 'forever blacken her memory' in my mind. I sent the articles and wrote that I was still her friend."

They halted before the entrance to Judge Hutto's office. He looked into her eyes and noticed how clear and unmuddied were the whites of them, next to the deep violet irises.

"I'm a little surprised," he told her.

"Because I condone sin?"

"You didn't. But women usually are so—so——"

"So vicious toward their own sex?"

"Perhaps."

"Trade unionism," she said unexpectedly. He smiled.

"Ages before you men even thought of a union we women had one that's about the most rock-bound the world ever saw."

"Marriage?"

"Yes—a woman's property right in her man. Every other woman knows it. The woman who violates the property right is the object of that particular viciousness you spoke of—because it's so important that the property right be maintained."

"So men are just so much livestock to be owned?"

She laughed. "Oh, I'd hardly consider *you* as livestock, Mr. Constable."

"Dave," he suggested.

She accepted it brightly. "Very well—*David*."

He felt a pleased sensation of accomplishment.

"You were telling me that women have a whole system of ethics differing from the ethics that men understand," he pursued.

"Perhaps that's true."

"That explains something that's always puzzled me. The old lawlessness that seems to be a part of woman."

"You mean unscrupulousness," she corrected.

"You're agreeing with me?"

"To a degree," Julia said. "Women will do what no man would think of doing—for someone they love. It happens all the time. Right here in Jericho, even." She smiled at him. "I leave you here. Goodbye."

Later that day he again walked past the store which had displayed Mr. Pickwick in its window.

Mr. Pickwick was gone.

Dave went in and made inquiries.

Yes, the clerk said, a nice piece of Royal Doulton. They were rare. The last one had been sold that day to Mrs. Porter Grimes. She collected them.

6.

That David Constable openly defended J. Wilber Bratten and Kay Middlekauf did not surprise many people. His tangent views were well established. He hated to see a man, or a woman, kicked after they were down. And he was not averse to prodding the town's Pharisees.

"Outside of the bad taste—or bad judgment—of the location they chose, it's not the first time such a thing has happened—even in Jericho," he said. "No reason to treat it as if it were a brand new episode in the history of man. As the old editor told the young reporter, you can write editorials against that sort of thing, you can preach against it from the pulpit, you can even pass laws against it—but you're never going to make it unpopular with the public."

David Constable was regarded as such a Philistine that not even the church people were very indignant with him. But his attitude had little weight in helping the cause of Bratten and Kay Middlekauf.

Fortunately for J. Wilber, he had another, and far more purposeful defender.

Algeria Wedge's motives were different from Dave's. She cared not an iota for the moral aspects of the affair, or the mere question of fair treatment involved. But she did care about the effect of it on the First Church of Jericho.

Algeria had an unfailing loyalty to what she adopted as her own— her husband, her set, her political party, her church. Whatever injured one of these touched her very closely.

There was no sentimentality in this. It was part of the fabric of her life. In the past, Algeria had sometimes experienced the realization of weakness which many ambitious women have felt in seeking achievement in a man-dominated world. But she had never permitted herself the luxury of depression for long, and in these later days she had begun to find a source of gratification in the very accomplishment of difficult matters in the face of obstacles.

It is a finer and more delicate feat to induce many persons to act according to your wishes without their realizing it, than merely to call upon crude authority for obedience. Influence over people was power to Algeria. Influence is bought by one's becoming important in many places. Each organization to which she belonged was a microcosm of Jericho. Jericho was a small cell of the state. And the state was a member of the nation.

Tucker was now thoroughly committed to his campaign for Congress, hardly yet knowing her role in bringing him into it. As a matter of fact she did not dare yet confide in him the full scope of her audacity. Her dreams were without bounds: always Tucker was the center of them, the means by which she hoped to achieve.

The lower house of Congress was but a stepping stone to the Senate. A United States Senator has infinite possibilities for advancement. The Cabinet—with a little luck—might almost be counted on. It was true that the Republican party always nominated for President someone from New York or Ohio or Illinois—the great populous states. But frequently the party leaders looked to the Middle West for vice-presidential material.

A Senator from agricultural Kansas, with a good record—and Algeria would see that Tucker's record was good—might be a very acceptable nominee for Vice-President. And accidents before this had translated Vice-Presidents into the White House.

Algeria actually dared dream. . . .

But here, in the inception, was difficulty. The First Church was vitally important as a starting point—a solid fulcrum on which to brace the lever to hoist Tucker to high places. She had put endless time and effort into it for that reason. Tucker usually attended Sunday worship, and sometimes passed the plate; but it was Algeria who did all the real labor of keeping the Wedge name prominent in major church activities. She avoided the jealousy of other women—she was scrupulous to do this, now that she had something real to gain by it—refusing honors politely and graciously. Petty offices meant nothing; she was quite willing to allow other women to be presidents of little group organizations. But she was consulted on nearly every important decision made by any of these. Even J. Wilber, up to the time of his shocking contretemps, had frequently asked her suggestions and assistance for the choir—and she had freely and intelligently given them.

With few exceptions those women who once had been terrified of Algeria Wedge had become her vocal admirers. She no longer dominated all social affairs in Jericho. Other leaders were beginning to bask again. In the First Church, Algeria was unfailingly gracious, warm with praise, quite extraordinarily patient in listening to unimportant matters, a generous giver; and the very sight of her—as Mrs. Widcomb often flatteringly said—in her Sunday pew, with her gray eyes and her invariably handsome hats, was an inspiration to the whole congregation.

Algeria heard about Bratten and Porter Grimes's secretary as soon as Tucker did—which was as soon as the *Clarion* did.

Her first thought was an impatient: The stupid *fool!*

Her second was to talk with her husband on the telephone.

"What about J. Wilber and Kay Middlekauf?" she asked him.

"We're verifying details now."

"You're not going to *print* it?"

"Well—we've gotta be sure there's a clear-cut case, to avoid libel——"

"Tucker, you mustn't even *think* of publishing that!"

"Why not? It's a terrific story—prominent man and girl. To say nothing of the *circumstances*. Why it's national!"

"National" was Tucker's encomium for a happening. He meant by the word that the news was so important or interesting that it transcended the ordinary bounds of Jericho and would become a budget item on the Associated Press wires. Small towns like Jericho loved to originate national stories. It got the town's name in the date lines, and sometimes in the headlines.

Algeria pretended obtuseness. "What do you mean, 'national'?"

Eagerly her husband's voice came back over the wire. "Why—can't you see the headlines in the big Eastern dailies?"

In fifteen minutes she was talking to Tucker in his office.

"You can't use that story," she told him.

"But, darling——"

"After all, dear, we've known all the time that J. Wilber was mentally and emotionally immature, even if he's well into his forties."

True enough, Tucker admitted. J. Wilber hated reading. He was a game player. Card games. Even checkers. Anything to take his mind off himself. He loved croquet and had a court in his back yard. He belonged to the Jericho Country Club, and although he was a very ordinary golfer, he went in for it hard, spending considerable money on new clubs and new gadgets and new lessons. He was intensely exhibitionistic—a show-off. Everyone had observed his almost hysterical zest in performing before a group on a piano, and his antics when he led the singing at the Commercial Club were a little nauseating even to Tucker.

"J. Wilber was bored to death with his existence," said Algeria. "I feel a little sorry for him."

"That doesn't alter the fact that this is a big story."

"Yes it does, Tucker."

"Now listen, darling, I can't have you or anybody coming up here to tell me how to run the *Clarion*. . . ."

She waited patiently until he had run through this familiar plaint. Then she said:

"Let's be realistic. Do you want to go to Congress?"

He stared. "Why—of course—" he said weakly.

"Then kill that story! You've got the best excuse in the world. You just admitted you weren't quite sure of the libel aspects."

"There's always a little danger when no legal action has been filed in a thing like this," he agreed.

"Good. Then kill it. The First Church has been hit heavily enough. Whatever affects Tucker Wedge's church, affects his politics. Why, darling, the First Church is your stronghold! Everything you print will help the other crowd across town, and give aid and comfort to your opposition. Don't you see?"

Tucker was beginning to see.

He was sulky, but she had shown him the way. He did not know all that was in her mind, but he called in Clarence Snead and gave orders that nothing—not a line—about the Bratten affair should be printed, unless it was made safe by legal action.

7.

Algeria perhaps fumed inwardly, but outwardly she was calm. She allowed no shocked expressions to escape her. Upon her friends she urged Christian charity in judgment. She called upon Dr. Widcomb and his wife, to express regret and assure them of her support. They were almost touchingly grateful.

She even sent over to Mrs. Bratten, who had sequestered herself, a jar of very special jelly, with a graceful, tactful little note.

8.

The galling part of all this, to the adherents of the First Church, was that the great rival in Jericho, the Community Church, was a natural beneficiary of the scandal. The congregation of the latter institution was able only thinly to conceal its exultation at what had happened.

For a long time the Community Church had suffered under the snubs and airs of the First Church. The unfortunate episode of the young preacher in the Community Church pulpit who had cribbed his best oratorical lines from the great atheist, Ingersoll, had never been permitted to be forgotten; the Community Church winced under veiled gibes about this from the rival flock.

The Bratten affair, therefore, far from giving the pain that might have been expected to the devout of the Community Church, seemed to fall upon them as the gentle rain from heaven upon the place beneath. They appeared, in fact, to drink it up gratefully, almost to revel in it, and were heard exchanging happy comments.

This perhaps human but certainly un-Christian spirit was a source of resentment to Algeria Wedge and many others. Church rivalries have the quality of creating unique bitternesses. The fall of Wilber Bratten and his choir girl further heightened the enmity between the two congregations.

In the scheme of things at the Community Church, Margie Ransome occupied a place analogous to, and fully as important, as that which formerly had been held by Wilber Bratten at the First Church.

Margie was the Community Church soloist. She was seventeen years old, and nature had dealt bountifully with her. Her face was round, her features pretty and delicate; she had a sweeping black glance and a mop of curling hair so black that it had blue tints in it; and she possessed the poetry of carriage sometimes seen in young girls and young trees.

But the most beautiful thing about Margie was her voice.

When she stood up in the church choir loft and sang, many people were inclined to stop all thinking while they listened to her. Her throat swelled, and every note seemed to come as if caressed from her soft lips.

Margie's voice was of her, yet somehow apart, like a trusted and beloved friend or companion. It did things almost without her bidding

—things which other people said were wonderful, and which were thrilling even to herself.

About her voice she was building new hopes and great aspirations; and this was because of Julia Norman.

Julia was Margie's friend. The young girl worshiped Julia, and it was from Julia that she heard the fairest, the most intelligent, and in a manner the most thrilling summation of her musical gifts.

It was Julia who told Margie that her voice needed training. Julia, who loved and appreciated music, knew some of the things that were wrong and told the girl with equal honesty that, were her voice given the training it deserved, there were almost no limits to its potentialities.

For the first time Margie began to have great dreams. She saw herself singing, some day, in grand opera. At Wiesbaden, perhaps, or in the Paris Opéra, or at the Metropolitan, with Caruso. . . .

But she had scarcely begun dreaming these dreams when she encountered what seemed to be the immediate end of them.

Margie's father, Tom Ransome, was a portly dark man, with a crudely winning manner of talking—which did not, however, fool people as to his grasping ways.

He possessed wealth—as wealth was reckoned in Jericho—and was reputed to have sold more wheat lands than any other man in western Kansas. Each year he added to this wealth. He was sober, shrewd, even cunning, and he was hated by most of those with whom he had dealings because he was too clever for them and kept growing richer.

"He's the kind of a man who always shakes hands with a widow woman, before he forecloses on her mortgage," Porter Grimes said of him. As this was exactly what Porter Grimes did under similar circumstances, it hardly merited the bitterness with which he said it.

Actually, it was not strictly true. David Constable knew Tom Ransome well, and was his friend in spite of his unpopularity. Dave knew full well that Ransome had a hard side, which he turned to the world. But he had seen also a softer side, which was toward his family, and little Margie in particular.

But he counted his dollars very carefully, did Tom Ransome.

And when Margie came to him and begged him to send her away to have her voice professionally trained, he refused with abrupt finality. He saw no value in such foolishness. He wanted no daughter of his on the stage.

When it was explained to him that it was not play acting but grand opera toward which his daughter's ambitions yearned, he said that he had never attended a grand opera performance, and never expected to, but it was all the same—stage flummery with music. Maybe worse.

And he added that he expected Margie to get married and bring up a family like any other girl. He had never finished grade school himself, and when Margie graduated from high school he considered that she had all the education any girl needed. As a concession, he added, she might take normal training, and get a county teacher's certificate, so that she could earn her own living teaching country school a year or so, if she desired. By that time, he expected, somebody would come along and put a "Mrs." in front of her name.

That, without considering himself in any way callous or hardhearted, was the way Tom Ransome looked at Margie's future.

Margie's mother, a very shy, retiring woman, who hardly ever said anything, did not debate the subject with him.

To Julia there was tragedy in this. She comforted Margie when she wept, and did all she could to encourage the girl. In Margie's heart Julia was identified forever with her dreams and ambitions. Julia was Margie's confidante and adviser. She had been away from Jericho. She represented the whole outside world. Margie depended on her more than on anyone else for counsel and solace.

Youth is resilient, and Margie recovered from the intense depression her father's refusal had given her, although she never ceased mourning. Never had she sung better than she did that summer. In spite of the hot weather and the indifferent preaching, the Community Church had the biggest congregations of its history.

This circumstance was viewed with the more animus by the faithful of the First Church, because some of this increase was made up of defections from the First Church itself.

Looking sourly across town, there were a good many adherents of Dr. Widcomb's congregation who decided among themselves that the Ransome girl with the brilliant voice was a common, pretentious, flip little minx, probably no better than she should be; and new stories circulated about the hardfistedness of her father.

Of course, Margie could hardly have helped being spoiled a little. But her small vanities hardly deserved the criticism they received.

She was, without realizing it, a symbol—the chief focus of the Community Church's triumph, and of the First Church's anguish. At seventeen it is hard for a girl to understand that she is a cause for hatred, or the tortuous train of events that made her so. The knowledge might have come sooner, and under less bitter circumstances, had it not been for a surprising event which now took place.

9.

Matthias Widcomb was hard hit and suffering. Even the outrage he felt at the sacrilege which had been performed in his church could not equal his sense of loss at being deprived in one sweeping disaster, of the leader of his choir, one of his largest contributors, and a chief pillar of his congregation—to say nothing of a part of the odor of sanctity which had surrounded his house of worship.

The minister's cares seemed to bear him down. People remarked that the scandal had added years to the parson's age. His gaunt shoulders were more stooped than ever.

Few people, in those days, knew that he was conferring frequently with Algeria Wedge. What took place at these conferences not even Eugenia was privy to. But it was Eugenia who first noticed that the good man's figure gradually seemed less bowed and more buoyant.

There came a morning when a new and violent fury of gossip swept Jericho. J. Wilber Bratten, it was whispered, was back in town—had sneaked in on a train at night. Furthermore, his wife had actually received him back. He was living at the house.

This incredible thing was shortly verified. J. Wilber had been seen—momentarily—at a window.

That afternoon Lillian Bratten, on an unavoidable errand downtown, was cornered by Mrs. Horst and flatly asked if it was true. She replied as flatly:

Yes, Wilber was home. And whose affair was it if he was?

The contingencies which brought Bratten back had been foreseen by Algeria.

His return was a matter of necessity—he could not stay away, because everything he owned was tied up in the city. An insurance business is of such nature that it cannot be transferred, part and parcel, to another part of the country at will. Clients and customers are stable things, not to be shifted about. To keep them a man must remain with them. J. Wilber, in all the rest of his life, could not have built up another business such as he had in Jericho.

What amazed many in the town was the way that little mousy Lillian Bratten stood up for her husband—although she was the one, surely, who had been most deeply wronged. She faced down everybody—even the friends who tried to "sympathize" with her. For this, of course, she was criticized. Some went so far as to hint that Lillian Bratten herself was no better than she should be—else she certainly could never have accepted, as she seemed to have done, this monumental transgression.

But David Constable acquired a deep-seated admiration for Lillian, who had the courage to face a community that insisted on telling her how it could not see, could not understand, how her *pride* would permit her. . . .

Then another rumor ran in little ripples through the neighborhoods, over back fences, down business streets, into humble homes and fine houses. Something big was going to happen at the First Church . . . something on Sunday.

When Sunday came, every seat in the church was filled long before it was time for the morning service to begin. And every bit of standing room was taken, while a crowd, unable to enter, lingered without, trying to hear what was going on.

10.

Sharp at eleven o'clock the bell in the belfry rang a few times. It was the customary signal to latecomers that services were about to begin; but the warning was wholly unnecessary this day.

As the organ prelude began, the choir filed in and took its seats, the place of J. Wilber Bratten conspicuously vacant. The Reverend Dr. Widcomb ascended to the pulpit and gave the opening prayer; then announced a hymn, which was sung. Responsive readings, announcements, and other routine matters followed. The congregation began to display symptoms of restlessness.

During the singing of the sermon hymn, the preacher knelt with one knee on the floor behind the pulpit, his hand at his brow, in prayer. This was not customary. When he arose at the conclusion of the hymn and announced his text, the knowing ones exchanged significant glances:

The Eighth Chapter of the Gospel According to St. John, the Seventh Verse. From the story of the Woman taken in Adultery. Sternly the minister read:

So when they continued asking him, he lifted up himself and said unto them, He that is without sin among you, let him first cast a stone . . .

The sermon was solemn and impressive. Ordinarily Matthias Widcomb dwelt thunderously on the terrors of the Hereafter and the fate of the wicked. But his was a gentler theme today: Forgiveness, Its beauty, Its necessity, Its injunction upon man.

Before the sermon was well launched the whole church became tense, for the implications were too plain to be escaped.

As the sermon ended with a short prayer, silence hung like a weight over the congregation. For a moment Matthias Widcomb gazed sombrely over them. Then, above the profound hush, rose a sibilant, gusty sigh of sheer emotion.

The choir-room door at the front of the church had opened. It was rarely used, except during cantatas and such churchly theatricals as demanded a side entrance from which the pulpit rostrum steps could be reached. But no drama hitherto issuing from that door compared to the present one.

J. Wilber Bratten stood in the opening. One moment he peered out, startled, as if minded to go back. Then he thought better of it, and with head bowed and hands folded before him, came forth with slow and measured steps, to the foot of the pulpit right at the head of the center aisle. So silent grew the church, after that single great sigh of ecstatic excitement, that his footsteps on the soft aisle carpet were clearly heard. He looked up, his face twisted. His countenance seemed worn with suffering. He was like a man at the foot of the gallows.

On the rostrum above, the minister raised his long, black-clad arms. His voice filled the church.

"Hear ye all what the Word of God saith. 'Confess ye therefore your sins, one to another, and pray for one another, that ye may be healed. The supplication of a righteous man availeth much in its working.'" Matthias Widcomb paused, and his voice dramatically lowered. "Our brother has something on his soul to say to all of us."

In the emotion-choked silence the voice of J. Wilber Bratten was heard. Not the bull voice to which the people were accustomed, but a weak, shaking voice.

He was making confession.

At least it began as a confession. But he had not uttered three halting sentences before his face began to work. Two large tears squeezed out. He had to draw a handkerchief and remove the thick-lensed glasses while he mopped his eyes.

He tried again, and his voice broke. He caught his breath with a sob, and raised the handkerchief again.

In the harrowing silence someone in the congregation wept noisily. And in a single instant, it seemed, every woman in the church burst into tears, and many of the men with them.

Insistent cries sounded from the pews.

"No! No, Wilber!"

"Say no more!"

"It's enough—you've done enough!"

"We forgive you—God forgives you!"

Matthias Widcomb knew his moment. With his gaunt cheeks streaming, he descended from the pulpit and put his long arm around Bratten's weeping figure. At that J. Wilber lost every vestige of self-control and, placing his face on the minister's black broadcloth shoulder, he wept loudly and unrestrainedly.

The man of God raised high his free arm, and his voice rose above the sobs and ejaculations which filled the church.

"Brother Wilber—no man condemns thee—neither do I condemn thee! Go and sin no more! Thy faith hath made thee whole!"

From the pipe organ came a great chord. The whole crowded church, with wet eyes, broke into "Old Hundred":

> Praise God from whom all blessings flow,
> Praise Him all creatures here below . . .

And then they stormed up from the pews. Men clutched at J. Wilber's hand. Women crowded near to bestow upon him the kisses of sisterhood.

Never in all its history had Jericho enjoyed so great an emotional saturnalia.

J. Wilber shook hands and accepted kisses and continued to weep copiously. He was profoundly, supremely happy.

He was restored. From whatever the world might say in the future, he was as secure as a ship riding in the calm behind a breakwater when a storm rages on the sea. He had made his confession, full and categorical, and his reinstatement was complete.

11.

J. Wilber Bratten was happy. Matthias Widcomb was happy. The congregation was happy over one of the greatest sensations in memory. But one person was not happy.

Algeria Wedge.

She it was who had planned the strategy, even instructing the minister and the penitent in their roles. The performance had been tremendous, exceeding her hopes. Her riposte against the thrust of fate at the First Church had been sensationally successful.

But Algeria knew the damage which must be repaired. Long, very long, it would be before people ceased talking of this day. The sin of J. Wilber would be the subject of low humor. It might be years before the First Church lived this down.

Only Algeria had really speculated on who sent the note to the minister which caused the confounding of J. Wilber and his pathetic paramour. She had studied that note.

Rejoice in the wife of thy youth ... Let her breasts satisfy thee at all times ... For why shouldest thou ... be ravished with a strange woman, and embrace the bosom of a foreigner?

J. Wilber had been "holden with the cords of his sin" all right.

And Lillian Bratten had taken her husband back, showing forgiveness that seemed almost saintly.

In all Jericho only one person knew ... that it was Lillian Bratten's hand which had written that note to Matthias Widcomb.

Part Three

JULIA

CHAPTER I

1.

IN the high plains country, autumn is incomparably the best of the seasons. Spring is always in a tearing rush, with raw high winds, muddy roads, days on end of dust and grit in the atmosphere, and sudden violent thunderstorms. Summer is a bully, beating the helpless earth with a malevolent ferocity of heat and drought. Winter is a hag, savage from frustration, snarling at the land with ice-fanged blizzards in sheer insensate hate.

But in the fall come weeks of calm, sweet skies. The world seems to stretch and relax in blessed relief from the wrath of August. Rains fall, but they are gentle showers, cooling and life giving, lacking the violence of the storms of other seasons. The sun, which until now has seemed such an enemy, smiles with kindness; and on the far horizons are faint bluish shadows of haze instead of the mocking mirage which danced there during the dry bone months. The earth gathers unto itself joy and strength with which to resist the coming winter.

With autumn the climactic effort of the wheat harvest is well past. Fodder crops are in process of gathering, but this is a matter infinitely more leisurely, and farmers have time to visit at each others' fence corners, and swap gossip, and sometimes lies, and occasionally horses.

To Julia Norman, as she went up the sidewalk to Judge Hutto's home in the early September evening, the world had never been more beautiful—and yet in herself she felt a measureless discontent.

Now she was deep in Jericho; a part of the life of the town, welcome everywhere. She was accepted in the legal profession. The male lawyers, inclined at first to resent her, saw that she was modest and kept to her chosen role behind the scenes.

Socially, she was more than occupied. Algeria Wedge had "taken her up." Women like Algeria, who entertain much, like to gather about them persons who are attractive and amusing. Julia had beauty, and wit, and a gift for dress. Conversationally, she could hold her own even with Algeria, but this she did agreeably and sweetly, trying hard never to offend; and succeeding in performing this difficult tightwire walking act because she had a warm and generous nature, and a quick instinct for the feelings of others.

Therefore she was sought after. Older women called her "my dear" with quite genuine motherly affection; and younger ones felt only a minimum of natural jealousy.

For it was apparent that, though Julia was brilliantly attractive to men, she had, for some inexplicable reasons, no designs on any of the beaux of the other girls.

She had to be adroit. It is a matter of delicacy and insight to discourage young men without offending them—and in such a way that their previous sweethearts are willing to receive them back. Even so, she had not been entirely successful. Already three bachelors and an impressionable widower of mature years had made proposals, and been brokenhearted for two weeks or more after she refused them. On a few occasions she had been taken driving by gentlemen with less honorable intentions, and had to be firm with them.

Yet she had a feeling of futility in spite of her busy existence. She was a career woman, with a measure of success. It was not enough. She did the same things, day after day, and she wondered where it was taking her. Nature used beauty to stimulate and entice her senses. Her soul fluttered, to rise to the skies, but could not lift itself from the ground. She was twenty-three and life was passing her by.

2.

Mrs. Hutto's front-door knob was of brass, and polished like a mirror.

Julia did not knock; she turned the knob and entered. She was almost a daughter in this house. It was her place of refuge.

In the hall a bright, clean rag rug greeted her; and an old-fashioned hall-tree on which hung one of the judge's mohair coats and two or three battered hats. Beside it stood the brass umbrella stand containing a wonderful collection of articles—two or three of Mrs. Hutto's parasols; the judge's rusty old umbrella; and many canes of different shapes and characters.

Owing to his arthritis and his age, the judge never walked without a stick, and in his long life he had collected many. Julia noticed the goldheaded malacca which had been presented to the judge by Chauncey Depew. There was also the bamboo with an ivory handle. It contained a sharp little sword of tempered steel in its shank, and according to the judge dated back to the time of the first Napoleon.

Judge Hutto was now past his eightieth birthday and he had not been well enough to go to his office all week. Julia carried a leather case filled with papers for him to look at.

She removed her hat at the mirror in the hall, saw that her hair was neat, and went into the sitting-room. She liked the restfulness of this place, and stood admiring Mrs. Hutto's magnificent braided rug. The old lady had made it herself, so it had a history; she never tired of relating how this bit of wine-colored broadcloth came from Cousin Carrie's dolman coat that she wore to the St. Louis World's Fair; and the one yonder was out of an old suit of the judge's—a bit bright for him, the old woman would cackle, and it had even been suggested that she made him buy that blue suit so it could eventually go into the rug. And so on. It was a labor of love, and of years, that rug; and it was almost as filled with reminiscence as a family picture-album.

On the sitting-room table were a few books, and a stereoscope with its box of double-view picture cards. Two large engravings of George Caleb Bingham's paintings, "Stump Speaking" and "The County Election," were on the walls. The judge said they illustrated democracy in its crudest but perhaps purest form.

Julia heard slow steps, and the judge's voice chirped:

"How are you, girl?"

It stabbed her to see how slowly he moved, with his old bent back and his cane, and his skin so transparent that the tiny blue veins could be seen in his temples and on his eyelids. Yet he never relaxed his waspish geniality.

"I brought the papers on the Holcomb will and the Lupton estate, and three abstracts for you to approve," she told him.

"Who's representing the Lupton heirs?"

"Turnbull and Collins."

He snorted. The judge had long ago given up courtroom practice; but he was forever quarreling with Julia because she would not take such cases.

"You women! Willing enough to speak up for yourselves but timid as rabbits about others! Now *why* didn't you handle that yourself, Julia, and pocket the fee?"

"We've been over that."

The judge grunted and dropped the subject. They began to go over the papers. While they were in the midst of it, Mrs. Hutto came in, bearing the mail and the evening *Clarion*.

"When the Judge gets through monopolizing you, Julia, I'd like to get you to look at my new black bombazine," she said.

"Of course."

Mrs. Hutto handed the newspaper to her husband and sat down to examine the three envelopes which had come in the mail. In spite of her large figure and harsh visage there was something amusingly childish about her. Very quickly she decided that two of her letters contained bills—and placed them on the table. The third, however, was addressed to her in a handwriting she could not quite identify. For a time she gave it the most earnest scrutiny. It seemed almost familiar—but not quite.

"Could it be from Agatha Wartle, thanking me for the flowers I sent when her daughter Ann had her baby?" she mused aloud.

"Can't say, Mrs. Hutto," said the judge, who was immersed in the newspaper.

"No," said Mrs. Hutto decidedly, answering her own question. "I remember now, Agatha's already thanked me."

"Had you considered opening the envelope as a means of solving your puzzle?" suggested the judge with a gleam of a smile.

But his wife ignored him. It was not in the old lady's nature to do anything so direct.

Judge Hutto's white brows suddenly knit with concentration. He read a moment. Then, surprisingly, he chuckled.

"Listen to *this*," he cried.

"What is it?"

"The *Clarion*'s after Dave Constable, horse, foot and artillery. Whew —what a trenchant cutlass Tucker Wedge is swinging in *this* phillipic!"

"Read it," commanded Mrs. Hutto, and Julia raised her head with a sudden heightened interest.

The old man cleared his throat and read aloud:

FEATHERING HIS OWN NEST

When Rufus J. McCurdy, alias Gotch McCurdy, was convicted yesterday, on his own plea, of liquor in possession, he received only a nominal thirty-day sentence in the county jail—on the recommendation of the county attorney.

This sentence, so ridiculously light, demands an explanation, in view of the reputation and record of this man. McCurdy was caught with a dozen bottles of contraband liquor on his premises, and has been a notorious trouble-maker for years.

A thirty-day sentence, to a man like McCurdy, is no more than an incitement to further activities in the same kind. But this is by no means the most serious or outrageous aspect of the affair. The McCurdy episode is only a typical example of the way the county attorney's office has been mishandled for years.

It is intolerable that the resources of a public office should be used to forward the interests of criminals and crooks. But it is infinitely worse that David Constable, who by mischance happens to be county attorney of this unfortunate community, should be allowed to use his position as public advocate to build up a scaly, slinking criminal practice for himself to take over as soon as he is kicked out of office.

Need *The Clarion* recall to its readers that the man McCurdy was once the client—and the only client—of David Constable? Is Blair County to continue to suffer from laws which are not enforced and crime which is encouraged, so that a jackleg lawyer like Constable can feather his nest?

Julia listened to the reading with a shocked mind. The attack seemed so violent, so causelessly vicious. She could feel indignation rising in her, mingled with something like fear, as the judge's voice continued to utter the malignant words. For a moment, after the old man lowered the paper and gazed at the two women, there was silence.

"Well!" gasped Mrs. Hutto at last. "They make David Constable into a criminal."

But the judge suddenly chortled.

"It's the kicked dog that howls," he said. "This editorial's a yawp of pure consternation."

"What do you mean?" asked Julia.

"It means only one thing—that Dave Constable's suddenly developed into a bigger menace than Porter Grimes or Tucker Wedge and their myrmidons ever dreamed."

"But people may believe it!" objected Julia.

"Some fools. But it will make most people mad—as it obviously has made *you,* my dear."

"Hmmf!" sniffed Mrs. Hutto.

She cocked her head to one side and gazed through her nose glasses at the baffling letter in her hand. Then she turned it over to consult its back; but the postmark was too blurred to be made out. She held the envelope at arms' length, then brought it close to her nose, examining it as a squirrel examines a nut—or as if she might surprise in it somewhere a secret code.

"Hmmf all you want to," said the judge. "Dave's obviously taking care of himself better than I believed—until I read the effusion of this peerless palladium of the people's rights."

He tapped the *Clarion* contemptuously with his fingers.

"David Constable's a fool!" exclaimed his wife. "I'd like to shake him good. Always with the wrong crowd—that Farmers' Co-op! Pooh!"

She returned her attention to the letter. Julia watched her with affectionate amusement. Sitting bulkily back in her chair, Mrs. Hutto tapped the corner of the puzzling envelope against her teeth, her eyes screwed ceilingward, while she counted with her thumb against the fingers of her free hand, as if going over the names of all the people she knew who might have sent the missive.

"The fact remains," said the judge, "the harder a newspaper is hit, the louder it squeals. It's pretty obvious that they've discovered Dave is going to run for Congress—and maybe lick them!"

"I don't understand—" said Julia. "The Republican district convention in August nominated Tucker——"

"And Dave wasn't even a candidate. Why should he be? That convention was rigged and controlled by Porter Grimes. Dave was too smart. He had another move. Mrs. Hutto, what you call 'that Farmers' Co-op' is solidly organized over the district and solidly behind Dave. I'll bet they're getting signatures on a petition right now to run him as an independent—and if they do—watch!"

"Hmmf!" said Mrs. Hutto again. She heaved herself up, carried the letter over to a window and held it to the light in a fruitless attempt to read the writing through the envelope. Failing, she sighed discontentedly and returned to her chair.

Julia had listened intently to the Judge. Her inexperience with politics kept her from realizing fully the forces which were at work under the surface. What the old man said amazed her.

"But—Mr. Constable hasn't even announced—" she said.

"That's to his advantage. He's in the maneuvering spot. Oh—he's quiet, is our long-shanked friend Constable, but the grass doesn't *exactly* grow under his feet!"

"You really think this editorial won't hurt him?"

"Julia, my dear, the high priests of Republican standpattism are just beginning to awaken to the fact that in addition to being a brilliant prosecutor, the gentleman who opposes them has been laying up some pretty fancy political hay. *That's* the why of this piece of billingsgate in the paper."

Julia felt a sudden sense of excitement, almost of jubilation.

Mrs. Hutto was sitting, looking moodily out of the window. Suddenly she fixed on the envelope an expression of reckless resolution, tore it open, and read the brief note within.

"Sally Harris!" she cried. Intense disgust came into her face. "Just saying the Library Club's been postponed. Hmmf! Some people certainly don't mind wasting your time!"

She was still fuming when they went in to dinner.

3.

The calendar said September 10.

When it came time to close the office, Dave rose from his desk, put on his hat and picked up a large cardboard box.

The date was not important to anyone else. But to him it was important.

He placed the box in the seat of his car and was about to get in behind the steering wheel, when he saw Julia Norman.

She was looking at him in the superb way some women have of looking—lips half-parted, brow clear, a hint of a smile in her eyes—so he waited.

The sight of her gave him a warmth within that nothing else did. Julia in a blue fall suit, Julia in a lemon-colored gown, Julia in a white silk dress— She seemed always to have the power to make him feel as if it were a fresh spring morning. And he did not know anything lovelier than that.

She came so directly toward him that he thought she had something of importance to say to him. But she only said:

"Are you driving back toward town?"

"I'll take you wherever you want." He stopped.

"No, you're going somewhere. Anyway, I just happened to think that I was loving this walk——"

He smiled suddenly. "Are you in a very big hurry?"

"Why—no—not very——"

"I'm going on a little errand—a mile out into the country and back. It won't take more than fifteen minutes, and I'd like to talk something over with you——"

She was glad. "I'd like the ride!"

After the car was under way, she remembered she had not asked where they were going. She did so now.

"To the cemetery," he said.

"Oh?"

He drove silently for a few minutes. Presently she said:

"What was it you were going to talk about?"

"Some people want me to run for Congress."

"Why don't you?"

"Do you think I should?"

"Why—if you're interested in politics—I should think——"

"That's just it," he said. "I wonder if I'm sufficiently interested in politics to give up my life for it."

She did not answer; he could see she was thinking.

"If I happened to be elected to Congress," he went on, "I'd be a politician the rest of my life."

"You wouldn't like that?"

"Julia, I don't know. I love politics. I enjoy the heat of a campaign, I can take a defeat if it comes, and I confess I'd be exhilarated at going to Congress. Furthermore, there have been petitions circulated in the district—by the Farmers' Co-operatives, managed by Webb Pettis chiefly. They want a spokesman in Congress, and they say they've got more than the required five per cent of the qualified voters to put me on the ticket. They've got a week to file the petitions with the secretary of state in order to get my name on the ticket as an Independent Republican. But——"

"But what, David?"

"There's something I haven't proved to myself." He smiled whimsically. "Do you know I'm not sure whether I would be successful in private practice?"

She was surprised and puzzled. "Why—I can't understand——"

"I came out here when I was a young man, to be a lawyer. But I never really got started in law practice. I've been a public official almost all the time. Sometimes I wonder very much what would happen if I started to swim in the sea of legal competition——"

She laughed. "That's ridiculous. Everyone knows you've been building yourself a 'scaly, slinking criminal practice.'"

He glanced at her, then laughed. "You've been reading Tucker's editorial."

"What about that Gotch McCurdy case?" she suddenly asked.

"Julia, they broke into Gotch's sleeping-quarters and seized six quarts of whiskey. He hadn't tried to sell it. Maybe he was going to—but there was not an iota of evidence he had made an effort—yet. To me, breaking into a private dwelling is a crime worse than almost any other. John Adams said the American Revolution began in 1761, when James Otis delivered his great argument against the British 'writs of assistance.' He said the search by revenue officers of private homes was a gross violation of the common law. It *was*. And it still is! Furthermore, the way the dry squads go about enforcing their law, insults my sense of justice. Why always raid the homes of the humble, like Gotch? Why not raid Porter Grimes—or David Constable? That's the reason why I made the recommendation to which the *Clarion* took such exception."

Eagerly her mind followed and agreed with his argument.

She nodded. Then another thought came to her.

"Do you—hesitate to run against Tucker Wedge?"

He was silent for a moment and the smile faded.

"Because of our former friendship?" he asked at last. He shook his head slowly. "I did not break that friendship," he said. "But it is broken—destroyed completely. The fact that Tucker Wedge is a candidate, if anything, would only make me more certain to go into the race—to defeat him!"

Julia said: "David—I wish you would announce. Right away."

He studied her. Presently she said: "It's something bigger than you. I heard you talk to the farmers at Bedestown. It's important that you—that someone like you—goes to the Congress of the United States, to say some of those things you said to the farmers."

Still he did not speak.

"There is one more thing," she added. "You have an enemy. But it's not Tucker."

"Who is it then?"

"Algeria."

His eyes hunted her face. "Why do you say that?"

"A woman is the best judge of a woman."

"And that's your judgment?"

"Do you remember something I told you once about a woman's knowing no ethics when someone she loves is concerned? That is how Algeria is."

"She thinks so much of Tucker?" His voice sounded strange, almost wistful. "I had not really considered that," he said after a moment.

"Of course," Julia amended, "it's not entirely unselfish. What helps Tucker helps Algeria."

"But still, there's something there—a great concern, great plans." He fell silent, brooding, his eyes on the road ahead. "I envy him," he said at last.

"Algeria Wedge is the most capable woman I think I ever knew," she agreed, with something like a sinking of the heart. She went on, generously. "She's wonderful, David—superb! It was she who gave Tucker the ambition for Congress. I don't blame you for admiring her."

He smiled now. "That isn't why I envy Tucker."

"Then I don't understand——"

"Julia," he said, "let me tell you why we're going out to the cemetery tonight. There was a little girl—just a thin little thing with big eyes —who lived at my house for a little while last winter. Her name was Edie. She died——"

His voice grew deep in timbre and he paused.

"It was a year ago today that she came to me. She gave me something I hadn't known anything about—love. Since she went away— I've had a chance to know what I lost."

He stopped, cleared his throat.

"That was what I meant when I said I envied Tucker," he ended.

"I'm sorry," she said. Something about him touched her deeply. All at once she knew the reason for a thing about him which had puzzled her. An extraordinary, almost motherly sensation of pity for him came over her. She felt suddenly as if she were face to face with a solitariness of soul such as she had not conceived of before.

She felt the necessity of changing the subject from this unspoken thing between them.

"We were talking about Congress," she said.

"And you said Algeria was my real enemy. But why should she feel bitterly toward me?"

"I don't think she does. Her enmity toward you is a perfectly impersonal thing—that's why she could be so deadly. You're an obstacle to be removed. She will remove it if she can with perfect cold-bloodedness."

He nodded, his mind rapidly accepting and sorting out this new array of facts she had given him. He realized that Julia had perfectly expressed to him something he had only imperfectly expressed to himself. Many things suddenly were explained.

So Algeria was his real adversary? Dave found himself suddenly admiring the woman and her consummate skill and daring. He traced back the happenings of the past. Why—now he could see it. She had done something, evidently quite deliberately, which he had not thought possible—sundered him from Tucker Wedge. And in a way from which there was no recourse.

Furthermore she had maneuvered their battle until it was on her chosen grounds. A man cannot fight a woman with a woman's weapons. Dave could not afford even to admit that Algeria was his adversary.

He laughed suddenly, without mirth.

"So you think I ought to announce, Julia?"

"I do."

"I think," he said slowly, "I shall do so."

4.

The sun was near the horizon when they reached the cemetery's dark cedars. Small red clouds floated in the western sky, and the far plains grew mysteriously dim and blue like a remote sea. About them leagues on leagues of flatness seemed to be losing their pale yellow-green as the violet evening shadow stretched its fingers across.

Within the cemetery Dave stopped the car, and stepped out of it, carrying the cardboard box.

"I'll be gone only a few minutes," he told her.

"Couldn't I—go along?" she asked.

It was pure impulse on her part. Without answering he opened the car door for her.

A few yards away an iron paling surrounded a small plot. Dave held the box under his arm to unlock the padlocked gate.

"I had a little stone put out here," he said, almost apologetically. "This is my first chance to see it."

The grave of the little girl . . . Edie.

A subtle change came over him as they entered the enclosure. He seemed to have lost consciousness, almost, of Julia.

She saw the headstone beside the small grassy mound; it was of a design so odd that it struck her—an open book on a pedestal, sculptured of very white marble. So real was it that it seemed she might almost turn the pages.

"She loved books," said Dave.

An ache came into Julia's throat as she read the inscription chiseled on the marble book's open pages. Edith Meader, it said, and gave the date. Then:

> *Goodnight, dear heart. The*
> *sweetest dreams be thine.*

The man stood, bowed over the grave.

His gaunt figure shortened itself suddenly to its knees with a strange awkward humility. The cardboard box was on the earth beside him and he began to open it, his big fingers fumbling with the cord as he worked with the knots.

The lump grew in Julia's throat until she thought it would choke her. She watched him take the lid from the box. There were flowers in it—cut flowers. Carnations and marigolds.

In the west, from the sun which now lay below the rim of the earth, a single red spear of light thrust upward toward the first of the glimmering evening stars. . . .

5.

All the way back through the purpling evening, Julia was silent. She had looked into the secret corner of a man's heart, and her own heart was flooded with pity at what she had seen.

She wished she could say something—anything—to soothe his unhealed hurt. Once she opened her lips, but closed them again. Something stronger than her inclination, an imperious shyness, held her silent.

As the twilight faded, he switched on the lights. The car, whirling down the road, picked out with its questing glare the dark-green walls of hedgerows on either side, the weed-grown ditches, and, once, an early night rabbit, which, dazzled by the sudden illumination, ran frantically ahead until almost overtaken, then summoned a last-moment gathering of its wits, and leaped, limp as a rag, out of the way.

Now they were in town. The car came to a stop. Ugly walls, spotted with window-squares of light. Smell of onions and kitchen grease. The girl faintly shuddered.

"Home," she said. "Humans have to have a cave of some sort to live in."

"Thank you for going with me, Julia."

"It was good—the ride and the talk——"

"I'll see you in."

"That's not necessary——"

He was out, opening her door. Consenting by her movements, she began gathering up the little things a woman always carries. He took her arm as she stepped out and for a moment she leaned against him. He caught his breath. She glanced up. Perhaps it was the street lamp, but his face in that moment looked ashen.

Her room was on the second floor. She handed him her key.

Now that the final moment of parting had come, he discovered in himself a great reluctance to go.

For a moment they both stood silent.

"Thank you," she said at last.

"Good night."

He turned slowly, as if it required of him a supreme effort of will power. Her pale hair shone softly in the hall light. She still remained in the open door and he moved suddenly toward her again.

"Julia . . ."

She came like a fragile flower, blown on a gust of wind.

Her lips brushed his cheek.

All at once his arms were about her. Her body, light, and soft, and breathlessly vibrant, was close against him. Her cheek was under his lips and her fragrance in his nostrils.

For half an instant she still turned her face away. Then she surrendered. Her lips opened to his kiss, wet and sweet, hot as fire. In his ears was a great rushing, as of a wind. He knew nothing but the starved anguish of his arms, and the balm of her body within them. . . .

Sanity returned. They stood back from each other, breathless.

In her eyes was a new look. Unnamed protest, unnamed hopelessness, unnamed question. Soft urgent fury, demand, fear.

He realized they were standing in an outer hall. Anyone might have seen them.

"I—forgive me—" His voice shook. He turned to the wall and drew a trembling hand across his eyes.

He heard beside him her soft whisper.

"I did it. It was all me. You must not blame yourself."

Hardly understanding, he looked at her. She stood close to him, small yet somehow protective.

"I knew this must happen—some time," she said.

It was as if she recited some great obvious fact, without even thinking.

"Julia—" he whispered.

He took one long awkward step nearer her.

"I love you. And it's no good, Julia. But I love you."

She murmured something in a voice so small he could not hear.

They kissed once more; then stood a moment, simply staring at one another.

None of the ecstasy or jubilation of a suddenly discovered love was in their look.

Only misery. Profound, aching misery.

CHAPTER II

1.

HE had his supper alone downtown, hardly knowing what he ate. Afterward he returned to his office and tried to work.

It was past midnight before he went home. He let himself into the house with his latchkey and switched on the lights. Mrs. Dunham and Belle long ago had retired; they did not even hear him come in. His comings and goings had ceased to interest them. They were asleep now. The two canaries in the dining-room were asleep in their hooded cages. Mrs. Dunham's cat, a yellow heap of fur, was asleep in Dave's old chair. The goldfish were asleep, or as near it as fish ever come.

Not a thing in this house savored of Dave. The women and their interests permeated it. Suddenly it nauseated him, and he switched off the light.

He felt his way up the stairs to his room and there he lay awake in his bed for hours.

Something Julia had said kept coming back to him: *I knew this must happen—some time. . . .*

What did those words mean?

They twisted through his consciousness until at last the thinking dulled his mind and he slept fitfully.

Shortly before dawn he heard a rustling sound, long sustained. At first he thought, as he half-awakened and lay with the torpor of weariness still upon him, that his tired mind was imagining it. But the rustling sound grew heavier and prolonged. It spread out like a veil of soft whispering, overlaying all other of earth's noises, large or small. At last it aroused him enough so that he rose and went to the window. Gray light was coming into the sky. It was raining heavily. This was not the swift dashing rain of the plains, which comes with drama and excitement, but a slow, all-pervading, cold weeping from leaden skies, without wind or lightning. It fitted profoundly the depression of his spirits.

No use to go back to bed. Sleep was out of the question. Dave dressed and went downstairs. The women still snored in their rooms. Silently he made a breakfast of toast and coffee by the stove, and as silently departed for his office.

Nobody, at this ungodly hour, was in the courthouse. His office was close; still reeking with the stale tobacco smoke he had left from long puffing at his pipe during the hours of the night before when he tried to solve the turmoil in him.

He threw open the windows to the rain. A rich, damp smell came in, as if the air held in its arms a new vitality from the life-drinking soil. Ordinarily that smell gave him joy, but now he was incapable of any kind of joy.

Julia loved him.

It was momentous; almost incalculably amazing. Yet she had made him believe.

He still could not understand how it happened.

Of one thing he now was determined. Never again could he dare risk another situation such as that of the evening before. He had to steel himself to seeing her as little as possible in the future. And he must not think about her.

Having come to this decision he discovered how very difficult it is to put a woman out of mind. Wherever his thought went, it came about inevitably in a circle to Julia.

One topic alone that he had discussed with her was safe and good: politics. He bent his mind on this; and through it, succeeded at last in channeling his thinking into a less dangerous course.

He remembered her words concerning Algeria; and with the recollection came almost a triumphant thought. For months his feelings toward Tucker had been bitterly confused. There had been times when the injustice of the treatment he had received rankled deeply until he was filled almost with hate. But at other times it was very hard to school himself into looking upon Tucker as an enemy; the long years of friendship had struck their roots deep.

But now that he knew Algeria's role, Dave's viewpoint was unexpectedly simplified. Why—Tucker was no more than a uxorious man. Many men were dotingly fond of, and submissive to, their wives—but it was a weakness Dave did not respect. He found that the thought freed him suddenly of the lingering last loyalty which hampered him. Contempt did what anger could not do.

His fight was clear for him at last. In the summer months he had discovered in himself a great new resource. Many people were interested in him, working for him, talking about him. It had come upon him almost without his realization. Only secondarily had ambition brought this about. His first speech—the one to the Bedestown Farmers' Co-op—was an expression of his beliefs, delivered boldly, without any reason beyond his conviction of the necessity of uttering the truth as he conceived it.

But the speech had sent its ripples into the farthest corners of the Congressional district. Other farmers came. Sometimes townsmen. Many more invitations to speak were received than he could fill. But when he did speak he poured out the same doctrine he had given at Bedestown.

The Regular Republicans became interested in him. Hecklers were planted in one or two of his meetings. But his long years as a prosecutor in the rapid give-and-take of courtroom battle stood him in excellent stead. It took a ready-witted interrupter, indeed, to hold his own with Dave Constable in an impromptu argument.

Dave knew that the reports of his speeches and of the growing interest in him had gone to Porter Grimes. And to Tucker Wedge. And . . . to Algeria.

His own ambition was aroused now. He was spokesman for the Insurgents. Without his encouragement, Webb Pettis and the farmers had been for two weeks circulating the petitions for him. They waited his answer, and he was ready to commit himself to the career of politics they asked of him. Julia had convinced him.

Dave heard his staff beginning to come in. The courthouse was coming to life; the day's work about to begin.

He decided to make a formal statement of candidacy at once. Mentally he began to draft his letter to the committee, preparatory to dictating it to Cully. He would, once again, underscore his fundamental battle line: the people against property; the horny-handed men against the smooth-handed men.

In the midst of this his telephone rang. At the voice he heard when he lifted the receiver his face lit up; then grew grave.

"What? It *can't* be!" he cried. Then: "When did it happen? Thank you."

He hung up the receiver slowly.

It was Julia. She had just told him that Judge Hutto was dead that rainy morning.

2.

There really was no surprise in it. Judge Hutto was in his eighty-first year. He went to sleep in his bed and simply did not awake.

For months life had burned dimly in him. His blue eyes lost their vivid brightness, fading as if a film had been drawn across them. Each day his skin grew more translucent, until it seemed that, with a little effort, one could almost see through his frail body. In his infrequent appearances on the street he appeared to depend less on his two withered legs, whereon his trousers all at once appeared overlarge for him, than on the stick he used to support his bent frame.

To Dave, however, the most alarming symptom had been the judge's growing acceptance of his own coming end. Dave one day encountered him moving feebly along, and paused to converse.

"You're looking fine, Judge," he said. The conventional lie.

Judge Hutto gave a wintry smile. "No! Not from *you,* David. From you I expect nothing but the unvarnished truth."

"I do think you appear a little stronger——"

"You think nothing of the sort. I am fully aware—and fully reconciled." The judge paused, and chuckled mirthlessly. "Not that I welcome the inevitable."

"Judge——"

"Let me talk, Dave. The profound underlying pessimism of the old is something you must be old to imagine. When you are young you have the strength to hope. But quite aside from the jolly fact that as soon as you are born you are in a quagmire you never get out of until you die, age brings you to the edge of the fathomless abyss yawning to receive you into its blackness. Even mire seems at times preferable to dark. But you know you are at the end of your trail."

"I never heard you in this vein before," said Dave, perplexed.

The old man patted Dave's arm.

"You needn't fear that I'm going to make you a repository of my feelings about the silly tragedy of human existence. After all, life may be pretty grim for each of us—in the farthest chambers of his heart—yet it is pretty worth while for all of us. The good of existence is tangible enough. I shall continue yet a little while to read, exchange thoughts with my friends, watch the mental and emotional antics of my fellowmen, see the beauty of leaf and cloud, marvel at the friendly stars on clear nights, and thank the God who made and loves it all. No, I am not unhappy. I see much, that is all. Perhaps I am really much happier than the ruck of unthinking fools who optimize all over this dumb, protesting land of ours."

He passed on, moving slowly, with a flash of his rare brave smile.

And now he lay dead.

Dave got his hat. He spoke to Cully:

"Judge Hutto passed away this morning. I'm going to the house."

3.

The downpour had ceased, but the sky still hung low and gray, with a promise of more rain.

Two or three automobiles already were parked on the wet pavement before the Hutto house. Dave approached the door.

Dark wreath, tied with thick black crepe, above the polished brass knob.

The door opened. It was Julia. Of course—she was taking over the duties of the household for Mrs. Hutto.

Julia smiled wanly in the hall. Decorous, prim smile; set in a china face. Stiff, withdrawn body in black.

"They are in the sitting-room." The formal voice with which one speaks to a stranger.

"Thank you," he replied.

She took his hat.

Several persons were in the sitting-room. He observed that Jasper Peddigrew and his wife had come to pay their respects. Peddigrew was a candidate to succeed Dave as county attorney, an office he had held years before. His pig eyes took in Dave with cold hostility and his nondescript mustache worked.

Mrs. Widcomb, the minister's wife, was present to support the widow, although the preacher himself, who had been there all morning, had gone. The rest were neighbors whom Dave scarcely knew.

In a wide-bottomed rocking chair sat Mrs. Hutto, wearing her black bombazine dress. She took Dave's hand in her soft pudgy palm, very seemly and proper, showing no signs of weeping.

"Mrs. Hutto—he was like a father—to all of us——"

This was the very kind of banality he had wished to avoid. To say something which does not sound inconsequential against the all-pervading majesty of death is well-nigh impossible.

"I know, David," the old woman said calmly. She clutched his hand. "Don't worry about me. I have lived a long time and I have learned one thing: to accept life."

Feeling uncomfortably out of place, he sat on the sofa. Talk seemed foolish; yet they made some feeble efforts, mentioning drearily the rain and such harmless topics. Other visitors came in. With a slight surprise, Dave heard Mrs. Hutto, over and over, repeat the same thing she had said to him. I have lived a long time. I have learned to accept life.

He waited a decent interval and prepared to leave. This time the tears did come to her eyes as she took his hand again.

"He was so good . . . to me. . . ." she whispered.

That was from her heart. For a moment the real anguish, the real loneliness, broke through. With a welling gush of sympathy, he gripped her hand.

She regained herself.

"Julia wants to say something to you when you go out," she said.

Julia's word was a natural request.

"Mrs. Hutto wants you to be one of the pallbearers."

"It is an honor."

Again she gave him the stiff smile.

He thought: trivial politenesses. We stand here talking them, and all the time your face is hinting many strange things to me. What is your opinion of me today—now that you have thought over last night? Did you sleep no more than I did? You look wonderful in black. A jeweler uses black velvet to set off a matchless stone. My dear, my dear —you should wear black—you should always wear the black of night, to set off that lovely head. . . .

He was at the door. She gave him the stiff little grip of her fingers, and released his hand quickly.

4.

On Saturday, two days after the judge's death, the church was filled with the faint, sickly scent of many flowers, and there was no sound but the whisper of ushers in the rear, and the funereal rustling of dresses as women moved in the pews.

The courthouse was closed. The Jericho Bar Association attended in a body. Dave sat with the pallbearers. He saw Mrs. Hutto, her unwieldy old body bent forward, and beside her Julia's bright head in a small black hat. The girl had been with the old lady continuously since the judge's death.

Mrs. Hutto bore up well. At the commitment she stood sturdily beside the grave, her only emotion shown by the way she clutched Julia's hand. Her head was bowed, her gray hair stirred in the breeze beneath her black bonnet, but she did not weep.

". . . *Earth to earth, ashes to ashes, dust to dust; in sure and certain hope of resurrection unto eternal life . . .*"

It was over at last.

The crowd began leaving the cemetery, entering automobiles, driving off briskly on new interests, new pursuits.

Dave glanced over the iron palings around Edie's grave.

Fresh flowers . . . why, someone had put a shower of bright blooms . . . calendulas . . . by the white sculptured book.

5.

In the evening he told himself that he was going to the Hutto house to learn if he could perform any further services. But though he tried to deceive himself with this reasoning, shame and guilt clawed at him as he approached the door.

In the trees, late September insects creaked. The clouds which had overhung the sky for two days were gone and the stars burned brightly. As yet the moon had not risen.

Tentatively, he pressed the bell.

There was a light in the house, but at first no one responded. He decided to go, and turned away with a strange mixed feeling of disappointment and relief. Then he heard a step and the door opened. She stood there, so close, looking at him.

"Why . . . David . . ."

"Julia, I came up—to see—" he began awkwardly.

"Mrs. Hutto is not at home. She's spending the night with Mrs. Wartle."

"Oh."

He lingered miserably on the threshold, gazing down at the hat he held before him in his two hands. She did not speak.

"I see," he said at last. "Well——"

He bowed his head and started to turn away.

"David!" Her voice broke with pain and terror at his going.

He went to her, moved by some power entirely outside himself. He groped for her hands blindly and drew her to him.

"David!" she said in a helpless whisper. "Not *here* . . ."

"Where then?"

"Oh, I don't know. Somewhere else. Not in this house. Take me away. Take me away only a little while. . . ."

"My car," he said urgently.

She hesitated achingly. Her mind said no, but her body assented. She bowed her head.

6.

In the profound prairie night, David Constable halted the car far out, where a low mesa stood above a wide shallow valley.

He switched off the lights. Darkness suddenly possessed them; made them a part of itself. The sky was deep sapphire blue, with a diamond dust of stars flourishing all the way across it. Infinite distances away, whole worlds beyond, a faint sound arrowed through the air. A lonely coyote, yapping thinly.

Since their hurried, unconsidered flight from town, neither of them had uttered a word. Now they sat, still chained in a silence that built and grew, until it became almost unbearable.

He turned toward her desperately.

"Julia," he whispered. "Oh, Julia—Julia——"

She came to him, into his arms. His lips felt the firm smoothness of her cheek.

"Why is it . . . this hunger, this pain?"

She pressed closer to him, but still she did not speak.

"I want you, darling," he said. "And I can never have you . . . never. . . ."

His voice trailed away, infinitely sad.

Suddenly her face was wet with tears. In his arms her slim body tensed and twisted. Her lips joined his with unrestrained, fierce passion.

All in an instant she was transmuted from softest velvet to white fire. To his hunger leaped her hunger.

7.

Long after, they were able at last to talk.

She sat as far as she could from him in the car and her voice was little and rigid.

"It happened. We weren't strong enough. Maybe now—that it's too late—we can recognize it and face it—and deal with it——"

He was still the male, the selfish procreating animal.

"Why?" he asked. "Why—since it's already happened—must it be dealt with in any way—except the way we want?"

"It's utterly wrong. You know that. And so do I."

He began to recover judgment. But still he fought against admitting this inevitable thing.

"Julia, I do love you. And now I know that I never have loved anyone else."

She said: "I suppose—coming immediately after what's happened —this is a great compliment."

"Don't talk that way, darling. I know how you're feeling. But things like this have happened to people before—and turned out all right. Haven't they?"

She spoke slowly, as one infinitely his superior in the wisdom of life: "I never knew anything like this to turn out right yet."

Still he would not give in.

"Julia—" he began. In agony he reached for something, anything. "If it did happen—don't you see—we both wanted it—we were ready for it. I won't let it end now. I'll never let you go. Not after this——"

In the dimness, compassion seemed to come on her face.

"I've made you miserable, David—and I would have made you only happy."

He tried to understand, but could not.

Then all at once he did understand.

She was a woman and mortified utterly. Because she had given herself, and felt she had given herself cheaply . . .

Her voice came, harder than before with the universal savage self-hate of woman who has given her body . . . and who for the first time overwhelmingly realizes what she has done.

"I acted like a strumpet. Why don't you ask me . . . why?"

"Because I *know*. You are generous. You did it because it is in you to give boundlessly. Julia—you humble me——"

It comforted her. Her voice lost its rigidity.

"Thank you. I hope—something of that—is true. But it wasn't the only reason."

"Why, then?"

"I couldn't help it. I have been in love with you too long."

He tried to understand. "In love with me . . . long?"

"Ten years."

The calm voice made him mute with amazement. She went on:

"Do you remember that afternoon at the tree, long ago? It goes back to that."

He put his arms about her. She cuddled to him now, small and almost childish. Her voice continued, almost dreamily:

"I was a strange child, a difficult child. I watched you, so sure, so humorous, so kind, and invested you with many-colored imaginings."

"I did not deserve it," he said, deeply moved.

"I never dared meet you, because we were poor and I was so wretchedly shabby. I've gone around the block many a time to avoid having you see the patches on my dress. You'll never know how I had to steel my resolution to come to you that day when Gotch McCurdy had father down at the livery barn . . ."

He drew his arm closer about her.

"I told you that because I want you to believe that you were the center of my life—even when we went away."

"But as you grew older—there must have been other men. You are beautiful."

"I won't deny that men have been interested in me. I tried to be interested in them. But they could mean nothing to me; even when they begged me to marry them."

He sat silent. Very simply, she went on:

"Most girls dream and talk about love. But I had no one with whom to share my confidence. I knew it was foolish, hopeless. As I grew older, I realized that childish infatuations usually disappear when the object of them is seen with the new altered vision of more mature viewpoints. So when I came back to Jericho, I almost trembled at the thought of meeting you again. And—incredible as it may be—you were . . . the same."

Her face turned up to him in the darkness.

"How could I keep from rushing to my fate—after those ten years?"

He kissed her wordlessly.

Very late they drove back to town. At parting they said almost nothing.

For hours he lay sleepless in the long, long silence in his room.

CHAPTER III

1.

CHURCH bells.

Julia woke to them Sunday morning. She lay listening. At times she found a rich joy in attending divine service—the orderly peace, the music, the decorous spirit appealed to her, rested her. The woman in her liked the sensation of security, and settled ways of life, and consent of long established custom.

But this morning the church bells brought something else. She remembered suddenly the night before. . . .

She had thought things were straightened out somewhat in her mind when she went to bed. There had been comfort in the power of David's arms, and the long talk with him . . . after.

Even as she had closed the door, after her goodnight to him, and turned toward her bed, her soul became the battle ground of great conflict. She had walked across to her mirror and stood looking at herself for a long time.

Every cheap story she had ever heard or read about girls who involved themselves with married men went whirling through her mind. Kay Middlekauf. . . . Why, she thought with a gasp, I'm no better than poor Kay. . . .

All at once she knew that she had always felt toward Kay Middlekauf a slightly patronizing superiority, as if it were due to her better judgment and more fastidious tastes that she had escaped the temptations which had trapped Kay.

After this, she had looked back into the mirror.

"The long and eminent line of Normans," she said aloud, softly. "Well, my instincts didn't pay much attention to the long line of Normans. Oh, Kay dear, how could I have been such a snob?"

Suddenly weak, she sat on her bed.

What does he think? What *can* he think?

He assured me . . . and I believed him. But after all he is a man—a vital, attractive man. How can I assume other women have not felt toward him as I felt? Perhaps this was only one of many casual episodes. God knows it must have been . . . ridiculously easy for him. Maybe—good God—maybe it was too easy to be interesting. . . .

Blank-faced, she stared at the wall.

Cheap . . . easy to get . . . push over. The words she had heard. The ultimate words of degradation for a woman. Whiplash words in her mind.

Panic came and grew, a torment.

How can I ever face him again? It seemed somehow noble . . . at the time. But now. Now I have lost value; in my own mind and in his. I cannot help having lost value. Women have to be so careful. . . . I have known it all along. The old sayings—they were based on wisdom hard won by us women through the ages. And I've heard it again and again—a man always has contempt for any girl he can take . . . easily . . . in that manner.

But at this low point her reason came to her rescue.

Look at yourself, Julia, and say if it wasn't beautiful . . . and wonderful. . . .

It's immature and childish to bring to bear now values I've long ago outgrown. I *cannot* have misjudged him. I can judge men—and David Constable has honor great and perfect. It was no mere light moment for him—any more than it was for me. And to me it was . . . as if that were what I'd been born for—the reason all along why I'd been put into the world.

So at last she had slept.

And now in the morning, lying in bed and listening to the church bells, her assurance was gone again.

The rationalizing of the night before had faded. A sense of guilt possessed her with renewed force. She wondered if her face would tell the world what had happened. The books said that sin always leaves its mark. . . .

That brought her bolt upright out of bed, staring into the mirror.

No. There was nothing different. The same clear-cut familiar face. Sleep, and her yellow hair hanging in two plaits down her shoulders, made her seem younger. If anything, she appeared more innocent. . . .

Wide awake now, Julia smiled at herself. How ridiculous for a grown woman to think and act this way!

She began to unbraid her hair, preparatory to arranging it.

2.

The scratching of the pen was the only sound in the room. David Constable bent his head over his work in careful concentration.

Always he felt shackled when seeking to express his thoughts in writing; it was not his natural medium. But he strove with a lawyer's precision to make his meaning clear, whether or not his phrasing was graceful.

He had spent the night wakefully. Dave was not confronted by the same questions with which Julia had wrestled. To him the experience of sex was not radical and new and terrifying; nor was he much concerned by the abstract moralities.

Although he had led a continent life, his acquaintance with the world was such that he was not oppressed greatly by a conviction of sin. If anything the tumultuous occurrence of the previous night endowed him with a flush of leaping ecstasy when he thought of it—the natural pride and triumph of a successful and enamored lover.

But there were questions of his own to consider.

He ceased writing to light his pipe, taking slow puffs as he sucked the flame from the curling matchstick into the tobacco, until the coal was well lighted, then blowing out a smooth white cloud of rich smoke. As he laid the burnt match in his ashtray, Julia's face was before him, the play of expression on it, as she laughed, as she wept, as she thought. There were many Julias; two in particular. One was the Julia of the fine, clear mind, the Julia who had won the respect of Judge Hutto for her balanced intelligence and her ability in pure abstract reasoning. The other was the Julia who thought not at all, who felt rather, who lived in emotion and surrendered to the imperious demands of her body. These two Julias made a complex and delightful combination; a combination which enthralled him.

He said to himself: What is my status toward her?

It was the fiftieth time he had asked himself the question, but he went through it once more, with careful, legal analysis.

She is young, he said. And I am more—much more—mature and experienced. Is it that she trusted herself blindly to me—and was betrayed by me?

He considered this, and unconsciously shook his head.

I suppose that, in the common way of thinking, I stand guilty of having wronged her. But she did not act to me as one wronged. She met me—with fire and eagerness. If I seduced her, she helped me with her own seduction. That is it. Hers was not the role of a helpless, victimized girl. Hers was a warm partnership; a withholding of nothing.

Julia was a revelation to him. Women are wonderful lovers in direct proportion to their imaginations. And Julia's imagination was exquisite and rich. The thought of her still dizzied him.

Dave was not worried by doubts as to how the girl thought of him, whether or not she respected him or held him in contempt. His was the male view. She had yielded herself. That was the ultimate proof that she loved; the one most final and complete token of regard, the greatest gift it is in the power of a woman to give a man. She loved him, and he returned her love so strongly that the thought of it shook him.

Out of this grew the complications.

Dave knew that suddenly he had assumed an obligation toward Julia. He did not yet exactly know what the outcome of this would be. He wanted her. But he was as yet not far enough along in his thinking to understand how he could approach this part of the problem.

Certainly it would not be on the basis of a sordid back-street love affair. That could be defilement of her. Julia would reject it; but he rejected it before she did.

He wanted to marry Julia; to have her for his wife.

But he was already married. What about Belle? Divorce?

This he had given careful study, and he knew that for the present he would not be able to advance evidence in court to prove grounds if Belle opposed it—and she certainly would oppose it. She cared nothing for his love. But she had told him once he was bound to keep her the rest of her life, and she was going to make him do it. This was a heavy problem; he put it aside for future thinking.

Meantime he had come to a great decision—one he arrived at with a wrench. He was giving up ambition.

Of a sudden he had discovered that his affairs were inextricably entangled. Julia was one thing to him—and all the other things which had been important to him were set over against her. Under the present state of his relationship to her he was sure he could not go into a political campaign.

Lately, as his organization had grown and evidences of his hold on the people had mounted, the victory in the congressional contest had become the most important interest in his life. There was the desire to prove to the spiteful *Clarion,* to Algeria Wedge, to Tucker, to the scheming Porter Grimes, how little they could affect him with all their underhanded tactics. He wished to justify the faith in him of Webb Pettis, and of men like Andy McAdam, Timberline Wilson, Will Pipkin—countless little men, to whom he was a hope and an idol.

But now he must choose between politics and Julia. A candidate for public office undergoes a microscopic examination of his private life; and particularly so in Kansas.

He would not be able to see Julia any more—if he ran for office. And at this minute it was more important to see Julia than anything else. For years he had lived a life without happiness, trying to make politics fill the place of happiness. Now he had found a splendid, shimmering promise of happiness, to which he turned blindly and hungrily.

So he made his decision—against Congress, against Webb Pettis and his countless other friends, against even the cause he stood for.

Perhaps he was making a mistake. If so, he would have to abide by the results.

This that he was at present writing, was a letter to Webb Pettis and the Farmers' Co-operative Associations, formally notifying them that in spite of the petitions, he would not be a candidate.

3.

Algeria was sitting in the library when she heard Tucker come in. She glanced up, and again noticed how bald he was growing.

"I've got news," he said, rather portentously. Much too portentously to her thinking.

Tucker had latterly begun to consider himself somewhat of an oracle. Usually it secretly amused Algeria, who knew much more than did he about the steps of his progression. But on this day it jarred on her.

"Really?" she said. Her tone and attitude indicated that she had more important concerns than his news—whatever it was.

His portentousness disappeared.

"It's politics." He gazed at her almost pleadingly. Algeria's approval was becoming increasingly important to Tucker.

"Well?" She permitted a small flicker of interest.

"Dave Constable's not going to run."

"How do you know?" She sat up, eyes widening.

"He notified the Farmers' Co-operatives."

"What did he say? Did he give any reasons?"

"We're carrying the whole story this evening." He was able now to enjoy a glow of satisfaction. The news *had* brought Algeria out of herself. All pretense of indifference was gone. "Here's a copy of the letter," he added.

She took it, her gray eyes scanning rapidly.

Desiring to clarify ... Congressional situation ... notify all proper persons I will not be a candidate ... sensible of the honor ... personal considerations ... impossible to devote the time and energy ... wish to thank my many friends for their loyalty and support ... all good wishes.   DAVID CONSTABLE.

She glanced up. "It was sporting of him to get out formally. He could have kept you on tenterhooks."

"I suppose so."

"I wonder why he did it?"

"That's not so very important, is it?"

A shadow of impatience came into her eyes. "Of course it's important! I suppose we're not children. Anything like this *must* have a reason."

"Well, he mentioned personal considerations. Business——"

"Nonsense! I suppose you realize, my pet, that this elects you?"

"Oh, I rather think I'd have been elected—in any case——"

"Let's not be stupid!" She withered him. "If you don't know it, I do —David Constable has the farmers believing in him. Let's face it, Tucker. He might have beaten you, organization or no organization. He must have known it. Yet he withdrew...."

"Perhaps his record as county attorney——"

"Is there really anything in that? Between ourselves, we don't have very much on him, do we?"

"Well ... no ..."

Keenly the woman pursued her line of reasoning. "It's something we don't know about. Is he afraid? For himself—for somebody else?"

He stared: but she kindled, suddenly elated.

"Do you suppose—" She hesitated, then rushed on. "Could it be possible that Dave Constable's—involved—with a *woman?*"

"Not Dave!" he objected rather stupidly. "He's never been interested in women——"

"Show me a man who's not interested in women! He's normal, isn't he? The mere biology of it—male and the pursuit of the female. If I know Dave Constable, there's nothing lacking in him!"

"But he's married——"

"And they're not even speaking—haven't been for months. No!" She was sparkling now. "It *must* be a woman ... if I could only discover ..."

Unaccountably her face fell. She had a weapon—if she discovered the key—but she could not use it.

She had been disarmed when David Constable withdrew from the campaign.

Yet her mind raced, going over the names of all the possible women in Jericho.

She came to one. Passed it. Returned to it. Considered it.

Julia Norman. H'mm.

Julia Norman. They were friends all right. She'd been on a program with him ... somewhere. Oh, yes. Bedestown.

And Julia Norman never took any interest in the young men Algeria brought to her.

Julia Norman had *other* interests. How amazingly sly!

The zest of the huntress was in Algeria's fine eyes.

Let's see. Julia Norman lives in the Westwood Flats. Who do I know that lives there?

Mrs. Dierks! The very person. She's sewed for me—why, I believe she told me I was her best customer.

On Algeria's agenda went a notation to get hold of Mrs. Dierks the sewing woman, first thing next day.

4.

He did not telephone Julia on Sunday, because, for some reason, he shrank from it. He did not know what kind of knots her emotions were tied up in.

He felt perhaps she would prefer being left alone.

Or perhaps a certain embarrassment held him.

When Monday came, he knew all day that the *Clarion* would that afternoon publish with a whoop of triumph the fact of his withdrawal from the congressional race. It was the sort of a thing that made him brace himself, mentally. He knew that when the announcement became generally known many people would be hurt and disappointed and angry. He toiled furiously all day Monday, catching up on an accumulation of work in his office, and trying to keep his mind off the afternoon newspaper story he knew was coming—and off what was sure to take place afterward.

He did not call Julia on Monday.

Tuesday was the day when, as he expressed it to himself, "all hell let loose." From early morning until late at night they were at him.

Webb Pettis must have started for Jericho from his farm as soon as it was light enough to drive. He was waiting at the office when Dave arrived.

It was not a good time for Dave. Webb did not understand. He had worked mighty hard on this, he told Dave, and he thought they could win the election. He was unbelieving at first when Dave would not change his decision, and finally he believed and grew short with his words, and got up and went away, leaving Dave feeling like a traitor.

After that the telephone rang insistently most of the time; and what time the telephone was not ringing, there were people in the outer office waiting to be seen. And all of the words said to Dave over the wire or directly, face to face, were about his withdrawing from the campaign.

So he did not have time to telephone Julia on Tuesday.

And here it was Wednesday. He had not seen Julia or heard from her since Saturday night. Four nights. And three days. This was the fourth day. In all that time he had made not one effort to reach her.

His conscience assailed him for this. He knew he should call her the first thing that morning, but he put it off. It was not that he did not want to talk to her. It was that he had a sneaking, inward fear that she would be angry with him, and hurt with him. Certainly she had every reason for being.

People—so many people—had been angry with him and hurt with him for the last forty-eight hours that his mind felt raw; as if the con-

tinuing abrasion caused by their irritation had worn away the covering
of his brain to the smarting, leaping nerve-cases themselves. It needed
one thing only to complete his torment: and that would be to have
Julia hold him . . . typically femininely . . . to account for his neglect
of her.

But all the time, he knew that somehow he must talk to her. At least
a dozen times he had the impulse to telephone her. Twice he actually
lifted the receiver. But both times he placed it back on the hook.

He had discovered in himself a surprising, abnormal sensitiveness.
Of a sudden he began to be apprehensive that she hated him . . . for
what he had done, for what he stood for.

So he did not call Julia all day Wednesday.

And then, just before closing time, Julia walked into his office.

She stopped at his door, and said "Hello," with a smile as casual as
if nothing had ever happened between them. She looked wonderful
in a long, tight dress of dark blue wool, and a wide black velvet hat
which turned upward from her face and made her skin seem fresher
and her eyes clearer than ever before.

Dave got up behind his desk.

"Julia—" he said. "I—I've been trying to get to the telephone all
day——"

She smiled again. "I knew you were busy. So I came up."

Not one word of chiding. So she was not angry.

She dropped into a chair and an intense relief flooded him. She
should have been furious with him and she was not. It was a kind of
generosity in which he felt she was almost unique.

"You are beautiful . . . and gallant . . ."

Her eyes fell slightly, then returned to his.

"I'm glad you think so—still. I had—wondered."

"About what?"

"A woman always wonders what a man will think of her."

"You've been reading books. Moralistic novels."

"No."

"You mean a woman actually gets that kind of a notion without
someone's putting it into her head?"

"It's not a notion. It's true."

"Why should a man be anything but more—more——"

"It depends on the man, I guess."

"Not on the woman?"

"Perhaps on the woman, too."

That was settled. They smiled into each other's eyes and he wanted
very much to come around the desk and gather her into his arms. But
he sat still. No telling what moment Cully might come blundering
into his office.

Cully did come in. But he tapped first, which he never did ordinarily. It gave Dave a curious disquieting feeling. Did Cully suspect something about them?

"Anything else, sir?" asked Cully when he entered. He fiddled with papers on the desk and turned his long horse face toward Julia. He could not keep his eyes off her.

"Quitting time?" asked Dave. "No, nothing more. Good night, Cully."

"Good night, sir."

Cully withdrew, almost unwillingly.

After he closed the door, Julia said: "I've been reading the papers."

Dave smiled, a trifle grimly. "CONSTABLE QUITS UNDER FIRE. That was how it ran, wasn't it? Good old Tucker—he never overlooks a chance."

She nodded. "That was what I meant."

"It seemed to surprise a few people."

"It surprised me."

"To tell the truth, Julia, it rather surprised *me*."

"Why did you do it?"

"I couldn't afford to make the race at this time."

"Afford?" For the first time her voice was almost sharp, as if in vexation. "You would have gone to Congress!"

He tried to laugh. "That's your—loyalty. Because you like me, you think everyone else does. You might be surprised to learn how many people dislike me very thoroughly. Actually I don't believe I had a chance to win. I was only running to give the farmers a kind of a voice——"

She did not laugh with him. "David, you can rescind that withdrawal. Please do it."

"I'm afraid it's too late."

"It isn't—I'm sure it isn't."

"Even if it isn't I can't do it."

"Why not—*why?*"

"For the best of personal reasons."

"David—won't you do it—for *me?*"

A coldness came over him. "I cannot do it, Julia."

At the iron in his voice, she caught her breath. Then she rose. "It's closing time. Will you take me home?"

He was surprised. "Would it be wise?"

"Why not? I have some business to discuss with you."

This was a new sort of boldness. She knew that gossip started quickly and almost without reason in Jericho. Yet Julia was so well balanced . . . he decided.

"Very well. My car's out front."

Together they left the courthouse. Something new was in her. Some kind of an unvocal contention. It troubled him as he put her into the car and went around on the other side to enter. As he did so, a red automobile swept by. Dave glanced up. Tucker and Algeria Wedge. Algeria, as usual, was driving. Neither of them seemed to notice him; but he got into his car with almost guilty quickness.

She glanced at him. As they drove down the street, she said:

"I don't think they saw."

"I don't care if they did," he retorted almost roughly.

"It wouldn't matter anyway," she said, with an inflection of calmness so strange that she drew a look from him. She did not explain. Neither of them spoke until they drew up before her apartment. Then he said:

"I understood you wanted to talk."

"Yes."

"But you've said nothing."

"I want you to come up."

Again he was troubled. As he hesitated, she said:

"Believe me, it will not matter."

"Julia, you've said that twice."

"Have I?"

"What do you mean by it?"

"I'll explain. But come on."

He followed her into the building. Across from the stairs in the lower hall he saw a door.

"Kay Middlekauf's old room," she said, seeing his glance. "Mrs. Dierks, a seamstress, lives there now."

They mounted the steps. Within her room she held out her hand for his hat.

The old hunger for her came sweeping back. He reached out to her, laid his big hands on her arms, drew her to him.

But she turned her face. Her cheek was cold and firm to his lips, not yielding.

"No," she whispered.

He released her, chilled by her stiffened body.

"That's—over," she said, her voice still low.

A French clock on the wall ticked slowly for the space in which a man might count fifty. Then he said:

"Julia—you can't mean that?"

Her face and tone were completely matter-of-fact.

"I'm leaving Jericho, David."

He blinked as if she had struck him. After a moment he said:

"Where—are you——"

"To Kansas City. Do you know the firm of Grossett and Strauss, lawyers?"

"Judge Grossett—in the circuit court five years ago?"

"Yes. They made me an offer some time ago. I've just accepted it."

"You mean you're leaving here—to take a minor law job in a firm like that? You can't!"

"I think I should—it's an opportunity."

"Opportunity? It would submerge you all your life! It's just what you *shouldn't* do. Why, Julia—you're getting started in your own practice here. A running start—Judge Hutto passed on not only his law library but his clients to you. I won't let you make such a fool of yourself!"

"I've closed the office here, and made all arrangements."

"When did you close the office?"

"Yesterday."

This was what happened when he neglected communicating with her. He began hunting for arguments against the thing she was contemplating. "Look, Julia. I have another thought. I'm going to open an office as soon as my term is over. I think I can count on being successful. Why don't you go in with me—would that appeal to you? It would be better than Kansas City!"

She shook her shining head.

"It would be just the worst thing in the world—for both of us."

"I can't let you go," he said desperately. "I love you. Doesn't that mean anything?"

Julia said: "You gave up Congress—because of me."

"That's not the reason!"

"David, you do very many things well—but lying isn't one of them."

For a moment he looked at her with something as ugly as terror in his eyes.

"Help me to understand," he said. "Is—this—because I quit the congressional race?"

"Not exactly. That was only a symptom—of something worse. I'm no good for you, David."

He protested sharply, aghast. "No good for me? You're the difference between misery and joy to me. You can't mean this! Why, darling—I'd give up anything in the world for you——"

"Even the people who depended on you?"

"Even that!"

She was silent a moment. Then she said:

"I won't let you give them up. I won't allow you to destroy yourself. You're too important to be wasted——"

"Nothing's important, except you."

"David, it isn't every day that a man comes along with the right thinking, and the courage to back it up—and the ability to be elected to an office where that courage and thinking will be of some benefit to the country. You must not even *think* of yourself—or of me!"

"That's not true!" He was pleading a case—a case of terrible importance. "A man has a right to consider what he loves—before anything else."

"What does a man love?" she asked queerly. "His business? A woman? Himself? A little, selfish man might think no farther than his petty concerns. But not you!"

"Julia," he begged. "I'm just getting things arranged in their proper places. I'm trying to be sensible and sane—to make plans——"

"About—*us*?"

"Yes."

"It's a little late to be sensible and sane—about us."

At her words his face changed. Almost curiously he stared at her. This was a thing he had never anticipated. While he had feared that she was angry with him, it had not once occurred to him that she would leave him—desert him.

It had never been in his remotest thoughts but that she felt toward him as he felt toward her: that there was any problem save the immense one for which he had the responsibility—of working out some means so that they could be together in dignity and honesty.

He was ready to surrender anything for this woman. It was growing manifest that she had not the same feelings toward him.

When at last he spoke, his voice was cold.

"Are you sure you aren't just running away, Julia?"

"From what?"

"From yourself. From a—let us say, an unpleasant situation."

"No!"

"I believed that you loved me," he went on remorselessly.

"Some things are more important than love. If I did what you want me to do now, the time would come when you would hate me, as you would hate yourself."

"That sounds very noble, Julia." He found himself sneering. "But let's face the facts. You're afraid—isn't that it?"

"Afraid? Of what?"

"Of the whole mess—of divorce, of gossip. Love doesn't mean nearly so much to you as keeping your dainty skirts from being smirched. Does it?"

She was stung.

"If I were afraid—just remember that I'm the only one who had anything to lose in this affair. You're protected. You're a man. The world forgives a man. But a woman *never* is forgiven. Remember Wilber Bratten—and Kay Middlekauf." She looked at him as if trying to see into him. Then she added: "But I am not afraid. If I had been I would not have gone this far."

He knew he had wounded her, but he made no effort to soothe the wound. He was hurt too deeply, too terribly himself.

Still with the same coldness, he said: "You had business to go over?"

"Mrs. Hutto's affairs. She wants you to handle them."

On opposite sides of a table, with a heap of documents between them, they began to work.

5.

Algeria Wedge, in her red car, drove past the apartment house.

She had seen Dave and Julia together, though she gave no sign. She said nothing about it to Tucker, even. When they reached the house she dropped him off on some excuse, and made a long rapid detour past Julia's lodgings.

Algeria wanted to satisfy herself about something.

Her purposeful gaze took in Dave's motor car in front of the building.

Now she knew part of what she desired to know.

Without slowing the speed of her automobile, she turned at the next corner and drove rapidly home.

There she went directly to the telephone and called her dressmaker, Mrs. Dierks, who lived in the room below Julia, at the foot of the stairs.

6.

They finished their work, and Dave took his hat to go. It had taken two hours, and there had been nothing but the strictest formality between them.

As he left her, Julia said one thing he was to remember later.

"David, I will never forget, never regret . . ."

But not even in this last moment so much as a parting kiss.

He did not see her when she took the train next day.

Thereafter, for a long time, he had difficulty in understanding that she was really gone.

CHAPTER IV

1

WIND tugged at the window sash, and heaved at the house until the timbers creaked. Dave put two more shovels of coal in his small stove and returned to his desk. It was growing late, and something was brewing outside.

Here in January, almost in the middle of the month, the plains had basked in enchanting Indian summer with soft hazes and pleasant breezes. The ground was not even frozen; and some farmers spoke of midwinter plowing. The morning of this day had been clear and bright, but Dave noticed an odd yellowish purple bordering the northern horizon. By the middle of the day small clouds were scudding down from the north, until at dusk the sky was a vault of lead. Then the wind came up.

Dave returned to his study of the brief. It was a very thick brief, and the title of it said nothing of its importance: *Upshaw* vs. *the State of Kansas.* But in that vast pudding-thick array of dull wordage lay a whole battlefield of the people against the moneyed overlords.

Dave did not know Upshaw, had never seen him. Harrison J. Upshaw did not live in Kansas. He was senior partner of a firm, Upshaw and Cape, warehousers, with grain storage facilities in Kansas, Nebraska, Minnesota, and Illinois. The firm's headquarters were in Chicago, and Harrison J. Upshaw had his residence in a handsome house on Lake Shore Drive. He also had a grown family—the sons were Yale, the daughters, Wellesley—and a senior wardenship in an aristocratic Episcopal pile of Gothic stone. He was a respectable citizen, an admirable man, filled with conscious goodness. He hardly realized that his fortune had been made by mulcting farmers in ragged overalls, who had thin, leather-faced wives, and unkempt children.

A few cents a bushel only was what Harrison J. Upshaw's warehouse took. Even had it occurred to him that those few cents a bushel meant to the farmers the difference between comfort and poverty, he could hardly have been expected to change his storage charges or his other policies.

Harrison J. Upshaw had an Investment to protect. He had Stockholders, whose interests were paramount. He had Trade Ethics, which would have been violated by a cut in rates. He subscribed to the principles of *caveat emptor* and *laissez faire*.

Upshaw, the pleasant, upright, and respectable, had been selected by some important people for an important purpose. The people who had selected him were the heads of various railroads, of the electric utilities, of the natural-gas companies, of water-control companies, of coal mines, of industries, and of investment banks; and the purpose for which he had been selected was to act as a spearhead to break the whole system of "reform" laws which had been swept into the statutes of Kansas on the wave of Populist indignation a decade before.

The smooth-handed men had been very wise and patient. They knew the value of biding their time; and that the horny-handed men, sooner or later, were certain to become divided, or to be too preoccupied with the need of obtaining food for their families, or too ignorant and poorly led, to maintain a united front.

So, having now allowed a reasonable time for these eventualities, and having in that time regained gradually and subtly a substantial control of the state political machinery through the tireless manipulations of men like Porter Grimes, the smooth-handed men were ready for their counteroffensive.

The appointed time now had come; because with the legislature firmly in hand, there would be no uprising which might remedy with new legislation any laws found defective by corporation lawyers.

Almost the only united force left for the little men of Kansas to rally behind, was the relatively new farm organization, the Farmers' Co-operative Association, which now spread well over the entire state. Years before David Constable had sowed the seed which had germinated in this healthy growth, in the mind of Webb Pettis. Webb Pettis was now state president of the Kansas Farmers' Co-operative Associations.

In this year the trade unions had dissipated their strength; they were involved in their own difficulties. So it was the Farm Co-ops, when Upshaw refused to obey the law fixing a maximum rate for storage of the farmers' grain in his vast wheat bins, who demanded vigorous action by the state attorney general.

The first step was simple. The firm of Upshaw and Cape was clearly guilty of violating the law. But the second was not so simple. The firm of Upshaw and Cape, through its battalion of lawyers, challenged the validity and constitutionality of the law itself. The district court of Shawnee County, in which was the state capital, upheld the law in the first test; and the Farmers' Co-operative Associations offered to furnish special counsel to assist the attorney general in the real test before the state supreme court in the spring.

It was the appeal brief from the Shawnee County district court to the state supreme court that Dave was studying.

Raindrops spattered on the roof and against the windowpanes. He raised his head. Rain in January meant cold weather in Kansas, and probably ice on the pavement. He could tell the wind was rising. It wailed about the eaves, and sometimes sudden blasts rattled the sash.

Dave forgot about the wind and read on.

The old, old argument. The fixing of maximum storage rates, pleaded the expensive lawyers of Upshaw and Cape in tedious legal language, constituted a taking of property without due process of law. How often had Dave heard that favorite cry; that appeal to the very legal guardianship which the predatory ones rejected in their own conduct; that demure masking of piratical intentions under pretense of devotion to the pure religiosity of the law.

Dave wished he could have the handling of this case.

He laid out his strategy. First, he would drive home the principle that the warehouse business—and any business which was clothed in like manner with public interest—justified public control.

But there was a second, collateral argument which must be contended with; this was the cunning one. Although the wheat bins of Upshaw and Cape were within the borders of Kansas—only a matter of some thirty feet within the borders, to be sure, since they stood almost on the line between Kansas City, Kansas, and Kansas City, Missouri—the warehouse company lawyers asserted that in those bins was stored grain from other states also, Nebraska and Missouri specifically; and that this placed the bins and their contents under the provisions of the Interstate Commerce Act. A matter for the Federal government and Congress rather than state control, said the lawyers with great cunning.

Here, Dave knew, would be the real battleground. Again he wished he could direct that battle. That, however, was out of the question. Four months ago he might have been the very man chosen by the farmers, because of the influence of Webb Pettis. But that was past. He had hardly seen Webb since the argument on the day following his decision not to stand for Congress. He had hardly seen scores of his other friends.

This was hard. But the hardest thing to bear was the knowledge that where his friends felt resentment toward him, his enemies held him only in contempt. A long way had David Constable come down. He had seen the cold sneer on Porter Grimes's face; and it was a bitter thing to endure.

Porter Grimes and his machine had been everywhere victorious in the November elections. Tucker Wedge piled up a landslide majority for Congress, because he faced no effective opposition. All down the line of county offices, good organization Republicans held sway—including Jasper Peddigrew, who had achieved his ambition once more to be county attorney.

These new county officers had just been sworn in during the past week. They were paint-fresh in their positions; they hardly knew the functioning of their offices yet.

Dave heard the storm grow heavier outside. He went downstairs to look at the base-burner, and took the occasion to open the front door. The rain was freezing. He could see ice on the porch, and a steely sheet of ice on the ground as the thermometer plummeted. In the darkness the earth was rapidly whitening—the rain was turning to snow.

He closed the door and returned to his upstairs room. For another hour he read. The whine of the gale lifted higher a note or two as he went to bed.

2.

When they went to sleep that night, the people of the high plains had no particular premonition of great danger. But during the dark hours the storm, instead of abating, gained in fury.

Awaking at dawn, Dave was surprised at the darkness. His breath was white in the cold room.

He rose and dressed, shivering: Then he went about the house, building up the fires. Once more he opened the front door, but quickly closed it again. The snow had thickened into a fine powder of razor-sharp crystals, a choking smother, swept along on a typhoon wind of incredible discomfort. He caught a brief glimpse of his own front gate. That was all. The smother closed before his eyes and he could not see even the houses on the far side of the street.

A blizzard, a great blizzard.

Continued for any length of time it could create a situation gravely threatening.

Dave said: "Good God!" and returned to the dining-room.

Belle and her mother were up now. They took uneasy glimpses out into the white fury, and glanced at him.

He answered their unspoken questions. "Bad storm."

While they cooked breakfast, he brought coal up from the cellar for all the fires. A truce reigned in the house, because of the portent outside. Mrs. Dunham fried eggs and frizzling strips of bacon. Belle had discovered that powdery snow was drifting in through microscopic cracks about the windows. She spent a long time after breakfast sealing those interstices with strips of rag pushed in by a knife blade. The sub-zero blast had gained such tremendous force that sometimes it shook the house in insane wrath, and the women wore faces of half-frightened wonder.

Dave decided against trying to go uptown in this storm. He went up to his room after breakfast, built up a roaring fire in his little stove, and threw himself again into the study of *Upshaw and Cape* vs. *the State of Kansas*. He took up a pencil and a yellow tablet with a red line ruled down the left margin, and began plotting points. It was mental exercise purely. He did it as another man might have worked out a chess problem.

The long day dragged to its end. Outside the storm still snored as darkness grew intense. He replenished the fires in all the stoves before he went to bed on this second night. He wished very much that he had an outside thermometer. Time and again he had thought of getting one, but it always slipped his mind. He had no idea how cold it was, but he guessed the temperature at far below zero.

Morning came again, with the same peculiar darkness where there should have been light; and his breath was thickly white. The fire in the little stove had burned out: he spent some minutes kindling a new blaze. Then he went to a window.

The panes were thick with rime. When he scraped a small space to see through, he at first had the impression that something was wrong with his eyes—he could not see out. Then he realized this was caused by the snow, blowing more thickly than ever.

It was unprecedented—the continuation of a blizzard at this fury. Dave was worried as he went down to rebuild the fires. After a time the women came down. Both were in a surly mood this morning. They snapped at each other during breakfast; but strangely, the truce toward him still remained.

When he had eaten, Dave wrapped himself warmly in overcoat, muffler, and big overshoes, with the intention of going to his office. But as soon as he stepped out of the back door into the white fog that bit with ice-fanged teeth through the heavy clothing to his bones, he knew it was foolish to attempt it. He fought his way to the shed where he kept his car. Snow had drifted in and the automobile was too frozen to be started.

So he returned to the house and spent the day again in his room, occupying himself with the affairs of Upshaw and Cape. He was beginning to arrive at a conceivably feasible line of attack in the case. But it gave him only a sense of futility—he was like an arm-chair strategist tinkering with assault plans while the practical soldiers did the actual fighting.

The third morning came with only a slight letup in the blizzard. It was incredibly cold, but he could see across the street now sometimes through breaks in the flying white snow.

This morning he did not even try to start his car. But he had had enough of the house. Dressed as warmly as he could he struggled on foot through the drifts downtown. For two days he had not been near his office. He saw only one or two people on the way—hurrying, heavily wrapped, with backs bent to the cold, showing white puffs of frozen breath as they crossed quickly from one shelter to another.

All of Jericho was snowbound, but Patterson's drugstore was open. He paused a moment at the thermometer outside. So far down was the mercury that he could hardly believe it. Twenty-five degrees below zero. Fifty-seven degrees of frost.

He had never seen it so cold in all his life.

He entered the drugstore. Old Doc Patterson stood warming his backside at the stove. The physician looked worn, his eyes sunken and his jowls covered with the white pinfeathers of an unshaved beard.

"Hello, Doc. Twenty-five below," said Dave.

"Colder than that yesterday. It's moderated some but the mercury's sliding again. It'll be thirty below tonight."

"You were down yesterday?"

"Certainly. Sickness knows no weather. I'm greatly worried."

"What about?"

"The country people. What's happened to 'em? David, there are shacks on these plains—I know them—that are no more than tarpaper and lath. What we're going to discover when this is over gives me vertigo——"

"Aren't the county authorities at work?"

"Not a move. The whole courthouse is new. Machinery's not even started. Nothing's been done—*nothing*. It's a horror, David. It actually is."

A sickness at the thought was in the old man's eyes.

Dave was shocked. He had been a private citizen just ten days, and the instinct of responsibility still was strong.

He had intended going to his new law office in the Jericho National Bank building, but instead he left the drugstore, lowered his head, and bucked the blizzard to the courthouse.

How familiar the limestone steps seemed—even covered with windswept snow. He struggled through the gale-buffeted door.

The building seemed ice cold. Its furnace was not adequate. In their offices a few county employees shivered. As soon as they heard he was in the building they began gathering about him. He was a familiar figure to them, someone who knew what should be done. He gazed about him at the faces, struck dumb by dread of disaster.

Except for Bradshaw Gates, the sheriff, they were all subordinates, clerks, deputies. The sheriff was new—an unsuccessful building contractor who had gone into politics with no qualifications for office, save that he knew where his orders should come from. But at least he was on duty and almost tearfully glad to see Dave.

"Have you done anything to get help started into the country?" Dave asked.

"Nope. Ain't been able to."

"Have you phoned to find out how things are?"

"Telephones down everywhere—that ice storm before the snow loaded 'em an' the wind snapped 'em like straws," the sheriff said. "Roads all blocked by drifts. In the draws the snow's twenty-five foot deep in places. Lots of families ain't been heard from."

Dave knew that Jericho itself was at a complete standstill. Fuel supplies were dangerously low. No train had come through in two days—there were no railroad snow-plows in the country for a storm of this kind. Business was suspended; all schools closed. The waterworks system was reported frozen. Even the postoffice was idle. In the town, families huddled together, usually in a single room of their houses, the other rooms battened in every possible way against the cold.

Dave said: "This is God-damned serious, Brad. You've got to do something."

"What can I do?" Gates' face, unshaved for two days, was woebegone, his eyes bloodshot. "I ain't got deputies enough——"

Somebody had to take command. This was chaos. Dave's eye took them in, all the county employees present. Bradshaw Gates with three deputies, and the jailer and matron who lived at the courthouse; half a dozen men from other offices, two or three unclassified hangers-on, a janitor. The county attorney's office was closed. Jasper Peddigrew was at home.

"I want everyone down in the sheriff's office," Dave told them.

When they gathered there, he spoke to them briefly. They listened. At this moment of deadly crisis he alone was prepared. They remembered him as dependable and strong, even when they had opposed him in politics. Willingly and gratefully they accepted his leadership, providentially at hand where there had been no leadership.

"This is as bad a storm as I've ever heard of out here," he told them. "Nobody knows what's happened to the people in the country. Maybe some of them are dead. It's sure that there's been terrible misery. We've got to get help to them."

With so short a peroration he began giving orders.

The orders were obeyed, implicitly, without question.

Messages went out. Jericho began gathering teams, men, sleighs.

Before noon a hundred men were at the courthouse. Dave gathered them in the district court, where he had a county map pinned to the wall. Nobody questioned his authority. He gave directions. Six, eight men would go with each sleigh. Shovels, food, fuel should be carried wherever they could be tucked in.

He stood before the map. Such and such sleighs with crews were to go west and south; others southeast and east. Two sleighs would try to break through to Bedestown, across the frozen river.

"Bedestown, it's my guess, will be pretty well organized, because Webb Pettis is up there," he said. "But help him as much as you can."

That left one road—the road south of the river, through the broken sand hills. He paused.

"That'll be the mean one. I'm going with that sleigh myself."

He waited for volunteers.

"I'll furnish the sleigh and team." It was Andy McAdam.

"Good, Andy."

Timberline Wilson would go along. Dave's eye looked over the crowd.

"Gotch McCurdy!" he said.

"I'll go." The big man nodded his huge head.

3.

Out across the white roads which radiated from Jericho like filaments of a spider's web, crawled the rescue sleighs.

Eastward from the town went five, with Andy's sled in the lead. The team's sleigh bells jingled with a false counterfeit of cheerfulness. In the killing cold, rime grew white on the muzzles of the horses; the frozen moisture of their breathing settled about their nostrils in an icy frost.

Dave drew his muffler over his mouth and nose, leaving only his eyes exposed. The others in the sleigh did likewise. They pulled the earflaps of their caps close, and drew the caps down over their foreheads. They thrashed their arms to keep up circulation. Within a mile ice had gathered on Dave's muffler and he was forced again and again to ease the space so that breathing was possible.

"Ke-rist, it's cold," complained Timberline.

"Don't lose your cap," said Andy unkindly. "That bald head of yourn is the biggest expanse of naked hide in Kansas, an' I don't want to see your brains freeze to death."

On the main-traveled road it was not so bad. Andy urged his team into a trot over a brief stretch of smooth snow. Dave held his mittened hand over his nose and blew softly to warm the space within.

"We'll hit the trouble when we turn off at the Rector corner and take the line along the river," he surmised.

"That ain't even a decent road in dry weather when there ain't no snow," agreed Andy.

The sleigh bells clashed merrily. The horses trotted, walked, trotted again. Behind, in single file, four other sleighs followed. Dave could see white jets of frozen breath like steam from the horses' heads.

At the first turn the last two sleighs in line took the south and west roads, according to orders. When the Rector corner was reached, Andy pulled up. Dave walked over in the snow for a final word with the drivers of the other two sleds.

"Looks like somebody's been up that road already," he said.

"Yeah. Does."

"You'll have no trouble, except maybe crossing the river. Webb Pettis is likely to have his headquarters at the Bedestown school."

"O.K. See you." The two sleighs slid off north with a plume of snow smoking up behind each runner.

He knew the family that owned the corner place. The Til Rectors. A thin, pleasant woman with reddish hair shot with gray came to the door.

"Mrs. Rector, is Til here?" Dave asked.

"No. He and Randy—our boy—left before noon with the cutter to try and get through to Bedestown."

"Guess we saw his runner tracks. Heard anything from over west?"

"Not a thing. You going that way?"

"Thought we'd try."

"The next place up the road is owned by the Callans," said Mrs. Rector. "I reckon they're all right. No young children and the place is in pretty good shape. After that, though—I don't know."

"Who's beyond the Callans?"

"Jefferson and Jackson Protheroe. Them twins. They batch."

"Beyond that?"

"The Oskissons."

"And then?"

"The Joss place. Tony Joss and his wife. I've been worrying about Ada Joss. Expecting, you know. Somebody sure ought to get to *them*. Likely to be hard—so many draws in the sand hills."

"Thanks, Mrs. Rector. When Til gets back, tell him we were here."

"Won't you bring your boys in? I'll fix coffee——"

"Like to, but we've got a long way to go."

"I understand." She hesitated. "If Til's home before dark, I might even come over with him. It oughtn't to be too hard, after you've broke the road—and I'm that worried about Ada Joss—the baby due any day now, and all——"

4.

As soon as Andy turned his team west along the sand hills, the trouble began. For a time they could see the tops of the fence posts along either side of the road. But within half a mile the horses began convulsive plunging, and stopped.

"All out," said Dave.

Scoop shovels flashed. In a few minutes the sleigh was through the drift, but within half a mile they encountered one deeper. It took twenty minutes to cut a way through that. The men gasped for breath as they labored. It was turning colder, and though the wind whistled keenly, the snow was not blowing so badly. Dave coughed as he sucked the sharp air into his lungs.

Another quarter-mile of comparatively level snow, raked by the north wind, but practicable for the straining team.

"Yonder's the Callan place," announced Andy.

Low, snow-covered roofs, and smoke eddying from the chimney, blown instantly flat by the icy gale.

They turned in.

A farmer with a ragged mustache which was one frozen icicle, waded toward them from the barn.

"You Tobey Callan?" asked Dave.

"Yeh."

"All right here?"

"All *right?*" a whimper of indignant self-pity. "If you kin call it all right when a man's lost thirty head of cattle——"

"How about the family?"

"None of *us* is dead, if that's what you want to know. The woman frostbit her hands, but——"

"Who's next over—the Protheroes?"

"Yeh. Them no-account twins. Live in a dugout. Tell me what I'm gonna do about my livestock. The government ought to be made to help us farmers out——"

"Everybody's lost livestock, Mr. Callan. It's people we're concerned with right now."

They left him still wailing about his losses as they drove out of the yard.

Another hour's struggle.

"Protheroe place ought to be jest over there," said Andy.

"Can't see it."

"By that cut bank."

They pulled up, hallooed.

Two gaunt, bearded men seemed to appear from beneath a snow-drift.

"'Light an' come in."

Surprising how similar they were, even to the length of their lank beards, and the way the very locks of hair curled.

"You all right?"

"Yep."

The men were comfortable, not particularly worried. Their dwelling, a dugout, most primitive of all plains domiciles, was safest in the two most terrifying manifestations of weather in the flatlands—the tornado and the blizzard.

It was growing near dusk, and Dave saw his men were cold.

"Go in and warm up," he told them.

Willingly they stumbled down crude steps into a foul-smelling hole underground. But it was delicious, getting out of the bitter bite of the wind. They stood close about the Protheroes' flat-topped stove, and threw back their coats to let the heat reach their bodies better. A coffeepot simmered. They ate cold fried mush washed down with the scalding black liquid.

"How far to Oskisson's?" Dave asked.

"Two mile," said Jeff Protheroe.

"Heard anything from them?"

"Nary word," said Jack Protheroe.

"How's the road?"

"Bad gulch at the boundary fence. Say, Jack, less you an' me go 'long an' see whut's goin' on."

"O.K. by me."

There were six in the crew now. As they came out of the dugout and climbed into the sleigh, the horses were stiff with cold and anxious to start.

"Tough on the team," grunted Andy. "See how they've ga'nted?"

"Can't be more than four miles to the farthest place," said Dave.

But darkness was coming—early, because an overcast dimmed whatever late rays the sun may have had.

"Git careful jest t'other side this leetle sand hill," warned Jeff. "Road falls off sudden. Soft snow there."

Andy pulled up. The Protheroes jumped out and went ahead, wading in the whiteness. All at once they were thigh deep and turned back.

"Right there," said Jack. "A job, diggin' through that place."

Big Gotch McCurdy demonstrated his usefulness here. He was chewing tobacco, and it seemed that he had grown a new beard—a crystal amber beard of solid ice—which clung to his stubbly chin. It kept increasing as time passed—like hard, brown, brittle glass. A sharp blow would have shattered it. But Gotch paid no heed to it, nor seemed to mind the appendage. It was a penalty tobacco chewers paid in such weather as this.

The livery-stable man did not speak. But each heave of his shoulders sent an immense scoop of ice flying, and the heaves came fast and were sustained with great endurance. Gotch could scoop twice as much snow as the best of them. Dave was the poorest scooper, finding it necessary to rest often. But McCurdy, with his curious brown goatee, fought doggedly on.

The cut deepened—so much so that they could no longer throw out the snow.

"Got to make benches," Dave said.

On either side the Protheroes cleared snowy shelves on which they stood. The men below heaved snow up to that level and Jeff and Jack pitched it out over the top. Even in the cold, they perspired under their clothing.

By the time they were through the draw, darkness had fallen. It was completely dark when Andy brought his team down and across on the run. The cold was more jagged. Timberline was complaining that his nose was frosted.

Out on each side of the sleigh hung one of the Protheroes, watching for the tops of fence posts which alone indicated the right-of-way.

"Shy off to your left," Jack would cry.

"You're antigodlin' too much toward the ditch on this side," Jeff would presently warn.

All at once one of the horses stumbled. Andy brought him up with a crackle of oaths. The beast plunged and blew. At once the little drayman stopped the team and went around to look. It was the off horse. The animal was limping badly.

Andy felt down the snow-encrusted leg, examined the hoof, came back shaking his head gravely.

"Pulled tendon," he said. "If it don't go bowed, I'm lucky. How far on to the Oskissons?"

"We ought to be seein' their lights right from here," said Jeff.

A shout from Timberline brought them around.

"Looky here!"

They went back to where he stood, behind the sleigh.

"Dead," said Timberline.

Together they lifted out something stiff and cold, something with frozen clothing on it.

"So that's what the hoss stumbled on," said Andy.

"Say—that thar's Kelly Oskisson!" exclaimed Jack Protheroe, who had scraped the snow from the dead face.

"Load him into the sleigh. We've got to reach that farm!" cried Dave, with sudden apprehension.

The frozen body seemed heavier than an ordinary corpse. Someone commented on it.

"Ought to be heavier—jest a solid chunk of ice," said Jeff.

Andy began easing his team along, watching the limping horse anxiously. The men walked behind, in the sleigh tracks.

"Cain't understand why we ain't seein' the Oskisson lights," said Jack.

They were almost on it in the darkness before they saw . . .

5.

It was Andy, up ahead, swearing. "Why—why—it's burnt. The house is burnt down!"

They rushed forward, relieving themselves with profanity.

Possibly the family had overtaxed the stove, trying to keep the wretched shack warm, or the stovepipe became red hot, or sparks caught the roof. The snow had drifted, partly covering the blackened litter of ashes and charred timbers.

"What about—the family?" Dave hardly dared to think.

"There was Missis Oskisson an' the two kids," said Jack.

"Maybe—in the barn," suggested Andy.

The low shed stood fifty paces away—not so much a barn as a shelter, made of posts and covered with a roof of coarse prairie hay and cornstalks. It had never been intended for weather like this. The men went toward it, hating to think of what they might find.

The whole interior was drifted with snow. No horses or cattle were in it. But—in a corner—they found three snow-covered lumps.

All dead. The woman and her two children, little shavers—a boy and girl, not yet in their teens. The children were curled and huddled about their mother. Even in death the woman clutched an arm about each of them, and horror and anguish were frozen into their attitudes.

"Didn't have no time to get their clothes," said Jeff.

The woman and her children were half clad only. They had tried to cover themselves with hay to keep warm. . . .

"Four—dead," said Timberline gloomily.

"What about the Josses?" said Dave.

Andy shook his head. "Don't know how I kin get this sleigh any farther. If the Oskissons had any hosses, they've wandered off in some draw—prob'ly daid. I'd hoped to get somep'n for my lame off-hoss. He's too stove up to go any further."

Dave considered this. The gravity of the situation was apparent. Judgment dictated that they remain where they were, or try to make their way back to the main-traveled road. But he remembered something else.

"Mrs. Rector said something—about a baby being due——"

The men looked uncomfortably at him. Nobody wanted to risk the battle to reach the Joss place in this weather on foot. Dave could not blame them. The thermometer must be down close to thirty below, and the wind had risen again, with choking smothers of flying snow. The road they would have to take had not been broken. . . .

He said: "There's shelter for the horses here, Andy. Stay here and work on that lame leg. Maybe you can get him going. You can build up a fire of some kind—but don't burn down that barn."

They heard him with that same uncomfortable silence.

Finally Andy said: "What ye figgerin' on, Dave?"

"I'm going to try to make it through to the Josses."

Another silence. Andy cleared his throat.

"Looky here, Dave. No use of you bein' looney. Jest because the Oskissons was burnt out ain't no sign the Josses is anythin' but comfortable. An'—an'—hell, it's likely to kill a man who tries to get through them drifts on foot."

"I think I ought to try it anyway," said Dave.

"We'll be pickin' ye up—jest like we done Kelly Oskisson."

"I've got to chance that."

Dave pulled his cap tighter about his ears and turned to go. He heard a hoarse voice behind him.

"Wait a minute. I'll go with ye."

Dave glanced back in surprise. Gotch McCurdy was coming after him.

"Come along," said Dave, pleased. "Andy—if you don't hear from us by morning—try to send help through some way. Maybe the Rectors will come along—Mrs. Rector spoke as if they might——"

With Gotch McCurdy beside him, he started off into the storm.

In silence they fought their way. It was the hardest kind of going. Even on the levels the snow was deep, and the wind like a saw-edged knife. When they reached the soft drifts they struggled through, sometimes up to their armpits in the loose white smother. This was what men used snowshoes for in the real snow country. But there were no snowshoes here. Every step was hard labor.

For a time they walked abreast. Then they took turns breaking trail, one following the other's tracks. Gotch still chewed tobacco, increasing the length of his brown beard of slimy ice.

Never had Dave imagined such cold. Once in a while he whipped his arms across his chest to stir the chilled blood; and frequently he rubbed his cheekbones and nose with his mittened hand. Again and again he felt a numbed sensation as he began rubbing, and each time when he stopped the cheekbones grew numb once more. He was certain that his cheeks were frostbitten.

He envied Gotch his imperturbable endurance. The big man shouldered his way along without visible expression.

Dave slapped a mittened hand against his thigh. The sting that followed in his fingers alarmed him. Numbness was creeping into his hands. This was dangerous . . . how much farther was it, anyway?

The wind wrestled with them, twisted them. Sometimes clouds of fine snow left them gasping, almost sightless. The cold sank iron fingers into them.

Doggedly, Dave concentrated on his progress. Each step became a separate effort of will, a planned exertion, to be accomplished before he could even think of the step which was to follow it. As the night grew blacker and the cold fiercer, he began to fear that he would stumble. If he stumbled he was quite sure he never would rise. He was not especially concerned about this. He thought about it in a dull and uninterested way, without alarm. He was very weary. He steeled himself to fight away the suffocating languor that rose about him like a quicksand; a deadly languor, which sought to drown his consciousness bit by bit; through which he struggled falteringly, step by step, summoning up a shred of will and yet another shred to drive him on. If he fell it would be over. Almost it would be welcome. But he would not let himself fall, no matter how he stumbled. His will power would not permit it. There was a goal of some kind . . . oh, yes. He must reach a woman who was suffering with child. . . .

And at that moment, Gotch McCurdy fell.

Dave was behind him and saw the bulk in the darkness slump forward into the snow.

The sight filled him with astonishment. So preoccupied had he been with himself that it had not occurred to him that Gotch might be feeling the same sensations, the same weariness and coldness he was feeling.

McCurdy—why, he was a giant, a man without nerves, a man of oaken thews, phlegmatic as an ox with no nervous system at all—he scarcely noticed pain and weariness that destroyed other men. But McCurdy had given out.

Drunkenly weaving, Dave went to him, took one of the man's arms and tried to lift him. The weight of Gotch was too great to lift.

Dave snarled at Gotch. He slapped the giant's face. The blow seemed to jolt Gotch into anger through his dull lethargy. He fought to get up, rose to his feet, and turned on Dave with hate.

Dave watched, too weary to care much, until he saw that McCurdy was up. Then he took the lead.

They had just enough strength. The cabin lights gleamed suddenly ahead.

6.

Dave heard something when he knocked on the door. It sounded like a woman's voice. He could not make it out, so he opened the door.

Gotch followed him in. For a moment they stood swaying in the middle of the room. Gotch stumbled over and sat heavily on a chair.

Dave closed the door carefully and looked about. Typical prairie shack. One room. The cheapest kind of lumber and tarpaper. Warped boards. Wads of paper and rags stuck into cracks.

Fire roared in a stove, but the woman was in the bed in a corner, quilts wrapped about her. The stove could not keep this shack warm.

"Tony—" she said. "Tony . . . ?"

"Mrs. Joss?"

"Yes. Ain't Tony with you?"

"No."

The eyes above the quilts widened with fear.

Dave had a sinking of the heart. That loglike lump of ice which had been Kelly Oskisson . . . was there another like it, back somewhere on the road?

"We just came up from Jericho," he told the woman.

She was a gaunt woman, with deep-bitten lines in her young-old face and hair a disordered, uncombed mass. A sharp paroxysm seemed to go through her.

"I—thought—my husband would come back with you——"

She seemed unable to comprehend.

"When did he leave?" Dave's fingers were thawing, and sharp arrows of anguish shot up his arm. Gotch straightened up a little in his chair.

"Night before last—before it got so bad," the woman said. "He went to Bedestown corner—for some flour an' stuff. He never came back."

"He's probably all right, Mrs. Joss. We've got an outfit breaking through to Bedestown. I expect your husband will be on the road home right now."

Another spasm went across her face.

"I—do you—" Terror was in her eyes. "Can you git a doctor?"

"No doctor nearer than Jericho, Mrs. Joss."

A little whimpering wail. Then she said:

"My time's—come ahead. Days ahead. The strain—an' the storm, I guess. Can—does either of you know anything about—*this* . . . ?"

Childbirth.

The woman was in the throes already.

Dave experienced a sensation of helplessness and dread. He spoke to the woman, striving to be cheerful. Then he took Gotch off into a corner.

"Ever see a baby born?" he whispered anxiously.

"Nope."

"Well, get ready. You're going to see one now. And I haven't the remotest idea what to do."

Gotch said: "I've seen mares—drop colts."

"Wonder if it's anything alike," said Dave.

"Must be. A kid comes out same as a foal." Gotch hesitated and added, cautiously, "So I been told."

"Well," said Dave, "she's going to have a baby. The pains have started. We've got to help her."

Gotch considered. "If it's anything like a mare—she'll do most of it herself."

Dave found himself deriving comfort from the words. Gotch had seen the grotesque processes of nature. The woman, clutching at the bedclothes in the corner, and crying, was going through that which dumb animals had gone through while the stableman took care of them.

It was not much comfort. But it was something.

"Get the place as warm as you can," Dave told Gotch. "Not too hot —watch that stovepipe." He remembered the Oskissons.

Then he went over to the bed. "How do you feel now?" he asked.

"Like—it would happen—pretty soon—" She twisted her body in the bed quilts.

Dave said: "Gotch, get some water good and hot."

He had no notion what to do with the water, but it was something doctors always called for. At least it made the woman feel that things were being done for her, as Gotch went outside long enough to scoop a big pot full of snow and bring it in to the stove.

"Gettin' colder," the big man said.

"You're just getting used to being warm," said Dave.

He sat on the edge of the bed and took the woman's skinny hand. Again her body tensed in a spasm and her face contorted. A long wail —it seemed to last minutes, the contortion, the spasm, and the wail.

Dave's eyes anxiously sought Gotch's.

"Hadn't we better—take a look?"

"Dunno what good it'd do. All the lookin' in the world didn't never hurry a colt in the foalin'——"

But Gotch came awkwardly over to the bed. Dave stood up and looked down at the woman. Her eyes pleaded with them.

He pulled the quilts up at the side nearest the stove. Good God, the woman was fully dressed . . .

He began turning up her heavy wool skirt, with the petticoats underneath. It was distasteful. He felt embarrassment and clumsy inefficiency, a sense of violating decencies long prescribed.

But Mrs. Joss helped him. With a pair of scissors Dave cut her underwear away.

"What do you think, Gotch?" Dave asked anxiously.

The liveryman came over.

"If she was a mare, now," he said, "I'd figger on action purty quick."
Dave was glad for this evidence of superior knowledge.

"What do we do next?"

"Nothin'. It does itself."

"We better warm up a blanket then. We've got to have somewhere
to put it—when it comes——"

The woman watched them with the stricken, impersonal eyes of an
animal. An animal helpless and afraid. She hardly heard them. Too
utterly was her mind turned in on herself, on the cataclysmic thing
that was happening to her.

Dave returned to her, tried to reassure her.

"Don't be afraid, Mrs. Joss. The human race has been going on a
long time. And it's just the last few years that mothers have had doctors at childbirth. You're going to be all right."

The kindness in him brought tears to her eyes.

"If—only—another woman—" she whispered, clutching his hand.

A hoarse cry burst from her; an especially violent spasm wracked
her body. . . .

It seemed forever. Grimly they fought in that cabin for a life. Two
lives.

Dave's face grew drawn and gray in the yellow lamplight.

Twice Gotch stumbled out for more fuel. He seconded Dave, as
concerned, as grimly determined, as he.

Once, in a breathing space between spasms, when the woman momentarily rested, Gotch said: "Gawd, I'd give a laig for a drink."

He went out again, for wood.

Dave thought: Odd how liquor changes a man like Gotch. He has
worked like a fiend, none of us could keep up with him. Now he is
filled with concern and zeal for this woman whom he does not even
know. That is Gotch sober.

But Gotch drunk, is another Gotch. Gotch drunk is a beast. Men
like Gotch have made prohibition a fanatical religion in Kansas.

Gotch came back in, his arms loaded with wood.

More time dragged on leaden feet. The spasms came more frequently.

In the last moments, the woman lost her panic, and became oddly
calm. It was her first child, but she took command.

Between pains she gasped out directions.

Outside, the wind howled like a pack of savage wolves, hungry for
Death. . . .

7.

Long, long after, the first gray daylight showed in the windows.
Dave heard voices.

Til Rector and Andy McAdam had broken through in Rector's sleigh. With them were Mrs. Rector, and Webb Pettis, and Tony Joss, and Timberline. They burst into the shanty.

Dave and Gotch sat sagging in chairs, faces haggard.

Ada Joss lay on her pillow, her hair over it in a tangled web. She opened her eyes when her husband, a small swart man, came over to her with Mrs. Rector.

"Everything . . . all right," she whispered.

Dave felt Webb Pettis' warm handclasp and heard his friend's voice. He nodded toward a bundle of blankets beside the stove.

"Boy," he croaked.

The baby had been born three hours ago.

CHAPTER V

1.

ON this April afternoon the sky was innocently blue. A week of rain had laid all dust. The prairie air was crystal clear and balmy. Sparrows bickered in the boxelder tree which was just putting forth fresh, virgin leaves outside the open window.

And Dave wrote a letter.

He paused and nibbled the end of his pen, staring abstractedly into nothing between short periods of writing. He felt he should not be writing this letter, but he could not help it:

My Dear Julia:

This town really isn't the same since you left. Your many friends miss you, and the Jericho Bar Association looks twice as ugly since it is without the one member it ever possessed who could add something to the credit side in beauty.

We had some bad weather last winter, and a good many farmers are hard hit. People you may remember, like the Dode Smiths, and the Amuels, and the Charley Bulls are cleaned right out. We have a record number of bankruptcies in court this spring.

He tapped his square front teeth with the end of the pen. The pen leaked and the inside of his index finger on the right hand was stained with ink.

Western Kansas had been denuded of life by the great blizzard as if a gigantic scythe had whipped across it. All through January, while snow still choked the gullies and eddied on the levels, and while crews of men labored in arctic temperatures to get trains running and restore wire communications, the farmers counted their losses with daily increasing dread.

Only by degrees was the full fearfulness of the toll evident.

From Calgary to the Red River, livestock had succumbed in incredible numbers. Loss of human life had also been heavy—scores were dead in western Kansas. The country lay stunned.

Dave wrote another paragraph of his letter:

If the wheat crop turns out well in yield and prices, we may still pull through. This, however, is problematical as the wheat still must run the gauntlet of drouth, chinch bug, rust, and hail. As for the price factor, you remember our discussions of what the farmer has to face in the harpies who prey on him before he can get anything for his crop.

He thought of the pitiable condition of the country. Countless farms had not enough horses or mules left to put in the spring crops. But the wheat—ah, the blessed wheat! Fortunately, as far as the winter wheat was concerned, the great snow had been only a benefit, keeping the cold from killing the plants.

Wheat was the last hope of the plains; the only chance for alleviating universal disaster. As spring waxed gradually, the farmers watched the wheat with an anxiety only they could have told, and when they saw at last that the good Turkey Red had survived, a new spirit was evident in the plains. Western Kansas lifted its head once more.

Dave's pen scratched again on the paper:

In this connection, Julia, some importance is attached to a certain legal case in which I figure in a modest way as co-counsel. You may have seen something about it in the papers or law journals. *Upshaw* vs. *Kansas*. It may develop into a test case on which the whole fabric of regulation of the utilities and other quasi-public institutions will be tried.

To Constable, the blizzard had brought two things: Self-forgetfulness while he fought against it; and a new strength when it was over.

In the first white-tinged fury of that storm he had regained much of the regard of the plains people which he had lost. Those who blamed him, for that last-hour desertion in the campaign of the previous fall, regained their confidence in him because of what he had done.

When nobody else was able to lead, Dave had taken the responsibility. Men talked much of his grim fight to rescue the sand-hills families. The story of his midwifery also had gone the rounds—and about this was some ribald jesting. But through it, Dave had risen in esteem. Even Gotch McCurdy rose to a new regard. Dave took the joking in good part, and the Josses brought the new baby to town and had it christened after him, David Constable Joss.

Out of these things he derived a certain pleasure. He had bitten off a big piece, swallowed it, digested it, and made it a part of his strength. His name extended now over half a state.

Now it was borne in on him how much wiser Julia had been than he; and how more honest she was than he. He remembered her words: *I won't let you give up . . . the people who depended on you. . . .*

It shamed him to think of the day when harsh things had passed his lips, and when she alone was thinking the truth and facing the reality. He had been brutal and vindictive. He would have given much to be able to call back what he had said.

When she went away from Jericho he was at the bottom. He had lost his friends, he had given up his political future, he had betrayed his cause . . . and on top of all that, he had lost the woman for whom he had done those things.

Well, at least he had regained his standing with the people whom he had counted as friends. This was the first step upward.

The real proof of this had come only a week before.

Webb Pettis headed the delegation of farmers, rough-faced and serious in their "store clothes."

Dave drew in his breath when he heard them ask him to act as special counsel in the now celebrated case of *Upshaw and Cape* vs. *the State of Kansas.* He found words at last:

"Webb, it happens I've spent all winter studying that case."

They nodded with satisfaction. For most of the afternoon they listened as he laid before them the process of thinking which he had crystallized, and the daring innovations and ideas he planned to apply. He was proud of this honor, but prouder of the trust it implied. The case might go to the United States Supreme Court—it might become the symbol of the struggle in which he was most interested.

Again Dave returned to his writing:

During this spring our new Congressman, Tucker Wedge, and his wife, have been the chief focus of interest out here. Algeria was kept busy when the worst of winter was over with a series of social courtesies that, I am sure, must nearly have caused her physical, if not nervous, prostration, except that she is such a remarkable woman. Tucker, at the same time, was in almost endless conferences.

Algeria appeared wholly occupied with her social activities, but between you and me, I suspect she was just as deeply involved in her husband's practical political problems. She is enormously charming and capable, as you have remarked, and one of the greatest proofs of her quality is the way she plays the role, in public, of the admiring and even awe-struck helpmeet, while, I am sure, going over every knotty question with Tucker in private. I have no doubt she has saved him some blunders. They went to Washington late in February.

In the *Clarion,* Dave and the rest of Jericho had been able to read a circumstantial diary of the activities of the Wedges since they arrived in the nation's capital.

The Tucker Wedges had taken an apartment in an "elegant" Washington neighborhood. Mrs. Wedge had been seen in the House gallery, looking on as her husband took the oath of office. Mrs. Wedge was a charming hostess at a congressional tea. Congressman and Mrs. Wedge were luncheon guests at the White House.

To Dave these things were trivial, but he was impressed by the surprising frequency with which the name of the new Kansas representative appeared in the serious political columns of the big newspapers. There was no doubt of it—Tucker was making a fine record as a "freshman" in the House. His political viewpoints were regarded with satisfaction by the conservative financial wing of the Republican party. He was a clever writer and speaker, and whatever he lacked in adroitness or daring was more than supplied by his brilliant wife.

Dave continued the letter:

As a special pleader for the Farmers' Co-operative Associations, I will be in Topeka the week of June 15. This is quite a way from Kansas City, and I do not suppose you are ever in Topeka. Still it would be pleasant to see you again and find out how you are faring.

He thought wistfully that Jericho had not changed much since Julia went. The fields went through their slow, sure rhythm, turning dark green after the whitening of snow, then growing rankly toward the yellowing of summer harvest. Men and women came and went, had their being, conducted their affairs, gossiped, hated and loved, begot children, died and were buried. The departure of one honey-haired girl seemed to have little meaning. To anybody but Dave.

The last thing she said was as fresh in his mind as if she had just said it: *I will never forget, never regret. . . .*

The memory of her was still with him. Time had not diminished his heritage of longing.

He penned a last sentence:

I am missing you, Julia.
                                        Sincerely,
                                                DAVID CONSTABLE.

He folded the letter, addressed and stamped the envelope, and walked downstairs to the mailbox on the street outside the office building.

Within an hour he wished violently he had it back.

He felt that the letter was unwise. Julia had not asked him to write. Had she not made it very plain that she wanted to hear no more from him? It was a stupid letter anyway. . . .

The letter, however, had gone.

2.

Sunday evening, after a week of unseasonably warm and sticky weather early in June, Dave came out of the house and sat alone, smoking, in the porch swing.

Mrs. Dunham had strapped herself with gouty fingers into her corsets and taken Belle off to Sunday evening services at the Community Church. The house was silent.

To the west, the high clouds still were tinted with soft flame from the sun which already had set; and a single brilliant evening star blazed in the darkening sky above.

Dave could hear distant voices, soft and diminutive. A girl laughed. The youngsters were in the streets. School was just over but they continued to flock and preen together for a few days, before separating for their summer pursuits, unwilling to surrender their close companionship of the previous months.

He remembered the letter to Julia. He need not have worried about it. If she had received it, she was ignoring it.

For days after mailing it, he had waited with painful expectancy for his daily mail, surveying each envelope in the hope it would bear a certain handwriting. No such envelope came.

After a time it became apparent that she was not going to reply. And he did not know why she should. The Jericho episode of her life was past and gone; she had other interests and concerns.

Probably she had plenty of masculine attention where she was now, he thought with a sudden throb of jealousy. Smart young Kansas City attorneys, with college fraternity pins and Quality Hill connections, and the measureless superciliousness of youth.

If she thought at all about Jericho, it would be with distaste.

He put aside the jealousy. And he told himself that refusing to answer his letter was the only sensible thing for Julia. Again he was ashamed that it had required the girl's clearer judgment to force him into a sane course of action. What could she want with a furtive correspondence?

A woman gives greater hostages to fate than a man.

Also, he felt, there was a course to which Julia would never consent —that of cheapness.

Feet came toward him in the darkness, a scuffling disorder of sound on the sidewalk. A girl squealed, and a boy giggled with reedy insolence. At this pinfeather age, newly discovered male sadism runs the gamut of pinchings and hair-pullings and other awkward effronteries; and female masochism responds with delighted wails and squeaks and histrionic manifestations of anguish, to encourage still further thrilling cruelties from the boys.

These must be the young people from the Christian Endeavor Society of the Community Church, who had just been let out to make way for the adult prayer service to which Mrs. Dunham and Belle had gone. Dave often heard the youngsters pass on Sunday nights.

A short distance up the block they stopped. He could not see them

in the darkness under the trees, but he heard more sniggerings and
another shriek of ecstatic outrage from one of the girls. The talking
grew lower, secretive.

Then a voice lifted suddenly, in harmony with the far fading light
on the horizon:

> Day is dying in the west,
> Heaven is flooding earth with rest . . .

The velvety soprano rose effortlessly toward the bright evening star.
That was Margie Ransome. Nobody else could sing like that. The
shadowy dusk, the distance, the quiet, invested the song with beauty
which the listening man subtly felt.

Other youthful voices joined the stately chorus:

> Holy, holy, holy,
> Lord God of hosts,
> Heaven and earth are full of thee,
> Heaven and earth are praising thee,
> O, Lord most high . . .

The voices seemed pure and unquestioning. From these young souls
faith seemed eminently fitting and proper.

For a moment the throbbing beauty of the song hung in the evening
silence.

Then someone sniggered again, there was another outcry.

Several girls screeched at once in mock terror at some new barbarism
of the boys and there were masterful shouts from changing young
male voices.

The spell was broken. Dave sat puffing his pipe, half-amused, half-
regretful.

A chorus of good nights. The group was breaking up. He made out
a muted, pleading dispute.

"Margie, kin I take you home? . . . Aw, Margie, you was gonna let
me. . . . Kin I take you, Margie, kin I?"

Margie replied, clearly, that they all could come.

More good nights and young feet came on toward Dave. In the
shadow of his porch he could make out Margie Ransome, passing his
house on the way to hers, acutely conscious of the delicious hostility
toward each other of three somewhat pimply cavaliers who followed,
surrounding her in the darkness.

Happy child, he thought. Untroubled, fortunate, lovely child. Life
had yet to lay its hand upon her. Dave hoped the hand would touch
her lightly.

3.

Margie, seventeen, in her last year of high school, was dewily pretty, and knew it. Perhaps she was even a little vain.

Dave would hardly have wished her otherwise. To him, vanity was a trait of femininity not entirely without its pleasantnesses. Because she is beautiful, woman is a little vain. Because she is a little vain, she studies to enhance her beauty. And nobody in his right mind would ever say that there can be too much feminine beauty in this world.

There was nothing serious about Margie's vanity. Actually, she was almost humble about it . . . with the humbleness of the untried maiden who knows her power over adolescent youths, but still is unsure of herself with maturer men.

Margie sang publicly whenever occasion offered; she laughed easily —too easily—at any excuse; like other girls, she "gushed," sometimes in a sudden whirlpool of utterance, a flood of words all at once, every sluice open at the same time. And always, consciously or unconsciously, she practiced her little tricks and wiles and arts on anyone who happened to be around her. To Dave it was a pretty thing to watch.

The most complete contrast to Margie, among the women Dave knew, was Algeria Wedge. Long ago Algeria had given over any conscious effort to enthrall for the sheer thrill of it. She was coolly discriminating in dispensing her charm, reserving her efforts for those whom she thought worthy, or who could be useful to her.

Yet Algeria, past her youth and perhaps a little bored with life, was unconsciously at her best when she encountered other people. She had that habit of listening, as if whatever was being said to her were the most important thing in the world; her gracious ways were instinctive after so many years of use; she used her fine eyes to their most charming advantage; and she always was perfection itself in her grooming. And all this was as unconsciously a part of her, as her heart or mind.

Julia Norman was too youthful to be unconscious of her face and figure. Once she had told him, almost primly, when he complimented her:

"A woman must know it if she is not unsymmetrical."

On another occasion, apropos of something entirely different, she had smilingly quoted a verse of Ambrose Bierce:

> To men a man is but a mind. Who cares
> What face he carries or what form he wears?
> But woman's body *is* the woman. O
> Stay thou, my sweetheart, and do never go!

But Julia's loveliness came as much from her heart as from her physical beauty. She had been lonely as a child, had matured earlier and in more searching fires than most girls; but it had made her the reverse of bitter. She gave of herself freely and with eagerness; and her warmth was such that it drew not only men to her, but also women. The thought of her brought a rush of feeling to Dave which he beat down, since it was useless.

And that brought him inexorably to the unloved and unlovely women of his own household.

Of all the women he knew, only Belle and her mother lacked that saving grace—the instinct to please. Neither of them cared any longer what anyone in the world thought of them.

Dave was hardly more than a boarder in his own home—a paying boarder who provided everything. He knew Belle and Mrs. Dunham hated him even more than before his open estrangement, but he could not stomach any other relationship.

The law bound him to a woman who grew daily less prepossessing, more slovenly; who was dedicated now to self-indulgence and self-pity; who turned more each day in to herself, succumbing increasingly to her own indolence, timidity, and inertia. Because he was bound to Belle, he was bound with almost equal force to her mother. He carried his household like an over-burdening load on his back.

Had circumstances been different he would long since have left them, moved to the hotel or elsewhere, and continued to support them but without seeing them. It was Julia who was responsible for his continued endurance of existence in that house.

He had made up his mind to climb back to the place from which he had fallen when he made that ill-advised decision to drop out of the race for Congress the previous year. Politics is a hard and exacting master, requiring often severe sacrifices. A man in politics had to be almost as careful of his reputation as a woman; and for Dave to "desert" his wife—even if he continued to support her—would have been the ultimate factor to complete his destruction. The public always sympathized with the woman in such a case, never taking the trouble to look at the justice or injustice of her position. It was convention; everyone subscribed unhesitatingly to it. "Wronged Womanhood" was a banner flourished high. For the sake of his political future, David Constable still maintained the form of conventional married life.

He had succeeded at last in numbing himself to Belle and her mother. He lived in his single room, with his books and his pipes, and left the rest of the house to them and their menagerie of pets.

He put in incessant hours on *Upshaw and Cape* vs. *the State of Kansas.*

In this coming week he was to argue that all-important case before the seven lawyer-politicians who constituted the Supreme Court of the great State of Kansas.

4.

Margie Ransome, swinging her hips lightly, followed by her three adolescent escorts, might have been considered the most fortunate girl in Jericho.

Life was at high tide. She was the center of every party, picnic, or social event of any kind to which she went. If the other girls were jealous of her, they concealed it, and gushed over her, for her leadership was not to be challenged.

The criticism of her by older women, which had risen during the Wilber Bratten scandal, had died down.

Men did not criticize Margie. They looked at her and smiled on her. She found them both fascinating and frightening. The callow crop of high-school youths tumbled to obey the crook of her finger. With surer, older men she was still shy, but the admiration of men is easily evident to a woman, and Margie, knowing she enjoyed this admiration, was gaining daily in confidence.

Had she known David Constable was sitting on his dark porch as she passed, she would have tossed him a musical "good night." She knew and liked and was somewhat awed by him. To her he was full of courtly and somewhat obscure jests; and she never quite had the courage to show off before him, with that mixture of daring and impudence which was hers, for he gave her the disquieting impression of viewing these small efforts with amusement. But she knew him as kind.

David Constable was one of those who stood at the very top of her galaxy of men. At the bottom was Gotch McCurdy.

Gotch McCurdy's face was the one face that frightened Margie. Margie was afraid of the evil which hung around him like an aura, and of the whisperings about him, and of the very fact that his look followed her on the street.

The one really great secret shadow in Margie Ransome's life was her own home. She never said anything about it, but she felt it. She had almost given up now the hope of doing anything with her voice. Her father was adamant.

Tom Ransome had grown, if anything, less popular than before. But he paid no attention to it.

He kept his daughter as well dressed as any girl in town, and after Algeria Wedge, Margie was the first of her sex to learn how to drive a car, so that her father's big dark Buick became a further buttress to her popularity.

Margie loved Tom Ransome. She loved her mother, too. But she wished her mother were a little less of a recluse, a little more sociable. This was at the bottom of Margie's discontent.

Myra Ransome, Margie's mother, almost never went out. She was a silent woman with only one great interest—gardening. Hers was a wonderful garden, for western Kansas, and she tended it with a zeal which was almost endless—and almost pathetic.

The Ransome house with its brown-shingle walls was surrounded by flowers and trees. A place of beauty and retirement. Sometimes it seemed almost a hiding place.

Guests were never invited to the big brown house. Margie could not understand this in her parents.

Sometimes she begged to have just one party in the garden—it was really beautiful there, with its Chinese elms and Russian olives, and tamarisk which turned pink in the spring. But she was always met with refusal, and her mother became so tight lipped and tense, that Margie was almost alarmed Mrs. Ransome did not explain. But she was hostile to any visitor.

There was one saving factor. Jericho merely put down th Ransomes as "peculiar," and did not criticize so much as speculate.

5.

As the day for the hearing of the appeal in the case of *Upshaw ana Cape* vs. *the State of Kansas* approached, there was a small flurry of comment on it in the state's newspapers.

The newspapers did not know much about it. Many tedious cases are heard at every session of the state Supreme Court and hard-pressed reporters prefer "human interest" to legal abstraction.

Such newspapers as did make comment rather prided themselves on having had the perspicacity even to discover that there was such a case, and that it had any importance at all. They were inclined at first to advocate strong prosecution and exemplary punishment of the recalcitrant Upshaw and Cape.

What was this out-of-state firm trying to do anyway? Did anybody in Kansas know its officers? How did it arrive at this cavalier attitude toward the statutes of the Great State of Kansas, as made and provided?

On the big papers in Kansas City and Topeka and Wichita, a few earnest young subordinate editorial writers pawed through dull literature to find cogent arguments favoring vigorous action against Upshaw and Cape and all their works. They wrote editorials—which were cut down to two paragraphs by editorial chiefs and placed at the bottom of the column along with other scrapings from the barrel, deploring

"Famine in China," and giving an admiring nod to some crotchety old couple for having "Completed Fifty Years of Wedded Bliss."

Shaggy-headed, elder country editors, who were chiefly concerned over how they were to pay for their next shipment of "boiler plate," wrote perfunctorily, and in sardonic vein, about "Eastern capitalists," and expressed a pious hope that the attorney general's office would be severe with those who thumbed their noses so impertinently at the Sunflower State.

Not yet had the newspapers discovered the real import of the case of Upshaw and Cape. This would require time. The process already was under way, but it was not yet apparent. It was under way as a leavening which extended slowly from golf courses, and lounges of exclusive clubs, and discreetly elegant homes, and bank directors' rooms —through the business offices of the newspapers, on up into the editorial rooms, where at last dawned the profound truth that Free Enterprise was being threatened by the law which the firm of Upshaw and Cape was challenging.

Time would come when earnest young subordinate editorial writers would be as diligent in searching dull literature for arguments defending Upshaw and Cape in their Courageous, Farsighted, and American defiance of governmental interference, as those young editorialists now were in assailing the same gentry. And on that day senior editors would no longer cut down the offerings of their subordinates to two paragraphs at the bottom of the column, but would allow them full scope for the expression of their considered—and revised—opinions, at the very top of the column, right under the masthead. At the same time shaggy-headed, elder country editors, having also seen the light, but remembering that their readers were in large number aggrieved farmers, would compromise by simply forgetting about Upshaw and Cape, and devoting their full time to worrying over their "boiler plate."

But this time was still to be. Meantime, David Constable took a train for Topeka, the state capital.

CHAPTER VI

1.

Upshaw and Cape vs. *the State of Kansas* dragged toward its drowsy close.

For two days a succession of brilliant, eloquent, and high-priced corporation attorneys had upheld the cause of the warehouse company. Now the attorney-general's office was making its plea in behalf of the challenged rate-regulating act.

A country lawyer carried the burden of summation. The seven eminent jurists of the Supreme Court listened in their several ways to the tall, lanky man with the leisurely manner, the long, whimsical face, and the occasional drollery.

Chief Justice Van Bloom, who was seventy and looked eighty, nodded continually and woke himself with starts and sleepy glances about, to see whether or not he had been observed.

Justice Cassner drew curlicues, slightly pornographic, on sheet after sheet of legal cap paper, then carefully scratched them out and threw them into a wastebasket below the polished oak desk.

Justice Noel yawned every ten minutes, scratched himself with the profound melancholy of a flea-ridden pot hound, and threw himself back in his chair.

Justice Rankin gazed cherubically—and with a mind completely blank—at the fly-specked ceiling.

Justice Stafflebach was not sitting.

Justice Fulkin, who was years younger than his very distinguished colleagues, having just reached the age when he was becoming discontented with his wife's lack of interest in his bedroom prowess, propped himself sidewise and gazed longingly—and irritably—at the forms of women in summer dresses, which he could glimpse infrequently through the branches of the elms below the open windows of the Supreme Court room.

Justice Twitter placed his fingers tip to tip and regarded them with a stupendous frown, which might have indicated concentration on the arguments of David Constable, special counsel in the attorney-general's office—but really masked an inward worry over a torpid liver.

It was to Justice Twitter that the special pleader addressed himself.

Dave had no delusions that the jurist was hearing a word he said. But he had to have some kind of target.

Court reporters, with painstaking pothooks, were taking down each word of these proceedings, and the record was going to be important for the future. Wherefore, Constable was making it as complete and persuasive as possible.

Toward the rear of the courtroom sat a knot of silent men with tanned faces and clothing which did not fit comfortably. One of them, with black Indian eyes, was Webb Pettis, state president of the Farmers' Co-operative Associations, which had become a power in Kansas.

The courtroom was stuffy. The day was hot. Flies droned lazily. Subdued distant sounds of a sleepy town came through the open windows.

Dave paused, occasionally, to pass a handkerchief around his throat under his collar. He was glad when Court recessed for luncheon.

2.

In the hotel coffee shop he ate sautéd sweetbreads and conversed with Webb Pettis.

"What's your guess, Dave?" asked Pettis.

"We'll win—this round."

"How do you know?"

"Notice the honorable members of the Court?"

"I reckon."

"They spent more time considering you and the farm members present than they did listening to me."

"So?"

"They were less concerned in the logic of the case, than in estimating the voting strength represented by your crowd of sunburned friends."

"I sort of did notice 'em lookin' our way, now you mention it."

"The justices without exception desire to be reëlected to office," said Dave. "And the Co-op carries too much voting weight to be turned down."

Webb considered. He was shrewd and an excellent judge of human nature, but this was his first experience with a tribunal as awe-inspiring as the Supreme Court of Kansas, and he found it difficult to believe that a consideration of such simplicity would affect its deliberations.

"What happens after that?" he asked at last.

"Upshaw and Cape will appeal to the United States Supreme Court."

"That's next, eh?"

"The Kansas Court," said Dave, "will uphold the principle of public control of concerns heavily weighted with public interest. The United

States Supreme Court will accept jurisdiction on the contention that this affects interstate commerce."

"Have we got a chance in Washington?"

"Just about a chance." Dave added: "I hope."

"You sound a little down in the mouth."

"I might as well tell you, Webb, that we're up against something stronger than logic, stronger than truth, stronger than anything. We're up against a philosophy of political economy. Everything depends on whether the Supreme Court of the United States has a leavening of liberal thinking."

"What do ye think?"

"I'm a little afraid we'll run into mental hardening of the arteries."

"What about them Sherman Anti-Trust decisions?" argued Webb.

"A different matter. Public opinion's too strong against the monopolies to be ignored. The public's not awakened to this question of ours —yet."

They finished their meal in thoughtful silence.

"If they beat us in Washington," said Dave at the end, "we have only one hope."

"What's that?"

"To elect a state legislature in Kansas that's so strong for the farmers, it will rewrite the code in such a way that it will conform with the Supreme Court ruling and yet maintain the chief principles involved."

"Pretty big order, that, Dave."

"I know it." Dave was sober. "Kansas has, at times given the liveliest hopes for the processes of democracy. She's been keen, aggressive, liberal, a leading state in the nation. Look at Populism. But that was when she was fired up with a holy fury."

"Which she ain't now?"

"When the people's bellies are full they find it pretty easy to sink back comfortably and let things run themselves. The state goes back to the old rulers. 'As a dog returneth to its vomit,' you know."

"Have ye forgot the blizzard, Dave?"

"I'm not likely to."

"Stummicks in western Kansas is purty lank this year."

3.

Dave walked back to the statehouse alone. He had his ticket and berth for the return to Jericho in his pocket, and his bag was packed. The train left at nine o'clock at night. He had hoped for Webb Pettis' company, but Webb was taking an earlier train for Wichita. The Supreme Court would not announce any decision for at least two weeks.

It was hot and Dave walked up Kansas Avenue, keeping as much as possible under the awning in front of the stores to take advantage of the shade. His mind was on a conference he was to have in the attorney-general's office before the court resumed sitting at two o'clock. Not with the attorney-general, but with his assistants. The attorney-general himself was a pompous old frog, who had not been in private practice in twenty years.

When Dave came to Topeka at the start of the hearings, he had received from this dignitary a perfunctory greeting and been turned over to the subordinates. There were three of them—bright young men, all with the superficial gloss of the University of Kansas law school on them. Two of them were Betas and the other a Phi Delt. They were one in the ennui of youth, and in their superiority as dwellers in a big city—Topeka's population was around fifty thousand—toward him as a denizen of a country town.

David Constable came to them as a lawyer serving in a private capacity, representing the interests of his client, the Farmers' Co-operative Associations. But by this alliance to the state attorney-general's office he assumed at once almost the sole responsibility for carrying on the case against Upshaw and Cape.

Very rapidly he altered the attitude of the three bored young deputies in the attorney-general's office.

He had not questioned them on the case five minutes before he brought them out of their lethargy; in fifteen minutes they were three young men who were very anxious to avoid any further personal examination by this Westerner who knew the case forward and backward, up and down, as they would never know it, and who possessed a mordant sarcasm toward ignorance. By the time Dave was through with them, they looked on him with the uneasy respect that a troop of gaudy young lancers might display toward a suddenly unmasked battery of heavy ordnance.

They became obedient and deferential; and took orders and followed instructions with exemplary speed and care. They were good boys, Dave felt. He had no further trouble with them. As a matter of fact they were almost embarrassing in their admiration of him; and after the short course in law methods he gave them, were destined to be far more useful than before to the taxpayers of Kansas.

All at once Dave stopped in his slow walk up the street. Beneath a shadowing canvas awning, something in a shopwindow had caught his eye. His mind suddenly abandoned all consideration of the attorney-general's office and all aspects of *Upshaw and Cape* vs. *the State of Kansas.*

It stood smiling at him.

Four inches of pottery. Green greatcoat, gaiters, spectacles, flat hat, shawl.

Mr. Pickwick in painted ceramics.

He remembered how Julia had stood, head tilted, gazing wide eyed. At a Pickwick figurine exactly like this. And he remembered how she had laughed as she told him a woman sometimes liked things quite useless and quite frivolous.

For two minutes he stood looking at the droll figure in the window. Mr. Pickwick. Julia.

He resumed his progress up the street toward the imposing capitol. Within half a block he stopped.

He turned back and walked rapidly to the store. This was ridiculous, foolish.

"I saw a little pottery figure in the window——"

"Yes," said the clerk. "One of our Dickens figures. Mr. Pickwick."

"I believe so."

"We have a nice assortment of those, sir. Royal Doulton. Sam Weller, Mr. Micawber, Fagin, Peggotty, Scrooge——"

"I'm only interested in Pickwick. How much?"

"Three dollars."

"I'll take it."

When he completed his argument before the honorable Supreme Court of Kansas that afternoon Dave felt the little lump of the package in his coat pocket.

4.

Charming vistas of the Kaw River Valley rushed past the car window. Undulating river. Oak clad hills. Fat cattle in lush meadows. Stone farmhouses. Corn already tall.

This was the rich Kansas. The beautiful Kansas. The smug Kansas. The train hurried. *Click-click, click-click.* Iron wheels incessantly clacking over rail joints. Coal-smoke smell. Banana smell. Cracker smell. Squalling children and women going past to the ladies' washroom.

In this part of Kansas there was little in common with the hungry, strenuous, lean West. Kansas was two, perhaps three different places, really. This eastern half was, geographically and physically, a part of Missouri. The south central portion belonged to Oklahoma. Only the West and Northwest possessed truly and inescapably an entity of their own.

Dusk descended. Pale yellow light from station windows whisked past in the gathering darkness. Dave lost the swoop of telegraph wires going hypnotically by.

It was a two-hour ride from Topeka to Kansas City.

5.

The taxicab twisted through brightly lit streets, through dimly lit streets, up a steep hill and down. It stopped. The driver said:

"Here's yer address, Mister."

Dave stepped out and paid his fare. Then he looked up at the brick building. He had found the address in a telephone book.

Modest neighborhood. Small old houses. One or two apartment buildings. A shabby grocery store on the corner.

He went up gray limestone steps with the sensation of a man walking in a dream. All this was fantastic. He had not planned it. It just had happened. He should be this minute boarding a train in Topeka for the West. Instead he was in Kansas City, in the small lobby of an apartment building he had never seen before.

Little metal mailboxes in rows on the wall in the entrance hall. A name on each. Above each a bell button.

One by one he read the names.

There it was. Prim engravers' script on a calling card.

Miss Julia Norman.

He pressed the bell button and stepped over to the speaking tube.

Now that he had performed this act, his throat seemed to constrict with conflicting emotions. In one way it was a victory, ringing that bell. In another, it was the greatest admission of defeat he had ever made.

He waited.

"Yes?" the tube said suddenly. Nasal voice, distorted.

He said: "Julia . . . this is Dave Constable."

The voice did not at once respond. Then it did.

"David?"

"Yes. I was in town. I wanted to see you. Are you busy?"

"N-no." She hesitated appreciably. Then: "I'll ring the buzzer. Open the door and come up. Second entrance to the right on the third floor."

He turned the knob at the harsh squawk. Apartment sounds within. Phonograph down the hall. Milk bottles at the doors.

He was in an agony lest someone should come out and see him. Though he had not the least notion what difference it would make if anyone did. Nobody here could possibly know him. He reached the third floor. Knocked on the second door to the right.

In the moment of waiting he suddenly discovered he could not remember how she looked. He wondered if she would be changed. Her voice on the speaking tube had sounded different. She had invited him up . . . without eagerness. Would she be annoyed? A sort of despair seized him and he swallowed, over and over.

The door opened.

Julia said: "Hello, David." With a note of wonder. She gave him her hand. Firm little grip. Then he was inside and she had closed the door and taken his hat.

For a moment they just looked at each other. Standing there, ill at ease.

Julia wore a white taffeta robe, high at the neck and belted in at the narrow waist—infinitely feminine and enticing.

Her cornsilk hair gleamed. Her eyes were still wells of clear violet with wide black pupils and curving dark lashes. All his old hunger returned, and with it the sick feeling that now it must always be a hunger.

She was seeing the good familiar figure of the man. Wide, bony shoulders, fine forehead with the old errant lock of hair across it. Splendid gray eyes and mouth with lines of humor and kindness.

"Won't you sit down?"

Ridiculously impersonal and primly polite, the way she said it.

It was not what she wanted to say. She did not know what she wanted to say.

That letter in April—it had required an effort not to reply to it. But she had remembered the date of the Supreme Court hearing. And she had hoped he would come; yet feared that he might.

"I was so surprised to hear your voice." She tried to laugh. "I could hardly believe it."

"Yours sounded—mighty good."

That left her silent for a moment. Constraint grew.

His eyes went about the room. Beautiful good taste. The kind of taste he would have expected of her.

She saw the glance and was glad because it gave her something to talk about.

"These apartments are all built in the same pattern. Living-room. Bedroom. Bath. Kitchenette and breakfast nook."

Bright, chatty voice now. Almost too bright. And completely impersonal.

"You have all that here?" he asked.

"Yes. They're livable. But I hate apartments. You seem to be living all the time in your neighbor's lap."

"It's very pretty, the way you have it."

"Not as I'd like to have it. I haven't the time to put on it. Nobody is living with me, and I spend much of my time at the office."

They sat there, being tricked into inconsequentialities and banalities. He could stand no more of this. He rose.

"I think perhaps I'd better be going along."

She rose with him.

"It was pleasant, seeing you again, Julia. I'm happy that you're doing well."

His hand went unconsciously into his pocket, and the fingers encountered something small and hard.

He turned as he was about to open the door.

"I had almost forgotten."

He brought out the little package from his pocket.

"I found this. In Topeka."

With a strange expression she unwrapped the little package.

"Mr. Pickwick . . ."

Her voice was a hushed half-whisper.

She looked up at him and her eyes were filled with tears.

Of a sudden she bowed her head and put her hands before her face, the little pottery figure still in her fingers.

"Julia——"

She turned to him, blind with tears.

"David—oh, David—you *remembered*. And I—didn't even answer your letter. . . ."

She stood, frail and wonderful. He moved toward her, his face gone suddenly haggard.

For minutes they stood close locked, body to body, mouth to mouth, as if they could not get enough of each other.

She drew her mouth away, gasping.

"Mr. Pickwick—" she said with a breathless little laugh. "We're smothering him——"

He allowed her to put the figurine on the table, not releasing her, and felt the miraculous suppleness of her waist as she bent. From the table Mr. Pickwick regarded them benignly.

All at once they were saying all the things they could not say before. The dam burst, their words and thoughts rushed out in spate.

Time lost its meaning. They forgot concern, forgot fear.

She clung to him suddenly, silently; with new fierceness. His heart pounded deafeningly in his ears. In his arms her body shook, and their lips bruised against each other.

She knew what would happen. The inevitability crowded out any hesitation.

A mighty theme of unearthly music played through her. Music . . . wild music . . . carrying in its matchless overtones the boundless realms of the universe, all the longing and fulfillment, the insatiable desires and hopes of the world.

Slowly at first, then in mounting surges, the tremendous chords swept her. The music began in timid pulsation, soft violin notes of attraction, then mounting in desire and passion, with woods and harps, and at last the brasses, climbing and climbing, through sobbing sighs, hope and pain, laments and wishes, delight and torment; until it seemed that in this unworldly orchestration her heart would burst if it did not soon reach to the mighty summit ... and yet she wished that summit never to be reached ... never.

In delirium she sustained the mightiest onslaught of the full crescendo, the most powerful endeavor by unseen forces and aspirations ... to interpret the ultimate. And at last ... the peak. ...

6.

This was their hour, made magnificent by disregard of all consequence, and the reckless gamble for happiness.

Afterward they had coffee in the sitting-room, and talked for hours. Julia seemed to feel neither fear nor depression. She was happy for the time not to think, not to consider the future or the past or any time but the present.

It was he who felt once more a shadowing doubt and sorrow. With renewed sharpness he began to understand how bitter long all the future would be to him.

After awhile he said: "I must go."

"Stay a little longer," she begged, her arms about him, her nose burrowing in the hollow of his neck.

He remained.

"This moment's so important I want to prolong it to its last second," she said seriously. "For there'll never be another."

He made a gesture of protest, but she spoke again:

"It's true. I've put aside the ordinary emotional refuges of women. This I've looked squarely in the eyes—because I had to. What happened tonight ... we cannot risk again."

"I suppose you're right," he said gloomily.

"You have thought the same thing, darling. There is a great future coming for you. This rate case—it is more important than anybody thinks. I know what it means." She put her cheek to his, and pressed his head to her with her soft palm. "Tempest and trouble and venture, and resolve. The great fight is coming and you will be in it. You have taken up the responsibility. You must not look back. Ever."

He held her achingly close. He could not get over his wonder at her. So frail, sweet, almost childish—a shadow under her eyelids, mouth so exquisitely modeled, form so slender.

Yet she was strong.

At the end, it was she who put her arms about him, kissed him devotedly, soothed him, smiled on him, and finally bade him farewell.

"No letters, even?" he asked in parting. "Just an occasional let-ter——"

"No letters. No nothing." She shook her head, smiling. Then her face went suddenly wistful. "Oh, David, darling—you *do* love me?"

"More than anything——"

"I want you to like me better than—anyone——"

It was over in a bewildering flash. She broke off in the midst of it, and looked at him mirthfully, as if surprised at what she had said.

"A woman! Isn't that exactly like a predatory, competitive woman?"

He could not resist her. They laughed together. And so parted.

CHAPTER VII

1.

DAVID CONSTABLE one day stood in a marble building in Washington and took an oath. He was thus admitted to practice before the highest tribunal in the nation, a considerable honor for a country lawyer; but he cared less for the honor than he did for his responsibility. To him this case was of gravest importance, and the difficulties before him seemed very great, the pressure against him tremendous.

The newspapers had discovered *Upshaw* vs. *Kansas* belatedly, but now they were trying to make up for all previous lack of attention. Leading editorials in the rock-ribbed journals put up a devastating barrage, calling attention to the danger inherent to the whole fabric of the System of American Business; declaring the law an example of crackpot legislation; asserting that a great state like Kansas should cleanse its books of any such outlaw interference with Free Enterprise as this attempt to regulate rates had patently revealed itself to be.

David Constable received considerable attention from the press in Washington. But the articles written about him and printed in every large city in the East were not so unpleasant as he had half-expected. This was because the reporters took a liking to him. The wisp of hair on his forehead, his gaunt figure, his pipe, his drawling anecdotes made him colorful copy, and the correspondents loved him for that.

Dave saw no reason to call on the Wedges during his short stay in Washington, and he received no invitation from them.

But he was discussed by them, quite seriously.

Algeria was looking past the present and back to the voters of Kansas; and she was worried over the publicity Dave was receiving. She had never for one moment discounted him as a prospective antagonist for Tucker. In this she was almost alone, but she had an immense respect for the Jericho lawyer and she proposed to leave him no advantages she could take away.

The newspapers, therefore, suddenly had another story to print. Congressman Tucker Wedge of Kansas had issued a statement about *Up-Shaw* vs. *Kansas* which was a forthright attack on the disputed law and all it stood for.

Delighted, the newspapers delved into backgrounds; and discovered suddenly that Congressman Wedge and Attorney Constable came from the same district—the same town in fact. To have the Congressman who had been elected—the reporters looked back at the records—by a truly tremendous majority, and must therefore be the real spokesman of his district, issue a categorical denial of all the Attorney's contentions in the rate case, was more luck than the standpatters expected or deserved.

The newspapers missed nothing in the story. It had front-page space and big headlines, and the pictures of the two antagonists were published side by side. A feud in the Short Grass. The men were bitter enemies—someone said they once had been intimate friends. Great copy for newspapers.

Congressman Wedge's strictures were given full play. "A statute . . . placed upon the law books of the state . . . on the impulse of a temporary insanity . . . the outcome of a momentary, but only a momentary, socialistic hysteria . . . from which Kansas is devoutly thankful it has recovered." And so on.

Congressman Wedge expressed the pious hope that the Supreme Court would throw out the objectionable statute, and went so far as to predict that Kansas never again would be "swept away by the false gods of radicalism."

In the newspapers the assailants of the rate-regulating law had things very much their own way. But before the Supreme Court, David Constable showed so great a familiarity with all the labyrinthine twists of state and federal corporation law, and argued his points with such impeccable logic, that the silken robes of the nine august personages on the august bench rustled with approval.

But almost from the very first Dave knew the fate of his case was foregone.

The Kansas rate-regulating statute was held unconstitutional insofar as it affected interstate commerce, three Justices dissenting.

2.

"A man who-o-o——"

The speaker stood on his toes, sweat dripping from heavy jowls, as he bawled at the crowd.

Tobacco smoke permeated everything; it seemed to radiate from the iron girders and the concrete floor of the ugly municipal auditorium in Wichita. This building was used indiscriminately for livestock exhibitions and conventions, and the smell of the stable filled it, but that did not bother the delegates, for this was the state Farm Convention.

Harp Howell was the speaker, a rancher from Medicine Lodge who had gone broke like many others in the face of railroad-rate differentials, packers' margins, wheat speculators' profit taking, mortgages, blizzards, and droughts. He was mad, blind fighting mad; and he had an idea he wanted to get across to this farm convention.

"*A man who-o-o rep-uh-sents the wish-us of the com-mun pe-pul, the rights of the fa-a-armer and the work-er, the leader in the battle aga-a-ainst the money blood-suckers.*

"*A man who-o-o——*"

The acoustics were terrible. Harp Howell was one of the few who had been able to make his voice heard clear to the back seats in this auditorium. He had been speaking for fifteen minutes, and he would speak another fifteen before he reached the point where he would name "the man who-o-o." But the delegates knew already what name he was going to give them, and the lassitude that all day had gripped the assemblage dispelled itself in a mounting tension.

David Constable, seated on the platform, took a sip of water from a glass on the table, and was glad his hand did not shake with his excitement. He had a curious unwilling expectancy, a doubt if what was going to take place was desirable, a certain relief that indecision was over and he was in for it now.

"*A man who-o-o——*" bellowed Harp Howell, beginning another interminable panegyric. Dave wished he would finish.

A strange, almost inexorable eventuality, this. He glanced over at Webb Pettis, toying with the gavel. Webb was permanent chairman of the convention. He and Dave controlled it. What they had done together would make history—had already made them marked men, both of them.

It seemed to Dave that he had lived politics all his life. But it was only eight months since he had devoted to it the greater part of his energy—the eight months since the Supreme Court decision had wiped the rate-regulating laws off the statute books of Kansas and left the state with no control whatever over utilities, transportation companies or other concerns heavily involved in the public interest.

The day David Constable received word of the Supreme Court ruling was the day he went to war; and it was the day Webb Pettis and the Farmers' Co-operatives went to war with him. It had not started as any personal campaign for office. It had started merely as a farm movement to grasp again the lost control of the state political machinery and repair the damaged system of laws.

But whether Dave desired it or not, it had become a personal matter. His fury made him a speaker of deadly effectiveness. Back and forth across Kansas he stormed, wherever he could find an audience to listen to his gospel—and the farmers were rising and howling their support for him now, wherever he went.

He had become a symbol—the personification of the fight against

piratical utilities and the money power. He had given the farmers a
sense of cohesive force and the understanding of the task to be performed.

And that was the purpose of the speech Harp Howell was shouting
at the convention. The speech was designed to put this convention on
record—to put the entire farm population of the state behind the candidacy of David Constable for the United States Senate.

"*A man who-o-o-o—*" Harp Howell dragged it out longer that time.
He must be nearing his conclusion.

Dave knew that he was being discussed all over Kansas. The name
of David Constable had suddenly risen as a threat to the soft-handed,
smooth-voiced, smiling men. The resultant accord among the big-
business leaders was a thing of amazing, deadly efficiency.

Already he had felt the edge of their rancor. He had been assailed
by the press and by the Old Guard politicians. He had been carica-
tured, lampooned, and blackguarded.

But that was only the beginning. Because the soft-handed men realized that now they were in a suddenly vulnerable position. Fate had
treated them scurvily. The old Senator, the bulwark of reaction, whose
fences were kept in a state of repair so perfect that to defeat him was
almost impossible, had at last felt the palsying hand of age. He was
very ill—he could never run again. The vacant senatorial post was
wide open.

Men like Webb Pettis and Harp Howell were fighting for Dave
Constable's candidacy, because the farmers had a big plan, a bold plan.
Seize control of the state's dominating party, and cleanse it, and use it
as a vehicle of reform. That was why Dave was in the Republican race.
The horny-handed men were making a tremendous gamble for high
stakes. A man like Constable, with statewide popularity, might sweep
with him into office enough men of liberal views to control the next
legislature.

The smooth-handed men had their candidate also, and the resources
not only of the state but from outside the state were being placed behind him.

He was a man with experience in legislative work, a man with common sense, who would listen to reason.

A safe man.

Tucker Wedge.

Dave considered this corrosive fact. Whatever he did, fate seemed
always to throw him against Tucker Wedge. And Algeria.

His mouth closed grimly. This time the issue was clear and the
showdown inevitable. There would be no stepping aside by him this
time. He was impelled by every circumstance—desire to vindicate him-

self, anxiety for the cause he held at the central focus of his life, personal ambition, the promises he had made—to defeat Tucker Wedge and the smooth-handed men. This time.

A sudden great roar shook the air. Harp Howell was looking toward Dave, extending an arm, smiling.

Dave rose. The convention was on its feet, screeching its lungs out, in wholehearted, crazed enthusiasm. Men paraded up and down the aisles. A bass drum's thumping was dimly heard in the tumult, the only sound audible from the brass band which had struck up.

Dave walked to the edge of the platform and raised his arms, a smile fixed on his face.

Once in a long while the people of a state arose and spoke out for themselves. Perhaps this was such a time.

His eyes fell on the press tables where telegraph keys chattered frantically, sending the story of all this over the state—over the nation.

A farm revolt was news. Big news. Disquieting news.

3.

It would have been ironically amusing to Algeria, had it not been so annoying.

She had returned to Jericho with a sense of high accomplishment, of a goal almost reached.

And when she arrived, she was a center of discussion, not because of the brilliant things she had done in politics—but simply because she had introduced an innovation in dress.

Algeria knew that there were big men in Washington who addressed her with genuine respect because they had been shrewd enough to recognize the power behind Tucker Wedge—the capable, clear-eyed, charming woman who was his wife.

It was not quite time for this recognition to become general. But that time would come, and the recognition would be sweet. Algeria knew herself now, and what was in her. Politics had turned out to be the field for which she had always searched, for which her talents were peculiarly fitted. She had conversed at receptions in Washington with men who controlled the politics of Pennsylvania, and New York, and Ohio, and Illinois. And they spoke to her as men and brothers, because she understood their language.

Algeria was quite sure that in the inner circle of politicians she was more highly regarded than Tucker. Because they knew her adroitness, her will power, and her political insight. Some day Algeria would become known as the first woman ever to boss a state politically. That time was almost at hand, and she felt a great anticipation of the day when the nation would know her for her own achievements.

Yet, here in Jericho, she was talked about only because her latest costume took Jericho's breath away.

In a single season the flowing skirt and shirtwaist had been replaced all over America by a strange outlandish mode, the chief feature of which was a skirt so narrow that the wearer was forced to adopt the hobbling, toddling gait of the geisha of Japan.

"Sheath-skirt" was the fashion designer's name for it; but America has never permitted its phrasing to be curbed by couturières or anyone else. America concocted an inelegant name, and it stuck.

Hobble skirt.

Women, handicapping themselves so they could not possibly take a full stride, nevertheless were somehow newly attractive to men.

Out of nowhere sprang a song, heard in construction camps, on harvest fields, at cattle roundups, in factory enclosures. Its tune was the then popular "Casey Jones":

> Come all ye rounders, if ye want to flirt,
> For here comes the lady with the hobble skirt;
> Ye kin hug and squeeze her jest as much as ye please,
> But ye'll never git that hobble skirt above her knees . . .

In this summer the sight of women tottering self-consciously along with the hobble half-step was still enough of a novelty to cause men's necks to crane. Yet Algeria arrived in Jericho with something which at a single stroke made every new dress in town a back number.

Clarissa Grimes, who with Porter Grimes met the Congressman and his wife at the train, was the first privileged to see this unbelievable new costume. The sight caused her eyes to bulge.

Algeria saw her saucer-round gaze and smiled.

"Think it's too daring, dear?" she asked.

And when Clarissa lamely protested her own broad-mindedness, Algeria said:

"Everyone, honestly *everyone,* is wearing it in New York and Washington."

Clarissa Grimes could hardly reach a telephone quickly enough to begin spreading the news.

What Algeria had brought to Jericho was a refinement on the hobble skirt. Hers was so haltering that the most ultrafashionable of the dresses in town looked full and old in style by comparison. Locomotion in it would have been impossible, as an ordinary skirt. And therein lay the breath-taking thing about it.

The skirt was *slit.*

The women took in this fact, and gabbled all at once together. Slit at the *side,* would you believe it—right up to the very *knee!* And those six-dollar silk stockings! As if, really, to *invite* men to look!

Having seethed virtuously, every Jericho woman rushed away and set her dressmaker into sudden activity, for she felt she would perish if she did not at once have a dress to match the audacity of the Congressman's wife.

The slit skirt swept Jericho as it did the nation. In the discussion, which grew instantly heated, politics for a time took a subordinate place. In that hot summer the excitement stirred over the slit skirt was equivalent to that which might have been induced by a small war.

Criticism was immediate, sharp, and prolonged. Editorial writers— but significantly not those of the Jericho *Clarion*—made sardonic and ungallant comments. One crotchety editor went so far as to suggest that it would not be long before women were wearing their skirts right up to their knees, and they might as well do it as what they were doing. Whereupon—very properly—he was boycotted by the insulted womanhood of his city.

Legislatures debated bills governing the moralities of women's garb, but these usually perished before being committed to papers, because the lawmakers found the subject to be a very hot potato indeed.

Smart young preachers who made a habit of hitching on the coat tails of almost any current event for the sweet sake of publicity, preached sermons against the new style.

But all of this was without effect other than providing the nation, and Jericho, with a spiced conversational item. Women continued their willful way unperturbed. The slit skirt was like a fever which ran its course.

4.

Algeria was late at the meeting of the Library Club at the Grimes house. She made it a policy to be late. It is an invaluable means of obtaining notice.

She was to speak to the Library Club on her experiences in Washington, and she wore a new dress. Her wardrobe was the envy of her friends, although the shock of the novelty she had introduced had departed.

Algeria was growing quite skilled in informal little talks, in which she referred intimately to famous people and gave her listeners a vicarious intimacy with ambassadors, society queens, statesmen and visiting nobility, for which her audiences proved most avid. The speeches were valuable politically, and just now she and Tucker were busy building political fences.

There had been one mistake—a serious one—made in Washington. That was Tucker's statement against the rate-regulating law. She blamed herself for it—the idea had been hers, to counter the publicity David Constable was gaining. At the time the position seemed good politics, but since they had returned to Kansas she and Tucker were beginning to discover they had been a long way from their constituents in opposing the regulation of utilities and industries. The mistake had to be repaired and Algeria was doing her full share in the labor of doing so.

As soon as she entered Clarissa Grimes's house, she knew that something extraordinary was on the mind of every woman present.

Fifty feminine faces filled with eager vivacity. Fifty feminine tongues all going at once.

Algeria smiled. She liked to see a crowd of women all letting go, words flowing spontaneously, nobody paying any attention to what anyone else said, all having a good time.

Her late entrance was hardly noticed. No ordinary chitchat could create all this animation.

As soon as she had exchanged greetings with Clarissa Grimes, Algeria said:

"Now tell me."

"Tell you what?"

"What that's all about." Algeria waved a hand at the chattering crowd, and smiled at Clarissa. "If every one of them hasn't something scandalous to discuss, I don't know women."

Clarissa squealed. "Is it possible you haven't *heard?*"

"About what?"

"The Ransomes?"

Algeria shook her head, smiling. "Remember me? I'm just back from Washington."

"Ooh—it's just got out. Everyone's simply *floored*——"

"Come on, Clarissa!"

"Well!" Clarissa drew a deep breath, mouth and eyes wide. "I wouldn't be telling this for *worlds*—you know that—if it weren't all over already. I *don't* gossip, and I *hate* women who talk this way, *but*——"

"I know. You utterly abhor scandal, Clarissa. *But?*"

"Tom and Myra Ransome aren't married!"

Clarissa surveyed Algeria in triumph, to see how she would take this. But at first Algeria, for all her quick intelligence, did not understand.

"Not *married?*"

"Never have been! She's his *housekeeper*—his *mistress*—isn't it shocking?"

"Why—they've always been known as Mr. and Mrs."

"That's why it's so utterly *astounding*. It seems they never took the trouble to have a ceremony. He hired her to keep house. Then he started *sleeping* with her." Clarissa caught her breath. "After all," she said temperately, "I don't blame *him*. Why *should* a man marry a woman when he can get absolutely *everything* he wants without going to the trouble?"

"How can you possibly know this?" demanded Algeria.

"Some people from Kingman, Kansas, where they used to live. Oh, there *can't* be any mistake. Those people knew them too well. The Ransomes moved out here from Kingman and represented themselves as man and wife. *Everybody* accepted it."

"Naturally." Algeria was beginning to believe.

"Of course *everyone* feels so sorry for the poor child. *Dear* little Margie. So sweet and pretty, I've always thought. Of course, she's a little show-off—but that's natural, I suppose at her age. This makes her into a—a *bastard.*" Clarissa almost whispered the word. "Isn't it horrible?"

The horrible nature of the disclosure did not kill the note of jubilation at the triumph of being the first to tell it to Algeria.

It *was* horrible. Algeria thought rapidly.

She did not know Margie Ransome well, but a thing like this would ruin the child's life. Algeria made no pretense of being above enjoying a bit of gossip, and even furthering it. A normal feminine outlet, after all, and not confined to women, either.

But this was serious.

Mrs. Hutto, who was president of the club, moved into the center of the room, her hat on, her glasses hanging on a little hook of gold on her ample bosom, her stern, large face bearing its official look.

"Ladies," she said in a firm, sonorous voice, "it's time we started, and our speaker's here."

The chatter did not cease at once. Mrs. Hutto waited grimly. Gradually the ladies, acceding reluctantly to her dominance, lifted faces suggestive of children obliged to leave play.

"We have with us this afternoon our good friend Mrs. Wedge—" Mrs. Hutto began.

The last voices died; the figures in the chairs rented from the Farthing Funeral Home, became rigid; there was a final sibilant whisper in the back row.

Algeria began to talk.

Her speech was shorter than usual, because all the time she was speaking, thoughts were running through her mind. The Ransome scandal was certain to rock Jericho. Tom Ransome's wealth and unpopularity would play a part in this. Community resentment would make itself felt in ugly ways. And Ransome was a friend of David Constable. There was small doubt that Constable would take his friend's part. Animosity engendered might easily attach itself to him also.

There was another factor: Margie Ransome had enemies, too. Every girl who had been outshone by her resented her. Every mother whose daughter had been eclipsed shared the feeling. Furthermore, there was the old malice remaining from that period when Margie was a symbol of triumph in the Community Church, and a reminder of shame to the First Church.

This was going to be a blow to the Community Church akin to that which the First Church had suffered in the Wilber Bratten affair, Algeria reflected. With something so dynamic loose in the community, no one could tell what might happen. Algeria considered thoroughly all the possibilities.

It was too bad, she assured herself, that a girl so young and innocent as Margie had to be involved in a scurrilous matter of this kind. But Algeria had nothing to do with starting the story. And—since the eggs already were broken—Algeria saw no reason why, if she could think of a way, she should not make from the broken eggs an omelet. She began earnestly to think of some recipe for that omelet: it should be an omelet strongly seasoned with political significance if she had her way about it.

CHAPTER VIII

1.

THERE were days when queer silences fell as Margie Ransome came into rooms where there were other people. Days of strange actions, when her friends did not smile and wave, but looked straight ahead and walked quickly on. Of oblique remarks, with voices kept carefully meaningless.

At last one day she stood before Tom Ransome.

"Is it *true?*" she demanded.

Her father exchanged with her mother a sick glance. For a moment the big man sat silent, his swarthy face glum.

"Where did you get this, Margie?" he asked.

"Mrs. Widcomb—told me—not to come near her girls——"

Margie's tears were welling. Numbed by shock, she had for days been unable to ask the question of her parents.

"So," said Tom Ransome. "It come out after all . . ."

"It *is* true then?" Margie cried wildly. Up to the last moment she had hoped they would deny it—treat this black rumor with the scorn it deserved—perhaps have the people who spread the malicious story in the courts.

Tom looked at her.

"I'm—then I'm—*illegitimate?*" the girl sobbed.

The word had power to terrify and destroy.

He shook his head with stubbornness. "Don't let nobody ever tell you that you ain't a legitimate child," said his heavy voice. "Part of it's true, I guess. Your ma and me ain't never been married by a parson —with a marriage license. But we're as legal man and wife as any in Jericho. Common law. Your ma's got all her rights, and you've got all your rights—same as any other wife and daughter has."

"But—daddy—*why* . . . ?"

His eyes fell. "Margie, you got to try and understand some things. People don't always do the same way. Your ma and me, we kind of fell in love. At first it was—well, a kind of temporary basis, you might say. She didn't know if it was for keeps; neither did I."

His voice grew almost sullen.

"Then we was going to get married. Put it off a little—this move to

Jericho came along. Out here we just called ourselves Mr. and Mrs. Ransome. Everybody let it go at that. Don't you see? When people thinks you're married already it's kind of embarrassing to get married all over again. And one day—we found you was on the way into the world."

His eyes lifted to hers, his face was tender, beseeching.

"What was we to do, honey? Getting a marriage license then—after all them years—wouldn't have done no good. I was in the middle of a big real estate deal—thought I couldn't afford no scandal." He groaned. "Wisht to God now I'd let it go to hell. Myra and me, we talked it over. Concluded to let things go as they was—everything had been all right before."

A long silence.

"Anyway," growled the big man at last, "we *was* man and wife—in the eyes of the law we was. I looked on her as my wife, and stuck to her and supported her and protected her. She looked on me as her husband, and worked for me and was faithful to me. We both said the world could go to hell."

Margie said nothing. After a time she rose and went to her room. Her head was spinning. She believed. At last she believed.

2.

Margie locked herself in her room and cried until it seemed the tears she shed washed all the strength out of her.

Once her mother came to the door and tried to speak to her. Then her father. She would have nothing to do with them.

When she had so exhausted herself that she could no longer weep, she lay silent a long time and tried to think.

She considered oblivion—suicide. It seemed a desirable sanctuary.

She had known a girl, a pathetic creature pregnant with nobody to marry her, who hanged herself with a clothesline in her father's barn.

There was Tom Ransome's shotgun in the closet off the hall. One could take off a shoe, place the muzzle against the forehead, and press the trigger with a toe . . .

And in the bathroom was an iodine bottle with skull and crossbones on it.

But when she rose from the bed, red eyed with weeping, she found she could not bring herself even to look at the bottle with its grisly symbol. She was only seventeen. Vitality surged in her too strongly.

She sat on her bed a long time, staring drearily at nothing.

When darkness came she took off her dress and drew on a pair of overalls and a boy's shirt from her closet—clothes she had worn when she rode with her father in the country. The sensitive swelling of her breasts filled out the shirt, but the overalls, of the bib type, helped hide this telltale evidence of femininity. She crowded her thick hair up under a man's old felt hat, and exchanged her slippers for a pair of coarse farm shoes.

After that she opened her window screen, let herself down in the darkness until she hung by her hands, and dropped. It was quite a fall, but the flower bed was soft, and the only hurt she received was a slight scratch on her cheek.

The moon was coming up. She supposed it was about nine o'clock, and she remembered that the Red Ball freight pulled through the yards in about an hour. People sometimes caught rides on freight trains—men—hoboes, tramps, bums. If men could do it, Margie thought she could. She hoped people would think she was a boy.

As she started alone in the night toward the freight yards, shadows seemed so menacing that she shrank from them. About a quarter of a mile down the track from the regular depot was a freight shed. She decided to hide there, waiting for the train.

As she paused in the shadow of the building she heard, from far away, a long, hoarse bellow. A prickle of fear swept over her. With the coming of that distant train she would cut off all her previous life with a cleaver stroke.

It was lonely at the silent freight shed. Town noises came faintly, and the passenger-station lights seemed remote. She climbed up on the loading dock and stood there; and it seemed that everyone in the world was miles away. The girl's wistful face turned toward the comforting sound of distant motor cars and distant voices.

A weak animal's instinct for protection and concealment took possession of her. She did not like waiting outside until the freight train came.

There was an open doorway. She peeked in. Black in there—but at least it seemed more private. She entered timidly, groped for a box, and sat down on it, her back to the wall.

Through unconscionable eons time trickled slowly, each second a year, each minute an age. A distant clock boomed. Ten times. That would be the courthouse clock. The freight was due at any time now.

Then something brought her all at once standing upright in the darkness. Footsteps. Footsteps on the loading platform.

Margie shrank in a corner, terror choking her.

She tried to reassure herself: Nobody knows you're here. Nobody's seen you. No reason why anyone should bother you.

In spite of all this she cowered.

The steps halted. Then resumed slow progress. Feet neared the shed door. Margie almost screamed, but held herself mute, choking back her voice.

A beam of moonlight lay across the floor from the doorway. In it suddenly a man was standing.

He peered into the shed. Fear greater than all previous terror clutched her. She knew the man.

Gotch McCurdy.

The moonlight fell athwart his ugly face and in spite of herself she gasped. An infinitesimal sound, but Gotch heard.

"Thought I seen you," he said to the black interior.

He had not located her, but he was sure she was in the shed. Leisurely he blocked the door with his body.

There was a long silence.

"What ye doin' in there?" he demanded suddenly, harshly.

A taint of sour whiskey crept toward the girl. The man was drunk . . . Gotch was dangerous when he was drinking, everyone knew that. She shrank farther back, not answering, holding her breath.

"I seen you go in here," he said deliberately. "I follered ye."

He waited. When she did not speak he grinned. A huge paw went into a pocket, brought forth a match, struck it.

The girl's white scared face sprang out in the sudden illumination.

"Get away from me!" she said, hoarse with terror.

He held the flaming match up to his face which had the brutal lines of drink in it. Slowly, inch by inch, his eyes went over her body. Comprehension came into his expression.

"Huh! A girl." He threw away the burnt-out match and immediately lit another. "A *girl*." His tone now congratulated himself. "Who are ye?" He came a step into the shed. "You're the Ransome girl, ain't ye?"

Margie's horror suffocated her.

Gotch took another heavy step nearer, a grin on his thick lips. The stench of bad liquor coming from him was suddenly nauseating.

"What—do you want?" she managed to stammer.

"Nothin'. Nothin' much." He seemed to be trying to soothe her. "I jest want to talk to ye——"

"I don't want to talk!"

He grinned again. "High an' mighty, ain't we?" he said deliberately. "An' we're nothin' but a woods colt!" He took another menacing step toward her. "A woods colt ain't got so much to be high an' mighty about."

He chuckled. Margie understood him. She retreated still farther into the shed, and shook at the look on his face.

"Ye be nice about it, now," said the drunken animal. "No use puttin' up a fuss. It ain't goin' to do you no good. I kin be purty nice to a gal —if she's nice to me. An' I kin get mean, too, if I get mad——"

With a curse he flung down the match. It had scorched his fingers.

In the sudden darkness, Margie felt him reaching for her. Instinctively she twisted under his arms and heard his head thump against the wall. He swore horribly and turned to catch her like an immense hairy beast.

The way to the door was momentarily open. Margie darted toward it like a frightened rabbit. McCurdy bounded after her.

The dock lay white in the moonlight.

Margie doubled to the left as she cleared the door. A row of packing cases blocked her.

She turned to leap off the dock, but the man who was after her had cut off her escape in that direction.

She wailed a hopeless plea.

"Don't—please, Mr. McCurdy——"

In the moonlight his eyes glittered with triumph. Margie was cornered against the wall.

Gotch crouched, his legs bent like a wrestler's making ready to spring, his arms spread. He began a slow, unsteady advance. Margie tried to scream; her voice froze in her throat.

Suddenly he came, in a bull-like, squattering rush, eyes gleaming, yellow tusks flashing, stubble beard bristling with black lust and fury.

Margie stumbled back, her hand behind her. It touched something, closed on it . . . the handle of a shovel, left leaning against the wall.

Desperately she clutched it, swung it upward. With every ounce of strength in her slender body, she dashed the iron head of it squarely into Gotch McCurdy's face.

The man went down without a sound.

His huge limbs sprawled, his legs quivered momentarily, then grew rigid.

A darkness welled slowly out of his mouth—blood.

It formed a little pool on the moon-whitened planking, suddenly shot out a thin red arm that ran to the edge of the dock.

3.

Margie stood staring stupidly down at the sprawling figure on the freight dock.

It seemed so ridiculously easy . . . so unbelievable . . . that her puny strength should stretch the giant out like that. The shovel must have struck him on the temple, and the man's drunken rush contributed as much as anything to the force of the blow. Gotch McCurdy lay in the moonlight like a great log.

Margie stooped fearfully over him. She was gingerly in her approach, ready to leap away at the slightest hint of a movement. She still shivered in terror at the thought of being caught in those gorilla arms.

How huge the man was. One of the great, outstretched legs was almost as large as her entire body. Margie peered into Gotch's face, upturned to the moon. A bruise, already purpling, showed on the side of the wrinkled forehead.

She straightened up. A new terror beat in her throat. Was . . . he dead? She was sure he was. Blood coming out of the mouth was a sign of death someone had told her. She had . . . killed.

Margie fought for her breath. She began to think:

Murder—they hang people for murder.

She gathered courage again and knelt beside the inert body. From the nostrils and half-open bleeding mouth came a revolting fetor of sour liquor; but she could detect no sign of breathing, nor could she feel anything like a heartbeat, as she placed a hesitating hand on the great arching chest.

Suddenly she rose to her feet. For some minutes, as a background, unnoticed in the terrible excitement immediately involving her, she had been subconsciously aware of a sound. It now came sharply into the fore part of her mind. Snorting, clanking, splintering ding-dong of a brazen bell. The freight train. The Red Ball was pulling past on the other side of the switch yard. It was the train she had wanted to catch, but now it was going . . . going. . . .

With her heart pounding, Margie fled desperately from the freight house, away from the lights of the city, toward the long trundling of the square-topped cars which made an ugly moving pattern against the night sky.

Fear replaced fear in her.

She stumbled over uneven places, dodged this way and that to avoid obstacles in the darkness, turned her ankle slightly and limped as she ran.

Her breath came short. It set her thinking: How would it feel if her breath did not come at all? How would it feel to be hanged?

"Ah, dear God," she moaned.

Suddenly, quite unexpectedly, she was leaping among the tracks, bounding and tripping over a treacherous underfooting of iron rails and wooden ties.

A pungent smell of smoke. Just ahead, rolling slowly but with un-hesitating purpose, was the train of cars. She glanced fearfully up and down the freight yards. Nobody was near. Far up, beyond the head of the train a distant lantern winked.

A name, in white letters, on the side of a car: KANSAS CITY & SOUTH-ERN.

But this was not the Kansas City & Southern line. The name gave her purpose, though.

The train gained headway, but Margie ran harder, gaining on it.

Up ahead the engine lurched faster. With a clattering of coupling blocks which began at the tender and traveled toward the rear of the train in a rapidly mounting crescendo of sound, the whole string of cars gained sudden speed.

They were sliding away. Margie hurled herself forward.

Her clutching fingers felt iron handles. Closed.

She leaped and was jerked through the air.

Miraculously, her foot came down on an iron bar; the lowest rung of the ladder.

She clung to the Kansas City & Southern car, gasping, as the train sped out of Jericho.

4.

After a while she got back her breath and was able to climb around where she could stand on the bottom of another ladder, between the cars, close to the couplings.

She thus placed herself in shadow, out of direct view of the train crew, if anyone happened to glance down the train.

She knew now that her arms were shaking with weariness. For the first time, also, she realized that she was crying. She had been crying a long time; how long she did not know. Her face was wet. Her throat ached from sobbing. She felt very weak and clung to the ladder in dread lest she lose her hold.

The train swayed and lurched, the movement increasing as it gathered speed beyond the city. Margie's head spun with dizziness, the reaction from her long run and from her hunger.

She began to be afraid she would fall between the cars.

Her imagination pictured what would happen to her if her body plummeted down there . . . bloody rags under the wheels.

It made her cling more despairingly to her ladder, using up strength uselessly, so that her knuckles and forearms ached with dull throbbing. With horrified fascination she stared down at the roadbed, dimly glimpsed, lurching under her in the darkness. There was something hypnotic in that smooth, sinuous passage. She shut her eyes tightly. . . .

5.

"What ye doin' down there?"

The voice above was so loud and startling that Margie convulsively tightened her grip on the rough iron handles. Her face turned upward, pallid in the gloom.

Peering down was a rough, harsh visage. A railroad lantern, held down to illuminate the space between the cars, threw into relief the features of the man, investing them with heavy, sinister lines. All the shadows fell the wrong way on the face. The top of the forehead was shadowed by the bushy, protruding eyebrows. The man's nose appeared huge and grotesque because of the shadings which extended upward from the lantern's rays. His mouth had a brutal look and the lines about it were etched more deeply because of the unnatural angle from which the light beat upon them. His mouth opened, a dark cavern.

"Come on up here!"

With frightened, instinctive obedience, Màrgie began to climb toward the throaty growl, going reluctantly, not daring to disobey, her eyes on the face above.

A big hand reached down, seized her arm roughly, and hoisted her on the sloping roof. The lantern rose and Margie felt the eyes of the man going over her.

"I'll be dogged!" The brakeman was astonished. "A gal!" He studied Margie by the light of his upheld lantern. "Only a kid," he said next. "Well, you're an odd 'un." His voice was gruff, but with the lantern light in a more normal relation, his face no longer appeared so sinister.

"Where ye think you're headin' for, sister?" The visage hardened.

Margie felt a faintness. She had not the least idea. Then suddenly she remembered the lettering on the car—this car—which she had seen just before she caught its iron ladder.

"I—I guess—" she said weakly. "Kansas City——"

"So! Bummin' to Kansas City!" The brakeman's voice grew savage. "Ridin' other people's cars, an' tryin' to slip by an' get honest folks in trouble by cadgin' rides, eh?" He hesitated, scowling. The lantern had shown him the tears on the girl's face.

"I—no—" Presented in this new light to her, Margie did not know how to reply to the question.

"Don't try to lie out of it!" broke in the brakeman with a sort of dogged harshness. "A female hobo, eh? An' ye'd be perfeckly willing to sit by an' watch a man with a wife an' six kids get fired off the line for lettin' ye sneak aboard the Red Ball. Yes, ye would!" He seemed to be whipping himself into a kind of fury.

The engine ahead tooted a couple of times and the train began to slow. Margie hoped it would stop, or at least slacken its speed so she could drop off. She tried to edge away from the accusing lantern.

"Don't try to get away!" Margie froze into immobility. "I know your kind. How old are ye?"

"S-seventeen——"

"Seventeen, eh? An' a no-good little tramp already! I suppose that jest because you're a gal I ought to shut my eyes an' let ye ride? That's the way ye look at it, ain't it?"

"No, sir. I—I'll get off as soon as the train slows down enough——"

"Oh, ye'll get off, will ye?" The brakeman made an absurd mimicry of the girl's voice. "Ye think that'll soften me up, now don't ye?"

"N-no, sir."

"Ye do, too! Lyin' ain't goin' to help ye. An' let me tell ye, my fine, fenaglin' young lady, you're badly mistook if ye think Jim Fitzwilliams will soften up toward *any* bum, *she*-bums included, what's stealin' rides on the Johnny O'Brien."

She could not help it. Tears filled her eyes and she bowed her head. Overwrought, shaking with weakness, she clung to the catwalk, sobbing, blind, despairing.

The brakeman looked at her, holding up the lantern to see her better.

"When did ye eat last?" he asked suddenly.

Had she been asked to give her name or tell why she was running away, Margie would have lied. But the sheer irrelevancy of this question surprised the truth out of her.

"Not—since morning." She fought to stop crying. The train began jolting to a halt. Far ahead, through her mist of tears she could make out the hulk of a water tower. Dim figures labored over the engine's tender. The cars were at a standstill.

"Get yourself down off this car, immediate!" growled the brakeman.

Margie obeyed. Preceded by the man she descended the iron ladder. She stood on the ground beside the train, looking at her captor, wondering if she dared bolt and try to escape. All fight seemed taken out of her.

When the brakeman moved she cowered instinctively away. A blast or two came from the engine up ahead.

"Not since mornin', eh?" said Jim Fitzwilliams. From the distant front of the string of cars began the progressing clatter of coupling blocks, taking up the slack as the engine started the train once more. The sound moved rapidly toward them and the brakeman turned on Margie.

"Get into that there car," he ordered.

A door stood open, dense blackness within. Margie stared, uncomprehending. Closer came the rattle of coupling blocks.

"Want to keep me here all night?" snapped the brakeman bitterly. "I'm hind shack on this train an' I got my work to do. Get into that car afore I—throw ye in by the britches—which may the Holy Mother forgive ye for wearin'——"

He seized Margie's arm and hurried her toward the opening.

Unresisting, too dazed really even to wonder what her fate was going to be, she scrambled in. The car already was lurching into motion. The brakeman gave her a shove. For a moment of sick fear she thought he was coming in after her. Instead she felt a paper parcel into her hand.

Jim Fitzwilliams was gone. He had waved his lantern, caught a passing ladder, and climbed to the top of the train.

For minutes Margie, crouching in the blackness of the box car, found it difficult to understand what had taken place. Then, by feel and by smell, she examined the package the brakeman had pushed into her hand.

It contained a sandwich of bread and bologna. Jim Fitzwilliams' own lunch.

6.

Old Doc Patterson chewed on his spectacles. The glasses had made red furrows on either side of his tired nose, and his white surgical gown was tight across his belly.

"The corner of the shovel took him in the left temple," he told Constable. "Massive hemorrhage in the lateral cerebral tract and destruction of brain tissues. He'll be gone in a few hours."

Dave gazed down at McCurdy. A nurse in stiff, starched white sat beside the hospital bed, keeping icepacks on the man's head. Gotch's face looked strange and distressed in its swathing of bandages. His lungs fought stertorously for air.

"Will he get back his senses?" asked Dave.

"Extremely doubtful."

"Then this stands as a deathbed utterance?"

Dave glanced again at the sheet of paper in his hand. It contained Gotch McCurdy's statement, gasped out when he first was brought to the hospital.

It was the Ransome girl done it. She was skipping town and I tried to get her to go back home.

That was all, except for the signatures of the witnesses:

NATHAN J. PATTERSON, M.D.
ERCELINE WINROD, R.N.

A switchman had found McCurdy shortly after midnight on the freight-shed loading dock.

"He was dying when they brought him to the hospital," said Doc Patterson. "He wanted to say something—we took that down. Then he went into coma."

"This is a lie!" exclaimed Dave. "Look, Doc—can't you bring him back long enough for me to get the truth out of him?"

The physician shook his head.

Dave went out into the night. It was hours yet before dawn. When he returned to his office Tom Ransome was still waiting there, haggard and fierce.

"He's about gone," Dave told him.

"Did he say anything more?"

"No. He's unconscious and slipping fast."

"God! Can they fasten that on Margie because of his say-so?"

"A deathbed statement's hard to combat in court, Tom."

"God, my poor woman!" the big man moaned. "God, she's like to gone crazy. God——"

Dave gazed at him, babbling there with distraction, and the look in his eyes was something Tom Ransome did not understand.

"Tom, I'll be with you whatever happens—to the finish," he said. Ransome grasped his hand, not knowing why the promise was made, but blindly grateful for it.

"Before we do anything else," added Dave, "we've got to find Margie. A girl in a boy's clothes—she ought to be easy to find."

Tom Ransome only clutched his head in his arms.

7.

Gotch McCurdy lingered two days. Doc Patterson said it was a miracle. Even with his brain rotting in his skull the stricken man's herculean strength fought off death.

But he was gone at last, and with that a new factor entered.

Six citizens, friends of Dr. Rister, the coroner, and impecunious enough to be glad for the patronage of one dollar for sitting on a coroner's jury, brought in a previously prepared verdict:

We find that the said Rufus J. McCurdy came to his death as a result of injuries caused by a shovel, said shovel being at the time aforesaid in the hands of one Margery Ransome. . . .

The same day Jasper Peddigrew, as county attorney, issued a warrant which in ponderous legal phrases charged Margery Ransome with having unlawfully, feloniously, willfully, knowingly, and with intent and malice aforethought, committed a murder, by inflicting upon Rufus J. McCurdy certain injuries and contusions which caused and/or contributed to the death of the said Rufus J. McCurdy.

The necessary ritual of legal verbiage being thus accomplished, the hunt for Margie Ransome overlapped the surrounding counties and spread across the state.

Murder is the most unequivocal of all crimes. Violent death is raw, savage, and primal, and it arouses raw and primal instincts—blood lust, and the hunter's craze, and herd ferocity. The murderer is an enemy, a fugitive; he must be pursued, trapped, punished. No excitement equals that of a man hunt. On the faces of persons merely reading about it in a newspaper, the eyes narrow, jaws set, lips thin to cruel lines as atavism resurges.

When the quarry is a handsome girl, the additional fillip of sex is added. Human impulses then are sometimes hard to gauge.

Dave was not surprised, although it angered him to find that most of those to whom he talked in Jericho were very willing, even eager, to believe in Gotch McCurdy's "death statement." A few were skeptical simply because they found it hard to believe that a girl as frail as Margie could have wielded an implement as heavy as the shovel with enough strength to cause a fatal injury. These, however, found their arguments unpopular. Everyone, nearly, seemed greedy to believe the worst.

The usual lewd stories went around. Margie Ransome was a sly hussy, it was openly said. She did her singing in the church choir with that sweet and innocent expression of hers, to cover up her shamelessness. Circumstance to these stories was given by nodding women who asserted darkly to each other that blood always tells—a child born out of wedlock could hardly be anything but wild and lawless.

A strange mutation of public opinion occurred concerning the dead Gotch McCurdy.

Jericho had regarded him as a ruffian, a criminal, little better than a dangerous outlaw.

Now, however, viewed in the light of the morbidly stirred new interest, he suddenly became, in the general estimation, a citizen worthy of respect, even affection. And this even to those who had once been most bitter against him. His "death-bed statement" was repeated, discussed, savored. According to that utterance, Gotch had been trying to induce Margie Ransome to return to her home where she belonged, when she struck him fatally. It was proof of an underlying kindness which, Jericho agreed, all too few had recognized in the stableman.

McCurdy anecdotes began to be related. He had loaned his greyhounds to rabbit-hunting boys. He had *almost* been converted once, by the weight-lifting evangelist. He had given this or that down-and-out vagabond shelter in the livery stable. This kind of talk grew until Gotch McCurdy almost assumed the stature of an unappreciated philanthropist.

It remained for John Farthing, the undertaker, to sound the final note, however, to the sanctification of the memory of Gotch McCurdy. After he had laid the liveryman out for burial, Farthing came near to tears in recalling what a superior hearse driver Gotch had been.

Immediately all Jericho remembered that McCurdy—in top hat and long black frock coat—had driven to their final resting places many citizens who had passed on to their reward. That was in the days when he owned the only hearse in town; and the fact that he was paid good wages for the rental and driving of the hearse, and that he was usually fair-to-middling drunk when he so officiated, did not in the least minimize the recollection of him as a sort of Charon for the elect of Jericho in that period.

This remembrance completed the transformation of Gotch McCurdy from a graceless rascal into a beloved public figure—a figure for whom the entire community now began to be convinced it felt an aching sense of loss.

Had anyone, in his lifetime, told him the kind of a funeral Jericho would give him, McCurdy would not have believed it. All pews in the First Church were crowded. Gotch possessed no family; so his congenial and disreputable companions, the hangers-on at the livery stable became the chief mourners, and were seated together at the front, where they clustered somewhat uneasily, and itchily, glancing about as if they feared they might be discovered and ejected; and at the same time giving forth an aroma of moonshine whiskey so rich that it permeated the entire solemn atmosphere of the church.

The Reverend Matthias Widcomb preached a moving funeral sermon. His text was that old favorite: "I am the Resurrection and the Life," and he exercised admirable skill in employing half-truths and oblique implications to limn the picture of a man who, perhaps, had been misunderstood because his virtues were hidden 'neath a rough exterior; but who, in the deepest sense, was a True Christian because he followed the Great Commandments, and was gone to a Sure Reward. Many in the congregation wiped their eyes, and sincerely regretted having once spoken of Gotch McCurdy as a disgrace who ought to be hanged, or at least permanently lodged in the penitentiary.

A long and moving account of the funeral ceremony appeared in the *Clarion*—written with the best tear-jerking journalese. The heaps of flowers at the grave were described, and Gotch was referred to editorially as "a product of his time and place, a man who went his way, fearing nobody, sometimes making mistakes—as do all of us—but inevitably and unquestioningly a true son of Jericho, who met an untimely and tragic end in a kindly effort to do a good turn for a family he scarcely knew."

After the funeral and the *Clarion* article, indignation increased on the streets. And now the real animus behind it began to appear. Margie Ransome had been a shining mark for spite and envy; and her father was much hated.

It was openly and loudly asserted that the authorities were making no serious effort to apprehend the girl because Tom Ransome's money was buying them off. Threats were made. Tom Ransome went to sleep at nights with a loaded shotgun beside his bed.

CHAPTER IX

1.

JULIA could not have told what made her heart leap when the telephone rang.

Hundreds of times that telephone had rung in her office, and never before had she felt the quick, breathless surge that she did now at the short trill of the bell.

Months had passed since that night with Dave. Each day she went to the office. Her services were highly satisfactory. Her employers often complimented her. But she seemed to be working with one half of her mind only. The other half was passive, occupied with dull wonder at herself and what life had done to her.

Now, all at once, a lightness of anticipation possessed her. She could not explain it. One doesn't explain premonitions.

Julia picked up the telephone receiver.

"Miss Norman," said an airy voice. "Jericho, Kan-sas, is calling Miss Nor-man."

She knew. The premonition had been correct.

A wait, and she heard ghostly voices on many distant wires. "Your call is ready, Omaha. . . . Op-er-a-taw, I'm still waiting for my call to St. Joseph. . . . Sorry, Mister Thayer is not at this num-bah. . . . Wichita, puh-lease ring two eight oh thrrrree."

Then another voice, far away. "Hello?"

She felt a kind of wandering panic.

The voice grew stronger. "Hello? Hello."

She said: "Hello. David—this is Julia."

"Hello, Julia!" he cried. There was joy in his voice. Then he hesitated. "Julia—how have you been?"

"Fine. David, it's a rotten shame about the Supreme Court."

"I expected it all along. But Julia—this call—you must forgive it. I could think of nobody else——"

She could not help the feminine counter: "So—as a final resort—you called me?"

"But Julia—" His voice was astonished. "You told me——"

"I know, I know." She laughed a little, but not very mirthfully. "What do you want of me, David?"

Again the hesitation. "Many, *many* things . . ."

She clung to the telephone and made her voice behave.

"But, David—what particularly."

"Julia," he said after a moment. His voice became stronger now, more direct and businesslike. "I want your help in finding someone. Margie Ransome."

"Margie? Oh!"

"You knew that Gotch McCurdy was killed?"

"Yes, indeed. The papers here have had quite a lot about it. What's that preposterous thing about Margie?"

"Julia, Margie . . . killed McCurdy."

She was stilled by the certainty in his voice. At last she said: "How can you know?"

"I'm morally sure. You knew McCurdy. He was drunk."

"How can I help?" she asked, groping for his meaning.

From infinite remoteness he said: "I have reason to think the girl's in Kansas City."

"But why?"

"I traced her through a freight brakeman. My own private line of information. The sheriff's office has no idea—yet."

"What am I to do, David?"

"She's got to come back. On her own volition. To face the charges. This is important for her case."

She said: "And you want me to find her?"

"You're the only person I can trust. Will you?"

"Of course."

Another voice broke in. Impersonal, chill voice of mechanical feminine officialdom.

"Your three min-utes are up."

"Operator," protested Dave, "we're not finished."

"I will keep the cir-cuit op-en. Kindly do not talk lon-ger than necessary." Glib repetition by rote.

"Hello, Julia," said Dave.

"Hello. I'm still here."

"Thank you. The case doesn't look too good at this end. McCurdy made a death statement accusing the girl."

"Don't be silly, David. This is a natural for a defense attorney. No jury's going to convict that girl when she testifies. She had a reason— you know she had—she only needs to tell it."

"It's not that simple. You've forgotten Jericho. There's a whole lot more in this than a girl facing a murder charge."

She drew in her breath. "I begin to understand. Are you going to defend her?"

"I must. And I may be just the worst possible counsel for Margie."

"How, David?"

"Politics. With me in the case, every aspect of it will be tinged with politics. They'll be after me—through her. It might be easier for any other lawyer in the state to acquit her."

She thought a moment. "Why do you take the case, then?"

"Tom Ransome is my friend, and he will have nobody else. But there's another reason that's more important."

"What reason?"

"I kept Gotch McCurdy in Jericho, Julia. I defended him. I made myself responsible for what he did. A sort of sneaking attachment for him—proud of myself, I guess, because I could make him do what nobody else could. And there was a stubbornness about it, too. Nobody was going to tell me whom to befriend. That sort of an attitude. If it hadn't been for me, McCurdy would have been gone years ago. Whatever happened—and nobody knows what did happen—I was as much to blame as if I'd been there myself. His death—the way it happened—was my fault. Don't you see, Julia? I'm morally obligated. I've got to clear that girl if it's the last thing I do!"

"I see," she said. Then: "I'll do my best."

"Find her. Wire me when she takes a train back. I'll meet her."

"I'll come back with her, David."

"No!"

His vehemence astonished her.

"Why not?"

"It wouldn't be wise. Not just now." He was silent for a moment. She could almost hear him thinking. At last: "I'm not making myself clear, am I?"

"Not very."

"I can't very well explain it. This place is upside down. Nobody knows what will happen. The farther you're out of it, the happier you'll be—and I, too. I know it doesn't make sense, but——"

"All right, David."

He said goodbye. She hung up, slowly.

2.

Julia sat behind her desk and looked up at the man.

He was a private detective. He was huge, gentle voiced, slow witted, impossibly ugly, and loyal.

His name was Sammy Fogel, and Julia marveled at his ugliness each time she saw him. He was an ex-wrestler, Jewish, and his head had been crushed and malformed by the brutalities of the so-called sport to which he had devoted his big body in the days when he still was able to think clearly—before head-scissors, and flying mares, and headlocks had damaged his brain. He had the walking-beam shoulders of a wrestler; they and his great torso stretched out the ill-fitting gray suit he wore. At either side of his head protruded ears twisted like Brussels sprouts. His nose was dished and beaten out of shape, his lips were bruised to an unnatural thickness, and his eyes receded into his skull under deformed brows.

Sammy was assigned only to strong-arm jobs by his agency. He had been sent to Miss Norman because the case looked simple.

"I t'ink I mebbe got a lead, Miss Norman," he said.

"Where?"

"Like you said, she's a singer. I done the joints all the way up Twelft' Street, an' along Baltimore, an' Grand, an' South Main. This kid kinda answers the description, but the name's different."

"What does she call herself?"

"Bonnie Francisco. She's at Joe Moccasso's night joint."

"How can I see her?"

Sammy scratched his close-cropped head.

"I ain't talked to her, like you said. She don't even know I been watchin' her. Guess it wouldn't do to bring her up here——"

"No. I'll go down to Moccasso's."

Sammy shook his head. "Miss Norman, that ain't no place for a lady——"

"I'm not a lady. I'm a lawyer."

3.

Together they walked slowly down Twelfth Street, listening to the hurdy-gurdy sounds of it, seeing the over-dazzling lights, the over-bright color, the overhectic bustle of the vice palaces.

Twelfth Street in Kansas City was a four-mile, brawling, garish honky-tonk—wide open and raucous, running from the Stock Yards clear to the Black End. The big "parlor houses" were south of it, toward the river. So were the big gambling establishments.

The bulk of Kansas City's night life, however, ran along Twelfth Street—the theaters, the nickelodeons, the penny arcades, the dance halls, the saloons, and the burlesque joints.

"You really didn't oughta to go into places like this, Miss Norman," protested Sammy Fogel for the tenth time.

"I've got to see the girl," said Julia. "The girl I'm looking for has only one way to earn a living—by singing. Nobody knows her but myself. So I must have a look at Bonnie Francisco."

"O.K., Miss."

They turned into the cheap joint.

Even Sammy's dished-in nose wrinkled in disgust. The air was rank with tobacco smoke. Around a small dance floor stood little tables, crowded with blowsy patrons of both sexes, drinking, smoking, and clawing each other. On the floor a tall, black-haired girl with a glassy grin was pulling tawdry garments off her wriggling body, swinging fat white hips and singing a suggestive song to the limping accompaniment of a four-piece "orchestra."

Julia halted near the entrance. One or two drunks stared at her from the bar, but most of the crowd was watching the stripper, removing her clothing with an excess of twisting and feigned coyness. The girl continued until the last flimsy article came off, and she stood, mother-naked, twisting, squirming before the crowd. The grin of glass did not change as she scurried behind the curtains with the patrons yelling and whistling after her.

The orchestra—piano, bass fiddle, cornet and violin—thumped a new tune. A few couples shuffled on the dance floor. Julia watched with detached semi-interest the "hostesses" at work around the tables—the girls for unattached men to dance with, or buy drinks for, or take upstairs. The place seemed the ultimate in depravity.

A new act came on. Coarse jokes from a scaly "comedian"—pitched to the level of degeneracy. A chorus of battered female creatures, with dirty costumes and fixed grins, looked worn and old as they went awkwardly through stiff gyrations.

Julia began to be conscious of more and more stares from bar-flies and table patrons. She was accustomed to being looked at by men, but this depraved appraisal was unpleasant. She experienced a crawling sensation between her shoulder blades.

The crass comedian, who doubled as master of ceremonies, bowed to his titter of applause.

"Now, friends—a little girl, with a great, big voice. A hand, friends. Miss—Bonnie Francisco!"

Like a circus announcer, he held an arm toward the curtain.

Julia forgot the stares, the insinuating whispers.

Margie Ransome stepped out from behind the curtain.

But what had they done to Margie? Lips a scarlet smear. Cheeks hectically painted. Hair rolled over a huge wire "rat" into a monstrous pompadour. Tinsel, shoddy dress.

From where Julia stood it seemed that one week had already cheapened the freshness of the girl into something tawdry enough to be in keeping with even this vile place.

But then Margie began to sing. And Julia's sinking heart took courage again. When Margie sang the cheapness and tawdriness somehow disappeared. She forgot herself, her bloated audience, her ugly surroundings. It was no anthem she was singing, but her voice soared:

> In my harem, my harem,
> There's Rosie, Posy, Josie——

Even with a song like that Margie took possession of everyone who heard her. The gross men and blowsy women sat silent at their tables.

Julia pulled at Sammy Fogel's sleeve.

Sammy stepped over to the proprietor, a greasy young Italian, in a gleaming white shirt front and black tails.

"Hello, Joe."

"Hi, Sammy."

"Who's the dame?"

"Out-of-town gal," said Joe Moccasso.

"Like her looks."

"Wastin' your time, Sammy."

"Yeah?"

"Won't do nothing. Cold as undertaker's ice. Won't even take no drinks with the customers. If I wasn't payin' her peanuts—five bucks a week—I'd bounce her."

At that moment Margie Ransome saw Julia. For the first time her eyes went to the back of the room. Julia knew it the moment the girl's gaze reached her. Margie recognized Julia and was frightened.

From the crowd came a storm of applause. Margie bobbed to it, and disappeared.

"Sammy," said Julia, "we must go backstage."

"Miss Norman," said Sammy, "this is Joe Moccasso, the guy that owns this joint. Joe, Miss Norman would like to go back—to see that gal who just sung."

"Why—delighted," said Mr. Moccasso, all gleaming gallantry when he saw Julia. "But she'll be out for her encore in a minute. Then I'll take you back."

But Margie did not come back. Moccasso looked annoyed.

"What's a matter with her?" he said. "She can't treat my customers that way. I'll——"

He started off. Julia nodded at Sammy and he followed, with her close behind him.

"Hi, Kiddo. Where ya goin'? Buy you a drink?"

Soft insinuating calls from men at the tables. But nobody was loud about it. That dish-nose and Brussels sprouts ears of Sammy's discouraged too much boldness.

Backstage, a dirty little runway led between the dressing rooms. Half-naked harlots stared and giggled. Cockroaches scuttled over the walls. The young Italian knocked at a door.

"Lookin' for Bonnie?" asked a black-haired girl. She was the strip teaser. She posed unabashed in a thin negligee through which her breasts were plainly visible.

"Yeh, Monica. Whyn't she come out for her encore?"

"She skipped."

"Whaddya mean?"

"She ducked out the backstage entrance right after her number."

"Why that little . . ." Moccasso began wrathfully. The strip-teaser grinned and thrust her hip at him.

"Do you know where she lives?" asked Julia.

Monica's grin vanished. Woman against woman.

At Joe's order, she named an address.

Julia filled her lungs with fresh air as they stepped out from the backstage entrance into an alley. Even the garbage smell seemed pure after that night club.

Sammy looked doubtfully at her.

"What you want to do now, Miss Norman?"

"Go to that address."

Sammy hesitated.

"I don't think you'd ought to," he said plaintively. "It's wuss'n this joint."

"I don't see how it can be."

"It—ain't safe, really. Tough people there."

"What about Margie? She's there."

"Miss Norman—let me go. I'll make a pinch—a fake pinch. She won't know no different. I'll bring her to you. You shouldn't ought to go to a place like that."

"You said that before."

"I mean it this time."

"Sammy, I've got to talk with Margie. And arresting her is the one thing I must avoid."

4.

It was everything Sammy had said. Dirty old brick tenement. Stink of excrement and sour whiskey.

Even Julia paused, almost daunted.

"You see?" said Sammy.

A streetwalker dawdled past them, conscious of a man in shabby overalls who was following her. She stopped, turned, and pretended to gaze into a darkened storewindow, swaying her hips a little. The man in overalls halted beside her.

Half-fascinated, half-disgusted, Julia watched the approach, the reply, the greedy smile of painted lips. The man in overalls went up the steps into the building, clutching the chippy's arm with an odd, shamefaced possessiveness.

Drunks lurched boisterously. A beggar came slowly toward Julia—a blind man, playing an accordion. Some doleful tune. "Nearer My God to Thee." Religious. They nearly always played religious tunes, very slowly, like dirges. Sammy dropped a dime in the tin cup fastened to the beggar's shirt front.

"Thank 'ee," the blind man said.

"Superstition," said Sammy apologetically to Julia.

The beggar went on up the street, the accordion growing fainter.

She looked up at Sammy. His bulk and the almost frightening ugliness of his huge head suddenly were very comforting.

She realized that Sammy was anxious, and for good reason. This part of town at this time of night was not a place for a nice woman.

"What now?" asked Sammy.

"We'll go in."

He shrugged his shoulders and led the way, glancing about warily. She stayed quite close to him in the half-lit hall.

Four rooms on the first floor. Three of them locked. A morphine-maddened hag snarled at them from the fourth.

Up dangerous rickety stairs they went to the second floor, and looked about the narrow hall.

A woman opened a door and stood, half in, half out, watching them silently. Tough-looking bat, with peroxide hair like rope ravelings. Cigarette in her discolored teeth.

Sammy walked over.

"Know anything about a gal roomin' here—a young gal?" he asked.

The rope-haired creature goggled at him.

"Naw—what's she like?"

"Brunette, seventeen, purty, sings. Goes under the name of Bonnie Francisco. Works at Joe Moccasso's."

She looked at him insolently. "You a dick—or a pimp?"

"What's it to you?"

The prostitute backed into her room. "I ain't talkin'."

But Sammy had his large foot in the door.

"Listen," he said. "I ain't interested in *you*. But I'm gonna find that gal."

"Uh-huh," said the woman as if now confirmed in a theory. "I *thought* she was somebody's gooseberry. That the wife? I ain't sayin' nothin'."

"This here's nobody's wife," said Sammy. "She's a lawyer."

"Oh, yeah?" The prostitute smiled thinly.

"An' that gal ain't nobody's gooseberry. She's jest run off from home."

"Go wan! You tryin' to tell me she's still a bud? Nemmind. I'll take your word for it. Only, brother—if you wanta keep her that way, get a move on. The dame don't live kin work on Twelfth Street without gettin' her safe blown——"

"Shut up! Ain't you got sense enough not to talk like that before a lady? Now look—you tellin' me, or ain't you?"

"What'll you do if I don't?"

Julia saw a door open—open just a crack, and quickly close again.

"Sammy—that door—" she said.

Sammy had seen it too. With amazing speed, considering his size, he leaped and thrust a shoulder against it. The door flew back on its hinges.

It was Margie. Eyes of a deer, cornered in this last hiding place.

"Go away—please go away—" she said to them.

Her voice was pitched strangely with fear. She was tearful.

"Margie," Julia said, "I came to talk with you."

But the girl would not listen. She began to sob.

"Look, kid," pleaded Sammy. "We're your friends, see? You're in a jam, ain't you? We only wanna help you——"

"I don't want help! I'm all right. I'm doing what I want to do. Now—leave me alone, won't you?"

She was distraught. Julia said: "Sammy, wait outside."

When he was gone, she turned to Margie.

"You go, too!" cried the girl through her tears.

For an instant Julia bit her lip, feeling embarrassed. She was not so very much older than Margie. Hardly enough to warrant her telling the girl how to run her life. Julia had not been so very successful, she thought, with her own affairs. But something must be said—said right now. It had to be exactly the right thing, or it would fail. Julia thought of what to say, lifted her head and began.

"I heard someone sing tonight. It wasn't much of a song. But it was a voice—a wonderful voice." She paused. The calmness of her tone had in a degree soothed the overwrought girl. "I've heard some great voices, Margie, but I don't think I ever heard a more beautiful natural voice than the one I heard tonight."

This was flattery—the most artful flattery—and yet Julia meant it with all sincerity. She believed in Margie's voice.

"You must not waste a voice like that," she went on. "You owe something to it—very much to it, Margie. It was given to you, but it doesn't belong to you. Perhaps you don't care what happens to yourself—but you must care what happens to your voice."

For a moment Margie believed. But thought returned and with it the sullen look.

"What are you talking about?" she said in a hard, brittle tone. "You know nothing good can ever happen to it—or to me—now."

At that moment Julia had her inspiration. "Margie, sometimes things happen which seem very bad, but really are good——"

"What is there good about *this?*"

"It may be the chance you needed for your voice."

Utter astonishment replaced the bitter resistance in Margie's tear-stained face. "How—how can you say that?"

"First—you must go back to Jericho."

"No! I'll never——"

"Margie, dear. You must trust me. It's the only way."

Julia, watching Margie's face, saw the conflict in it, the inward thought, the readjustment of ideas.

At last: "Would—would you go with me—Julia?"

Julia nodded.

Margie came to her weeping, in a storm of relief, of new hope, of gratitude.

5.

It was hours after the train left Missouri that the plains began to discover themselves to Julia. She had looked forward to them eagerly.

The rich, tree-embossed earth of eastern Kansas was far behind. Moist plowland, and groves of elms and oaks, were back there somewhere along the endlessly parallel gleam of the steel rails. Here the train seemed to crawl across a featureless country, low hills in the distance, yellowish and apparently sterile, yet covered with summer-cured buffalo grass. The country seemed abandoned. Here and there a few cottonwoods straggled along crooked water courses, emphasizing rather than diminishing the poverty of the soil. An occasional settler's cabin appeared remotely.

At long intervals they passed through little hamlets, desolate looking and afflicted with a dreadful sameness. Frame depots, water tanks, grain elevators, thriftless stores along deserted main streets. They were identical in almost everything, even to the town loafers leaning in the shade, talking idly and spitting tobacco juice.

It would have seemed a dreary prospect to some, but Julia watched it from her car window with mounting exhilaration.

Always the plains had appealed to her. They were so magnificently immense; satisfying some inward feeling. She pressed her cheek against the smooth glass, her face in repose, her eyes on the impossibly distant horizon.

Facing her sat Margie. A different Margie now. Simple dress, face clean and fresh, her hair as it always had been, a glorious mop of black curls, without a rat to mar it. She was still desperately frightened at what lay before her.

Julia wondered what would become of Margie. She wondered what would become of herself. She should not be here, riding across the plains to Jericho.

She knew she should not; David had told her she should not. It seemed part of some fate that had closed about her. She felt a dread, but she could not escape it.

I am in love, she thought. Once I was not; now I am. Love is something that really does not exist at all. You cannot touch love, or handle it, or measure it, or even understand it . . . any more than you can do those things to the imponderables of absolute time and space. Yet love is real and tangible, almost the most real and tangible thing in the world.

I knew it was David before I picked up the telephone . . . I knew it across five hundred miles of cities and forests, and rivers, and plains. The knowledge was more immediate than the electric impulse that brought his voice.

His voice . . . it gave my life purpose, where it had no purpose before.

Yet I am mad, being here on this train, going to David. I should be sane, at least. There is no use arguing that my return to Jericho was necessary because I had to accompany Margie. I could have persuaded Margie . . . but I could not persuade myself.

She saw running along the railroad track an irrigation ditch which had been led out into the wide valley from the river, and her eyes observed the curious contrasts created by it. Within the embracing arm of the ditch were fields—crops in severe rows, and stacks of alfalfa hay, giving an appearance of fecundity and abundance to the land inside the embrace of the irrigation canal.

Outside the embrace, however, as far as her eye could see, appeared only a limitless sterility.

My life is outside the scope of irrigation, Julia thought. Sterility. Withered grass, wide stone expanses, immense airy dry flats stretching away. There was a time, only a little time, when I was in the embrace. I was ready for love—ripe for love. And I loved . . . the wrong man.

Wrong? Could David ever be the wrong man? I cannot believe it. Something is crazy about the entire scheme of things, and I do not know . . . I wonder if I will ever feel emotion again. I long to feel— to feel intensely—even if it is tragedy. A life of no feeling? Rather no life at all!

So she sat, continuing to gaze out of the car window at the wonder of the plains. The sun was just setting. Clouds heaped tremendously

in the west, and the descending sun played on their tortured and unnatural evolutions. Some of the swelling bosses were dazzling white;
others ran a wild gamut of scarlet, flame, and gold. Bases were purple,
deepening in the inestimable depths of the valleys to ebony. The train
seemed to run wheel-deep in a sea of bloody light.

The mystery of the cloud heights, with their innumerable clefts and
swellings, was like the mystery of all life.

And Julia was going back to Jericho—when she had no business
going back to Jericho. She was going, on a decision made almost
without thinking, but from which she was unable to turn back.

She had dreaded and looked forward to this day. Her own conflicting sensations exhausted her. The great kaleidoscope of colors in the
west faded into pastels, then grays.

Darkness descended.

Julia sank back almost in relief. She would rest . . . until they
reached Jericho.

6.

The moment she and Margie left the train, Julia had a strange sensation of foreboding, of entrapment. She could hardly understand it.
The feeling seemed to dull everything.

She saw David crossing the brick platform toward her. The sight
of him had been something she had been waiting for, hungry for,
hardly expecting, really—something almost like a hope deferred until
it was almost ready to die, then suddenly, throbbingly revived.

But now, at this minute, she could only think that he looked taller,
leaner, and—yes, older. Her gladness was numbed.

Even when she felt her hand in his, she could not respond. She
heard his voice, and managed to answer something. Glare of night
lights from the depot caught her wide-brimmed hat, and the pale
wash of her hair, but could not penetrate to her dazed soul.

He released her hand and it dropped limply by her side.

From the waiting room a big, worried-looking man hurried. Tom
Ransome. Margie flew into his embrace and wept wildly there. Even
this seemed to create little impression on Julia.

She heard the tail end of a sentence from Dave:

". . . Go directly to the courthouse. Bail is arranged. After that,
Tom, you can take your daughter home."

Julia still was unable to understand herself. Jericho looked as always.
Only a few persons were at the station, but she recognized Andy
McAdam busy with the baggage, and saw his grin and wave.

Other impressions were dim: the car sped away up the street; familiar fronts of Jericho stores showed momentarily in the light from

the street lamps; her heels clicked on the sidewalk before the shadowy courthouse; only the office of the district court clerk, on the second floor, was alight.

She heard Dave speaking, Tom Ransome, Margie. All this was unreal and hazy.

Afterward she was alone with Dave on the courthouse steps.

"I'll take you to Mrs. Hutto's," he said.

"No. It's out of your way. I'll call a cab——"

"Nonsense."

He drove the car with both his big hands on the steering wheel, looking straight ahead to where the headlights brought the street rushing under their wheels. She sat very primly, far on her own side.

After a time she said: "The Kansas City papers had a great deal about you."

"Indeed? Hardly complimentary, I suppose."

"Well, the *Journal* seems friendly——"

"Ah? But the *Star* and the *Post?*"

"Not very."

They laughed a little, restrainedly. How curiously and unnaturally they were acting, speaking mechanically, without real meaning. It was her fault.

As they neared Mrs. Hutto's Dave said:

"Julia, you've got to sit in on this trial with me."

The proposal suddenly brought her alive, made her mind clear. Her old unwillingness to enter the courtroom arena returned to her.

"Why?" she asked quickly.

"I need another lawyer. You're the only one who is as fully concerned over this case as I am."

"But I'm a brief lawyer."

"A lawyer, primarily. And your first duty is to the client. I need you, Julia."

"But David—I—I have no courtroom experience. I can't think of it!"

His voice was deep and calm. "Yes, you can. You think of it tonight. I'll want to talk the case over with you tomorrow, and we'll discuss this further then."

The car slid to a stop, and stood, the engine still puttering. A light glowed in the parlor window of the house.

"Mrs. Hutto's sitting up for me," Julia said, almost hurriedly. "You won't need to get out."

As if to forestall something from him, she opened the door and stepped to the curb.

"Thank you. Good night," she said.

She knew he was studying her in the darkness, but she could not see his face. Suddenly she felt very silly.

"I'll come to your office tomorrow," she assured him, trying with her voice to make up for this strangeness through which she had been passing.

"Good night, then," he said.

She went up to the house in the darkness. Behind her, the car drove away. She did not look back.

CHAPTER X

1.

ALGERIA never came down to breakfast without doing her hair.

Women who put sloppy lace caps over an untidiness of uncombed witch's locks and drake's tails turned her stomach. She did not understand how men possibly could abide them.

When she entered the dining-room, her graying hair was as beautifully, meticulously neat as if she were just going out for the evening. She wore a full-length silk dressing-robe.

Tucker already was well into his eggs and bacon.

"Just got a phone call," he said. "Clarence."

"What was it?"

"Quite surprising."

She withered further nonsensical prolongation. "Really, dear, if you've something to tell me, need we play childish games?"

He smiled feebly as she lifted the silver coffeepot.

"Well, then—Margie Ransome's back in town."

"She was caught?"

"No. Came back of her own accord. With Julia Norman."

"Really?"

"David Constable met them——"

"This is extraordinary!" Her eyes were alight now with intense absorption, and he felt a small triumph after all.

"Dave arranged the bail. Margie's gone home now."

"David Constable was there." Algeria's voice was almost absent. She poured a cup of coffee and took a piece of toast. Coffee and toast were all she ever ate for breakfast. One cup, black. One slice, dry. A lifelong abnegation for her figure.

Her even white teeth bit into the crispness, but she scarcely tasted the food. All at once she gave a sigh—of relief, or perhaps of elated discovery.

"Constable's defending the girl?"

"Of course."

"Will Julia assist him?"

"Looks that way."

She thought a moment. Then she laughed, almost gaily. She could not have hoped for so much good fortune. . . .

"Where's Julia staying?"

"Mrs. Hutto's."

She sipped her coffee. Now the light in her face changed to the gleam of intrigue. With growing zest she considered this information.

Whatever bore on David Constable was of immense importance now. Algeria had sampled public feeling; far better than did her husband, she knew how dangerous Constable was. She looked upon him with no malevolence, but with an impersonal and deadly concentration. In her mind she began arranging facts she knew and things she suspected, a mesh of cross-linking circumstances. The fascinating machinery of unpresentable motives and actions were what made the dull, correct façade of politics interesting to her.

"Will they convict the Ransome girl?" she asked suddenly.

"I hardly think so."

"I suppose," she mused, "it would be impossible to convict her of *murder*. She'll swear that McCurdy was attacking her. But what about some lesser charge—manslaughter?"

"I didn't know you had it in for the girl?" He was rather stupidly surprised.

"I haven't the slightest interest in her. It's just a peculiar problem."

"Margie Ransome's entitled to justice, Algeria. Like every other freeborn citizen, she deserves a fair and even-handed trial before a jury of her peers——"

She gave a shudder of distaste. "Don't be a professional public man, dear—not with me. Please."

She knew exactly how to deflate him.

"What's on your mind?" he asked after a minute.

"That this may elect you senator."

"I wish, dear, you wouldn't talk riddles."

But now she smiled brightly and shrugged a shoulder at him, her good humor all restored.

"I've nothing, really, to base it on. Just a woman's instinct."

He knew her too well. "Algeria, what are you up to?"

She rose from the table and paced back and forth, her silk garments swishing and whining about her.

"Nothing." She smiled to herself and at him. "At least I don't know what. It all depends on—what happens."

She was lying. But she knew Tucker did not possess the cold realism this sort of thing required. Only one man in Jericho did possess it. Porter Grimes.

She glanced at the little gold watch pinned on her dress.

"Oh, dear. I'm late, and I have a very busy morning. Let me know if you hear anything more on the Ransome case, will you?"

Tucker finished his breakfast alone, but without the relish with which he had started it. His face seemed to be a field for conflicting thoughts, some of them not entirely pleasant.

2.

Julia said: "I'd rather not."

"The newspapers will be full of this case," he urged. "It will be a big trial."

"I know that. But——"

"Your firm in Kansas City will be gratified at the professional reputation you would get."

"I suppose so."

"And Julia——"

"What?"

"I want you in this case."

Their eyes met, clung together.

"There's something I must tell you," he went on. "When I knew you were coming, after your telegram, I was afraid."

"Afraid?"

"I'd spent months trying to put you out of my mind." He paused. "I didn't succeed."

They sat with the wide desk between them, and she pressed her fingers to her palms, seeing the whitening of the nails.

"I have even less right to think of you than before," his voice went on quietly.

"Why?" His words suddenly left her with a sense of desertion, pain. She waited, her heart almost chilled in her, for his reply.

"I've committed myself to this campaign," he told her. "A lot of people are depending on me. I am not my own man any longer."

"I went away once . . . not to interfere. Yet you want me—in this case with you."

"Because it's the last time for us to be together, Julia."

"It's always the last time, David. We've said it before."

"This time it *is*. It will be on a professional basis. The . . . other . . . is past. This case is a natural for a defense attorney. They're going to try to pin some kind of a conviction on poor little Margie—make an example of her—because of the queer, deformed way some of the people in this town think, and because my political enemies believe it would hurt my prestige to be defeated in court. I'm going to get her off—*we're* going to get her off—if you'll agree, Julia."

She looked into his eyes. "I agree."

She rose.

He came to his feet with her. And the movement seemed to release an emotion pent and held in iron check.

"Julia." He said her name softly, caressingly, almost in a whisper.

She stood rooted, watching him with a curious helplessness as he came around the desk to her. She felt his hands on her body as he drew her against him. Roughly he kissed her and her mouth trembled. Then his lips were against her throat.

"Please—" she sobbed.

"Julia—I can't help loving——"

She cried almost weakly. "Oh, God—I never intended this."

All at once he released her, stepped away. She stood trembling as he walked to a window and looked out.

For a long time he stood staring out, and she could only guess how profoundly shaken he was.

At last he turned, came back, and stood behind his desk. His eyes did not meet her. His face was rigid, the lines in it suddenly deep bitten.

"Forgive me," he said hoarsely. "I didn't intend that either. I will not let it occur again."

She was silent. Then he added:

"I suppose this will change your decision?"

She shook her head, expressionlessly. "I will act."

"Thank you," he said quietly.

She went out.

3.

When Belle Constable turned into Cox's Department Store, she did not see Algeria across the street.

Algeria, just coming out of the Jericho National Bank, smiled to herself. She had just finished a long conference with Porter Grimes, who would have an understanding with Jasper Peddigrew, the county attorney. About the prosecution of the Ransome case there was to be nothing half hearted.

That was the first step in Algeria's plan. She now contemplated a move of consummate boldness. It concerned the woman who had just gone into Cox's store.

Algeria stepped into the street, with the instinctive lifting of her skirt, a gesture innately graceful and feminine. She was not conscious of it. She did it as she did everything else, with style. Every move she made attracted attention to her, even when it was no more than crossing a street with a slightly lifted skirt.

The entrance to Cox's store was cool; and the clean, almost medicinal smell of dry goods came out of it. Belle was standing at one of the counters across the store. Algeria crossed to her.

It was the notions counter at which Belle stood. Needles and pins, and spools of thread, and elastic, and shoelaces, and buttons, and hatpins, and emery cushions, and sewing baskets. The infinite minutiae of which women's lives are comprised.

Belle glanced up. A frozen look of withdrawn hostility came in her face when she saw Algeria.

"Why, Belle! How do you do?" Algeria said aloud.

Her voice had a lilt, as if Belle were a dear friend whom she had not seen in a very long time.

"How are you," said Belle coldly.

"I saw you come in and I thought—it's been so long—I'd just follow you and speak." Belle watched her with complete suspicion. "I've wanted so often to chat with you—I've really neglected *all* my friends I'm afraid—Washington and Congress, you know. But when I saw you just now, I simply made bold—on the spur of the moment!"

Nobody could carry off a thing like that as Algeria could. Belle was unable to keep from thawing. She believed Algeria had some purpose in this, but it was, after all, not unpleasant to have the enemy thus come to her, for whatever reason.

"I was just looking," she said, unnecessarily.

"I, too! We might look together. And afterward—won't you have lunch with me—say at the Tea Room here?"

If it had not been so easy, Algeria could almost have been proud of herself. She had snubbed this woman for years; and the woman came around so eagerly. Goodness, how stupid Belle Constable was. Algeria had met many singularly dull women in Jericho, but this one surpassed them all.

She labored on her conversation, mixing interest, amusing things, and bright friendly charm. Talk grew easier. Constraint gradually departed, and something resembling cordiality took its place. Thirty minutes later they were lunching together in Cox's Tea Room.

To Belle it was something like a triumph. Almost dazed she listened, and it was gratifying to hear the hints Algeria dropped into the conversation—as one might drop floating petals into a current, not disturbing the flow, but accomplishing certain changes in the pattern. The hints did not constitute an apology exactly, but in their sum they comprised something in the nature of an explanation—of Algeria's attitude toward Belle. They had drifted apart—some inadvertence on which Algeria could not at the moment place her finger. But now—after all—Algeria gave an intimate little laugh—they *should* see more of each other. Of course, there was politics. But husbands were husbands. Algeria admitted Belle into full confidence. Women need not let the little bickerings of men affect their attitudes toward each other. Men were childish after all, weren't they?

A new exhilaration took possession of Belle. Secretly, she had hated Algeria above anyone, because secretly she admired her more than anyone. Now, to be understood—and to have Algeria become intimate as well as cordial—Belle tried to appear not to notice how other women gave a start of surprise when they came into the Tea Room, and how their heads went together when they saw her with Algeria.

Mrs. Judge Hutto waddled in, followed by a tall young woman with amber hair.

Mrs. Hutto gave them a nod and headed straight for a waiting table. Julia, however, spoke pleasantly before going on.

"Attractive, isn't she?" said Algeria, watching the girl's straight back.

Belle, looking after Julia, conceded that to some she might be called attractive.

"Personally, I can't see it," she added.

"Nor I," Algeria agreed. "But that type seems to have some mysterious fascination for men."

"I suppose so. Still I can't see how *any* man——"

"It isn't what a man has on his mind. It's what a girl like that has on *hers* that does the damage." Algeria paused. "Isn't she working with your husband on this case?" she asked.

"Why do you ask?" said Belle quickly. Something in Algeria's manner faintly disturbed her.

"No reason. Only—girls are so wretchedly spoiled nowadays. They have no compunctions—as long as it's a man——"

Belle was silent, brooding. Algeria surveyed her with the faintest hint of amusement in the deeps of her gray eyes.

"Have you finished your luncheon?" she asked. "The check's mine. Now I'll give you a lift home."

Several women nodded and smiled as they passed out. It almost restored Belle's feeling of satisfaction.

But not quite. When Algeria let her out at home, Belle was still thinking.

4.

At every session, the courtroom was crowded, and by the fourth day of the trial Julia knew that, for reasons unstated, the prosecution was dragging out the proceedings to unreasonable length. An unconscionable time was taken in selecting the jury. Long hours were spent haggling over the most minor legal points.

Julia actually had expected when she came to Jericho, that upon the recital by Margie of the circumstances leading to Gotch McCurdy's death, the case would be dismissed. But it was not so simple. Someone was hostile to Margie. Someone—behind and above Jasper Peddigrew, the county attorney—desired strong prosecution. Peddigrew also was affected by his own hatred of David Constable. Poor Margie Ransome—without knowing or desiring it, she had become a point at issue, the first test of strength, between two new and bitterly inimical forces in the state, of which David Constable represented one. The other was not apparent on the surface.

The importance of the case was recognized and shown by the unprecedented attention paid by out-of-town newspapers. Two correspondents from Kansas City papers, one from Topeka, two from Wichita, and one from Denver were on the spot, besides the Associated Press. As a result the press table in the courtroom was crowded.

The reasons for this abnormal interest were several. Among them were the sensational circumstances, the scandal concerning Margie's parents, the physical charm of the defendant herself, and above all the personality and political significance of her chief counsel.

This was more than a mere murder trial. A hard-fought criminal case sometimes provides unparalleled opportunities for disclosures concerning not only the prisoner at the bar but other principals. A whisper that was more than a whisper had been murmured in the ears of certain great editors, that the proceedings of the Ransome case might be eminently well worth watching. Politics—hot politics—was involved in anything touching David Constable.

Sometimes, listening to the case, it almost seemed to Julia that Dave was on trial instead of Margie. With continual spiteful insistence Peddigrew asked every prospective juror if he knew or had ever known David Constable—and in the manner of his asking there was more than an implication that a heavy taint attached to the character of any man who would acknowledge such acquaintance. To this Dave paid little attention; he had expected it. Julia was sorriest for Margie Ransome, twisting her handkerchief at the defense table, and for Tom Ransome, sitting anxiously beside her.

The attitude of the town amazed Julia, in spite of Dave's warning. She had forgotten how small communities nurse and savor and squeeze the utmost out of any suggestion of evil.

Unfortunately, Tom Ransome's defiant attitude toward Jericho's prejudices had done nothing to help. The Ransome case had provided the town with a morsel to chew and taste and digest slowly and thoroughly through an infinite amount of talk. Tom Ransome and his "wife" still lived together, openly, in a state of sin as Jericho viewed it.

The man had gone into the legal aspects of his union. Friends, including Dave, had suggested to him the propriety of a church marriage even at this late date, but he refused to consider it. In the eyes of the law, he declared, Myra was his full and legal wife. To marry her all over, would be to admit that in the previous years, including the time of Margie's birth, she was not his legal wife. On this he stood stubbornly.

Myra Ransome had become more than ever a recluse, and this far from moderating the criticism against her, only made it more bitter. Myra, to a good segment of Jericho's upright feminine population, was little better than a prostitute. To be a man's *mistress*—a word so dreadful that it was spoken only in whispers—was surely a form of whoring. People now remarked significantly that they understood why the woman spent all her time in that garden of hers—it was a lurking place for a guilty conscience.

As for Margie, Julia observed that her round prettiness seemed sometimes only a liability. An unpleasantly sex-twisted morbidity appeared in some persons. The very handsomeness of the girl seemed to make it more necessary to Jericho's moralists that the court make an example of her.

This feeling was fostered and encouraged by the *Clarion*. As the only newspaper in Jericho, the *Clarion* was regarded by many of its readers as an immutable rock of journalistic rectitude and wisdom.

Its news stories concerning the Ransome trial were carefully written to skirt the edges of libel, but its readers knew how to peruse between the lines, and it was generally taken for granted that far more than could be told, in the columns of a journal so moral and upright as the *Clarion,* lay behind the details published. When newspaper readers in Jericho scanned the articles about the Ransome case, all hedged about after the manner of approved journalistic practice with equivocations, such as "alleged" and "according to" and "on reputable authority," nobody should have blamed them for peering through this dense undergrowth of verbiage and allowing their imaginations to conjure up all manner of monstrosities in the shadows there.

Yet had it not been for a continuous secret pressure from unspoken sources, the case against Margie Ransome might have collapsed rather quickly. Public opinion had been most skillfully played upon by the *Clarion,* but the American public is not by nature vindictive. More and more persons were beginning to feel that Margie Ransome had suffered enough.

This was not, however, reflected in the attitude of the prosecution. Jasper Peddigrew and his assistants were grimly bent on obtaining some kind of a conviction. The county attorney had received his orders. Under the provisions of the law, he was demanding conviction of Margie on a charge of murder in the first degree, by malice aforethought, deliberate or premeditated. The criminal code allowed the jury to make its choice of the degree of homicide. It might vote for a conviction in the second degree, which was murder committed under provocation of sudden passion. Or it might decide upon voluntary or involuntary manslaughter. The prosecution asked for the ultimate, in hope of obtaining something less; for any kind of a conviction would be a victory for Peddigrew.

5.

Day after day, while the state presented its case, Julia sat at the counsel table and watched Dave hammer the witnesses. She had thus far not made a single motion, objection, or conducted one of the cross-examinations. But she was ready at his elbow, with the correct notes, the correct transcript of previous testimony, the correct citation, exactly as a skillful surgical nurse is ready at the surgeon's elbow with the right scalpel, the right clamp, the right sponge.

She saved him immense labor and time. It was her first direct professional association with him, and her admiration for him as a lawyer increased daily. He had the ability to pack a perfect load of inference into a single question asked of a witness, and this skill stemmed from his immense knowledge of the circumstances and legal precedents of the case.

Night after night Dave was at his office, reading, digesting, studying, annotating the heaps of stenographic pages from that day's hearing. Frequently Julia joined him. Their relationship was strictly, carefully, professional now. When Dave went to the courtroom next morning, the material they had studied together was photographically impressed on his memory, so that he could pounce on the slightest deviation in testimony, and confound a witness by laying his finger definitely on pertinent page and passage almost without referring to his notes.

He seemed confident. But to Julia it appeared that Jasper Peddigrew's prosecution was gaining ground. The switch-yard employees testified to finding Gotch McCurdy dying on the loading dock. The shovel which had caused the death was introduced as an exhibit. Post-mortem findings were presented. Most damaging was the deathbed statement by McCurdy, which was read in a dry, professional voice by Dr. Patterson.

The prosecution rested.

Dave called a witness to show that on the night of the slaying, McCurdy had been drinking.

Then Margie took the stand to tell her story.

In the tense atmosphere of the jammed courtroom, the girl answered the questions in a timid, halting manner. She had gone to the freight yards. McCurdy had followed her. He had attempted to seize her. In self-defense she had swung the shovel.

Peddigrew took the witness.

What was she doing in the freight yards?

"Running away," said Margie.

"Running away? Running away from what?"

The girl stumbled and stammered.

Perhaps, sneered Peddigrew, she didn't want to say? Perhaps she would rather tell the court why, after striking the fatal blow, she did not report the occurrence?

Margie tried to tell him that she did not realize she had struck Mc-Curdy so hard.

Peddigrew leaped on that. And not realizing, he asked triumphantly, did she catch a freight train immediately out of town, not even calling for help? Wasn't it the truth that she knew herself, at that very moment, to be guilty of murder? Wasn't it?

During the brutal cross-examination, which left Margie sobbing, Dave was on his feet continually with objections. Again and again Judge Henry Poster, a fair man, and a sound, if not brilliant, lawyer, upheld the objections, but Peddigrew found ways to get around them and the lashing examination went on.

Julia, at the counsel table, watched Dave's face. His eyes were serious, his mind concentrated sharply on the clash of wits. She had the feeling that this to him was as coldly pure an intellectual matter as any abstract problem in higher mathematics.

She looked at Margie, shrinking and twisting in the witness chair, and wished it were possible for her to be as calm, as unstirred as Dave seemed to be. Julia was not calm. Her two fists were clenched in her lap.

It was an hour before Peddigrew triumphantly dismissed the girl. Her admission that she had fled, knowing that McCurdy was unconscious on the dock, instead of reporting the alleged assault attempt, was damaging.

"We've got to counter that," Julia said in an undertone to Dave. "Call me to the stand."

He shook his head. "I don't like the way Peddigrew's acting. He'd do anything. And you'd be a target for him."

"I can take care of myself—with Mr. Peddigrew or anyone else. Call me. It's our best chance to break down that line of testimony."

He looked at her. "All right," he decided. He rose. "The defense will ask Miss Julia Norman to take the stand."

The crowded courtroom sat forward with new interest and there was even a stir at the press table. The exceptional good looks of the associate counsel in this case had not escaped the newspaper men, and frequent comment on this had been made in the stories they telegraphed to their papers each night. But Julia Norman had been disappointingly static in this case. Now at last she was going to do something. They poised pencils over copy-paper pads.

Julia took the chair and was sworn. She gave her name, her occupation, her place of residence, and said that she had known Margie well while living in Jericho.

"You talked to Margie in Kansas City?" asked Dave.

"Yes."

"What did you discuss?"

"She planned to return to Jericho."

"And you returned with her?"

"I did."

"Tell the court under what circumstances she returned."

"Margie Ransome was informed that murder charges had been filed against her. She decided to return to Jericho of her own accord, without pressure from anybody, because she wished to answer those charges and prove her innocence."

Julia's clear testimony obviously made an impression on the jury. Dave bowed to Peddigrew. "Your witness, Mr. Prosecutor."

The county attorney swelled portentously as he advanced.

"Miss Norman, you say you talked with the defendant. Is it not nearer the truth to say you hunted and found her?"

"I did find her."

"Was she at that time a fugitive?"

"Perhaps."

"A fugitive from what, Miss Norman?"

"A fugitive from slander and cruelty and prejudice, Mr. Peddigrew!"

"Ah? Occasioned by what?"

"Circumstances over which she had not the slightest control—her birth."

"I understand you, Miss Norman, to assert that the people of this city of Jericho slandered the defendant and were cruel to her? I was not aware that Jericho was so vicious and depraved." He sneered. "But you, I take it, say it is?"

"No."

"Then what are we to understand from your statement, Miss Norman?"

"I do not hold the entire town to blame for the actions of a few."

"Very generous of you, Miss Norman. *Most* generous. Who are these culpable people to whom you refer?"

David Constable was up with an objection, sustained by the judge.

"Your honor," said Peddigrew, "I have a purpose in this line of questioning."

"What is your purpose?" asked Judge Poster.

"To show prejudice on the part of the witness."

"There is no prohibition of prejudice in a witness."

"There is, please your honor, if such prejudice destroys the value of the testimony."

"Nevertheless, objection sustained."

Peddigrew was thwarted, but his malice had been revealed. He took a different approach.

"Miss Norman, what is your relationship to the chief counsel for the defense in this case?"

"Associate counsel."

"Is that *all?*" The sneer again.

Dave rose, his face pallid with anger. "May it please the court, the implications in that question are such that I must resent it, as I think every right-thinking man would resent it! I object to the question and move it be stricken."

"Objection sustained," said Judge Poster.

Peddigrew shrugged his shoulders and dismissed Julia.

Through the courtroom passed nods and nudges. Heads bent over the press table as reporters scribbled frantically. A hundred interesting speculations had been aroused. Beneath the surface of this case something highly significant had suddenly been scented, and the readers of the downstate and outstate newspapers would get the full benefit of innuendo from the pens of these correspondents on the morrow.

Dave whispered to Julia: "It was a mistake to call you."

"We had to have the testimony."

"Yes—but it gave Peddigrew a chance for his ugly tricks."

"It was a chance we had to take," she said.

6.

The first flash of apprehension came to him that night when he went home.

He did not know that Belle had spent that afternoon, and many others, mysteriously absent from the house in the company of Algeria Wedge. He did not know that she had listened to a story told by a little sewing woman, Mrs. Dierks.

He did know that there was something like triumph added to the bitterness in the face of Belle when she confronted him at the door.

"I suppose you're happy now," she said.

"What do you mean?" he asked with exasperated weariness.

"As if people already weren't doing enough talking——"

"What are you driving at, Belle?"

"Read that!" She thrust a copy of the *Clarion* into his hand. It was so folded that he could not help read the passage recounting Julia's testimony and Peddigrew's sneering questions.

He summoned all his patience. "Newspapers will say anything."

"That's *true* isn't it?"

"Don't be ridiculous, Belle!" he snapped impatiently.

"Ridiculous! *Ridiculous?*"

"Julia Norman is a lawyer—and that's all she is as far as I am concerned."

She sneered. "No more than a lawyer? And you see each other every night?"

"Yes. In my office. With two secretaries present. To go over the next day's case."

"And that's *all* you go over together?"

His eyes blazed. "Don't you imply anything about Julia——"

But Belle retreated rigidly, a mingling of hate and triumph in her eyes.

He went up to his room. For a time he sat still, thinking.

Did Belle know something? What could she know?

Presently he went to his desk and tried to write some letters, answers to an accumulation of correspondence. Tremendous amounts of letter writing must be done by a man in politics. Stacks of mail from selfish little men; men who by constant excited effort, constant talk, constant stimulation of interest in something that most normal persons forgot about as soon as elections were over, claimed to be able to deliver blocs of votes, great and small. They were writing Dave, telling him what they would do for him. Not one but had a greedy personal interest in putting himself on record with the man who might become senator.

This was the way politics were conducted. Dave sometimes felt a great question in his mind. Elections were supposed to be, under democratic processes, the expression of the will of the people. But in reality they became contests of selfish interests—the massing of many little, self-seeking blocs, into larger blocs held together by related interests, and the whole cemented into two huge, contending, dominant blocs, animated by conflicting, mercenary, rapacious desires.

The curse of American politics was the politicians. Sometimes Dave wondered how the nation had so long survived. By the mercy of God an occasional great man rose to leadership in moments of crisis—but that was rare. Otherwise the greedy men, the men with axes to grind, the men solidifying the clutch of special privilege, seemed always, by one means or another, to win the elections. The people seemed not to care. They voted—their prejudices, or petty issues, or to please a friend. He considered whether or not it was worth the struggle to try to bring to reality anything so evanescent as an ideal—in this kind of an atmosphere.

It was necessary to shake himself out of this frame of mind. Avarice and intolerance and lust for power must always be combated—for that purpose alone, the struggle was worth while.

Always the powerful schemed against the weak. The smooth hands against the horny hands. It was an issue old as the world, and only because a few men had thought it worth while to fight, had the world been kept measurably free. David Constable felt himself to be in goodly company at least.

In spite of the nameless worry in him over Belle and her suspicions, he slept fairly well that night.

CHAPTER XI

1.

THE ponderous machinery of the law neared the end of its grinding. The last of the testimony was in. It was late in the afternoon and final arguments of counsel would be made on the morrow.

David Constable was confident. He believed he would obtain a clean acquittal. Just now he was up at the judge's desk, reading a demurrer into the record. The demurrer would shortly be overruled by Judge Poster. It was only another of the interminable parries in the legal duel.

Julia was glad the case was nearly over; glad that she was beginning at last to believe with Dave in victory. A shadow had been on her. She could not explain just why, but she lived in fear of something which might happen—something unnamed, of the nature of which she had no inkling.

Margie Ransome had recovered from her ordeal on the witness stand the previous day. She, too, was caught in Dave's optimism. She smiled at her father.

Julia remembered the scene at the Ransomes' the evening before. It was the crystallization of her own thought—the one she had expressed to Margie, in order to persuade her to return to Jericho.

Tom Ransome had listened as she told him what she had thought concerning his daughter's future. Margie deserved the thing she wanted —training and a chance for her to use the wonderful gift of her voice. Hitherto Ransome had set his face uncompromisingly against it, but to Julia he listened.

It was Margie's chance to rebuild her life, regain happiness, Julia said to him. He should send her to Chicago. Better, to New York. Julia would obtain the name of a great maestro—some teacher of the voice who was of international note. Margie must have an audition. This could be arranged. Afterward things would take care of themselves, because the maestro would be eager to have Margie as his pupil. On such pupils as Margie a maestro's reputation was built, Julia felt sure. And Margie, with her voice schooled and developed, would, out in the great world, forget the bitterness and heartbreaks of Jericho.

This was Julia's plea. Tom Ransome and Myra nodded. They would do as she said—if she and Dave only would obtain an acquittal for their daughter.

Now as the time approached to give the case to the jury, Margie's fate became a very personal thing to Julia. Julia had persuaded Margie to return to Jericho and face the charges; Julia had obtained for Margie the promise of opportunity. Nothing must happen now to spoil it.

2.

There was a slight disturbance. A lean, brown man in a blue sateen shirt with a yellow tie and yellow sleeve holders, entered the enclosure before the bench. She recognized the man: a deputy from the sheriff's office.

He spoke to Dave, and Dave paused to incline an ear.

Stunned consternation came over his face. The deputy jabbed toward him a folded paper which Dave accepted mutely.

As if hypnotized, Julia watched the deputy turn, until his close-set eyes, in the narrow face, caught hers. She wanted to flee, but she could not.

He took three long, hurried steps to her, and extended another folded paper. She took it mechanically.

"You're served," the man muttered.

He walked out of the courtroom through the door behind the bench.

Julia was sure she knew what the paper was, but she dreaded to look down at it.

At last she did look. A subpoena.

She was summoned as a witness. *Belle D. Constable* vs. *David Constable*. A complaint for divorce.

It could mean only one thing.

Julia knew that she was flushing.

Involuntarily her eyes went around. All those people in the courtroom—could they possibly know what was in this paper?

Not yet. She felt an irresistible desire to escape . . . before they could learn. The shame of it overwhelmed her at this first moment. To be named . . . as a corespondent. What a filthy thing to happen. She must leave at once before the word got whispered around. Else she would never be able to endure the concentrated stares.

The court was recessing.

Not waiting to see David, she hurried out with the crowd.

She was in a trance almost, hardly feeling the jostling, conscious only of the terrible, irrevocable disaster for herself, for everything she was.

3.

The Jericho *Daily Clarion* did full justice to the Constable divorce case.

It was what is known as a "juicy story"—probably the juiciest of its kind in the *Clarion's* entire history.

What made it the more beautiful from the view of the eager young journalists who, under Clarence Snead, made up the staff of the *Clarion,* was the fact that for once all restraints were off.

Newspapermen are thwarted souls. Trained specialists in the discovery of scandal, they are constantly frustrated, because newspapers, for their own reasons, protect the names of certain individuals in their communities.

Any veteran reporter is privy to enough of the internal rot of humanity to blast a town apart, if he published a tithe of what he knows. But newspapers have a formula for dealing with such things. The ignorant, the unimportant, the humble are fair enough game, although a story loses value in direct ratio to the lack of consequence of its chief figure. Only rarely, however, is a prominent name involved in newspaper stories. This is not because the prominent live more circumspectly than the humble, but because of the weights and levers and shields which the prominent are able to bring to bear in avoiding publicity.

As an example, the *Clarion* had not published one word about J. Wilber Bratten.

But in the Constable case the bridle was off the horse. Journalism could go as far as it liked.

It went quite a way. The *Clarion,* that afternoon, made a very sensational "story" of the filing of the divorce action. There was a front-page "banner" headline, a two-column "lead all," and a full column of type, running over on Page Two. In a separate box the full text of the divorce complaint was printed, a violently vilifying accusation.

It was that text that made the Constable divorce story good.

The aggrieved spouse had announced adultery as her cause for action —a good, forthright allegation, usually masked under the euphemism of "extreme cruelty." In this case the wife named the woman she accused as her husband's paramour. A beautiful and, just then a very prominent, woman in Jericho.

The petition minced no words. It mentioned a date, and said:

Plaintiff is informed and believes and so charges that the defendant, David Constable, did commit adultery with one Julia Norman.

Plaintiff is informed and believes and so charges that the defendant

David Constable did at other times and places commit adultery with the said Julia Norman, and that the said Julia Norman did meet the said David Constable at divers places and on divers occasions arranged between them, and did there and then cohabit with him in a vile, immoral, lascivious, illegal, and lewd manner, contrary to the laws of the State of Kansas, and contrary to moral precepts.

Plaintiff is informed and believes and so charges that the said Julia Norman did by such cohabitation and fornication and adultery cause said David Constable to forget his marriage vows and turn from his wife, the plaintiff in this action, all to the great injury, harm, and suffering of said plaintiff, causing her grief and sorrow, and occasioning great nervousness, anxiety, loss of sleep, and suffering on her part . . .

The charges had been drawn by a skillful hand. The signature was Belle Constable's. But the mind behind that array of vicious accusations was far subtler than Belle's. Algeria had been present with her own lawyer to help frame the divorce petition.

Dave did not go to his home that night. He went instead to the Apex House. He desired quiet, time to think. But there was given him no time to think.

They came to his door—men who had backed him, men who wanted to know, men who were his friends.

"For God's sake, Dave, what are we going to do? . . . We gotta take some kind of action. . . . This'll ruin you. . . . It'll blow the whole ticket clean out of the water. . . . Why don't you file some kind of a libel suit? . . . Anything to take the heat off you? . . ."

Long distance telephone wires were hot from Topeka. For the other newspaper correspondents had been as eager, as active, as the reporters of the *Clarion*. It was a statewide story, a nationwide story. Topeka, Wichita, Kansas City, Denver newspapers proudly published "exclusive" accounts of the Constable divorce scandal. Other newspapers depended on the Associated Press, which had the defect of being more objective and less sensational than a Staff Correspondent could be. But even the Associated Press gave so much prominence to the story that Farm Heads and the Constable Senatorial Committee were in hysteria.

Dave must issue, immediately, a categorical denial of his wife's accusations, the politicians telephoned him. What was he proposing to do? Any kind of counteraction would help. But for heaven's sake he must do *something*. Did he realize how this was upsetting the carefully considered plans of many important people?

Dave walked the floor. There was nothing he could do for the moment. He was trying to think of an answer. He had to consider, he needed time. . . .

Topeka whined and howled. The mass interests of accumulated blocs of controlled voters, which had built their hopes on Dave, were wounded in their vitals. Men cursed him, pleaded with him.

All over Jericho he knew that people were gathered in knots, with one subject of overruling interest. The Constable divorce. That Norman woman. When had Dave Constable and that female done all this cohabiting the paper talked about? Women shrilled over telephones; men bunched on street corners.

Reports, hearsay, rumors. Hints, whispers, insinuations. Thrilling, exciting, satisfying.

Gossip ran like a grass fire. David Constable and Julia Norman had been "sleeping together ever since she came back from Kansas City." She was staying at the Hutto home; old lady Hutto knew all about it, was encouraging it. Dave Constable had maintained Julia Norman as his mistress in Kansas City. That delicious word *mistress,* again . . . it had power to stimulate imaginations to the point of drooling.

A magnificent establishment of Sin built itself up in the Jericho mind. Kansas City stood for Sin to the state, anyway. It was the City —distant, bawdy, incomprehensible. Kansas City had red-light districts, and open saloons, and places where naked women danced. Vice was terrifying—and at the same time fantastically attractive.

The tide of resentment returned with a new fury.

Dave Constable was a skunk—carrying on like that with the Norman woman, right when he was asking people to vote for him.

He had wronged his wife, hadn't he? Jericho heretofore never had particularly concerned itself over Constable's wife. But now it remembered gossip about her. The gossip said the poor woman was neglected by Constable, never taken anywhere by him. Why, she was a pathetic creature, no better than a servant in her own house, people said. He treated her like dirt. . . .

Night came down on Jericho, with the poison twisting and eddying in every corner of it.

4.

A few minutes after midnight, Mrs. Hutto, in a wrapper and with her hair in two thin gray pigtails, answered the insistently ringing doorbell.

"So it's you, David."

He came in, closed the door behind him.

"Mrs. Hutto, I must see Julia."

"David, what is it—tell an old woman what this is all about?"

He shook his head. "Later, Mrs. Hutto. You must be a friend to Julia. This is politics. But I must see Julia at once."

She conducted him to the parlor and lit a lamp on the table.

"Wait here," she said.

He heard the stairs creak as she ascended. From above: "Julia?"

Julia's voice replied, but it was low and indistinct because a door was closed.

"Dave Constable is here."

A moment's silence. Then the door upstairs opened. He heard Julia clearly now.

"Where is he?"

"Down in the parlor."

"I'll go down."

"Do you want me——"

"No. Go to bed, dear."

"I'm not sleepy. If I——"

"Dear, I don't need you. I shan't be long."

Dave, sitting in the parlor, uncomfortably gazing at the portieres, could hear the old woman's gusty, disappointed sigh, and her unwilling footsteps as she went to her own room.

Heels tapped in the halls, and he rose as Julia came through the hangings at the door.

"Julia . . ." He stopped.

She came into the room. Hair of pale amber in the lamplight. Eyes large and dark.

"I couldn't come before," he said.

She said: "How could it happen . . . *now?*"

In her he sensed a dangerous brittleness.

"I don't pretend to know how," he told her. "But somehow Algeria was involved in it. This horrible mess explains several things . . . why they made so much of prosecuting the Ransome girl. Why the case was dragged out. They were getting something ready. They had to have time."

"I see."

"It is all aimed at me. To destroy me politically."

"What about me? And Margie?"

"It is cruel—but the people who planned this did not even consider you."

"We are unimportant. Not even side issues."

"You must not be bitter. Please, Julia."

"What about Belle?"

"Oh, Belle. Yes, there is malice in Belle. You *are* the chief issue to Belle. That is the way with her."

"Belle wanted to ruin me. At least that gives me some consequence." Julia laughed a tiny mirthless laugh. "This will be an open divorce trial. And I will be the prize exhibit. You needn't tell me—I am not unacquainted with the law. I must answer that subpoena. I can't even leave the state. And this time when I go into court it will not be with protecting armor of a lawyer. I will be just another woman—a woman with a soul which is naked and ashamed."

He said: "Have you examined the date . . . alleged?"

"No."

"It was the day we went over Mrs. Hutto's affairs at your apartment——"

"That day?" she cried wonderingly. "Why——"

"Nothing . . . happened. That day."

For a moment she was silent. Then she said sombrely: "No. They hit upon the wrong day. But it does not change the essential guilt."

"Are you telling me that you suddenly feel guilty—when you did not feel guilty before?"

"No. That is not it. I felt the wickedness all along. But it happened such a time ago. I should have known it could not be forgiven. There had to be retribution."

She seated herself, her eyes downcast, her hands in her lap.

He took a step nearer her.

"Julia—can you ever forgive me?"

"Forgive? I don't even blame you. You did what a man has in him the nature to do. It was my own fault that I let you. It was my own fault that I came back here. I—really didn't need to come to Jericho, you know."

He was distressed by something in her voice.

"I love you," he said. "I want you to believe that."

"I believe. But it's—somehow too late——"

"No, not too late! This will die down. When the divorce mess is over, Julia—I want you to marry me."

She looked up at him. "Could there be any happiness in that—now?"

"Why not? We would have to set our teeth and live this down, of course. But even Jericho can forget——"

"*Jericho?*" Her voice was sharply incredulous. "You're not—actually proposing that I live here—as things now are?"

"*I* must live here." His face had become dogged.

"Why? You can go into any city in the United States and be a major success in the practice of law."

"I am committed to something here. Something bigger than I am."

"Bigger—than I?"

He looked at her, not knowing how to answer.

"Politics!" she exclaimed bitterly. The next words blurted out: "Don't you realize you're through? Disgraced? Do you think the people of holy Kansas will accept a candidate with a scandal on his name? You forfeited leadership. Why—you aren't even important—now!"

Then she felt she had hurt him and was sorry.

He said gravely: "You are right. I have failed the people. All day I thought about it—in the bitterness of futility, in the feeling of desertion. But there is an answer."

"What kind of an answer can there be?"

"It is this, Julia. A leader is not someone of supernal qualities, who invents, activates and brings to pass great ideals and great movements; but one who is, at the moment of climax, in a position where he may accept the leadership, and is willing to take on himself the responsibility."

He looked at her earnestly, as if to see whether she agreed. Her expression did not change. He continued:

"Every great advance made by men has been the fruit of long and discouraging reverses—like the waves of a tide, receding and advancing, until at last the crest of them sweeps to fulfillment. Individual men are unimportant to these great surges. No man in himself is indispensable, ever; but insofar as he crystallizes beliefs and gives expression to ideals—if only badly and unimportantly—he furthers the movement. I have faith that, in spite of reverses, the people will go on fighting. If I have, as you say, forfeited leadership, other leaders will rise. I still must maintain the right to work—behind the scenes, if not in front of them."

For a long time she stared at him.

"No!" she said at last, sharply, as if answering a question. "I won't do it! It's all right for you. You're a man. But I'm a woman. Think! If you were a woman how would you feel?"

"I know how you feel."

"Then you see how it is. You have to make a choice."

"It's your fight as much as mine, Julia."

"You've . . . made your choice?"

"No. You made it."

She felt cold, and then hot. Then somehow it didn't seem to make any difference.

She said: "Well, this was not what you came to discuss, was it? You wanted to go over the Ransome case."

Very brisk, businesslike and impersonal now. She felt his eyes on her, trying to understand her.

"Yes," he said. "I'm concerned over the case. Today I was sure we had won. I could feel that jury. But now I don't know. The human mind—even a juror's mind—is a strange and unpredictable mechanism." He paused. "You will not appear, of course. I couldn't ask it."

"It might even have an adverse effect, mightn't it?" she said bitterly. "The scarlet woman in the court of law . . ."

"Don't, Julia."

"I am incapable of being hurt any more, David."

He looked upon her with immense pity.

"Poor Julia," he said.

"I will get my notes for you. And—speaking as a lawyer—I believe I should not appear in the courtroom tomorrow. It might further prejudice Margie Ransome's cause."

Afterward, when she saw him to the door, she gave him her hand, stiffly. They were like strangers in parting.

5.

Dave's heels echoed on the stone flags. It was nearly time for court to open, and the courthouse halls were filled with people. Face after face turned toward him.

Aged, obscene, two G.A.R. veterans eyed him from the entrance of the G.A.R. Hall. One thumped his cane on the floor. They were creaky, rheumy old men, with bad breaths and bad tempers. Together they laughed; high-pitched senile laughter. And whispered as he passed.

People turned to stare after him, and those in front were too studious in their indifference—gazing away, studying posters on the walls, feigning not to see him.

A man slapped his thigh and said explosively: "If I had the doin' of it, by God, I'd——"

Dave turned quickly. The talk stopped dead and he could not see who had uttered the exclamation. He went into the courtroom.

He knew now the roads his dishonor would take.

Overnight, Belle had become a political symbol. Wronged Womanhood. The vindicators of Belle were providing for her a statewide celebrity. Orators would sob over her martyrdom and call on the voters to repudiate the man, and the cause, that had demeaned her. Poor, stupid Belle . . . and she would never understand what it was all about.

Dave leaned over the counsel table and spoke to Margie.

"Don't worry about things." He tried to make his voice sound convincing. "They're after me, and that should make it better for you. The pressure is off you now."

Then he sat down, waiting with set face, to take his punishment.

Through the long morning Jasper Peddigrew lashed and thundered at the jury. Most of his speech was directed at Dave. The county attorney at last had his chance to pay back old grudges. He stamped, and roared and shook his finger and his head. Words built up a pillar of malice. Dave did not even try to follow the speech, it was so far from the basic issues; but he could see that the jury, strait-laced, middle-aged, had its faces set against him.

Already he knew what he himself would say in the afternoon. As in a windy dark he sat, and his thoughts rushed out along his lines of reasoning. Before him was the whole question of obligations and loyalties.

For a day and a night the voices of men had battered at him, the words of men on the printed page, the knowledge he had of his broken condition, and the state of everything he represented. Overnight the press table had been crowded double with new reporters. Other papers had sent correspondents rushing to Jericho. Extra space had been provided. A telegraph instrument had been set up by the Western Union in the hall to take the frequent bulletins the reporters sent out for their papers.

Dave had decided on one of two courses. He could fight the divorce allegations and remain in the race for Senate. Or he could retire from the race.

The latter course was easier; but if he resigned, others would be injured—the lesser candidates would be deprived of the head of their ticket. On the other hand, if he remained in the race—and his election seemed impossible now—it was inevitable that Julia Norman would have to remain in it with him.

Her name would be dragged through the slime of election filth. She would be pilloried, made a byword from one end of the state to the other.

Already this was happening. As Jasper Peddigrew raged and frothed, every word of his speech went out on the wires. He was very glad that Julia was not present. The ordeal would have been frightful. He remembered her as he had seen her the night before—the brittleness. She seemed near breaking, and he was deeply concerned. It had not been the Julia he knew who had talked to him. The woman was distraught, frightened, taut.

Dave's mind dwelt wretchedly on this matter as the county attorney's speech went on. He wondered what he could do; what action he could possibly take to avert utter degradation for Julia. The law held them both in its processes, and Belle's malice was exceeded only by the malice of Mrs. Dunham.

Dave knew well that it would be the ultimate desire and intention of the two women to torture him—and Julia—to the utmost.

The divorce case would be a public spectacle. A witch burning.

Julia would have to undergo the humiliation, the subtle mental torments of the courtroom. The human nervous organism never feels so keenly in the physical as in the spiritual realm. It does not suffer so much, nor so long in the former as in the latter—and particularly when it is that of a sensitive woman.

David could vision the sneering smile of the lawyers; the expectant, lascivious greed in the faces in the packed courtroom, as Julia was questioned:

Miss Norman, were you with Mr. Constable on such and such an evening?

And did he go up to your room?

Miss Norman, please tell the court what you did there.

Nothing? Oh, come, Miss Norman. What a waste of time! Did you, perhaps, spend it in working out a chess problem?

Let me see, Miss Norman. There is testimony to the effect that the defendant, David Constable, was in your room, with the door closed, for a period of two hours. Do you admit that?

And you still assert that nothing untoward occurred?

Miss Norman, I must ask you a blunt question. Did you not on that occasion have sexual intercourse with this man?

Have you not at other times had illegal, illicit, intimate sexual relations with him?

Haven't you? *Haven't you?*

That would be how it would go.

He imagined Julia's pale, drawn, tortured face. However much she might deny, the attack would go on. The crowd would listen greedily. And the newspaper reporters would be there. From all over the state. That was the devilish purpose of the whole thing.

Every question, every word, every expression of the girl's features, would be recorded, embellished, described. She would be made to appear guilty of every lewd implication.

Dave closed his eyes. He could not stand that. Julia had told him that she was finished—through with being a part of his life. It was all over between them. But he could not endure to see her tortured. He grasped for straws.

Perhaps—*perhaps* he might bribe or frighten Belle into taking a divorce without a public hearing. He would promise anything, if she would only permit Julia to leave Jericho in peace.

Jasper Peddigrew's pillar of words came to an end. The court recessed at noon to reconvene at two. He had two hours.

6.

Dave came to the front door of his house with the feeling of being alien. Everything about it was familiar—the brass knob, the screen slightly sprung so that it stuck out a little at the bottom, the white paint beginning to scale on the panel. Yet he had an odd feeling that he was seeing it only in the imagination.

For eight years he had lived in this house, opened and closed that door thousands of times; but now it was no longer a familiar part of his life. He did not belong here now.

He half turned the knob; thought better of it, and rang.

The door opened slightly. Mrs. Dunham's swelling figure showed within. She glowered at him with angry red eyes.

"Get out of here! Get off this place!"

She tried to slam the door, but he put out a hand and held it.

"I'll be only a minute. I want to talk to Belle."

He forced the door back and entered.

Behind Mrs. Dunham in the hall stood Algeria Wedge.

This he had not expected. For a moment she looked him over, with the cool, sure, almost amused way she had.

He had no words for her.

"Where's Belle?" he asked Mrs. Dunham.

The old woman pursed her fleshy lips. "Belle doesn't want to see you."

"I've got something important to tell her."

"Nothing you've got to say is important."

His look at her was combined of exasperation and despair. Again he caught the curious, speculative glint in Algeria's eyes.

Suddenly he shouted, loudly and violently.

"Belle! Belle! Come here! I want to talk to you!"

The sound of his voice filled the hall. It caused the two women to step back from him.

To his surprise, Belle suddenly appeared, her hands oddly held behind her back.

In her wide face was an expression of intimate hostility, fixed rejection.

"Belle," he said, "I came to see if I could——"

His gaze took in Algeria and Mrs. Dunham.

"Can we talk alone—just a minute?" he asked Belle.

She returned his look coldly. "No."

"All right," he said. "I came here, Belle, to beg of you to drop this suit. I'm willing to do anything you want——"

He stopped and swallowed. Algeria's stare grew more curious.

"You can have the property. Everything. Is that fair?" he went on. "If you're determined on the divorce, I'll not fight it—providing only one thing."

He waited. "And what's that one thing?" she asked.

"That you don't drag this case through the courts. Don't do this——"

Her face was working. He knew the signs—she was building up one of her uncontrolled rages. Still she stood with her hands behind her back. When she spoke her voice was low and thick.

"And all this for that—cheap, dirty, two-faced slut?"

He looked at her, then looked away. He had no desire to see her any more, but he forced his eyes to return to her.

"Belle," he said, controlling his voice with an effort, "I'm going to tell you something. We've lived together all these years. I've always kept my feelings in the background and let you have your way. But for once I'm going to fight back. There's more at stake here than a woman's reputation, or a spiteful revenge on me. You're too ignorant to know it—but you've let somebody talk you into doing something that affects a lot of people. If you persist in making a spectacle of this divorce, I promise you it will be the something you'll never forget—or get over. There are two sides to every question, and I can be as nasty as you can." She retreated from him slowly, and he followed her. "It might interest you—and your friend, Mrs. Wedge, here—to know that your date—the date you allege in your petition—was a day when I was going over some business papers with Julia—and furthermore, I can prove it——"

His eye caught her movement.

Hands brought suddenly out from behind her back.

He glanced quickly.

A revolver. *His* revolver.

She held the nickeled thing with both hands in front of her.

Why, he thought with a sort of hazy wonder, she took that gun out of my own desk upstairs.

"Belle," he said, "don't do anything foolish——"

He kept walking toward her, his face stern. She continued to hold the revolver with both hands, pointed toward him.

"Give me that gun, Belle," he said. He held out his hand.

It felt as if she had struck him a heavy blow in the stomach with an iron bar . . .

His knees sagged with a sudden unexplained weakness. He sat heavily on the lowest step of the stairs.

Acrid fumes, powder smoke, prickled in his nostrils. Strange that he seemed not to have heard the report.

Impersonal thought came: the shock of the bullet must have numbed all my sense perceptions.

Another thought, intensely personal:

Bullet . . . *then I am shot.*

Not wishing to see, but knowing he must, he slowly forced himself to look down. On his white shirt front a dark red stain widened.

Voices keened in his ears. A great world seemed rushing—rushing blindly through space, incredibly, to its own destruction.

Beneath him the floor grew billowy, soft, gaseous. He slipped away through it, sinking, sinking.

I must . . . I want . . . I would never have dreamed this would happen . . .

Everything slid away from under him in blackness.

7.

Three women gazed hypnotically at the figure on the floor. Dave had rolled from the stairs to the carpet. He seemed very long—unnaturally long. As if the blow that brought him down had created an elongation of his body such as is created by the constricting coils of the anaconda.

Also he seemed very flat: almost as if he were partly buried in the Wilton rug. He lay face down, one arm beside his head, the other clutched at his belly where the bullet had gone.

Algeria drew a great breath. Then with a quick, swooping movement she was on her knees beside him. She tried to turn him over but could not.

"Dave—why—*Dave!*" she cried, as if she could not believe it.

Dave did not answer.

Her eyes took in Mrs. Dunham. "Help me!" she commanded.

Face pasty gray with fear, chin shaking, the old woman lumbered forward. Together they turned over the prostrate figure.

Dave lay on his back now. Very white. Very still. Very grave. His eyes were closed. He did not seem to breathe.

Algeria saw Belle.

The woman stood as if fastened to the spot from which she had fired. In her hand was a subdued glitter of nickel. The stub-nosed revolver, its muzzle round and sinister.

Belle opened her mouth.

"I—I—didn't mean—I don't know why I——"

Pathetic mumbling stammer. Algeria found she suddenly could not stand the sight of her. She felt for Dave's pulse; made out no life. She rose to her feet.

"Your telephone's in the dining-room?" she asked.

Neither Belle nor her mother stirred. Belle still held the gun with both hands before her, in a sickly daze.

Mrs. Dunham seemed to rouse from her paralysis.

"What are you going to do?"

"Call Dr. Patterson."

Mrs. Dunham licked her colorless lips.

"Wait. We got to think. What'll happen—to Belle?"

"I don't know. But I do know this man is dying. Do you want to make the call?"

"I—I—can't——"

"Then allow me to pass."

Algeria went to the wall telephone in the dining-room and put through her call to the hospital.

She heard Dr. Patterson's yelp when she spoke.

"Shot? Dave Constable? I'll be there at once!"

Algeria hung up, and rang again for central.

The two women had followed her into the room and stood together at the door.

"What—are you doing now?" asked Mrs. Dunham.

"Calling police headquarters."

"No! Don't——"

"A man has been shot. If I don't report it, Dr. Patterson will. Probably he's done it already."

"But—they'll—" Belle's voice quavered. "Will they arrest me?"

"If they don't it will be a gross dereliction of duty!"

"What will they do?"

"You'll go to jail."

"Jail? But I—I didn't mean——"

"You didn't?" Scorn curled Algeria's lip. "You're one of those women who go through life excusing any cruelty, any crime, on the ground they didn't mean it! Well, whether you meant it or not, you've probably killed a man. Try that excuse now and see how far it will get you!"

"He's—not dead?"

"Shot through the stomach, it looks like. That's death—if not now, soon. That's *murder!*"

"Oh, no!"

"You've murdered a man, Belle Constable, because he was too good for you."

Belle looked at the long slack figure huddled against the bottom step. She cowered.

"Oh, what have I—done to myself?"

Even in this moment her own selfish problem was what rose uppermost in her mind.

Behind her, her mother began to sob in craven terror.

What will we do, oh, what will we do, what will we do now, oh, look what you've done, you've done it, you did it all by yourself, I had nothing to do with it, oh, great God why did I ever bring into the world a daughter who would do a thing like this, great Heavens why am I so punished, oh, what have I ever done to deserve——

Belle turned slowly. The nickeled thing still was in her two hands. A voice said: *"Shut up, or I'll kill you, too."*

Not until she saw the ugly horror and fright in her mother's doughy face, did she know it was her own voice which had spoken.

Algeria came decisively across the floor.

"Belle, give me that gun."

She held out her hand.

With the same mottled, deadly look, Belle turned on her. For an instant they probed deeply into each other's eyes.

Then Belle looked down at the shining, deadly weapon. With a great shudder of revulsion, she flung the pistol from her, covered her face, and sank on the sofa, weeping hysterically.

Algeria picked up the revolver from the floor. Then she came back to Belle.

"Stop sniveling," she said.

They heard steps outside.

8.

Voices about Belle Constable. Men. Men with hats on. Men looking at the furniture, at the wall, at the long figure on the floor.

Where did the men come from? She heard her mother talking, talking. Why did she talk so much?

Somebody said: "You'll have to come with us, Mrs. Constable."

She looked up, hardly seeing. Man in a blue coat with a star.

Oh, she thought, you're arresting me. For murder. I have murdered my husband. It was a thing I did not intend to do, and even now I do not know why I did it.

Yes, I do. It was Algeria. Her fault.

Belle rose and went dumbly out, not even putting on a hat. Other men in the yard. Some with pencils and pads of paper. She was placed in a car. The courthouse.

She wished she could think. She wished she could explain to herself what she had done.

I am a murderess, she said over and over to herself, and Algeria Wedge and my mother are to blame.

It was true, though—about Dave and that woman. How could Algeria be so sure if it wasn't true? That sewing woman, Mrs. Dierks. She kept watch of the room for two hours . . .

But Dave said they were going over somebody's legal papers.

Algeria. Algeria Wedge. Algeria had been sympathetic. So sympathetic. Time to do something about this, she had said.

But how? Belle had asked her, dabbing her eyes with a lacey handkerchief Algeria lent her. It had a light, delicate scent. Gardenia.

That happened in the first days. When Belle had just discovered about Dave and the Norman girl.

Algeria said: Divorce. She seemed all-wise, filled with accumulated experience. Name that girl, Algeria said. Name Julia Norman. Tell the truth about her. Charge her with adultery. You can do it in a legal action, even if you can't prove it. I have a lawyer who will draw up the papers.

Then, after the suit was filed, the newspapers had their say, and the feeling of entrapment and disgrace rushed in on Belle . . .

After that it was her mother. Her mother was at her in savage triumph.

I knew it, I knew it, Belle Constable. I knew from the first this would turn out this way. I warned you. I did all a mortal mother could, to convince a wayward, selfish, headstrong, disobedient daughter. Now you've made your bed. Oh, you've made your bed all right. And you've got to lie in it. I just hope you get good and sick and tired of it. Oh, why did Almighty God visit upon me to have a child like this, oh, why, oh why, oh why . . . ?

The ceaselessness of it. The unending reiteration. The despair of ever escaping it.

And then Dave came. And she got the gun. . . .

They were coming back to her again. The men. She sat in the matron's office. There was the jail—over there with the steel bars. They were going to put her in the jail.

Belle babbled. Babbled everything, sometimes coherently, sometimes incoherently, to the men with the notebooks and stern faces.

CHAPTER XII

1.

WHEN the telephone rang in the hall, some inexplicable foreknowledge sent Julia to the balustrade upstairs.

Mrs. Hutto answered it. She looked up, face gone white.

Julia came down . . . slowly.

"Sit down, dear." Mrs. Hutto's voice was husky. She hung the receiver on the hook and came over to Julia.

The old woman moistened her lips as if they suddenly had gone dry.

"Julia—it's Dave. He's been . . . shot."

Julia's heart leaped so that she felt faint.

"Oh, no! What do you mean? Shot? How would—who would——"

Mrs. Hutto said: "He's at the hospital."

"But who? *Who?*"

Mrs. Hutto said slowly: "It was his wife."

Julia felt a dazed sickness.

An unnatural voice said: "How serious . . . ?"

Mrs. Hutto shook her gray head. "The doctor says . . . pretty bad."

In a half-world, somewhere between nightmare and fact, Julia stood up, clenching her fists so tightly she could feel the nails biting into her palms.

Bad. He's shot badly. David. He may be dying. . . .

Like a hammer it beat through her brain. If David died, everything was ended. The warm knowledge that he was in her world. Just that he *was* there. Unthinking warm knowledge. Gone, and all warmth would be gone. There was no sense to it.

Julia went to the telephone and battled for information.

Cold, institutional voice at the hospital. Mr. Constable's condition is grave. We cannot yet give you particulars. Yes, he recovered consciousness for a short time after being brought to the hospital.

Mrs. Hutto was weeping.

Julia felt a great unwieldy bitterness.

It it *your* fault he was shot, she said crazily to herself. It was your fault just as if you had held in your own hand that gun.

The fingernails bit deeper into her palms.

He did this on my account, she thought. I know it. Now because of me he has been brought down to a white bed, with white-clad men and women bending over him, probing into him.

Another thought: I quarreled with him last night. And they say . . . he may not live.

She hardly realized it when she stood before the mirror to see that she was neat. Later she was out on the street, in her darkest clothing, walking fast.

Smell. Ether and disinfectant and sickly-sweet funeral odor of flowers.

Nurses in white dresses which rustled stiffly with starch, carrying food in trays, medicines, bedpans.

Cream-colored walls with a bare ecclesiastical look. Clock *tick-tocked* solemnly. Gibson Girl prints in cheap black frames, and a Cupid, and a notice: *No Visitors.*

Julia asked at the reception window, and Dr. Patterson in his rumpled white surgical gown came out to her. She dimly understood what he said.

". . . doing as well as we could expect . . . double shock, the bullet and surgery, and lost very much blood . . . but so far as I can determine no lesions of vital organs . . . very sick man, Miss Norman . . . but fine constitution and I feel justified in an optimistic view . . . should know in twenty-four hours . . . blood count and temperature. . . ."

Outside, on the street, an urchin went past, whistling.

Julia went slowly down the hall toward the room at the end where nurses and interns labored. On the wall the clock's hands stood at half-past one.

2.

He was tearing a cobweb away from his head. It was more than a cobweb. It was a veil of black. It was heavy black velvet, smothering him, so that he fought for air and light.

He tore at the black velvet and momentarily he rent an opening. Julia. Why, Julia was there. She was looking at him.

"Julia . . ."

"David—darling!"

Another voice: "You mustn't talk, please, Mr. Constable——"

He fought to hold back the dark veil. Something . . . there was something of enormous importance . . . ah, yes, he had it.

"Julia . . . Margie Ransome . . . two o'clock."

She was bending over him, lovely, compassionate. "Yes. I understand. The arguments. I will go at once. . . ."

Julia's face was receding. Her lips moved, she was trying to tell him something more. He could not hear. The black web closed over his head . . . this time he did not care.

3.

Even now Algeria did not look up. Her eyes were on some little fiddling work she was doing with needle and silk and delicate fabric.

Tucker finished talking on the telephone, and came back into the library. Algeria could hear the maid clearing away the luncheon dishes in the dining-room.

As her husband came toward her his face was flushed, his bald head gleamed.

"That was Porter again. He's just heard from Wichita," he said. "The state committee's standing on its head!"

"Ah?" she said.

"If you'd only said it wasn't true!"

"What Belle Constable told those reporters? That I helped her prepare her divorce action? It *is* true."

He groaned. "It had to happen when the town was full of downstate correspondents, and every one of their newspapers after our scalps! That story's over the state already."

Tucker began to pace back and forth in the library.

"Do you realize what this means?" he demanded. "The woman shot Dave Constable. And then she blabbered. God, I think that a stupid woman may be the most dangerous creature that stalks this planet!"

She glanced up, but he rushed on. "I don't know how I'm going to face Porter Grimes. He's bitter. He ordered them to drop the charges against Belle Constable. But it was too late. She'd spilled her guts."

"She's free?" asked Algeria.

"Of course she's free. Constable said he'd not appear against her. He had a lucid period after he went to the hospital. I guess he'll pull through."

"This shooting simplifies his divorce problem for him, I guess."

"What do you mean?"

"Belle's got a sword over her head now. She'll have to take her divorce and shut up about it."

"I suppose so," he said. "But what is that to us?"

"Nothing. A sort of poetic justice—that's all."

He glared at her. "That woman named names, do you understand? Yours, and Porter Grimes', and mine. She thought she could get some kind of immunity—but do you know what she actually succeeded in doing?"

"I have a pretty good idea."

"Every big downstate paper tonight will say that the Wedges and

Porter Grimes conspired to have Belle Constable file her sensationai divorce—for politics. And that she was goaded into shooting her husband. The reaction is going to be simply terrible. It's begun already. *That's* what you accomplished!"

"Don't speak as if it were inevitable cause and effect, Tucker. You surely don't imply I planned to have Dave Constable shot?"

Usually she could bring him up short with sarcasm. But now he did not even stop walking.

"No," he said. "That wasn't your specific plan. You didn't expect things to get quite so far out-of-hand!"

Her eyes stayed on her work. Little round hoop of wood with delicate stuff stretched across it. Her needle made a bright pattern on the taut fabric.

"You're saying I arranged it all," she said. "I had no idea of this. You know that."

Silence built up. The greatest of all silences that had ever come between them. Resolutely she kept her eyes on her embroidery, though she wanted to look at his face.

Tucker had stopped walking up and down, and something was going on in his face—some change of which, instinct told her, she should make herself aware. But she would not permit herself to look up. His voice came coldly: "You're not malicious—so much as just irresponsible. That's what's so horrible about it."

The needle kept flashing in the silence.

"You're so accustomed to making people do what you want, that you're drunk on it," he went on. "Everyone jumps, when you say 'Jump!'"

"You resent that?" Her voice was cool, trickling.

"Perhaps," he said bitterly. "Maybe a trained seal has room for resentment. It's been your circus, Algeria. I was only a part of it. You had me where you wanted me—in the middle of the ring—with a ball on my nose——"

She had dreaded this moment, but she made a last effort to palliate.

"Try to be reasonable, dear——"

"*Reasonable?*" He shouted so that she almost jumped. "A man's shot down! And you ask me to be reasonable!"

He looked down at the carpet and his words were like his thoughts running out of him. "Dave Constable—he was . . . the best friend I ever had." His eyes turned upon her, hard and accusing. "I guess you wouldn't know what that means—having a friend like that!"

For the first time she looked at him, closely, unflinchingly.

"Are you sure," she said very calmly, "that you're sorry for Dave—or for yourself?" Then she added: "Whatever I did, with its consequences, planned or unplanned, I did for you."

"For me?" he sneered. "For yourself, you mean! It was *you* who wanted to go to Washington, to make the big splash."

"You didn't . . . want to?"

"It never entered my head, until you suggested it. You used me as you've used everyone else. And got just what you wanted—until you meddled with something so explosive that it blew right up in your face."

"In *all* our faces," she corrected him.

"Yes. That's it." His voice sounded hoarse. "You take everyone down with you, don't you? Rule or ruin—that's it. So I'm ruined politically. And the organization's blown sky-high. Does it give you any feeling of pleasure?"

"Aren't you exaggerating, just a little, Tucker?"

"Exaggerating? I've talked to Porter. We've both spent the last hour or more on the long distance, talking to Topeka, to Wichita, to Kansas City. We know where we stand—Porter and I. We're out—clear out!"

"So soon?"

"So *soon?* Those downstate crooks were just waiting for a chance. We'd forced them to take us—me for the Senate, and Porter for National Committeeman. But they didn't like it. And now—they've already dumped us. The convention next month—I was so certain—oh, hell!"

So that was what Belle Constable had done with her frenetic babbling. Wrecked an expensively geared and complicated political machine. Destroyed Tucker's chances. Belle Constable. Stupid Belle. Selfish Belle. She didn't even know it, but she had tipped the balance of political power from one end of the state clear over to the other.

Tucker waited for Algeria to speak, but she did not interrupt her work. After a time he said, very slowly:

"I'm just—only just—beginning to understand——"

She put away the needlework at last, and rose. "You say you understand, but *do* you understand? I wonder if you realize, my dear, that you're a sort of work of art? Something I made—with my own hands and brain. You're like a picture I've painted. Maybe I painted badly—but at least I painted as well as I knew. A great many people have a notion that you're a big man, Tucker. But you know and I know . . . the bigness is just paint. . . ."

He looked at her strangely, as if seeing her clearly for the first time.

"It just came over me," he said. "You wanted to get away from Jericho—didn't you? You hated it from the first. That's why you used me—to get away. You would sacrifice anyone to that one end."

Over his face came a look that was knowing, hateful, almost triumphant.

"Jericho's got you now, Algeria! Like it or not, we're through with politics. I'm finished being a painting—for you or anyone else. I'm going back to what I know—the *Clarion*. And you—make up your mind as of this minute—that Jericho's your home. You're going to live here, and like it—you and I. . . ."

He turned and went out. She watched him go: a bald, short man, growing more obese each year. A definite dewlap under his chin. A mediocre man who had enjoyed incredible luck. A man without any flair, any genius, any touch of greatness. Just . . . ordinary.

And she . . . with all the things he lacked . . . she was condemned to oblivion with him. Bitterness flooded her. So close she had been to her ambition. Tucker had obeyed her, she had thought for him, planned for him, conspired for him. Even Porter Grimes had taken suggestions from her as if they had been orders.

But now . . . never again would Tucker be her ductile, useful instrument. All her life she had dominated. And at last people rebelled and their acquiescence ceased. This, of Tucker's, was the greatest, last most crushing rebellion.

She had met rebellions before. But she had been young then.

Almost with a start she looked down at her hands.

They seemed gray. The veins stood out blue and crookedly on the backs of them. Their natural color had failed, the skin looked bleached.

Old hands, she said to herself. That's just it, I'm getting old already, and I know it. Wrinkled skin. My hair is going to be white. I'll be *hideous*.

I've been afraid of this all my life. It is woman's greatest tragedy . . . and somehow it has come over me all in a day.

Again she took up the tiny hooped embroidery and the gleaming needle. But her hands rejected the fancywork.

She sat alone. For the time, even her superb courage failed. She drooped in the chair.

The library seemed dark. Its book-lined shelves and familiar furniture suddenly appeared to take on the remote coldness of a tomb.

4.

At the hitch-racks around the buff-stone courthouse stood a multiplicity of vehicles—automobiles, horse-drawn equipages of many kinds. The courthouse was the focus of fevered interest in Jericho today.

Strange how rapidly news traveled around. The *Clarion* had an extra on the street, with a carefully ambiguous story of the shooting of David Constable, but long before that nearly everyone in Jericho knew the full details of what had taken place.

Julia, stepping between a team of drowsing dun mules and a battered farm truck, heard the clock in the tower ponderously strike twice.

She was late, she must hurry. As she started up the walk toward the steps, she was conscious of many people. Men, chiefly. They lounged in the shade, or knotted in close conversation.

In their garb was an odd sameness—faded overalls, soft black hats tilted forward over squinting eyes, cheeks bulging with tobacco. Farm people.

She felt their eyes on her: male eyes. The men turned to look after her as she went up the steps.

Although she had schooled herself as well as she could to be indifferent, the nerves in her back squirmed and twisted. To stare was the way of men. Once it had made her uncomfortable; then she became indifferent to it, accustomed to that intent appraisal. It was an inevitable corollary of being a woman.

But today the old shrinking distaste was back, sharper than ever. The men swayed together, whispered greedily, measured her, mentally stripped her naked, speculated on her.

The collective male stare was almost worse than the individual female stares she had felt on the way down from the hospital. Every line of the vicious *Clarion* story of the previous day had been read, savored, discussed. Faces peered at her from windows as she walked past—from behind curtains held slightly back to mask the watchers. It made her stomach tighten. Those were women. They were saying: *There she is now. There's that brazen Norman creature.*

She tried to ignore them, but she felt a sick desire to escape and hide.

As if manacled to it, she was held to her course. She felt that this parade was required of her—the gantlet of obscene eyes, the whispers, the half-muted jeers. A part of her punishment. Shame burned in her cheeks. Always before, men had stared at her as though she were an alabaster vase of beauty. They stared now, as if she were something humble and filthy.

Hurrying, she entered the building, and the bailiff, looking surprised, helped her through the crowd at the courtroom door.

Sour smell of humanity. Murmuring voices: *That's the woman. That's the gal the shooting was over.*

Solid phalanx of cynical curiosity. The press table. Reporters whispered, sniggered, made notes on her, the way she was dressed, the expression of her face.

Jasper Peddigrew rose when he saw her. She tried to read his look. Surprise? Triumph? She did not care. . . .

Margie gazed up fearfully. So close to the critical time, and Dave Constable gone. . . .

"Margie," Julia said. "I'll do the very best I can——"

The case was about to open. Lawyers still stood before the bench, wrangling in undertones over motions.

Judge Poster looked up. It was time for Julia to speak. She rose. "May it please the court," she heard herself.

Her voice shook. On Peddigrew's face was a furtive smirk. Judge Poster waited with a polite nod. Patronizing, courteous nod.

Very well, Miss Norman, the smug men were thinking. Go ahead with your little effort. We will be magnanimous and not hold your unhappy misfortune too greatly against you. After all—you are the weaker vessel, to be pitied rather than condemned.

The weaker vessel—why did the Bible call women that? Julia did not want to be a weaker vessel. She was fully responsible; what had happened had been brought upon David and herself—by herself. She did not desire the indulgence of these men; their courtesy, their superior bows.

Faces in the audience were gray, without identity. Margie's eyes grew wider, more apprehensive. Someone's lips moved incessantly, but she could hear nothing that was said. It was Peddigrew whispering to his assistant. The jury was waiting—sitting back, expecting little from her, but virtuously determined to give this unfortunate woman her chance. They would listen, but they wished she would get it over.

Julia wrestled with doubt; she was charged with sudden impotence before these buffeting currents of prejudice and custom.

In that courtroom it seemed that nobody was her friend. The women everywhere were united in enmity toward her; they were the defenders of the conventions she had transgressed. The men were against her, too; she was an upstart in an arena long reserved for their own.

So Julia met the great moment of loneliness.

She heard her own voice again. High-pitched, not effective. Woman was not made for public speaking. The sneer widened on Peddigrew's countenance. For the first time Julia felt, on her cheeks, under her eyes, two hot spots of anger.

What did Peddigrew know, what did Judge Poster know, what did anyone know, of the laceration of intimate sensitive nerves of her being which she underwent in thus offering herself to public scorn?

A coldness replaced the hot anger. Cold contempt . . . in the coldness her self-possession returned, hard as an icicle.

Julia picked up a paper and suddenly began to speak.

"Gentlemen of the jury, none of you, least of all myself, expected to hear this summation from a woman. I didn't choose it; nor did this defendant. I am fully aware how exceptional it is to hear the voice of one of my sex in a courtroom, and I ask your indulgence—and your fair-minded attention."

With her opening words her feeling changed. She looked at the jury; some of these men she knew.

Face. Face. Face. Lean jaw. Loose jaw. Spade beard. Little spiky

mustache. Big drooping mustache. Fat chin. Weak chin. Vandyke.
And a pair of Dundreary weepers.

Barber. Bank teller. Contractor. Lightning-rod salesman. Chiro-
practor. Teamster. And six farmers.

Methodist. Campbellite. United Brethren. Lutheran. Presbyterian.
Catholic. Free-thinker. And one Jew.

Why, these were people—ordinary people. They were the same as
people on Cape Cod, Massachusetts. Or in Tallahassee, Florida. Or
Buffalo, Wyoming. Or Santa Barbara, California. Or Kansas City,
Missouri.

She had been afraid of Jericho. She had wanted to flee from it. But
Jericho was not unique of itself. Jericho was a part of America. An
entity of the Republic.

These were the people. Everywhere around her would be the people.
She could not get away from them, but she did not want to get away
from them. She had been wrong, all wrong. And David had been
right. She could not feel contempt or anger for the people.

Julia walked over to the jury box and began talking to the people.

"Mr. Constable, the chief counsel in this case, is—in the hospital."
Her voice caught, but she went on. "You must have heard what happened. I hope—as I know you hope—that he will survive. The doctor
believes he will do so. But it is because he was gravely wounded that
I am here."

She put up a slender hand and pushed a small blonde lock of hair
from her forehead. Face by face her eyes went over the men in the
jury box.

"You have heard calumnies against David Constable." She hesitated,
then continued bravely. "From the same sources, you have heard—
things said about me. I do not ask you to disbelieve these things or to
believe them. Time will make known the truth. But whatever you
may think of her attorneys, I beg you, do not allow it in the slightest
jot to affect the fate of the child who is accused here—Margie Ransom."

She forgot herself in her plea, and in so doing she achieved a remarkable thing. The twelve men in the jury box felt her presence, saw
womanhood appealing to them—not in the stern, peremptory voice of
a lawyer, but as a woman, with softness, and charm, and tenderness.
She was telling them how she felt, her views on justice and mercy.
The appeal was intimately concerned with herself—but it was not for
herself. It was for another she pleaded. The drama of sacrifice which
is woman. The man in each of them gave fealty to her. They listened
with grave and concentrated attention.

"You are not sitting in judgment on David Constable . . . or on me.
But I ask you to sit in judgment on something else—on actions which
are conceived in dark places!"

Every eye, every ear, every thought in that packed courtroom was now concentrated on the tense, slim figure before the jury box. She listed the events of the week—the prosecution of Margie when politics was served by it; the cunning timing of the divorce action. Finally the shot, fired irresponsibly, which laid David Constable low.

"All—all—were actions conceived in dark places!" she cried. "The fruit of treacherous political scheming by grasping and unscrupulous interests. Margie Ransome is only a victim—hounded and driven, not because she was guilty of crime, but so that the character of a man who was a threat to the oligarchy of money and power might be destroyed!"

At the press table pencils worked feverishly. The telegraph wires would be hot this afternoon, and a woman's words would carry far across a great state and beyond.

"As I stand before you, this is the truth. This is why I plead with you to consider on the one hand this child, who fought for something she holds dearer than her life; and on the other hand the intolerance which persecuted her for the birth that was no fault of hers—the prejudice built up by wicked tongues—the malice based on political selfishness—the evil thinking sheathed in hypocrisy! Which of these merits the condemnation of right-thinking men?"

The people sat in their seats as if chained. They were seeing a woman who gave the most vivid suggestion of courage and pathos—in her voice, her movements, the very way she held herself with face looking up, as if she offered for the cause she pleaded her life, her being, all the mysteries in her.

In that moment Julia was beautiful as a woman can only be beautiful when she typifies womanhood itself.

Her voice ceased.

She sat down.

She had done her best.

In the tense courtroom the dry voice of the judge buzzed. Jasper Peddigrew was on his feet, saying something, looking at her. Why . . . the state was resting its case. The judge nodded.

A tall man, ludicrously thin, with a ludicrous Adam's apple, stood in the jury box. The Adam's apple worked up and down his stringy gullet.

As from a great distance Julia heard.

". . . Find this defendant . . . not guilty. . . ."

She rose to her feet, and her throat ached, she wanted to sob so badly. About her people were saying things to her. Margie Ransome, weeping with happiness, clung to her. Tom Ransome was saying something very earnestly. Jasper Peddigrew was there; she could not understand, but his eyes did not scorn her now. . . .

For the first time she was aware of the storm of sound. Judge Poster rapped futilely with his gavel. The crowd was on its feet, cheering. It had been cheering her ever since the jury gave its verdict without leaving the box.

She hardly realized this. She felt worn, emptied of all emotion.

She walked toward the door. The crowd massed about her; stood back. A path opened.

Oddly, she had one clear impression. A little, white-haired man, just outside the door. He took off his hat to her almost reverently—a strangely moved, strangely excited, little white-haired man . . .

She was out in the sunlight. And then understanding came.

She knew she had won. Not only had she won Jericho, but she had won over herself.

The people had spoken to her. The roar in the courtroom was the voice of the people. She had expressed a concept of justice and fairness to the people, and the people had leaped to her support, had idolized her.

There was a time when she had feared, almost hated Jericho. But this was Jericho. This was a part of the Republic. Her part.

These people were her people. She was of them. Their fight and their fate was hers. David had told her this was so. And she had not believed him.

Now at last she did believe. She hurried up the street toward the hospital.

She must tell David. She would be with him. Forever.

She began to run as she hurried to tell him.